A Recipe
for Love

hera

 Penguin
Random
House

First published in the United Kingdom in 2025 by

Hera Books, an imprint of
Canelo Digital Publishing Limited,
20 Vauxhall Bridge Road,
London SW1V 2SA
United Kingdom

A Penguin Random House Company

The authorised representative in the EEA is Dorling Kindersley Verlag
GmbH. Arnulfstr. 124, 80636 Munich, Germany

A CIP catalogue record for this book is available from the British Library.

Print ISBN 978 1 83598 051 4
Ebook ISBN 978 1 83598 053 8

Printed and bound in Great Britain by Clays Ltd, Elcograf S.p.A.

Look for more great books at
www.herabooks.com
www.dk.com

For Alison, Juliet, Ally & Amelia.

Keep on keeping on.

Prologue

Tomorrow the world! Tomorrow the world was a joke between Bella Smith and her beloved nan, more than a joke — a hymn to their shared love of travel, excitement and the next great adventure. Neither of them ever stayed in one place for too long. Why would you? There was always somewhere new to explore. Bella had only been working at this particular hotel near Malaga for a few weeks. Her customary restless feeling hadn't yet kicked in, but it would. It always did.

The stag party in front of her definitely wasn't helping. Preparing food at table was one of the restaurant's signature moves, but it was far from Bella's favourite part of her job. For her, cooking was all about the food. Turning a simple Crêpe Suzette into a performance took something away. It was bad enough when her audience was a sweet family group, drowsily cheerful on sun and sangria and happy to nod along with the theatre of the thing. It was even less fun with a table full of drunk, handsy posh boys who kept trying to slide euros into Bella's waistband. She raced back to the safety of the kitchen as fast as humanly possible.

Pastry was her favourite section. Dessert was the wow moment in any meal. The time for food that nobody really needed but everyone truly desired. Dessert could be an explosion in the mouth, a memory of childhood, or simple comfort. She finished exhausted but satisfied, her final sugar basket spun and her last plate dressed, and was wiping down her bench when she was called back to the restaurant. 'There's a guy wants to talk to you.'

She tucked the loose strands of dark brown hair under her cap as best she could and made her way to the dining room. The staff were clearing up and resetting for tomorrow's breakfast. The diners were long gone, except for one figure at the table nearest the balcony, the table with the horrible stag do.

Bella headed over, girding herself for another round of drunken propositions. The stranger looked up as she approached. Bella stopped.

Everything stopped.

In among the noise of the restaurant – the clatter of crockery and the chatter of her colleagues – there was a moment of absolute calm. Two strangers' eyes locked and the world slowed down, as if time was choosing to move around this instant and leave a pool of stillness undisturbed.

After a second, or maybe a year, the man spoke. 'I wanted to say sorry. For my friends. They're not really my friends.'

He was handsome by any standard. Dark blond hair, cut short at the sides, flopping slightly over one eye at the front. Bright blue eyes, and the slightest little dimple in his chin. He was also absolutely not Bella's type. He was very *very* clean cut. Safe, you could say.

'I wondered if I could buy you a drink to apologise.'

'You don't have to.' Who was she kidding, trying to put him off? Of course she would have a drink with him. It was all she could manage to not close the space between them and press her lips to his this very second.

'I want to. My friends, well they're my cousin's friends really, but they really were dicks to you.' He wasn't wrong. 'Just one drink to say sorry?' he asked again.

'Fine.' She moved backwards as he stood up, to stop herself from falling deeper into his orbit. 'One drink.'

—

How had that only been seventy-two hours ago? For Bella a lifetime had passed in those seventy-two hours. One drink had turned into two drinks. That was fine. That happened. Two drinks had turned into three. Again nothing out of the ordinary there. Three drinks had turned into a nightcap in his room. A little out of character but not, Bella had to concede, an absolute first. There had been plenty of guys before. Guys who were fun for a night, or a weekend, or even a season. This was something new.

That one night rolled over into the next morning and then the next afternoon, and then, sometime as the light dimmed again time had stopped altogether and since then hours had dashed past in seconds and moments had stretched into lifetimes.

There are points in life when the stars align and a road previously unimagined rises up to meet you. Bella Smith had taken a job as sous chef in a hotel on the Spanish coast because it was near the beach and a guy she'd met two months before knew a girl who knew another guy who knew the manager, and why not?

She'd accepted Adam Lowbridge's invitation for a drink because she couldn't imagine saying no.

She'd turned off her phone and chosen to stay in this bubble of skin and touch and words because, entirely without warning, she'd found a place that her body was telling her she was meant to be and because the things that had been important yesterday – work and mornings on the beach and earning enough money to move on to the next place – no longer mattered at all.

'So where are you from?' he asked.

They were lying in bed, limbs salted with sweat and entangled with one another and the sheet, spent for the moment.

'I'm a citizen of the world,' Bella laughed.

'What does that mean?'

She rolled towards him, pulling herself up onto her elbow. 'It means we travelled around a lot. School was in Leeds but my nan never liked to stay in one place for too long, so I'm sort of from everywhere and nowhere. What about you?'

'Well, the opposite to that. I have roots so deep you would nay believe. Grew up by a tiny village in the Highlands.' He brushed a strand of hair away from her breast. 'I live in Edinburgh now though.'

'And you're going back tomorrow.' The thing they had managed not to talk about for the last three days hung in the air between them.

'Yeah.'

So that was that. People left. It was what they did.

'Unless I stayed?'

'What?'

'Unless I stayed,' he repeated. 'I mean I don't think I'd be my business partner's favourite person, but, apart from Christmas and these three days I haven't taken a holiday for about five years.'

'You don't have to stay.' Bella didn't look him in the eye. 'I'll be fine.'

'I don't doubt it.' He reached for her. 'I'm just not sure I would be fine at all.'

His serious tone cracked her determinedly unconcerned exterior. 'Could you stay?'

'Yeah. Would you like me to stay?'

Adam staying didn't resolve anything. He wouldn't stay forever. Nobody ever did, but anything was better than the hole that opened up when she imagined him going right now. She settled back into his arms and whispered her reply. 'Stay.'

–

And so he stayed, for another week, and then another two weeks, and then three and four, and Bella's days fell into a routine of early breakfast and late dinner services, and the space between morphed from her normal routine of lounging on the beach with her shift-working seasonal colleagues to afternoons wrapped in Adam's arms, limbs tangled in the white sheets of his room.

'What do you do while I'm working?'

Adam lifted his head lazily from the pillow and checked the time. 'I'll show you, if you want.' He grinned. 'You will think I'm a total nerd though.'

That was intriguing enough to drag Bella out of bed and into shorts and a vest. Minutes later she was being led by the hand through the foyer and out to the hire car Adam had rented after he decided to extend his stay in Spain. 'Where are we going?'

'You'll see.' He drove north through the city and pulled up next to a sign proclaiming the location of the Jardin Botánico.

'Gardens?'

He nodded. 'Excellent Spanish.'

'I can just about manage botanical gardens. Apart from that it's mostly paella, chorizo, you know, the important stuff.' She looked up at the sign. 'How much is it?'

'Don't worry about that.' Adam led the way to the ticket booth.

'I can pay for myself,' Bella insisted.

'Adam!' The man at the ticket desk looked old enough to have been decades into retirement, with thick grey hair and deep lines on his tanned face. 'And you bring friend!'

'Francisco, this is Bella. Bella, Francisco.'

She nodded a greeting. The man smiled broadly. 'A friend of Adam! You are very welcome, miss. Go through.'

Adam pushed the barrier and led her into the garden. 'Don't we have to pay?'

'I think Francisco would be offended if we offered. Come on.'

They walked past cacti and bright sun-loving blooms, to a grove of trees surrounding a long wide pathway.

'Oranges,' Adam pointed out. 'And olives down there. And then peaches and nectarines. Incredible fruit. They had leaf curl on the peach trees though.'

'They had what?'

'It's a fungus.'

'OK.' Bella inhaled the scents of the trees around her deeply. 'And you know about peach funguses?'

'I told you I was a gardener.' He put a hand to the trunk of the nearest tree. 'Plants are much easier than people.'

'I know what you mean.'

He turned to look at her. 'I didn't think you were the green fingered type?'

'Not plants. Cooking. Like whatever's going on, I can lose myself in food. There's a sort of calm.'

6

'Exactly.' He was still staring at her.

'What are you looking at?'

'You.'

'Why?'

'Because I like looking at you.'

Bella waited for the fizz in her stomach that told her it was time to move on. It wasn't there. Normally her relationships came with a time limit. Either things ran a natural course, or Bella would find herself looking past the here and now and imagining her next move, which she inevitably pictured happening alone.

Adam moved to her and took her hand in his. 'You know I really do have to go home on Tuesday, don't you?'

The day after tomorrow.

'I can't take any more time off. Ravi's already going mental.'

'I know.' Bella's voice cracked as she spoke. 'I…'

'What?'

'I…' This wasn't her. She wasn't a girl who begged.

'Tell me.'

'I don't want you to go.'

And then his arms were around her. 'I don't want to go either, but…'

She pulled back, nodding quickly. 'I understand.' It was what it was. People moved on. She started to walk back towards the exit.

'Bella, wait.'

She stopped and turned. Adam wasn't standing where she'd left him. He was kneeling. 'What are you doing?'

'Bella Smith, will you marry me?'

She laughed, because the very notion was insane. People didn't get engaged after a few weeks. Bella was not the engagement type at all. The whole idea was ridiculous.

And also perfect. She laughed again but this time it was a release of pure joy bubbling up through her body.

Adam cleared his throat. 'You know you haven't answered yet?'

'It's quick.'

He didn't argue. 'It is.'

'I never thought I'd get married.' Bella paused. 'What if I'm no good at it?'

'At being married?'

'At commitment. At forever. Me getting married would be crazy.'

'Almost as crazy as me asking,' he agreed. 'I don't act on impulse.' He looked up at her. 'But here we are.'

'Here we are.' It was madness. 'Where would we even live?'

'You could come back to Edinburgh with me.'

Edinburgh. She'd never lived in Scotland. She'd visited a cousin of her nan's in Glasgow once, but that was it. A whole new adventure started to unfold in front of her.

'Bel!' Adam was still kneeling in front of her. 'You can say no,' he whispered.

She took the final step towards him and took his hand. 'Ask me again.'

'OK. Bella…' He paused. 'I don't know if you have a middle name.'

She shook her head. 'Officially I'm Isabella though, but nobody calls me that.'

'All right. I love you, Isabella "Bella" Smith. Will you marry me?'

'Simple question,' she joked.

'Simple answer – yes or no?'

So simple in the end. 'Adam… do you have a middle name?'

He winced. 'I have loads. William Alexander Angus.'

'Wow. We will unpack that later.' She squeezed his hand. 'Adam William Alexander Angus Lowbridge, yes. Of course yes. I will absolutely marry you.'

Chapter One

Even inside the terminal building, the air at Edinburgh airport had an evening chill that reminded Bella they weren't in Spain any more. She didn't care. Her heart was warm and her hand was wrapped tightly in Adam's. The flight had passed in a haze of plans for their future. He was working as a garden designer, running his own business with a friend from college, and he had a flat just south of the city, which would be easily commutable to a whole host of restaurants where Bella could set about looking for work. Or start something brand new in this new place. She could write recipe books, or get a food van. Maybe she'd look for a job in an upmarket cafe – something daytime, and a bit more nine to five than a full-on restaurant kitchen.

'I think we should get married soon.' There wasn't a single reason to delay. And why stand still and wait when you could forever keep moving forward?

They were waiting for Adam's luggage to arrive on the carousel. Bella only had her carry-on rucksack, but even for a four-day stag trip, she'd discovered, her new fiancé wasn't fond of travelling light. 'You can get married super fast in Scotland, can't you? Like at Gretna Green?'

'I think you still have to give notice.'

'Well that's fine. Let's do that today. Then we can get married as soon as we're allowed.'

He pulled her towards him. 'You don't want a big reception and a massive dress?'

She shook her head. 'I want to be married to you.'

'OK.'

'OK?'

He nodded. 'OK. Well, it's ten o'clock at night, and so I think the office will be closed, and honestly I don't even know where we'd have to go or whether you can do it all online. But tomorrow. Tomorrow we will find out what we have to do and do it.' He kissed the top of her head. 'And you're sure? I mean you don't know anything about me.'

Bella refused to entertain the idea that she might have doubts. 'Aren't you sure?'

'I'm sure. I just… I don't want you to feel like I pressured you.'

Bella leaned back slightly to look him in the eye. 'I'm sure. I want to be Mrs Adam Lowbridge. Well, I'll be Ms Bella Smith, but you know what I mean?'

He laughed. 'About that…'

A frankly massive black shiny suitcase caught Bella's eye on the carousel. She grabbed the bag and hauled it towards them. 'It's just this one isn't it?'

He gestured at the matching wheeled carry-on case. 'Well, these two.'

She pulled her rucksack onto her shoulder and took the handle of the smaller case so he'd have a hand free to hold hers as they walked through to arrivals and their brand new life together. 'Is there a bus to your place?'

'Yeah. Cab's easier though.'

Bella had no idea how much half a taxi would be. She did know that she had less than three hundred euros in her bank account, which was what? A couple of hundred quid at most, and whatever Adam said about having enough to cover the flat and the bills, Bella was going to pay her way. Straight after they'd sorted out the wedding date, she would be out looking for something to bring some money in.

Arrivals at an airport never gave Bella those warm and fuzzy *Love Actually* feelings. The mass of people around her greeting and hugging were just obstacles she had to get around to find the bus stop or the cheapest, which usually meant dodgiest, taxi option. Not today though. Today she wasn't travelling solo for the first time in a lot of years.

'Oh! Flinty.' Adam stopped suddenly and leaned over the barrier to envelop a woman in a hug. Bella stepped back. She didn't know what this was, but it didn't seem like she was part of it. A sign hung from the stranger's hand: *Lowbridge*. 'What are you doing here?'

The stranger pulled back. She was an older woman, at least seventy, Bella guessed. Not Adam's mum, because he'd greeted her by name. Too old to be an ex or a sibling.

'Sorry. Bella, this is Flinty. Flinty, this is Bella, my—'

'Sorry Adam. I've got some bad news. Your grandmother asked me to come. Goodness knows how she knew what flight you were on.'

He shrugged. 'Grandmother has her ways.'

The woman smiled but it didn't reach her eyes. 'Come around. We should sit down.'

Adam froze. 'What's happened?'

'Oh darling, I'm so sorry. Your father died this morning.'

Chapter Two

No. Adam shook his head. No. His father wasn't the sort who would do something like that. He was... he was... constant. Whoever moved on, whoever left, whatever changed, his father was there. 'What happened?'

'I'm sure your grandmother will tell you properly. Or Darcy.' She trailed off.

'What happened, Flinty?'

'It was sudden.' She wasn't meeting his eye. 'Well, if he was ill I never heard anything of it.'

'Babe,' Bella's voice cut through the soup that was swirling around him. 'Come and sit down.'

He let her lead him, as compliant as a child, to a row of hard plastic seats.

'Shall I see if I can find us some tea?' she asked.

'No need, lass.' Flinty produced a giant thermos from her bag. 'I came prepared.'

A plastic cup was pushed into Adam's hand and Bella all but guided his hand to his mouth so he could take a sip. He could hear her asking Flinty questions somewhere out there but the voices echoed like recordings from some place far away.

'So what now?' Bella was asking. 'Do you know when the funeral will be?'

'Not yet.'

'Do we need to come and help plan that or is someone...?' His fiancée's voice trailed away. 'Sorry. Who are you?'

He heard Flinty half-chuckle. 'Was thinking to ask you the same thing. I'm Flinty. Miss Flint. Maggie, but none of these have called me that for fifty years.'

'Hello Maggie. I'm Bella. I'm Adam's...'

The silence she left pulled Adam back to the conversation. 'Bella's my fiancée.'

Flinty looked from Adam to Bella and back again. 'Your grandmother didn't say anything.'

No. She wouldn't have. 'My grandmother doesn't know.'

'Well, this is going to be interesting.'

'So what do we need to do now?' Bella asked again.

'Well, I was going to take this one back tonight so he could get stuck into everything in the morning.'

So this was it. He'd be ferried back to the family home and what followed from there was what had always been destined, wasn't it? If he could just have one more night. One night in his flat, with Bella. One night of the life he'd thought they were starting. 'You can't drive tonight. It's late.'

'I'll be fine. Never sleep more than three or four hours a night anyway, and you can nap in the car.' Flinty turned to Bella. 'I suppose you'll be coming with us then.'

Bella squeezed his hand. 'If you want me to?'

Bella was sun and joy and the life he'd desperately wanted to choose. A few weeks with her had opened up parts of him that he'd learned to keep shut down. The Adam he was with her was less anxious, more impulsive, more willing to take risks.

He tried to picture Bella back home, with his grand-mother pursing her lips, and the village calling her 'his *new* lady friend' for the next twenty years. It was too much to ask, but if he didn't, he was going back alone. 'Yes. Please.'

'All right then.'

Flinty stood and smoothed down her sensible tweed skirt. 'Let's get on the road. If we set off now you'll have time for a couple of hours' kip before Veronica's up and at you to get working.'

'It can't be that far!' Bella laughed. 'Scotland isn't so big.'

Flinty shrugged. 'Five, six hours depending.'

Five to six hours of driving and fifty to a hundred years back in time.

'Right then lad.' Flinty paused. 'Sorry. I suppose I shouldn't say that now, should I?'

'Lad is fine.' Lad was what Flinty had always called him. He was a growing lad, or just a lad being a lad, or a wee lad who needed feeding up. 'You didn't have to come, Flinty,' he told her. 'You're supposed to be retired.'

She puffed her cheeks out. 'Like either of them could manage without me, lad.' She shook her head. 'Sorry. Best to get used to things from the get-go,' Flinty insisted. 'Right then sir.'

'Sir?' Bella hissed the question as they followed Flinty's small but surprisingly brisk strides towards the short stay parking.

Adam had known this conversation was coming. He'd known it when he'd first seen Bella working behind the pass in the hotel's trendy 'open to the dining room' kitchen. It was the reason he hadn't approached her on the first night in Malaga. It was the reason he never approached anyone he thought he might actually like.

He'd known it was coming when he'd sat next to her and talked about his life in Edinburgh and studiously not talked about his life before that. He'd known it was coming when he'd let her pull him into her, but by then it was already far too late. He was already utterly, irredeemably in love.

And, he'd known it was coming when he'd asked her to marry him. Was it a sort of lie to have not mentioned it so far? Perhaps. But it was also a truth. He'd shown her who he was, who he actually was, not who he was supposed to become. 'It's not really a big deal.'

'But you're a sir?'

'Not really.' There was no way round it. 'A baron technically. Some people say laird, but officially it's a barony.' He fumbled the words out as fast as they'd come, trying to make them small and less laden with implications. 'You can pretty much call yourself a laird if you own any land at all, so it doesn't mean much.'

'But baron means something?'

Another shrug. 'A long time ago maybe.'

'You never said you were a baron,' she hissed.

'Well I wasn't.' That was technically true, but not the whole story. 'I guess I didn't think I was likely to be. Not for decades anyway. My father was…' The thought caught in his throat. 'I thought he was going to live forever, I suppose.'

He watched his fiancée – if she was still his fiancée – for some hint of what she was thinking. Eventually she nodded. 'Sorry. It's just a lot to take in all at once.'

Of course it was. There was no one on earth who wouldn't be having second and third and fifteenth thoughts right now. 'No. I'm sorry.' There was only one right thing to do. He could release her from whatever obligation she was feeling, even if it broke his heart to do so. 'You don't have to come.' She didn't reply straight away. Adam's stomach clenched. 'It's OK. I understand. If you want to walk away, you can take my flat keys, until you sort out what you're doing next. I know this isn't what you signed up for. I am sorry.'

–

It certainly wasn't what they'd discussed. They had discussed life in the city, and bars and festivals and Bella finding a cool new job. Bella wasn't sure she was suited for supporting a grieving family, for funeral planning or applying for probate or any of the general adulting that being adjacent to death presumably required. And then there was the other thing. 'What does being a baron actually mean? How did your family become…?' Her head was spinning. 'Do you have servants?'

And then she saw Adam's face, the tiny dimple at his jaw where she could see all the tension he was holding inside, the haunted look in his eyes that someone else – someone who wasn't built to fit in to the gap alongside him – might think was angry or stoic, but Bella already knew was pure fear. She shook her head. 'I signed up for you. If you go, I go.'

'You're sure? My family… they can be… they can be a lot.'

'If you go, I go,' she repeated, and saw the deepening furrow at his brow ease just a little. She squeezed his hand. 'I mean it's not forever. We'll go. We'll do what needs doing. You can spend the time you need with your family. We've got our whole lives.'

She hoped that was the right thing to say. She didn't want to make it sound as though losing his father was something small, but she hoped that reminding him that nothing was forever and that this horrible moment would pass would help him through. He nodded wordlessly.

Flinty led them to the most decrepit rusty Land Rover Bella had ever seen. It sat like a gremlin of decay amid the nice neat family hatchbacks in the airport car park.

'How is this thing still going?' Adam asked.

'Perfectly good car this. Plenty of life left in her. Jump in.'

Bella stepped forward.

'Not that door!' Flinty shrieked. 'That one does nay open. Well it does open, but then it does nay close again and you'll have to hang on to it all the way back.'

'Right.' Bella followed Adam round to the passenger side, where the open door let out a waft of eau de wet dog. Adam slid across the dog-hair-covered back seat, before she climbed in next to him. He reached for her hand. A wave of nausea grabbed her. He'd given her the chance to walk away and she'd chosen to stay on the ride. It was like the ghost house at the fair when she was a kid. About a third of the way through there was a route you could take if it was too scary and you didn't want to go on. She'd never taken that turning then. Why start now?

She pushed the unease back down. They'd go to Adam's family home for a couple of weeks, and then, once the funeral was over, they'd be back to the life they'd talked about. This wasn't an unending path into the unknown. It was merely a temporary diversion. She pulled his hand to her lips and kissed the back of it. 'Everything's going to be OK,' she said.

Despite Flinty's instructions to try to sleep, Bella didn't manage to do any more than doze during the first part of the journey. At first Adam kept up a smattering of small talk with the driver and with his fiancée, but as one hour on the road turned to two, and then to three, he became quieter and quieter until, by hour four, he was staring silently out into the night, apparently lost in his own thoughts.

Bella tried to nap, but the roads were narrowing and the turns getting sharper and the old rusty Land Rover jolted and shook them over every bump. Every time she thought they must be getting close to their destination, simply because it absolutely couldn't be possible for the lanes to get smaller or more remote, she was wrong. 'Are we nearly there yet?'

'Getting closer. Another hour and a half at this time of night. Quicker in the daylight when you can see where you're going,' Flinty added cheerfully.

Bella chose not to dwell on her driver not being able to see where they were going, but her fingers gripped a little tighter to the seat beneath her. Eventually the car pulled to a halt. 'I'd assumed you'd be in your room, but...' Flinty glanced at Bella. 'There's a room made up in the coach house if that would be more comfortable for...'

Whatever the end of that sentence was going to be, Adam cut it off. 'We'll both be fine in the coach house.'

Bella surveyed the dark grey building in front of them. The dark night obscured much of her view but she could see that the wall was high and the windows small. It put her more in mind of a Victorian prison than an idyllic Scottish retreat.

Flinty hauled their bags out of the car. 'Sorry. I didn't have time to make up your room. And I didn't know if you'd want to be in there or in... well in the laird's room. Although I'm sure your grandmother will have something to say.'

Bella let the chatter wash over her. So long as there was a bed and she could get to it soon, she really didn't care.

'And there's only one room made up.' Flinty glanced at Bella.

'One room will be fine.'

'I'm not sure your grandmother…'

'One room will be fine,' Adam repeated.

'Well, I'll leave you to it.' She stepped forward and squeezed Adam suddenly on the shoulder. 'I know this isn't what you expected, but you're going to do all right, lad.' She stepped back. 'I'll be up in the morning to do breakfast.'

Adam shook his head. 'You don't have to.'

'I will though. So no point arguing about it lad. Sir.'

'Lad's fine.'

'We'll see about that.'

Bella staggered up the stairs behind Adam and into the room that Flinty had prepared for them. Well for him, but still. It was cold and a little unloved but it had a bed and a wardrobe and a small chest of drawers. She sat down on a rather tatty old velvet-covered chair, which sagged beneath her weight. 'This has seen better days,' she joked.

Adam glanced up. 'Yeah. Should have looked after that better. It'd be worth a lot more.'

Bella shook her head. She'd seen her nan haggle chairs in much better state than this down to a tenner for a set of four at the car boot. 'Cos it's like a Chippendale or something clearly.'

'No.' Adam strolled over and ran his hand over the arm of the chair. 'My granddad reckoned this was by his son. Chippendale the younger.' He shrugged. 'Worth way less than the real deal.'

'You're joking?'

Adam frowned. 'I doubt we've got proper provenance for it anyway.'

Bella lifted herself very carefully from the seat. 'I'm really taking my socks off in an actual Chippendale.'

'Well—'

'Baby Chippendale. Whatever.'

'Yeah. Maybe.' He looked around the room as if seeing it for the first time. 'Sorry it's a bit sparse. My father never really bought things new. Furniture just gets moved around to rooms that aren't used as much.'

Right. Bella battled to take that in. The almost-Chippendale was Adam's equivalent of the mismatched set of pans her nan had liberated from her former neighbour's house when Mrs Standish had moved into the home. A slightly unloved hand-me-down that nobody really noticed and that nobody would ever miss. 'Any other heirlooms I should be aware of?'

Adam half-laughed. 'Seriously, it's all heirlooms. Everything here was here centuries before I was born.'

'That's incredible.' What on earth would it be like to have roots that deep? To be connected to every single object in a place by generations of history. Bella sat down next to Adam on the bed and wrapped her hand around his. 'You're lucky.'

'So I'm told.' He turned his head slightly away from her and rubbed a hand across his eyes. 'We should get to bed.'

He was right. Bella was exhausted and she could only imagine Adam felt the same. She quickly brushed her teeth, went to the loo, stripped down to her T-shirt and knickers, wrapped her body around his, and fell fast asleep almost as soon as the light flicked off.

For an hour or two at least. When she opened her eyes the first thing she saw was Adam, standing by the window, staring out, still wearing yesterday's clothes. 'Did you sleep?'

'I dozed a bit.'

Bella sat up in bed. 'So what now? Do we need to see your grandma?' His grandmother had certainly been mentioned a lot last night. That was fine. Bella had her own experience of a grandmother who doubled as a force of nature. She could charm a grandmother. Who else? 'Your stepmum lives here too?'

Adam nodded. 'Darcy.'

'Who else do we need to tell about your dad?'

'Oh, just the great and good of the Highlands and Islands.' Adam's already grey complexion paled further. 'And my mother.' He closed his eyes for a second. 'Grandmother will have dealt with the rest. She's very good at dealing with things.'

'She sounds interesting.'

'She's…' He shook his head. 'I don't know what any of us would do without her.'

He hadn't moved from the window. Bella swung her legs out of bed. The stone floor, only part covered with a ragtag of thinning unmatched rugs, sent a shiver through her. 'How are you feeling?'

'I don't know. Numb.'

She padded over to the window, blinking against the low morning light. They were looking out towards another building. Not just another building. A castle. There was a surrounding wall, and some sort of grand gate and a big square… what was the word? Keep?… with actual turrets at the corners. 'Woah.'

'What?'

What did he mean what? There was an actual castle right outside the window. 'Who lives there?'

'What do you mean?'

Understanding dawned all too slowly. Baron Lowbridge. He was a lord, or laird or whatever it was he'd tried to explain last night. 'Is that your dad's house?'

Adam nodded. 'Yeah. Well no. I suppose it's our house.'

–

Bella pulled on her linen trousers and a T-shirt from the roll of clothes in her bag, along with her kitchen clogs, and followed Adam through the gate, across the cobbles and into the castle through a heavy wooden door. That took them into a narrow corridor, past an apparently unused room with an unconnected washing machine in one corner and a square of ill-fitting carpet in the middle, and then into the kitchen.

Here the castle felt inhabited. Flinty was frying rashers on the hotplate of a huge old fashioned stove. The smell greeted Bella like a hug.

'I'm glad you two are up.' Flinty gestured at the bacon. 'I did this out of habit, and then I thought nobody was going to come and eat it.' She pursed her lips. 'He liked his bacon, your father.'

Adam nodded.

'Though maybe he liked it a bit too much.' She shoved the rashers to the edge of the plate with her spatula. 'Maybe you'd prefer something lighter. There's that bran stuff the lady has.' Her shoulders slumped a little. 'Or melon. I'll be doing melon for your stepmother in a second.'

Bella shook her head. 'A bacon sandwich would be amazing. I'm not even sure when we last ate. Bacon sand-wich?' she asked Adam.

He didn't reply.

Flinty did. 'Aye. Well if you go through I've got things set out in the small dining room.'

The small dining room? That implied the existence of a larger dining room. 'How many dining rooms do you have?' she whispered.

'Two?' Adam replied.

'You don't sound sure.'

'Well two dining rooms in the house. Plus the coach house, and they used to use the great hall for banquets.'

'The great hall?'

Adam nodded. 'It's quite small.' He caught her eye and, just for a second, sunny warm Adam broke through the tension. 'Like an entry level great hall.'

'Oh!' Flinty called them back. 'She doesn't know yet.' She nodded towards Bella. 'About all this.'

'Right.' Adam pulled a face.

'*She?*' Bella asked.

'My grandmother. She's, well, she likes things done a certain way.'

Bella followed Adam from the kitchen into a large hallway. Adam pointed to the grand double-width doors opposite a wide staircase. 'That's the main door. Not sure when it was last used. It's probably reserved for visiting royalty.'

'Get a lot of those, do you?'

He shook his head. 'Bit far from Balmoral for them to pop over for tea.'

The hallway walls were lined with paintings. The largest showed a square stone-built castle, surrounded by a high wall that extended out from the main building and, presumably, enclosed a courtyard out of view of the artist. Alongside that, just outside the wall another stone building faced the pathway that led to the castle. 'Is that here?'

'Yeah. Years old though.' He pointed to the pathway. 'That joins up with the road now, and someone – my great-grandfather maybe – extended the coach house and replaced the roof here.' He pointed to the top of the castle. 'So it doesn't quite look like that any more. And there's the dower house off the east wing, that you can't see here.'

'Dower house?'

'Where the dowager lives. Built for the eighth baron's mother I think.'

'Right. So you have whole extra houses about the place and you live in the sort of castle people come and paint pictures of.'

Adam shrugged. 'Not that many people.'

'So this is the only painting of your house?' she asked.

He did at least look slightly sheepish. 'Well, it's definitely the biggest,' he replied.

The painting wasn't the most striking thing in the hallway. The most striking thing was too much like something from a long-forgotten school trip for Bella to even begin to get her head around. 'You know there's a suit of armour at the bottom of your stairs?'

'I am aware.'

'Like where do you even buy something like that?'

Adam shook his head. 'You don't buy things like that. You just sort of have them.'

'Why?'

'Because you do.' He shrugged. 'I don't know. You can't really get rid of them. Would you fancy taking Colin to the tip?'

'The suit of armour is called Colin?'

Adam smiled. 'My dad started that cos it used to freak me out when I was little. Hard to be scared of a shape in the night that's called Colin.'

Bella patted the suit gently on the shoulder. 'Well hello Colin.'

'And Colin's not so bad. The one upstairs is much worse. His arms fall off if you look at him the wrong way.'

Further discussion of precisely how many medieval soldier suits the Lowbridge family owned was curtailed by a sudden flurry of fur and paws and woofs. Adam bent down to pet the very excited chocolate Labrador in front of them. 'Dipper! Hello girl. Who's a good girl?'

Bella crouched down and held out her fingers. Dipper obliged with a tentative sniff and exploratory lick before turning up her nose and padding away.

A second later she was barking again, jumping up and down in the space in front of them, focused entirely on a patch of air somewhere off to Bella's left.

Adam ignored her. 'Come on. Breakfast's through here.'

The small dining room was panelled in dark brown wood, and there was a very faint smell of damp in the air. The dominant feature of the room was the huge stag's head, mounted between the two tall windows staring mournfully down at the room. Bella couldn't help but feel he was judging them. The table was laid for four with proper china, painted in a delicate floral pattern, and gleaming silver. There was a place at the head of the table, two more down one side and one directly opposite them.

Bella moved towards the first chair, where she could keep the stag under surveillance without feeling like he was staring her right in the eye.

'That's the laird's place.' The voice came from the doorway, but Bella hadn't heard footsteps, so who knew how long the apparition glaring at her had been standing there? The woman was elderly, but the sort of elderly that would never acknowledge such an inconvenience as the passage of time. Her white hair was scraped into an impeccably neat bun, and she was smartly dressed in navy blue trousers with a rose pink sweater over a high buttoned-up blouse. Her spectacles hung around her neck on a fine gold chain. And she was wearing court shoes. In the house. At half past seven in the morning. Bella wasn't sure she could think of a wider cultural gulf than the one between her and a person who wore court shoes for breakfast.

Adam greeted the woman with a tentative peck on the cheek. 'Grandmother.'

She nodded curtly. 'So, the new Baron Lowbridge.'

'How are you feeling?'

'I'm very well.' Her gaze settled on Bella. 'And you are?'

Adam was at her side straight away, hand in the small of her back. 'This is Bella Smith.' Bella felt the intake of breath he took before the next part. 'My fiancée.'

If the senior Lady Lowbridge was shocked or surprised she did not let any such disquiet appear on her face. 'Miss Smith.'

She held out a slender hand for Bella to shake, and then turned her attention immediately to the table. 'I presume your stepmother is joining us.'

'How is she?' Adam sounded concerned.

His grandmother shook her head. 'Well, she made the most tremendous fuss yesterday.'

'It must have been a shock,' Bella suggested.

'But still.' Adam's grandmother pursed her lips. 'There are things we need to get on with.'

'Oh.' A new voice in the doorway to the kitchen made them turn. In an instant Adam was over there wrapping the newcomer into a hug. Adam's grandmother clasped her hands at her navel. Bella hung back, not sure where she fit in.

Eventually Adam released the stranger. She could have been anywhere from twenty-five, but elegant beyond her years, to fifty, with a really talented botox technician. She was model tall, with hair cut short in an Audrey Hepburn style crop showing off her sharp cheekbones and wide blue eyes, but her face was pale and those unmissable eyes had shadows beneath them. She was wearing what looked like traditional men's pyjamas and a long man's dressing gown over the top. 'How are you feeling?' Adam asked her.

The stranger shook her head. 'I really don't know.' She had more than a twang of an American accent.

Bella cleared her throat, perhaps a little more pointedly than she'd intended.

Adam stepped back towards her. 'Right. Sorry. Bella, this is my stepmother, Darcy Lowbridge. Darcy, this is Bella.' He paused. 'My fiancée.'

One perfectly sculpted eyebrow elevated slightly. 'Fiancée?'

'It's new,' Bella explained.

'Clearly.' A spark of life had come back into Darcy's demeanour at this news. 'Well,' she turned to Adam's grandmother. 'Did you hear that, Veronica? Adam's engaged.'

'Apparently.' Veronica turned to the table. 'Shall we?'

Adam hesitated before he took the place at the top of the table. Bella went to take one of the chairs nearest to her fiancée but Veronica and Darcy were already taking their places, so she was shunted down to the space next to Darcy, as Flinty bustled into the room. 'Oh, Lady Lowbridge!' She smiled at Darcy. 'I didn't realise you were coming down. I was going to bring you a tray.'

'Veronica thought it was better to keep doing things normally,' Darcy explained.

'Doing things *properly*,' Veronica corrected.

'Is there coffee?' Darcy was staring at her crockery like she was unsure what to do next.

Flinty took the cup from her hand. 'You sit down, petal. I'll do a cafetiere.'

Darcy slumped back into her chair. Bella stood up. 'I'll help.'

Veronica shook her head. 'Flinty has everything in hand.'

Flinty was laying out serving dishes on the dresser at the far end of the room. She stopped as Bella approached. 'You sit down, love. I can manage.'

Bella turned back towards the table. Veronica was glaring at her. 'I said that Flinty has everything in hand.'

Bella sensed she'd made a terrible faux pas but she was hazy on how. It seemed incredibly rude not to help when one person was doing all the work, even if it was their job. And hadn't Adam said Flinty was retired? She found herself stuck in no man's land, between Flinty busying herself at the dresser, and the family sitting stock still and silent at the table.

'I'll bring some coffee and your melon,' Flinty told Darcy, as she set down a teapot on the table. 'You can help yourself to the rest.'

Bella stepped back towards the array of food laid out for them. She'd worked in hotels that put on a less fulsome breakfast buffet. She picked up a plate.

'The laird goes first.'

'Right. And I walk two paces behind him, do I?' Bella laughed as she turned, and stopped when she saw Veronica's face.

'I'm sure that's not necessary, but there is a proper order.'

Bella glanced at Adam. 'It's fine.' He sounded exhausted. 'We're all adapting a bit today, aren't we?'

He ushered Bella in front of him.

She helped herself to crispy bacon and a light fluffy white roll. Adam hadn't picked anything up. 'You need to eat something.'

'I don't know what...'

She handed him her plate. 'Take this. I'll go again.'

As she took her seat next to Darcy, Flinty was putting a plate of melon and a cafetiere down in front of the second Lady Lowbridge. She stared at it with the same empty expression Adam was wearing.

'I was going to call Xander down so you could tell him your news. But...'

Adam squeezed her hand. 'He's gone.'

'I won't believe it.' She looked at Bella as if seeing her for the first time. 'Oh, I am sorry. We should offer you a drink.'

Bella shook her head. 'I've got tea.'

'Right. Good. Bit early for something stronger.'

It wasn't even eight a.m. 'It is a bit,' Bella agreed. 'How long were you married?'

'Fifteen years. Well, it would have been fifteen in June.' She shook her head. 'I'm so sorry. I keep thinking he'll be down in a moment. The smell of bacon always gets him down for breakfast.' She glanced towards the door. 'It's just that I was in the next room. I'd called through to him to ask if he'd seen my address book because it wasn't by the telephone, and I don't know why I wanted it, but I needed to call the plumber about that tap and his number is in my cell, but I was going to phone on the landline so I didn't quite think of that, and anyway, Xander yelled back that it wasn't in the estate office, and why on earth would I think it might be? And then there was this sort of moan and a crash and…' She stopped. 'I was just talking to him, you see.'

Bella did see. It was utterly unfair and entirely inexplicable that someone could be right there and then, at the very next moment, not there at all. 'I'm sorry.'

Darcy sipped her coffee and winced slightly at the heat. 'That's kind.'

They completed their breakfast in silence. Adam, Bella was relieved to see, did eat his sandwich. Darcy did little more than push her melon around the plate, before she retreated to her room. Veronica's appetite appeared unaffected by the death of her son. Eventually she drained her teacup, dabbed her white napkin precisely to the corners of her lips and announced that she must get on. 'I shall need you in the estate office,' she told Adam 'There are arrangements to be made.'

'I was going to show Bella round.'

Veronica glanced in Bella's direction. 'Well I'm sure that won't take all morning. I shall wait.'

Flinty reappeared a heartbeat after Veronica left, so precise a timing that Bella suspected she'd been in attendance in the hallway throughout the meal. 'So that's Veronica. The baroness,' she said. 'Well, the dowager baroness.' Flinty closed her eyes for a second. 'No. That's Darcy. I don't know what that means.' She looked at Adam. 'Are they both the dowager?'

'I have no idea. I always asked my dad that stuff.' He swallowed back something that could have been a sob. 'Then didn't listen when he tried to explain.'

Flinty squeezed his shoulder. 'Well, you were young. We all thought there'd be more time, didn't we?'

The weight of the sorrow in the house suddenly felt heavy on Bella's heart. 'Do you want to go for a walk? Clear your head a bit?'

Adam nodded. 'Let's give you the grand tour.'

Bella followed him back through the kitchens and outside. She found herself standing at the edge of a large courtyard, surrounded by high stone walls on all sides. Adam pointed back through the archway behind her. 'So the coach house, where we slept, is through there.'

'Right. Cos everyone needs a whole spare house on the side.'

He half-smiled. 'We're just really short of space.'

Bella turned around to take in the enormity of the building that surrounded her. 'So this is all your house.'

'Yeah. Well… it's not all house really.' He moved to stand behind her, turning her body back towards the kitchen. 'So that's the main wing.'

'Wing?'

He laughed. 'What? That's what it's called. So the front entrance is opposite the stairs and the dining room on the

other side of this part, and the living rooms are sort of…'
He paused. 'In that corner and a bit along the second side.'

Bella followed his pointing finger. 'Right.'

'The main bedrooms are upstairs. Darcy. My…' He
stopped.

Bella turned and wrapped her arms around his waist.

'I'm OK. My father's room was up there. Anyway…'
He didn't continue.

She leaned into his body. 'So what's the rest?'

'All sorts. A lot of these rooms…' He pointed towards
what Bella was thinking of as sides two and three to the
square. 'Aren't in use any more. There's the library, and
then the more public rooms, for like audiences with the
baron, and big receptions and stuff.'

Audiences with the baron? Where the baron did a
couple of songs and a big dance number to finish? 'Audiences?'

'A long time ago. You know, people wanting their
disputes sorted out or begging to be let off paying their
rent.' He looked around. 'And then servants' quarters
obviously.'

'Obviously,' Bella muttered.

He took her hand and led the way through a
passageway in the far corner of the quad. 'This comes out
sort of behind the coach house, and here we are.'

In front of them was a long low single-storey stone
building, alongside a wide square patch of open grass. 'So
you've got a field?' Bella asked.

'A paddock.'

Which was different because?

'And stables.'

'You've got horses?'

Adam nodded and then stopped. 'Well, I don't. I haven't ridden for years, but Darcy does. Only… I'm not sure, I think three or four horses here now.'

'Four,' the distinctive New York accent carried across to them from the entrance to what Bella now understood was a stable block. Darcy was still in her dressing gown, with wellies pulled on over the pyjamas. She beckoned them over. 'Sophie McCullen keeps hers here since, since all that business with her granddaddy's place. And Nina from the village still rides. Apart from that it's just Liberty and Larry.'

Bella peered past Darcy into the gloom of the stable.

'This is Larry.' Darcy stopped at the first stall and petted the nose of the large brown thing that nuzzled against her.

Did you even say brown when it was horses? Horse people said grey for white, didn't they? Bella didn't have a clue.

Adam ran his hand over the side of Larry's head. 'No offence mate, but how are you still here?'

'Don't listen to him!' Darcy instructed.

'He must be about a hundred and eight.'

Darcy demurred. 'Larry is just swell.' She paused for a moment, forehead pressed against Larry's head. 'It's good to have them here. Especially today. When you want to just hide away the shit still needs shovelling.'

'Since when do you shovel shit?'

'I help out.'

'Sure you do,' said Adam gently. 'How are you?'

'How are you?'

'I don't know.'

Darcy nodded. 'Same.'

Bella hovered at the entrance to the stables, not wanting to intrude or freak out the horses or stand in the wrong place or…

Adam turned towards her. 'Sorry. So yeah, horses. Do you ride?'

Bella shook her head. 'Not much riding in a flat in Leeds.'

'Don't say that,' Darcy replied. 'I learnt at a city stables in Brooklyn. Every weekend as soon as I was big enough to sit on a pony. There's no feeling quite like it.'

Bella definitely thought of riding as a posh country thing not a normal city thing. 'I'm not sure it's for me.'

Darcy shrugged. 'To each their own.'

Adam glanced at his watch. 'I probably shouldn't keep Grandmother waiting much longer.' He stopped next to Bella. 'Oh, but what will you…?'

She pasted on a smile. 'I'll be fine. I can explore on my own.'

–

In the kitchen Flinty was putting away the breakfast pots. 'Adam's gone to see what his gran needs.'

Flinty nodded.

'I think me turning up was a bit of a shock to her.'

'To all of us,' Flinty confirmed. She put her tea towel down on the big table in the middle of the kitchen. 'She'll warm up to you.'

'Really?'

'Probably not,' was the cheerful reply. 'But you'll get used to her.'

Bella picked up the last two cups from the draining board. 'Where do these go?'

'You don't have to be doing that,' Flinty told her.

'I don't mind.'

'Really.' Flinty took the cups off her and opened a high cupboard above the sink. 'Veronica – Lady Lowbridge – she does have a good heart. She's just not very warm and cuddly, if you know what I mean.'

Bella felt she knew exactly what Flinty meant. 'She's not like my grandma.'

'Was she more pockets full of Werther's Originals and spoiling her grandkids?'

Bella almost laughed out loud at the image. 'Noooooo. More of a lifelong rolling stone.'

'You were close to her?'

'My mum wasn't really around when I was growing up.'

Flinty nodded. 'Ah well, good you had somebody then. Have you told her about you and Adam?'

Actually no. 'I will. Soon. Next time I call.'

Flinty didn't reply.

'So what else can I do?' Bella needed to be busy. She needed to roll her sleeves up. Her absolute dream would be a full crate of potatoes that needed scrubbing and peeling and chopping – something mindless that she could lose herself in. 'I know my way around a kitchen.'

'Not my kitchen you don't.'

No. Of course. No point treading on toes when she'd only just arrived.

Flinty turned back towards her. 'Sorry. Not my kitchen, is it? Going to be yours soon, so you can knock yourself out. One of the few things Veronica and Darcy have in common is that they don't really get involved in here. I mean Darcy would live on her smoothies given the chance, and Veronica...' She trailed off.

'What?'

'Well, she's had fifty years of food being something that appears in the accounts and on the table. I don't think she has the faintest idea, any more, what happens to it in between.' Flinty looked around. 'Anyway I think I'll be doing trays for lunch today, so not much to help with. You got here very late last night. You should rest.'

Bella didn't point out that Flinty had got here just as late and she hadn't had the chance to nap on the journey. This kitchen was clearly Flinty's domain, and that was something Bella could absolutely respect.

'You could go for a walk?' Flinty suggested. 'Or explore the house a bit more.'

'The house?'

Flinty looked at her blankly. 'Big stone thing you're standing in.'

The castle. Why did nobody else seem to have noticed that they lived in a massive blooming castle?

–

The surroundings of the estate office were utterly familiar to Adam but, at the same time, strangely alien. As a small child this room had been Father's space. If Father was in here, he was not to be disturbed. Even as a teenager, using the office as a cut through from the back stairs to the main castle had felt illicit. He still, instinctively, hesitated in the doorway, as if he was expecting his father to grumble that he was busy, and for Flinty to come dashing down the corridor and chivvy him away with promises of biscuits in the kitchen.

His father's chair wasn't there. His father had always had a strange leather-backed thing that looked for all the world as though someone had bolted an old fashioned dining chair onto a set of wheels and plonked it behind the desk. But the chair his grandmother was using was new, a standard black office chair that could have come from any catalogue anywhere in the world. 'Where's his chair?'

'I beg your pardon?'

'His chair? The leather one?' Adam shook his head. 'It doesn't matter.' Of course it didn't matter. It was just a chair. Chairs broke. People bought new ones. Things changed. Things kept on changing.

His grandmother took her seat, what seemed to be her seat, in his father's place, behind the desk, and gestured to the seat opposite her. Dipper padded into the office and bounded up to the desk. She sniffed the carpet beneath the table, sniffed Veronica, and finally Adam. He held his hand out to his father's beloved dog. She nuzzled for a second, before turning away. He clearly wasn't the master she was looking for.

'Shall we get on then?' his grandmother asked. 'You need to learn the ropes.'

'Not today?'

'No better time.'

He'd known she was going to say that. Veronica Lowbridge was a woman incapable of putting things off. If a task needed doing, the task got done.

'I prefer to do the routine tasks first. Otherwise one ends up cherry-picking the out-of-the-ordinary things and the day-to-day can get neglected.'

'OK.' Adam let his grandmother talk him through the regular weekly tasks for the running of the estate. He received instruction on logging into the bank accounts and the estate email inbox, all the while doing his very best to ignore the way the grey walls seemed to be pressing in on him. His grandmother sighed pointedly.

'Look. That damned plumber has re-sent his invoice. And it still doesn't have the right total. I suppose that idiot girl quite forgot what with…' She shook her head. 'With everything else.'

The 'idiot girl' of course being Darcy, and 'everything else' being the death of her husband. Adam's father. Veronica's son. 'How are you doing?' he asked her.

'Very well thank you.'

Adam swallowed back a wince. 'I mean, how are you doing since Father…?'

'I know perfectly well what you mean. No point dwelling on things.'

His father had been dead less than twenty-four hours. 'It's hardly dwelling—'

'I need to take you through the accounting.'

'Had he been sick?' The question rushed into Adam's mind and straight out of his mouth.

'What?'

'Before… you know, had he been sick?' Darcy had made it sound quite sudden, but some days it seemed like the sun coming up in the morning was a bit of a surprise to Darcy so he wasn't sure she was a particularly reliable witness. The idea took shape in Adam's head that maybe his father had been ill. Maybe there'd been things he could have done, if he'd known. If he'd been here. 'Had he seen a doctor recently?'

'He was a man in his fifties. All they ever do is see the doctor. It's all prostates and backs and weak knees. One doesn't like to pry.'

As if there was anything his grandmother wouldn't pry into.

'I'm sure it was just one of those things,' she added. 'As I say, no point dwelling.' She pulled a hardbacked ledger off the shelf behind her. 'These are the household accounts, separate from the estate accounts.'

'This isn't computerised?'

'Your father was used to doing it this way.'

Adam scanned the neat columns of numbers. They danced under his gaze. In normal life, in his real life, Ravi dealt with this sort of thing. The figures were written mostly in his father's slanting scribble, with the occasional oasis of his grandmother's neat copperplate script. His father would never write in this book again. 'I can't do this now.'

His grandmother nodded. 'Very well.' She closed the ledger. 'Perhaps tomorrow. And I suppose we should concentrate on the funeral arrangements first anyway.'

The mention of the funeral brought one of the many thoughts that had crowded out sleep the night before to the front of Adam's mind. 'Has anyone let my mother know? I mean I know it's complicated.' Boy, did he know. 'But they were married for a decade.'

Veronica nodded. 'I sent an electronic mail to the address I have for her. I don't expect a reply. I presume you have a telephone number.'

'Yeah.' Adam's contact with his mother was minimal. 'I don't know if it's up to date.'

He pulled out his phone. What would he even say to her? The screen flashed with two missed calls, both from Ravi. He fired off a brief text explaining that he was in Lowbridge and would ring when he could, but not explaining why.

His mother was trickier. Adam's finger hovered over the call button and then froze. He texted instead.

Veronica had already moved on. 'I've already arranged for
the vicar – the *new* vicar – to come. I don't know if the
girl will want to come to that.'

'Bella?'

His grandmother frowned. 'No. Why on earth would
she want to come?'

'To support me?'

That suggestion was ridiculous enough to be met with
a simple small shake of the head. 'I meant the American.'

'Darcy? Yes. I think she will want to be involved in the
funeral arrangements.'

'Whatever you think. I'm sure you're more than
capable.'

Adam sucked back whatever response he might have
wanted to offer. 'It's not only up to me though is it?'

Veronica gave him a look of sharp consternation.
'You're the laird. Things are generally very much up to
you.'

Chapter Three

Bella didn't really consider herself a 'going for a walk' type of girl, but there didn't seem to be much else for her to do. Flinty had assured her it would make her feel better, which was sweet, apart from the fact that Bella hadn't previously been aware she was feeling bad.

She went hunting for a bathroom before she set out. Given the size of the castle, she reckoned, there must be loads. Bella started in the hallway, ignoring the door she already knew to be the dining room. First door, first sitting room, decorated in slightly concerning shades of dark green with yet another poor deceased deer's head above the fireplace. Second door, second sitting room – decorated in yellow this time. Third room, third sitting room, painted in a slightly more restful shade of pale blue. No bathrooms.

The next part of the corridor was lined with portraits of, presumably, past lairds and ladies. Bella tried the handle of the odd little door alongside her. Odd, because unlike the rest of the doorways, this was cut out of the wall itself and closed flush with no frame to mark it out. A casual glance could miss its existence all together. Bella tiptoed through and found herself in a plain stone stairwell.

She set off up the stairs, and came out of a very similar door on the first floor. The upstairs version of the long gallery was an open balcony looking down into the room that ran alongside. Bella leaned over to take a look and gasped. It was dusty, and there were stacks of plastic chairs in one corner that gave the feel of a deserted primary school gym, but what she was looking down into remained, unmistakeably, a ballroom. An actual ballroom. The full *Bridgerton* fancy dress, string quartet, deal.

'What are you doing up here?' Flinty bustled along to her, arms full of bed linen.

'You've got a ballroom.'

'*You've* got a ballroom,' Flinty corrected.

Bella shook her head. 'I was looking for the toilet.'

'There's one down there.' Flinty pointed behind her. 'Next to the top of the stairs. You must have come past it.'

'I came up here.' Bella tapped the weird little door in the wall.

'Oh, Veronica won't like that. Family don't use the back stairs.'

'What?'

Flinty nodded. 'I mean really nobody uses the back stairs. They're very steep and damn cold. But especially not family.'

'I'm not sure she sees me as family.'

Flinty didn't deny it. 'She'll come round.'

Bella followed Flinty's directions to the bathroom, went to the loo, washed her hands and turned off the tap. Which promptly came back on again. Bella turned it off. It came on again. Off again. This time she stood and watched as the tap turned over so slowly and apparently entirely on its own. So was this the tap Darcy had been trying to get fixed? Bella would not be defeated by plumbing. She turned the tap a fourth time, twisting as tight and hard as she could. The tap stayed off. She allowed herself a small smile of triumph before she turned away. She was barely through the door before the sound of the trickle of water reached her. She turned the tap a final time and marched away before the damn thing had a chance to start up again.

If Bella was going to go for a walk she would need better shoes than the clogs she'd made do with for breakfast. The choices weren't great. Apart from her chef's clogs she had flip flops and a pair of canvas sneakers with a hole in the toe. Sneakers would have to do. The walk from the kitchen back to the coach house had told her that it was a slightly cool, but thankfully dry, morning. She pulled a jumper over her T-shirt and set out.

Their journey last night had all been in darkness, so she was slightly surprised to realise that the castle was built on an outcrop that jutted out into what? She could see more land directly opposite them but the water moved and dashed around the foot of the castle hill like the tide was rushing in. Were they on some kind of bay? Whatever. On three sides of her there was water, so Bella, for lack of other choices, started her walk in the fourth direction, along a long cobbled single-track road that connected the castle hill to the mainland.

Flinty had told her to take a walk around the estate, but what did that event mean? Bella had grown up on an estate, rows and rows of identical brown little houses and low blocks of flats, with leaky windows and electrics that fused if you looked at them funny set around a communal 'garden' that was littered with shit and syringes. This estate wasn't going to be like that, was it?

She continued down the road to the mainland. The street, now a properly tarmacked – if somewhat potholed – road, continued up the side of an inlet that flowed from the… Bella was going to say 'sea' for now. On the other side was an initially flattish deep green field, that then rapidly rose up a hillside. Everything around her felt big. Big sea. Great towering hills. Spectacular deep grey sky. It was the sort of scenery that hit you in the face with how small you were. Bella focused on the white spots of sheep scattered across the hill, reminding her that she wasn't quite alone. She'd never had much to do with sheep. Lamb, she knew about. Paired classically with mint, but in her mind perfect with more North African flavours. Her mouth watered slightly as she mentally put together a tagine with apricots, cumin, coriander and a dash of cinnamon. Lamb she was good with. Actual sheep, not so much. She rejected the wilds of the field and set off up the road instead.

She'd barely made it ten yards before the sound of a vehicle coming down towards her made her step to the side of the road. The car in question was a brand new looking four by four which screeched to a halt alongside her. The driver's window slid down and Bella was faced with a mass of bleached blonde curls. 'Are you from the castle, pet?'

'No.' Was she? 'Sort of. I guess.'

'Brilliant. Quite exciting isn't it? A summons to the big house.' The bouncy cheer-filled voice paused. 'I mean not exciting. Not in the circumstances. No. Sorry. Were you close to the laird?'

Bella shook her head. 'I never met him. I'm…' She was what? 'I'm his son's…' Come on woman. Pin your colours to the mast. 'I'm his son's fiancée.'

The mass of curls frowned. 'But you'd never met his dad?'

'No.' That did sound odd, didn't it? 'We only got together quite recently.'

'Oh, that's a shame. I mean that you never met the laird. Well the old laird I guess. You've met the new one!'

Bella nodded.

'Well hop in then!'

'I'm sorry?'

'I'm assuming you'll want to be there to support your fella. I mean you're part of the family now, aren't you?'

Bella's confusion was definitely showing, but the stranger seemed oblivious.

'Hop in. You can show me where to park.'

Sometimes the only way was to be direct. 'I'm sorry. Who are you?'

The woman laughed. 'Sorry. Sort of used to everyone knowing. Daft of me. I'd forget me own head. I'm the vicar. Everyone calls me the new vicar, cos I've only been here eight years.' She pushed the mass of hair out of her face and leaned forward, revealing a neat little flash of dog collar at her neck. 'I'm heading over to talk about the funeral. I think he'd want you there, wouldn't he?'

Bella had no idea. On the one hand, obviously she wanted to support Adam however she could. On the other, she'd never met his dad and there were already two ladies of the manor rattling around the Lowbridge estate. What use was a third?

'Jump in. I'm Jill.'

'Bella.'

'Marvellous. So you're going to be the new Lady Lowbridge. That'll be confusing. Most people still call that Darcy "new" and she was here at least five years before me. I don't know her all that well. I see the most of Maggie. I think most people do. Of course she's retired now.'

Jill was a ball of cheer and energy and words that tumbled over one another to get out of her mouth. Bella jogged round the passenger side of the car and climbed in.

–

As Jill got out of the car at the bottom of the hill, and stopped to survey the castle, Bella confirmed her opinion that the vicar was mostly hair. Huge generous strawberry blonde curls that were piled on top of her head, and held, not entirely successfully, in place with a leopard print scarf.

'We're through here.' Bella led the way past the coach house and in through the kitchen corridor. Flinty was at the sink, up to her elbows in soapy water. She looked round as the entered. 'Oh!'

'This is Jill.'

'I know.' She nodded at the vicar. 'Morning pet.'

'Hi Maggie. Sorry for your loss. You must have known him a long time?'

'His whole life.' Flinty shook her head. 'It's all topsy-turvy – people passing on who you knew as babies.'

Jill squeezed her shoulder.

'You'd best go through and hope Veronica doesn't catch you.'

Bella frowned. How had she displeased Adam's grand-mother now? 'What do you mean?'

'Clergy don't come through the kitchen, love.'

Jill laughed. 'I'm not really one to stand on ceremony.'

'There's nothing wrong with doing things properly.' Veronica was in the doorway to the kitchen. 'Veronica, Lady Lowbridge. My son will also be joining us.'

The vicar sort of half-curtsied. Bella wanted to hug her. Veronica looked appalled.

'I'm Jill.'

'Reverend… Jill?'

'Well Reverend Douglas. But you can call me Jill.'

'Reverend Douglas.'

Bella could almost swear the reverend's bouncy curls flattened a fraction.

She followed Veronica and Jill through the grand front hallway into one of the rooms off the corridor beyond the estate office. 'Could you tell Flinty we'll take tea in the Blue Room?'

Bella bristled slightly. She wasn't staff. She wasn't even actually sure if Flinty was staff. People kept telling her she'd retired. 'I think Flinty's busy.' Not that she wouldn't drop everything to make Veronica's tea.

'Oh.' Veronica looked personally affronted at the notion. 'Well you'll have to make it then.'

'I'll get tea.' Adam came out of the room Veronica seemed to be about to go into. He held out a hand. 'I'm Adam.'

'Lord Lowbridge,' Veronica corrected.

Jill gave another anxious half-curtsey.

'You don't need to do that. And it's just Adam.' Bella's heart warmed a touch. Just Adam. That was who she was here for. Not for some baron or lord or laird or whatever the term was. Just Adam.

Darcy was hovering in the doorway behind him. 'And this is my stepmother,' he continued.

'Darcy, Lady Lowbridge.' Veronica was starting to sound utterly despairing at the informality.

Jill stepped forward. 'I'm very sorry for your loss, Lady Lowbridge. For all of your loss, of course.'

Adam nodded. 'Thank you. And I think you've met my fiancée, Bella.'

'I'm not Lady anything.' Bella smiled. 'And I can get the tea. You go through.'

Veronica stalked past the doorway Darcy was standing in. 'We'll be in the Blue Room.'

Bella grabbed Adam's hand before he could follow. 'Isn't that the Blue Room?' She peered through the door. The décor had a definite blue-ish tint.

He shook his head. 'That's the drawing room, which is blue. The Blue Room is that way. And is yellow.'

She opened her mouth.

'Don't ask.'

She squeezed the hand she was holding. 'How are you doing?'

'I don't know. Mostly I'm just doing what I'm told.'

By the time the tea was ready, the rest of the group were ensconced in what any sane person would definitely have referred to as the Yellow Room. Bella put the tray down on the low table in the centre of the room. She had a proper teapot, she had sugar in cubes in an actual bowl and milk in a jug. She had cups and saucers. Not cups and saucers that matched, but one thing she had learned from her search through the cupboards was that nothing matched. Everything, it appeared, was inherited and nothing had ever been chosen to go together. She waited to hear Veronica's verdict on what she'd done wrong. She tapped the spoon on the edge of the sugar bowl. 'Tongs for cubes, dear.'

Bella pretended not to have heard. 'Tea, vicar?'

The reverend was sitting alongside Darcy on one side of the room. Adam and Veronica were next to each other on the other. Bella squeezed herself in between them.

'We were just talking about the service.' Jill directed her comments to Darcy. 'I was wondering whether you'd be wanting a big service for the whole community.'

Veronica shook her head. 'This is a family occasion. Cremation and then a service of committal at the chapel here. I imagine some of the other lairds will come, but there's no need for a great hullaballoo.'

Darcy looked pale and tired.

Adam jumped in. 'Although I know Darcy was wondering about burial. There is a graveyard here. I think it's a long time since anyone has been buried there.'

'Right. Well there's no legal reason you can't have a burial on private land, if you have space. I think it has to be a certain distance from water sources and that sort of thing, but the council or the funeral director could probably advise you on that.' Jill paused. 'You'd need someone to dig the actual grave of course.'

'Would you prefer that, Darcy?' he asked gently.

Veronica sighed.

Darcy was staring at her teacup. 'If there's no grave where do you put flowers?' Darcy asked. 'There should be somewhere to put flowers. We did that for my grand-mother. Every year on her birthday my mum would take us down to the cemetery and we'd take fresh flowers. Isn't that what you're supposed to do?'

'If that's something you'd find valuable.' Jill nodded. 'Everyone grieves differently of course.'

Veronica put her cup down with a firm clatter. 'I don't think we need that. It seems rather showy, don't you think?'

'Well as I say, everyone grieves differently. I had one lady plaited her sister's hair into a bracelet.'

Veronica's horror was palpable. Bella fought to keep her face neutral. The dead hair bracelet thing was giving her the ick but she was not going to let Veronica know that they agreed.

Adam slumped back in his seat. The stress was written across his face. 'What if we had a cremation and scattered the ashes somewhere here? Then there'd still be a place to visit.'

'Ashes go into the crypt,' said Veronica.

There was a crypt?

'I'm not having Alexander locked up in that death cupboard.'

Bella stifled a definitely inappropriate giggle.

'He took me down there once,' Darcy added. 'It was ghoulish.'

'You can bury the ashes if you want. You could still have a headstone.' Jill clearly thought they had a path to a resolution here.

Veronica was not on side. 'The ashes will reside with my husband and his father in the crypt.'

'What would you like?' The question was directed from the vicar to Adam.

'I don't know.' Mostly he wanted everyone to stop fighting.

Bella rubbed her fiancé's arm. 'It's OK to say what you want.'

She felt his bicep tense just slightly. His voice was low. 'I don't know what my father wanted.'

Both Ladies Lowbridge were quiet for a moment, but Veronica was not one for giving ground. 'I'm sure he would have wanted what the lairds have wanted for the last two generations...'

'Well...' Jill tried again.

'I was his mother.'

'I was his wife.'

And there was that impasse once again. Even Jill's relentless positivity was floundering. Adam leaned forward, rubbing his fingers up the side of his nose. 'Did he actually say anything to either of you about what he wanted?'

'Well I'm sure…' Veronica started.

'What did he actually say?'

'Well nothing as such,' she conceded.

Adam turned to Darcy. 'Anything?'

She shook her head. 'We didn't talk about it.' Her voice caught on a sob. 'He thought he had all the time in the world, I think.'

'Right.' He leaned back.

'I'm sure whatever we decide will be all right,' Bella offered.

'So if we have a cremation, does that have to be in Inverness?'

Jill nodded. 'It's the nearest place. We can have a service there, or that can be private and you can have the service here before or after.'

'OK. We'll have a private cremation in Inverness. I'll go with him.' He turned to his stepmother and grandmother and addressed them like a primary school teacher at the end of a particularly trying day. 'You two can come or not. Then can we have a memorial service here with the ashes?'

Jill nodded. 'Of course.'

'OK. Is that all right with everyone?'

Veronica opened her mouth but thought better of it. Both women nodded.

'Good.' Adam pulled out his phone. 'I should phone the funeral director then, shouldn't I?'

Bella could hear the quiver in his voice. She reached for the phone. 'Shall I do that?'

His face was a mask of exhaustion. He handed her the phone. 'Thank you.'

A few minutes later she'd confirmed that the cremation could be done within the week and they could have the ashes returned to them in the urn of their choosing in ten days' time. 'So we've got time to work out where you want to...' What was the phrase? 'Erm, lay him to rest?'

'And let's try not to argue about it,' Adam implored.

Even Veronica's unruffled exterior looked a little bruised by Adam's new attitude. He turned back to the vicar. 'Is there anything else?'

'Well, normally we'd spend some time talking about the service itself. Hymns. Readings. Perhaps you might want to talk about your father yourself? It can be much more personal to hear from people who knew him well.'

'Of course the laird will give the eulogy,' Veronica confirmed.

Adam responded with a small nod, but the fear had returned to his eyes.

'Wonderful,' Jill continued. 'So maybe Mrs Low-bridge... sorry Lady Lowbridge...' She turned pointedly to Darcy. 'You might have some music or a reading that particularly meant something to your husband?'

Darcy had visibly rallied but seemed to sink back as she caught a glimpse of her mother-in-law. 'What if we have a think about it and email you?' asked Bella.

'That would be great,' Jill agreed.

Finally, after another interminable round of sorrys for their loss and awkward mangling of names and titles Bella showed Jill out and walked her across the courtyard to where she'd parked outside the coach house. 'I couldn't believe it when I got the call to come over here.'

Bella glanced back at the castle. 'Yeah. It's a lot to take in.'

'No. I meant, well I'd heard about the laird. The old one obviously, but I'd never been here. I mean I knew there was a chapel. Technically it's part of my parish, but I sent an email when I first came here and never got a reply. It sort of dropped off the to-do list, you know. More pressing things.'

'So you're the vicar for the village?'

Jill nodded. 'Yeah. Although I don't see many of them at church. Locharron's a long way to traipse on a Sunday morning. I think my predecessor used to do special services in the community hall or...' She glanced back towards the castle and left the rest unsaid. 'The hall's all closed up now though.'

'I didn't know that.' She didn't know much it turned out.

'No. Well you're new here. Properly new.' Jill smiled.

'Arrived yesterday,' Bella confirmed.

'And you really haven't been here before?' She hesitated. 'Just, you know, most people meet the family before they get engaged.'

'No. Bit of a whirlwind romance,' she explained.

'Fair enough.' Jill nodded. 'Honestly I barely knew there was a son.'

'I don't think he's been back for a while.'

'Well he's here now.' She opened her car door and then paused. 'Look. I know what it's like to be the new girl here. I grew up in Newcastle, and my first parish was

Salford and now...' She looked around at the mountains and the castle and the loch. 'All of this.'

Bella's mind wandered back to her nan's flat in Leeds, to falling asleep in the corner while her nan's mates painted placards and talked class struggle late into the night. 'It's different,' she conceded.

'I'll say. I mean there must have been lords and ladies and wotnot where I grew up, but you don't really think of them actually hanging around the place, do you?'

Bella laughed, releasing a tension she didn't realise she'd been holding in.

'So, if you need to talk or anything...'

'I'm not really religious.'

'That's fine. And I meant as a friend, not professionally.' Jill pulled a pen and a scrap of paper torn from an envelope from her capacious bag and scrawled down a phone number. 'Just if you need to chat.'

–

Bella wandered back inside after showing the vicar out. Adam was leaning on the kitchen island with his eyes closed. Flinty nodded as Bella came back in. 'I'll give you two a minute.'

'Are you OK?'

'Yeah. I'm sorry, about all this. It's not what you expected.'

'It's OK.'

He raised his arm and she slid into the space alongside him, nestling her body against his.

'I feel like I should know what he'd have wanted.' He rubbed his eyes. 'For the funeral. I never asked.'

'That's OK. People don't.' She pressed a kiss into his hair. 'Whatever you think is right will be OK.'

'Really?'

She nodded. 'It doesn't have to be perfect.'

'Adam!' Veronica's curt tone cut through Bella's reassurances.

He pulled away and stood up. 'I'd better get on.'

Darcy had already vanished, presumably out to the stables. Flinty bustled back into the kitchen. 'Maybe you could have that walk now after all?' she suggested. 'You could take Dipper. I don't know if she's been out today, what with everything.'

Bella was at a loss for a reason not to. She rounded up the dog, and accepted the harness and lead and the handful of poo bags Flinty offered, and set out. Bella retraced her steps from earlier past the coach house and up the lane to the road. As they walked, the climb was steeper than she'd appreciated before, as the land rose above the castle rapidly. In places the gentle river alongside her was more of a torrent as it dashed downwards over moss-covered rocks and formed sparkling white waterfalls before settling into restful pools. It was beautiful, and utterly uncompromising at the same time. Most of Bella's life had been spent in places that were created by people. She was a city animal. Forests and mountains and deserted beaches were fun distractions for a day out or a wild lost weekend but day-to-day life took place in nice neat brick and concrete boxes designed by people to keep all of this at bay. Bella laughed at her own unease. What would Nan say? Probably something about how the only way past fear of the unknown was to bloody well get to know it.

Could she let Dipper off the lead here? She had no idea whether she'd come back if Bella called her, and they were on a road, albeit one that seemed to get about two cars per day. She could also see sheep on the hillside in the distance.

You weren't supposed to let dogs worry sheep were you? Bella realised she didn't really know what sorts of things worried sheep. Were they a particularly anxious animal? She didn't think Dipper was likely to approach them with dire warnings about the imminent climate crisis.

She kept Dipper on the lead. The road was quiet, apart from the sound of the water dancing down the hill alongside her. Bella imagined coming out here with Adam and a picnic hamper. Cold beers. Fat, perfectly seasoned sausage rolls, with a hint of chilli or apple. Thick crusty bread with cheese and…

'You all right there, miss?'

The voice stopped Bella's thoughts in their tracks. The enquirer was on the other side of the river. He was an older man, maybe sixty, maybe older, dressed in a water-proof jacket and dark grey trousers of the kind that seem to have more pocket than actual trouser. His grey hair was clipped short.

'I'm fine.'

'You don't see many people out and about, you know, on that side of the Crosan.'

'The what?'

He nodded towards the river. 'The Crosan. This thing youse are standing next to.'

'Right. I'm just out for a walk.'

'Must have walked a fair way to end up over there.'

'Not really.' She pointed back towards the castle. 'I started down there.'

He let out a long low whistle. 'Did you now?'

'Yeah.'

'So you'll have met our Margaret?'

Margaret? A bell was trying to tinkle in her mind but not quite ringing yet.

57

'They call her Flinty.'

'Oh!' Of course. 'She made me a bacon sandwich.'

'Sounds about right.' He narrowed his eyes. 'You must be the English lass young Adam brought back with him.'

'I guess so. I don't think there's another one.'

'Well, look at you.' He shook his head and cast a glance up the way Bella was walking. 'Where are you trying to get to then?'

'Just exploring.' She thought for a second. 'Flinty said there was a village, somewhere. I figured if I followed the road it must be this way.'

'It's a long road though.' He pointed behind him. 'Village is a little way down there.'

'Why isn't there a bridge?'

He laughed. 'There is.' He pointed back the way she'd come. 'You take your life in your hands trying to cross it these days though.'

'Right.' She returned his smile. 'Well it would make it easier to get back and forth, wouldn't it?'

He shook his head. 'Not something many of us bother to do these days. The road bridge is up that way. You just have to keep going long enough.' A small white dog suddenly came bounding down the hill on the other side of the river and jumped excitedly against the stranger's legs. 'There you are. Well, if this one's finished scaring the squirrels I'll be getting back. If you make it as far as the village I might see you again, Miss…?'

'Smith. Bella.'

'Miss Bella.' He nodded and turned away, and then stopped. 'I'm Hugh. You'll find me and my missus in the shop at the far end.'

'I'm sure I'll make it eventually.'

'Right enough.' He half-turned and called back. 'Heard about the old laird. Tell all of them up there we're very sorry.'

Bella continued her trudge up the lane. According to friendly Hugh with the tiny white dog, if she kept going far enough she'd be able to cross over and find her way back down the other side to the village. The thought of a village was the only thing keeping her going. She was picturing roses around doorways and cute little teashops and a warm welcoming village pub. She checked the time on her phone. Nearly two. She hadn't had lunch. Maybe the pub would do food. A nice hearty steak and ale pie could be just the thing.

The path was steep and as she climbed higher the road was moist underfoot. The tread had worn off her trainers years ago and she walked more slowly for fear of slipping. It was getting cooler too. She zipped her hoodie closed and wrapped her arms around her body. It wasn't dangerously cold. She wasn't one of those ridiculous townies who'd set off into the mountains in high heels and a sun dress. She'd done enough festival camping with her nan to understand the adage that there was no such thing as the wrong weather, only the wrong clothes. She was comfortably warm enough to avoid medical emergency. She just wasn't comfortably warm.

The road was an obstacle course of potholes and sheep shit but she kept going. Right until she didn't. She stopped hard and sudden as her ankle turned into an unseen crack in the road. An expletive burst from her lips, and Dipper's lead dropped free from her hand.

She stood stock still for a moment, right foot planted on the ground, left toes resting against her other leg, while the dog sniffed and explored the undergrowth around them. Bella forced herself to breathe. In and out until the initial shock of pain subsided and left her with the aching throb. Finally she lowered her foot to the ground. If it was only an awkward twist she could probably walk it off. She hopped her way around to facing back down the hill, abandoning her goal of making it to the promised bridge and the steak pie of her dreams today. 'OK girl. Let's go.'

She bent as best she could to grab the lead only to see Dipper bound away down the hill.

Adding 'losing the family dog' and a 'possibly broken ankle' to her list of first day mishaps was not great news. 'Dipper!' she yelled. 'Dipper, come!'

The dog was a smaller and smaller dot in the distance. 'Dipper, here!'

Nothing. Great. Bella forced herself to take a breath. Dipper had set off back the way they came rather than into the flock of sheep in the fields above them. That was good. She told herself the dog would find her way home, more out of pure hope than expectation. All Bella could do now was attempt the same.

She hobbled a few paces down the road, placing her left foot gingerly and awkwardly. On the fourth step the throbbing pain exploded into a sharp jab of agony. She stopped, balancing again on one foot. She wiggled her toes inside her shoe and tentatively moved her foot from left to right. Probably not a broken ankle, but that was little comfort right now. She'd been walking for the best part of an hour, which meant she was an hour from her bed in the coach house, and that was at a brisk walk rather than an ungainly hop. There was no way she could walk that far.

Defeated, Bella lowered herself carefully to the ground. What was she supposed to do now?

She closed her eyes and took a second to think. There was no choice but to try to head back down. She fastened the laces on her left shoe as tight as she could to give her as much support as possible in an ageing canvas sneaker. A long walk was about to become an even longer hop. As she pushed herself painfully back to her feet she saw a sheep staring at her from the grass at the edge of the road.

'What you looking at?'

The sheep stepped closer, followed now by five of its woolly friends.

'I really don't need an audience.'

The sheep stared at her.

'I'll put you in a casserole. Don't think I won't.'

The sheep seemed unconcerned.

She set off back down the hill at a slow, awkward half limp, half hop. After three steps she had a sense she was being followed. After five steps she was sure. After seven she stopped and looked back. The small gaggle of sheep stopped too. 'What are you doing?'

They didn't answer. Obviously. They were sheep.

She continued down the hill, pausing every few steps to breathe through the pain and check on the progress of her ovine support crew. Ten minutes into the struggle down the hill she was starting to grow quite fond of them. Fifteen minutes in, the pain in her ankle overcame any distraction being followed by her own uninvited mini flock might have offered. She slumped back down to the ground. She had her phone! Why hadn't she thought of that before? She pulled the handset from her pocket. One weak little bar of signal.

She'd tapped the phone symbol and brought up the keyboard to call Adam before it struck her. She was an engaged woman who didn't actually have her fiancé's phone number. There'd never really been cause to ask, and other than that, all of her contacts were in Spain, or Brazil, or Australia, or – she vaguely thought – possibly on a research station in the Antarctic.

There was always her nan. Bella had no idea where she was right now, but if Bella called she would always pick up, night or day regardless. It would take a day to explain how she'd come to be sitting at the side of a road in Scotland with a sprained ankle and a sheepish fanclub, and once she'd done that, Bella realised with a sinking feeling in her gut, she didn't actually know where she was. Near a castle and a river somewhere in Scotland. About five hours from Edinburgh. To the west, she thought. She briefly considered an actual ambulance. She could imagine Veronica's horror at the level of fuss that would cause, but even if she decided to call 999 she would still have the 'not knowing quite where she was' issue to contend with.

It seemed that the only way she was going to get off this ridiculous hillside was if she walked down herself. At least it wasn't raining…

Bella didn't even have time to finish the thought before the heavens opened and the light mist she'd been surrounded by turned, in an instant, into fat juicy drops of rain. That was conclusive. The actual landscape had taken against her. It had sent her pointlessly up a crazy hill, busted her ankle and now it was soaking her to her bones. Not that sitting about feeling sorry for herself would change any of that.

She pulled herself to her feet again. She needed something to lean on. She ignored the bleating behind her. She needed something that wasn't a sheep to lean on.

She scanned the ground around her. No decent sized branches. Actually barely any trees at all.

She carried on with her awkward slow hop, pausing here and there to shout for Dipper to no avail. The ground around her was soaking now as well, and the risk of tipping into another pothole, or sliding on a patch of sheep poo – she shot her companions an accusatory look to go with that thought – seemed to get greater with every ungainly step. Maybe she should give in, embrace the wet and the dirt, and shuffle down the hill on her arse. At least it would save her from the risk of falling again.

Abandoning dignity and cleanliness, and a large section of her self-respect, Bella lowered her bum to the cold wet road. This was going to ruin her jeans and her hands were going to be grazed for weeks but it saved her ankle and progress got a little quicker. She was starting to pick up pace when a noise from down the hill caught her attention. A car. She shuffled as fast as she could to the side of the road to avoid getting flattened by the vehicle.

Would they even see her? She really needed whoever it was to stop and take pity on her. She could now make out the familiar hulk of Flinty's Land Rover coming into view. She waved her arms as violently as she could manage. 'Flinty!'

The car pulled to a stop, but it wasn't Flinty who jumped out. Her fiancé's mouth dropped open. 'What happened?'

'Twisted my ankle at the top of the hill and then it started to rain and then…' She gestured back towards her sheep entourage. 'I seem to have made some friends.'

'OK.' He nodded. 'Shall we get you in the car?'

'Please.'

He took her weight as she wrapped her arms around his neck and let him lift her back to her foot, leaning, without thinking, into the warmth of his hand against her. The hop to the passenger side was much easier with someone to lean on. In that, a fiancé was more use than a sheep. As she slid her bum onto the seat she asked, 'Where were you going?'

'I was looking for you.' He kissed her head as she settled into the car. 'Flinty said you'd gone for a walk and then it started pissing down. I thought I'd try to save you from getting wet.'

'And then you actually saved me.' She finally found a smile. 'My hero.'

'We aim to please.'

'I'm very pleased right now.' She closed her eyes as he turned the old lump of a vehicle in the too narrow road. 'Did Dipper come back to the castle?'

'Yeah.' Adam frowned. 'Ages ago. Flinty reckoned you must have brought her back but then you never appeared so I wondered if you'd gone out again.'

Bella laughed. 'Oh thank God. I dropped her lead when I fell and she ran off.'

Adam shook his head. 'The only person she ever behaves for…' He stopped. '*Behaved* for was my dad.'

'I thought I was going to have to crawl back and tell you all I'd lost the dog.'

'No. No. Honestly I don't think you could lose Dipper. She always knows where her next meal is coming from.'

The relief of being in the car, of knowing that Dipper was safe, and of knowing that Adam had come to find her, filled Bella with warmth despite her wet clothes and sodden feet. 'Oh,' she remembered. 'Another thing?'

'Yeah?'

'Can I have your phone number?'

'What?'

'I don't have your number. I mean I didn't have very much signal so it might not have helped but I just thought, people who are getting married should probably have each other's numbers.'

He smiled as he drove.

'What are you grinning at?'

'We're getting married.'

She found herself grinning equally dopily back at him. 'Yeah, we are.'

–

Back at the coach house, Bella agreed to Adam's suggestion of a hot bath to warm her up and then some dry clothes before they sought out a bandage for her ankle. The bath was hot and welcoming, and Adam perched himself on the lid of the toilet, ostensibly to keep an eye on the invalid, but, if he was honest with himself, more to stay in hiding from his grandmother.

'How far up the hill did you walk?'

Bella shrugged. 'Not sure. I was trying to get to the village.'

'Why didn't you go over the bridge?'

'What bridge?'

'Just past the coach house, before the hill rises.'

She frowned, and then nodded. 'Yeah. The man mentioned a bridge.'

'What man?'

'There was a guy across the river. He said the bridge wasn't safe though.'

That couldn't be right. If the bridge had needed repairs his father would have done them.

'I didn't see a bridge anyway.'

Adam laughed. 'Lowbridge? The name of the village and the house and the barony. Kind of implies there's a low bridge.'

His fiancée submerged herself under the water for a second. 'I didn't think of that.'

'I'll show you when your ankle's up to it.'

'That would be nice.' She sat up a little bit. 'Did your grandma say anything about me?'

He knew why she was asking. She wanted to assess the depth of Veronica's disapproval. It was, he feared, even worse than she thought. 'No. She didn't really say anything.'

Bella shrugged. 'Well it's better than her spending all morning trying to persuade you to get rid of me.'

'She wouldn't do that.'

'Really?'

He paused. 'My grandmother does not try to persuade people. She's more for telling them what to do outright.'

'She doesn't like me.'

'She doesn't know you yet.' He feared that Bella was absolutely correct. 'Are you having second thoughts?'

She grinned. 'Oh, I had those ages ago. I'm on to about seventeenth thoughts.' She reached a hand out and he leaned across to take it. 'All the thoughts are the same though. All of this is crazy but you and me works, doesn't it?'

'It does.'

'Good.' She squeezed his hand. 'What about you? What have you been doing?'

'My grandmother's crash course in estate management.' Bella winced.

'Your ankle hurting?'

She shook her head. 'My brain is hurting. Is estate management up your street?'

'It's what I was raised to do.'

Now she sat all the way up in the bath. 'That's not what I asked.'

'No.' He closed his eyes for a second. Bella was a fish out of water here, and she'd already been thrust into the heart of his grieving family. He should be looking out for her, not burdening her with his worries. 'It's fine. How about you? I'm sorry about...' He pointed at her swollen ankle.

She shrugged. 'So maybe there was a tiny moment where I thought the landscape was out to get me.'

It must have felt that way. Even with her sitting right in front of him, he was still struggling to picture his feisty, modern, impulsive Spanish beach girl fitting in at Lowbridge. And if Bella didn't fit, what did that mean for him?

She flicked water at him from her fingertips. 'I'm not going to be beaten, though. I will charm this place into loving me.'

His disbelief must have flickered across his face.

'I'm serious,' she insisted. 'You saw. By the time you found me I had a whole flock of adoring sheep fans following me around. I'm a modern day...' she paused. 'Little Miss Muffet?'

He shook his head.

'Didn't she have sheep?'

'No. Spider, and it freaked her out.'

'Who was the one with the sheep then?'

'Little Bo Peep?'

'No.' Bella frowned. 'The lamb girl?'

'Mary had a little lamb?'

'Yes! Eating out of my hand they were.' She grinned. 'Today some sheep. Tomorrow your grandma. You'll see.'

Adam wished he shared her confidence, but where Bella apparently saw only sunlight and new adventures, Adam saw dark clouds.

'So, like, can you go to college to learn to be in charge of a big posh estate then?'

Adam managed a smile at that. 'You can. I didn't, though.' Much to his grandmother's displeasure.

'What did you do?'

'Horticultural college. Grandmother wasn't best pleased but honestly plants were the only thing I was any good at. Took me four goes to pass GCSE maths with a good enough grade to get in there.'

Bella rolled her eyes. 'I was awful at school.'

'In what way?'

'Oh you know. The usual stuff. Got bored easily, and life with Nan was…' She sank down deeper into the water. 'It was so different to school. School was all rules and it felt, I don't know, small. My nan was all about having adventures.'

'My nan was not,' Adam joked.

'No. I got that.'

'So did you go to catering college or something then?' Was that too downmarket? He wasn't sure about the terminology. 'Or culinary school?'

Bella shook her head. 'Nowt so fancy. I worked in a cafe in town from when I was about fourteen. Just at weekends. Then when I was sixteen I got a job washing dishes in a hotel, and that turned into a bit of commis cheffing – basic stuff, chopping potatoes and peeling veg, and I kept going. If you can cook you can pretty much work anywhere. Chefs, hookers and undertakers.' She grinned. 'The only people who'll never be out of work.'

'Not like high-end landscaping in tiny Highland villages.'

'I thought business in Edinburgh was good?'

'It is. For now at least, but I'm not there, am I? Ravi can keep things ticking over, but a garden design business does need a garden designer.'

'We'll work it out.' She sank back into the bath. 'Let's get things sorted here. One thing at a time.' She gave a soapy shrug. 'And then we'll find our next adventure.'

Bella's positivity was infectious. He'd been swept along by her for the last four weeks, to the point where he, Adam Lowbridge, sensible, cautious Adam, had proposed to a woman he, by any reasonable standard, barely knew. He waited, as he'd been waiting ever since that question had left his lips, for the doubt to rush in, but it simply wasn't there. Instead her presence gave him an unfamiliar feeling of certainty.

He let her soothe him. She was right. It was the sensible thing to do. Get things in order here. Give his father a proper send-off. And then maybe he could get back to his real life? It wasn't as if his grandmother needed him to run the estate anyway. It wasn't as if she would actually let him even if he tried.

Adam moved off his perch on the toilet lid and knelt on the floor next to the bath, leaning over far enough to plant a kiss on his fiancée's lips. She snaked a damp arm around his neck.

'You'll get me all wet,' he protested.

She leaned over and wrapped her other arm around his waist, pulling him towards her and splashing water across his chest and back and onto the floor.

Chapter Four

The following morning Bella gratefully accepted Adam's offer to bring her breakfast over on a tray rather than her come over to the house on her sore ankle.

'Castle,' she corrected.

'Don't start that again.'

She sat up in bed, wedging pillows behind her as she heard footsteps on the stair, and letting the sheet that was wrapped around her drop below her breast in a way she hoped was saucy and alluring, rather than merely dishevelled.

Adam's grandmother pushed the door open. 'Oh my!'

Bella grabbed the sheet and hoiked it over her boobs.

Veronica turned towards the wall. 'I was informed that you were ready for breakfast.'

'I'm sorry.' Bella was still, she felt, at something of a disadvantage.

Veronica turned around somewhat gingerly. 'I'll put this over here.' She placed the tray on top of the chest of drawers at the furthest corner of the room. Clearly she hadn't got the 'breakfast in bed to save Bella's ankle' memo, but if it meant she left sooner then Bella would happily embrace an awkward naked hop to get to her cup of tea.

Veronica appeared to have other plans. She clasped her hands together. 'I thought this would give us an opportunity to have a little talk.'

Why did that sound like a threat?

'I am aware that the younger generation tend towards a somewhat more casual approach to things than might previously have been the norm here.'

'What? I don't—'

Veronica held a hand up. Bella shut up. It seemed like this was a *little talk* where Veronica was the one who got to talk.

'If you are to marry Baron Lowbridge…'

'*When*,' Bella muttered.

'…there are certain expectations of you. A role like Lady Lowbridge comes with responsibilities and expectations. One cannot expect to have the same friendships and freedoms that she might have enjoyed before.'

Anger was beginning to swirl in Bella's gut. Who was this woman to suggest that Bella wasn't up to being the lady of her precious Lowbridge?

'It is a life defined by duty, not by individual wants or fancies.'

This was ridiculous. 'I think I can marry Adam and still have a life.'

'Of course. I simply want you to understand what type of life that might be. It will be quite different from whatever you have enjoyed before.'

Bella folded her arms, which had the handy secondary benefit of securing her sheet more firming across her chest. 'I'll manage.'

Veronica's lips pursed, presumably at Bella's perceived insolence. 'Perhaps you will. But is that enough?'

'What do you mean?'

'Many people *manage* in this sort of situation, but perhaps Lowbridge deserves more than that. Sooner or later one can find that it is not enough to manage. One might find they wish to be somewhere where they can thrive.'

Was Veronica warning her off? The anger in Bella's gut hardened. She did not need lectures on how to fit in, or what sort of woman she needed to be to be a lady. She was Bella Bloody Smith and her nan had raised her to understand that people were people. No matter who they seemed to be or where they came from you could only judge them by getting to know them and finding out who they really were. Veronica was showing a bit of who she was this morning. Bella mentally marked the older woman's card.

'I'll leave you to rest. Do think about it though. Is this really the place you belong?'

–

Bella managed almost six hours of resting with her foot up. During that time she drank five cups of tea, demolished a plate of ham sandwiches she suspected Flinty might have intended her to share with Adam, and a hefty chunk of fruit loaf – rich and moist and, she acknowledged, better than Bella could make herself – and imagined six different terrible accidents that could befall her soon-to-be grandmother-in-law.

The whole conversation had been ridiculous. She and Adam were here because his father had died. They would stay for the funeral, but then there was nothing to stop them – whatever Veronica said about duty – from going to Edinburgh like they planned. Adam didn't even live here. Why on earth would Bella?

After every check-in and food delivery, Adam and Flinty both told her vigorously that she needed to rest. And she tried. She lay on the bed and she closed her eyes, but she kept finding herself sitting up, or picking up her phone.

There was a message from her nan. Bella smiled. That was their deal. Wherever they were, whatever was going on, her nan emailed or messaged once a week, and Bella replied, or vice versa. They were rarely long, verbose screeds on what was going on. They were just enough to let the other person know you were still alive, and keep that sense that somewhere out there was somebody you were connected to. Bella scanned the message.

> I'm still down in Somerset. Gwendoline and Darren are dead set on their full moon ritual plan so I'll probably stay here for that. Take care. And tomorrow the world!

Bella hesitated over how to reply. News like an engagement ought to be delivered in person, but doing it over text would save her from actually seeing her nan's unfiltered reaction. She started typing, and then deleted, and then typed again and deleted some more.

> Bit of a change from Spain – I'm in the Scottish Highlands. Long story but all is well (give or take a sprained ankle!) Tomorrow the world xxx

And then she did try to rest, before starting a list of things she needed to do to find a job in Edinburgh, then an entirely unnecessary list of things she could do in Lowbridge. When she caught herself already three quarters of the way through registering with an international recruitment site, she decided that rest wasn't really working out for her, and climbed out of bed.

Her jeans had been squirrelled away somewhere so she delved into Adam's ridiculously overpacked suitcase. His jeans looked like they had every chance of fitting her waist but not a hope in hell of making it over her bum, so she pulled out a pair of soft jogging bottoms instead. They were fleece lined. What sort of man took fleece lined trousers to Spain?

Fleece lined was just the ticket for the old stone coach house. There was a radiator under the window but it didn't seem to put out any heat at all, however much Bella twiddled the control. And the plug-in heater Flinty had found her created a delightfully tropical hot spot covering the six inches around the heater but didn't seem to warm the room itself at all. And it was *May*. She was already thanking her lucky stars they wouldn't be here for winter.

She dragged the jogging bottoms on with a T-shirt and her clogs. It wasn't a high fashion look, but she was clean and dressed and ready for action. So long as the action only involved one foot.

She hopped down the stairs, clinging on to the rail, and hobbled into the courtyard. She stopped and twenty or more pairs of eyes turned towards her. Sheep. Lots of sheep. The leader trotted over to her bleating plaintively, followed by nineteen of its closest mates.

'What are this lot doing here?' Flinty came out of the kitchen door, buttoning her coat.

'I don't know. They were just sort of here.' Bella limped towards Flinty. The sheep shuffled after her.

'Well they seem to think you're their shepherd.'

'I don't know anything about sheep.' The flock had stopped, the front row just inches from Bella's legs. 'What do I do? Where's Dipper?' Dipper would be helpful, surely. Sheep did what dogs told them, didn't they?

'Like she'd be any good. Couldn't herd a housefly. I think they want to follow you. They're a herd animal. They follow the leader.' Flinty smirked slightly. 'They've decided you're top sheep.'

'What?' Bella glared at her new woolly fanclub. 'Shoo! Shoo!' She waved her arms in the general direction of the gateway. 'Shoo!' The sheep stared. They did not move.

'What do I do?'

'Lead 'em back out to the hillside I reckon. Come on.'

Bella inched through the space between the sheep and the castle wall, and hopped awkwardly towards the gate. 'They're not going to follow me.'

Flinty was staring behind her. 'That's what you think.'

The flock trotted after Bella. She led them through the gate and then paused, hoping the sight of fresh grass to munch on the hillside would encourage them to head off their own way. They stopped and watched her. 'I can't be followed by sheep the whole time I'm here.'

Flinty was failing to hide her laughter.

'It's not funny. I can't spend my days wandering around the hillside looking for fresh... what's it called? Pasture?'

'Aye. I do see that.'

Bella stared at her helplessly.

'Why don't you just limp your way up onto the grass a bit, and then maybe once they've got some food to distract them you can sneak off?'

'Fine.' Bella managed twenty yards up the hillside, attended by her woolly entourage.

'Stay up there,' Flinty yelled. 'Let them get settled. I'll pick you up in the Land Rover!'

A few minutes later the battered old four by four pulled up alongside her and Bella jumped in, to a chorus of unhappy bleats. 'Thank you.'

'Where were you off to anyway?'

Where was she off to? 'I don't know. I was getting a bit bored.'

'Right, well. Adam and his grandmother are...' Flinty frowned. 'Well, I think they're occupied. I'm going down to the village. You might as well come along now you're in.'

'OK.' The village was building into something of a place of wonder in her imagination – a promised land of shops, civilisation and possibility.

'Right then. We'd best get on. I don't want to leave things too long and come back to a kitchen full of toilet roll...'

Bella could definitely picture Dipper going full Andrex puppy without proper supervision.

'...or all my egg cups upside down on top of the door,' Flinty continued.

What on earth? 'What was that about egg cups?'

The older woman shook her head. 'She only did that one time.'

'Sorry. What?'

'You'll see soon enough.' Flinty grinned. 'Now do you need anything from the shop?'

Bella rolled with the change of subject.

'I think I need to get some better shoes, and maybe a waterproof?'

'You don't have those?'

'I was living in Spain a week ago.'

Flinty nodded. 'But the rest of your stuff must be somewhere?'

'I've got all my stuff with me.'

'Just that wee baggy you brought from the airport? Well aren't you one for travelling light?'

Why carry more than you needed?

'You'll not be able to get those in the village, mind. Not new. We might be able to find you something to borrow for the time being. What size feet do you have?'

'Five.'

Flinty nodded. 'Well that shouldn't be too hard. Hugh might be able to order you something in. Or you can wait 'til you can get to an outdoor shop.'

'So where's the nearest?'

'From here? That'd probably be Portree, over on Skye.'

Skye. A tune jangled in Bella's head. *Over the sea to Skye…* 'Isn't that an island?'

'It is.'

'So the nearest clothes shop is on a different land mass?' Bella was rapidly redrawing her mental picture of Lowbridge village.

'Aye, but you can drive all the way since they opened the bridge at Lochalsh. Or we could ask in the village if anyone's taking a boat over. There's usually a couple who do each week. They might take you along.'

'What sort of boat?' Bella had images of hardy Highland trawlermen pissing themselves at the wee English lassie's lack of sea legs.

Flinty glanced at her. 'A boat boat. Don't worry. You're not going to have to row over there. They all have motors.'

A boat trip sounded like overkill given that she'd probably be back in Edinburgh with its pavements and shops and restaurants and general lack of insanity in a couple of weeks. 'If I could borrow something for now then?'

'Aye. I thought that'd be best.'

Flinty drove the narrow country lanes like a racing driver in a hurry. Once they were over the road bridge, Bella realised she hadn't got close to the village on her aborted walk. The road widened slightly and they started to meet the occasional car coming the other way. All of which pulled into the side of the road to let Flinty past. The local drivers had clearly learned that if you didn't get out of her way, it would only end worse for you.

Finally they started to come into what Bella assumed was the village, and then they kept driving, through a cluster of small stone-built cottages and along the shoreline, where a shallow shingle beach gave way to dark blue water. Bella leaned forward to stare at the view. Across the water was more land, an island or a headland jutting out into the sea. Everything was sparkling in shades of blue and green. 'It's beautiful.'

'Aye.' Flinty nodded. 'We're very lucky.' She drove on towards a strung-out row of newer houses. At what looked to be the very last of these, Flinty stopped the car and pulled in on a patch of gravel and mud to the side of the road. 'Here we are then,' she announced.

Where they were didn't look like anything very much. They'd stopped outside a white painted detached house. There were piles of wood, and bags of compost on the driveway. Flinty marched past those. Bella followed and finally saw where they were heading. Above what she had taken to be the garage, and what the original builder had definitely intended to be the garage, was a hand-painted sign that read, 'Lowbridge Village Store'. And under that someone had enthusiastically written, 'If we don't have it, we will get it. Ask us for anything!'

Given that the whole shop took up the space previously allocated to a mid-sized family car, that seemed like an ambitious promise. She followed Flinty up the gravelled driveway. As well as the bags of logs and compost, there were newspapers, a bucket of flower bouquets, a station for returning and refilling gas bottles and a table stacked with potted plants and a handwritten sign declaring, 'From Mrs Allen. 50p each or £1 for 3. Proceeds go to the Community Hall fund. Money in the tin please!'

The shopkeeper had stacked their stock high outside, but the inside of the store was like another world. Whoever ran the place was surely part Time Lord, because there was no logical way this amount of stuff could fit inside a garage without at least a dash of Tardis-style 'bigger on the inside' magic going on. Flinty was briskly filling a basket with fresh fruit and veg, meat from the fridge, and bread from the basket next to the cash desk.

Bella followed her around, trying not to knock over any of the ceiling-high teetering displays.

'We need cleaning stuff,' said Flinty. 'Washing up liquid and bathroom spray.'

There was no cleaning aisle. There were no aisles. There was simply stuff. Mountains and mountains of stuff.

'Come on.'

Bella trotted after her guide again, right to the back of the garage, and then behind what was obviously the last display. 'Where are you going?'

'Cleaning and toiletries. This way.' Flinty pushed open a small door.

'This is just someone's garden.'

'Well, this is someone's garden. It's not *just* someone's garden.'

The path from the garage down the side of the house had been covered with a rig-up of sun parasols and tarpaulins, to provide some protection from the rain, but it was still very much outside and very much a part of a, Bella presumed, private garden. 'Are you sure this is OK?'

'It's fine. Didn't all fit in the main shop.'

Garage, Bella thought.

'So they had to expand.'

Flinty tapped on a patio door as she went past. Inside a group of women were sitting drinking tea. They looked up as one as Bella went past. She raised a hand in greeting. Flinty continued and pushed open the unlocked door of what looked like a standard garden shed.

A garden shed filled with cleaning products, toiletries, tissues, loo roll and kitchen paper. Obviously. Oh, and stationery and office supplies tucked against the back wall. Of course. Flinty added the cleaning things she needed to her basket, and then thrust a nine pack of toilet roll into Bella's arms. 'Carry this.'

Bella nodded.

'Do you need anything? Shampoo?' Flinty waved her hand towards the sanitary protection. 'That sort of thing.'

Bella grabbed what she needed from the surprisingly varied range of toiletries, and balanced it on top of the toilet paper.

'All right.' Flinty led the way back to what Bella's brain was now dutifully accepting as 'the main store' rather than 'some random garage' and placed her basket down on the counter.

One of the women from the house was now behind the tillpoint. Two of the others were loitering by the salad vegetables. Bella was finding it hard to avoid the feeling that they were rather more interested in her than in the lettuce selection. 'Afternoon Maggie. How's…' The woman at the till paused. 'Everything?'

'Oh you know.' Bella got the definite feeling that the two women had exchanged a look. The sort of look that said, 'Well I can't tell you in front of this one.'

'I'm Bella.' Bella stuck out her hand. She was here, and she wasn't going to stand around quietly while she was discussed in a range of silent nods and raised eyebrows.

'Bella's a friend of the new laird. Adam.'

'Oooh.' The woman's interest shot up a notch. 'Hugh said he'd seen some lass on the castle side. I thought he was having one of his turns.'

'Does Hugh have turns?' asked Bella.

'Not really. Thought he might have started. He's the type that would.'

'Well that was me. I met Hugh.' Bella smiled brightly. 'And his little dog.'

'Queen Latifah.'

'I'm sorry?'

'The dog's called Queen Latifah.' The woman shook her head. 'Previous dog was Edward WoofWoof. Big fan of *The Equalizer* my Hugh. Original and reboot.'

The woman looked back at Bella. There was definitely interest there, but there was something else as well. 'So a new laird?' She shrugged. 'Not that it'll make any difference to us.'

Why would it make any difference? Obviously it was sad, but why would the death of some guy in a big house at the other end of a village make any difference to anyone apart from his immediate family?

'Same old, same old over there isn't it?' the woman confirmed.

'Anna…' There was an edge to Flinty's voice that Bella wasn't used to.

The woman raised her hands in an apparent gesture of acquiescence. 'Fine.' She turned back to Bella. 'I'm Anna. Me and Hugh run this place.' She nodded at her associates, still lingering in the fresh produce. 'That's Nina. She basically runs everything else. And Netty.'

Nina stepped forward and shook Bella enthusiastically by the hand. Netty followed and stopped half a step behind. 'I don't run everything,' Nina insisted.

'Well there's not much to run with the hall closed.' Anna's tone was bleak again.

'What hall?' Bella asked.

'The community hall. It needs a new roof,' Nina explained. 'So most of the community groups have had to stop. We have Ladies' Group here at Anna's, but most things need more space, don't they?'

Netty whispered something inaudible.

Nina nodded. 'You're right. She should. You'd be very welcome.'

All four women were now staring at Bella. 'I'm sorry. I didn't quite catch that.'

Netty whispered again. Still completely outside the range of human hearing. Flinty, Anna and Nina all nodded and turned back to Bella. Apparently only out of the range of one human's hearing.

She smiled apologetically. 'I'm sorry. Still didn't quite…'

'You should go to Ladies' Group,' Flinty explained. 'Good way to get to know people.'

'Maggie comes,' Anna added. 'Now she's *retired*.' She didn't need to make air quotes around 'retired'. You could hear them.

Should she really be joining village groups when she wasn't sure how long she was going to be here? She opened her mouth to demur and caught the expectant expressions on the faces around her. 'I'd love to.'

'Wonderful. Tuesday mornings, unless Anna has a meat delivery. Then we move to Wednesdays.'

Netty issued another incomprehensible interjection.

'Quite right.' Nina nodded. 'Not the third Wednesday of the month because that's when the mobile library comes.'

'So when's the next one?'

'Monday.'

Of course.

'Right. Let's get these things rung through. Was there anything you couldn't find?'

'No, but Bella needs some things.'

Flinty physically pushed her forward, like a mother encouraging her child to do her bit at the school talent show.

'Oh yeah. I need some walking boots or wellies. And a proper coat.'

Anna's face barely shifted but the tiny tightening around her mouth spoke volumes of her thoughts on the silly English girl who'd rocked up in the Scottish Highlands without even a proper jacket. 'There's wellies in the red bin out front. Donated, so put something in the tin for the hall appeal. The coat we'll need to order in.' She pulled a lever arch folder from under the counter, flicked through and pulled out two thin catalogues. She handed Bella the first. 'These ones I can get from a place in Portree so you can pick it up Monday.' And then the second. 'These are nicer and better value, to be honest, but I have to order in so it'll probably be ten days.'

'I guess quicker?' she asked Flinty, who nodded in response. She picked one of the less awful-looking coats from the very slim women's section. It was still objectively horrible, but it was also the cheapest on the page. Bella was going to need to do something that earned some money really soon.

'Right. I'll settle up then,' Flinty said.

'I can pay for my things,' Bella insisted.

'Put it through on the house account,' Flinty told the shopkeeper.

'I can...'

'You can sort it out with the laird when we get back.' Flinty looked tired. 'Just carry these out for me, will you?'

Bella did what she was told, remembering not to open the back door. Flinty was still inside the garage shop. The four women were now huddled around the till, all talking at once.

Listening in was wrong. Eavesdropping was definitely something her nan would disapprove of, but also something she would absolutely do herself.

And this conversation, right now, was really happening in a public place and Bella was 99 per cent sure it was about her anyway, so it was hardly eavesdropping at all. Bella took a couple of steps closer and managed to catch a few words as they drifted her way. 'Never mentioned her before...'

'Bet the old lady was having kittens...' quickly followed by a, 'Don't talk about Veronica like that,' from Flinty.

And then, 'So is she after his money then?'

Bella was seconds away from giving herself away by pointing out that she had no idea Adam was about to inherit a castle when she'd agreed to marry him, when a voice much closer to her ear, stopped her. 'Who are you and why are you staring at my mother?'

Bella spun around and all but yelped in surprise at the man standing behind her. The owner of the voice was six foot tall and almost as wide. 'I'm Bella, and I didn't know I was.'

'Oh. You wouldn't be the famous lassie from the castle?'

'Apparently.'

He nodded. 'So you're staring down the local coven to try and listen in to what they're saying about you?'

'No.'

His face cracked into a smile.

'Maybe,' she conceded.

'Eavesdroppers never hear good of themselves,' he told her, moving past her into the stop. 'Ma! There's a storm coming in. I thought you might need a ride back.'

Nina patted the giant's arm. 'Oh. Pavel, you're a good boy. You'll take Netty as well?'

'Aye.'

Bella, Flinty and Anna watch the trio depart. Anna let out an unexpected low growl. 'I would climb that man like a tree,' she murmured.

'Wouldn't most people?' Flinty replied.

Bella didn't respond. Muscle-bound beefcakes were well within her usual area of interest but whatever Adam had done to her senses that first night in Spain, he was still doing. Bella had walked the world alone for a very long time. Her only anchor was her nan. This was something different. This was a feeling as though something

85

inside of her was constantly aware of him, louder when he was close, but never completely silent. She was a planet orbiting his star. No. That wasn't it. Because whatever that thing inside her that had come alive when he touched her was, she absolutely understood that he felt it too. They were orbiting each other, unexpectedly entirely held together. Who needed a beefcake when they had an actual laird waiting for them at home?

—

'I'm glad you're going to come along to Ladies' Group,' Flinty commented as she pulled the Land Rover onto the road outside the shop. 'Good to get involved in the village. Shows them things are changing.'

'Changing?'

'Just, well, the old laird hadn't been able to get that involved for a while, you know?'

Bella did not know. Bella did know that for so long as she was here she might as well get involved. Who knew how long that would be? But she didn't have to be making plans for forever to be able to enjoy the here and now. 'What is Ladies' Group anyway?'

'It's women meeting up to gossip mostly. But they organise stuff like the community hall appeal and village events and what have you.'

'Like the WI?'

Flinty's expression darkened. 'Do not mention the WI.'

'Why not?'

'There was an incident with a Victoria sponge and a competition with the WI and the Locharron Townswomen's Guild. Anna does not like to talk about it.'

'Right.'

'They're all nice enough though. You'll enjoy it. I'm sure.'

That sense of positivity evaporated as they arrived back at the castle and were met by a loud American-accented screeching shout from the front hall.

'I am not going to move out. I'm Lady Lowbridge, and this is my fucking home!'

Behind Bella, there was the sound of Flinty's footsteps retreating briskly back to the kitchen. Bella wondered if she should follow, but held her ground. Darcy was in the middle of the hallway. Her anger was directed at Adam's grandmother. Adam was standing on his own in the doorway to one of the rooms Bella hadn't ventured into yet.

'She's not saying you have to move out.' Adam's tone was placatory, but the tension she'd heard when they discussed the funeral arrangements was back in his voice.

'That's exactly what she's saying.'

Adam's grandmother held up her hand. When she spoke, her tone was cool. 'There are ways that things have always been done here. The lady's bedroom is for the wife of the current baron. You are not the wife of the current baron so you will vacate that room, as every dowager before you has done.'

'Grandmother!' Adam tried to interject. He fell back in response to the look he received.

'Adam will occupy the laird's room.' She finally acknowledged Bella's presence. 'If at some point he decides to marry, then the lady's room will be available.'

'If?' asked Bella.

Darcy screamed over her. 'So where am I supposed to go? What if I decide I want the dower house?'

'The dower house is occupied.'

'So maybe it makes sense for Darcy to stay where she is?' Adam suggested.

'That's not how things are done,' Veronica replied. 'Perhaps the coach house would be suitable?'

Darcy marched over to her rival. 'Here's an idea. Why don't *you* move out? I mean, I'm the dowager now. What are you?'

'I'm the baron's grandmother. You are just some New York—'

'Stop!' Adam raised his voice for the first time in the conversation. 'It doesn't matter who sleeps where. It doesn't matter whether you both call yourself dowager or neither of you do or you take alternate weekends and school holidays and share it between you. Please...' He sounded exhausted. 'Stop.'

Veronica's tone had already been icy. Now it was at absolute zero. 'Do not speak to me like that, young...'

But Adam had already walked away. The silence hung for a moment in the hallway punctuated only by the sound of a door creaking and slamming. Bella looked from one woman to the other. She still didn't really know what the row was about, but she remembered the *if* Veronica had associated with the question of Adam marrying, so she was minded to side with Darcy.

But neither of them were her immediate concern. Her concern was her fiancé. 'Excuse me.' She shuffled past Darcy and made her way across the hallway, and out of the door Adam had vanished through.

The room was cold, which wasn't surprising. The whole building seemed to be permanently freezing. One wall was covered with bookcases, half filled with the sorts of books that Bella associated with school trips to stately homes – clothbound and clearly unread for generations but still deemed dangerous enough to require caging behind metal grilles. The last bay of shelves was open and full from top to bottom with account books and modern lever arch files. On the desk at the centre of the room there was a computer that looked like it had been recovered from the ark and a stack of papers. Dipper peered out from behind a chair.

At the far side was another door. Adam must have gone out that way. Bella opened the door and stepped out, pausing a second to let Dipper follow. The rain had stopped, finally, and the air was at least warm enough now for her T-shirt and jogging bottoms to be sufficient. Adam wasn't in the yard outside. She couldn't see him in the field that was visible from the doorway. She limped around the side of the castle, scanning in every direction. If he hadn't headed off across the field, he must either still be close at hand or have made his way up the road towards the bridge uphill. Bella set off, slowly, on the increasingly familiar walk.

She was only a minute or two away from the castle itself when she caught sight of him, not on the road, but down towards the river. The bank dropped in a shallow slope at first. She looked to follow him, but the ground was wet and muddy from the day's rain. She called out, but he was too far away. Her chef's clogs were not designed for running but she managed a short awkward jog, wincing slightly on her still-sore ankle, to get within earshot of her fiancé. 'Adam!'

He stopped, turned and immediately ran back down towards her. 'What are you doing? You shouldn't be walking.'

'I'm fine. I wanted to make sure you were OK.'

Everything about his demeanour – his slumped shoulders, the bags under his eyes, the absence of the easy smile he'd worn in Spain – told her he wasn't.

'I'm fine,' he said. 'I just needed a break from the screaming.'

'Are they always like that?'

'Kinda. I think my father used to be able to get them to be more polite about it.'

'Well it's a difficult time.'

He half-laughed, but there was no joy or humour in it. 'So I keep being told.'

She took his hand. 'Anything I can do?'

'I think I need to take a break. I might go for a walk.'

She was balancing awkwardly on one foot. 'Do you want me to come with you?'

'And fall down another hole?' He shook his head. 'No. I'll be all right. I just need a few minutes to clear my head.'

She pressed a kiss to his lips and hoped he understood that it was more than a kiss. It was a promise that they'd be away from all this living their own lives very soon. He rested his forehead against hers a second before he moved away. 'I'll be back soon.'

Bella turned back towards the castle, expecting Dipper to stay out in the excitement of the outdoors with her new master. Instead the dog followed Bella inside.

Chapter Five

Bella limped back to the castle kitchen. Flinty was chopping carrots. The repetitive slice and tap of her knife against the board instantly soothed Bella's frayed nerves. 'Can I help with anything?'

Cooking always centred Bella. Even the most mundane prep tasks brought her a peace she seldom felt outside the kitchen.

Flinty shook her head. 'I'm fine here, love.'

'Right.' The feeling that Bella was surplus to Lowbridge's requirements edged up on her again. The thought of actually living here as lady of the manor, in the way Darcy seemed to, sent a physical shudder through her. What would she do all day?

'Why don't you take a proper look around inside?' Flinty suggested, in a tone that instantly cast Bella in the role of troublesome child who needed to be entertained and kept out of the way. 'You only got as far as the second ballroom corridor last time.'

'Sure.' She wandered through to the main hallway before Flinty's comment hit her. The *second* ballroom corridor. Did that mean the second corridor near the ballroom, or did it imply the existence of a whole other primary ballroom somewhere else in the labyrinth this crazy family insisted as referring to as 'the house'?

Opposite the entrance way was the staircase. The *front* staircase, as she'd now learned. Based on an instinct that Veronica was most likely to be in the office or one of the innumerable living rooms on the ground floor, Bella headed up the stairs.

At the top of the stairs was a grand landing, with doors and further corridors in every direction. Bella froze. Presumably these were bedrooms. You couldn't wander into a random bedroom. Years working in the hotel trade had definitely taught her that.

She turned back towards the staircase, before a sound from further down the hallway stopped her. It was a sob. She was sure it was a sob. She stopped and listened. It wasn't coming from the first door, the room nearest to her. She crept down the hallway. At the second door, she paused. Another sob, louder this time. Bella tapped gently on the door and pushed it open.

Darcy was sitting cross-legged in the middle of the floor, the raggedy-looking man's dressing gown wrapped around her shoulders, clutching a shiny-covered paperback. She didn't look up as Bella came in.

She moved alongside her. 'Darcy? Are you OK?'

Darcy looked up, as if noticing her companion for the first time. 'I gave him this for his birthday.' She opened the book to the bookmarked page. 'He said he'd been wanting to read it for ages. He didn't get to finish it.' She turned the book over in her hands. 'What should I do with it now?'

'I don't know.'

'Veronica says we should clear this room out for Adam.'

Bella shook her head. 'Oh no. We're fine in the coach house.'

'Veronica said…'

'It's not a problem. It's a really big house.'

'It's a castle, sweetie.'

Bella all but punched the air. 'I know! Adam keeps calling it a house.'

Darcy managed a watery smile at the long-running dispute between her and the rest of the family. 'His dad always said the same. I'd say castle and he'd say, "Well, barely."'

'It's definitely a castle. We should have a ticket booth and charge admission.'

'We used to.' Darcy took a deep breath. 'But then Covid, you know.'

'You didn't reopen?'

Darcy shook her head. 'Alexander didn't really have the heart for it. He was never that keen on having people around the whole time. This was supposed to be his room.'

Bella looked around. The dark wood furniture did have a distinctly masculine air, but there were clear signs of Darcy's presence. Tubs of moisturiser on the night stand. Women's clothes discarded on the chair in the corner.

Darcy pointed towards the door in the side wall. 'That goes through to a bathroom. Like a…' She wrinkled her brow. 'Is it Jack and Jill? En suite to two rooms.'

Bella nodded.

'And then through the other side is officially my room.'

'You didn't share a bedroom?' Bella asked the question before she checked herself. 'I mean that's fine. Whatever works…'

'No. We shared this room.' Darcy giggled slightly. 'Veronica doesn't know. I'm thirty-eight years old and I spent my whole marriage pretending to my husband's mother that we slept in separate rooms and then sneaking through here.'

'Every night?'

Darcy nodded. 'I used to mess the sheets through there up, but after about three months Flinty told me not to bother cos it was only making laundry, and Veronica would never dream of just charging into someone else's boudoir.'

Bella frowned. 'So the whole bedroom thing? You could stay in here and me and Adam could go in your room?'

'Oh no. Not sharing a room is apparently key to a healthy marriage.'

'How do these people ever produce heirs?'

Darcy giggled. 'I think they have a butler carry a little sample through on a velvet pillow.'

'And the lady just lies back and thinks of England?'

'Scotland.'

'Right.'

'Of course we never did.'

'Sorry.' She was a second behind.

Darcy wiped her eye. 'Produce an heir. Or rather spare.'

Bella winced at her own insensitivity. 'I'm sorry.'

'It's OK. We wanted to.' Darcy shook her head. 'It never happened, and Alexander wasn't keen on having doctors poke into all of that. He said that if it was meant to happen it would.'

Bella wasn't sure how, or even if, to fill the silence that followed.

'It's a ton more straightforward with horses. Just send them off to stud and they come back in foal.'

'Right.'

Darcy rubbed her hand across her cheek. 'Do you want to come out to the stables with me?' She looked around the room. 'I thought it would be easier in here. I thought I'd feel closer to him.'

'You didn't?'

Darcy half-smiled. 'I did. It just wasn't easier.'

'I'm sorry.'

Darcy pulled herself up to her feet and they made their way down the stairs and out across the courtyard – through a door Bella would happily have sworn wasn't there yesterday – towards the stables. 'Oh, is your ankle OK for this?'

Bella nodded. 'It's improving.'

'It's such a joy to live somewhere I can keep horses. I could only dream of it growing up.'

'In New York?'

'Yeah. Grew up having one bottom bunk with someone above me and someone right next to me, and now all of this. Until I met Alexander, I thought New York was everything.'

'And now?'

Darcy leaned against the fence alongside the paddock. 'I think Veronica thinks I'll go back there. I don't know. I can't think beyond right now.'

'You don't have to. And you can stay here as long as you want.'

'Is that what Veronica says?'

Bella sighed. 'Well, it's not up to her, is it? Adam will say the same. This is your home. You do not need to go anywhere.'

'You're kind, but there's a way these things work. The dowager moves into the dower house. The laird and lady live here. What should happen is that I should go to the dower house, but then where does Veronica go? You're not supposed to have two dowagers, are you? My Alexander died too young.' Her previously matter of fact tone cracked. 'I'm not ready.'

Bella bent her head towards Darcy.

'And I don't want to leave my girl. Liberty.'

Of course. The horse.

'Or Larry. Who'd be fool enough to look after him if I wasn't here?'

'Then stay.' Of course Darcy should stay. Bella turned and looked back at the castle. She could now see a staircase down the outside to a lower level that seemed to have grilles across the entrance. 'Is that a dungeon?'

Darcy followed her gaze. 'Oh, don't be silly. That was the kennels for a long time.'

'How many dogs did you have?'

'Well before my time there was a hunt. Adam hated it though. Don't think Alexander was really that keen himself.' She paused. 'So after the hunting dogs had gone it was just Wren and whichever pups we kept.' She looked for a second as if the tears were going to come again. 'Only Dipper left now. We lost Wren last year. That broke Alexander's heart.' Almost on cue Dipper came darting across the courtyard.

Darcy bent down to pet her. 'You're the last girl standing now, aren't you?'

Darcy was sweet when she wasn't screaming at her mother-in-law. Bella wanted to comfort her. There was only one way of giving comfort that Bella really understood. 'Let me make you some lunch.'

'That's very kind.' Darcy smiled. 'Oh, you didn't really think that was a dungeon, did you?'

'No.'

'Right, because the dungeon's over under the scullery.'

Of course it was.

–

Adam wished Bella had joined him on his walk. Her presence was a balm but also a distraction from the nagging voice that had lived in his brain for as long as he could remember but was now moving from a whisper to a shout. It was the voice that told him that whatever breeding, and the rules of inheritance, and the imperious insistence of his grandmother, said, he was not cut out for this.

He couldn't even keep the peace within his own family. What chance did he have managing a sprawling estate? Going through the accounts was like trying to learn to read Greek with his eyes closed. And the in-tray in the office of letters and bills and goodness knows what else made him thank the heavens for his business partner back in Edinburgh a thousand times over. Ravi was an organisational genius. And Adam was a good horticultur-alist and a decent designer. They both knew they needed the other. Here he was expected to be able to do it all, and that was before he'd even got started on the layers of responsibility and public duty that seemed to come with 'being the laird'. The family, the estate, the village – they were all spokes on the wheel. Adam was the hub. If he failed, nothing else held together.

From what he remembered of his grandfather, and, to a lesser extent, his father, being the laird involved a lot of wearing tweed and shooting game, neither of which really appealed to a man who'd scandalised his grandparents quite enough by briefly going vegetarian as a teenager.

He walked around the outside wall of the house and up towards the fields, but rather than continuing up the hill, he followed the line of the castle wall. This was a walk he'd done a thousand times with his father. The path split as the wall turned a corner. To the left, taking you further around to the far side of the house, there was another wall, with a small wooden door cut into it. To the right, the path went up hill along the coastline to the north, and then followed the clifftop around to the large headland that enclosed the sea loch and protected the house and the village from the elements.

He turned to the left, following the wall down to the old wooden door – the gateway to the castle's walled kitchen garden. The garden had been established in the 1800s by the son of the seventh baron, desperate to prove that modern gardens and imported tropical plants weren't the exclusive preserve of those fancy English lords and ladies. The pineapples hadn't lasted long, but the garden had thrived.

Adam stopped with his hand on the round metal handle. This garden had been his father's pride and joy. It was where Adam had first put his hands into the soil. It was where he'd learned about the rhythms of the seasons and the thousand and one ways in which a novice gardener could conspire to kill the things they planted, and the thousand and one ways nature had of surviving despite his interventions.

This garden was also where Adam and his father had spent most of their days in those strange disjointed weeks and months after his mother had gone. They hadn't talked. Adam's father had never been a great talker, but they'd worked side by side, planting, weeding, thinning out, tying up, and eventually harvesting. The cycle of the year from spring into summer and then autumn had carried them through the confusion and the emptiness that his mother's departure had left in her wake.

His hand rested on the worn wood of the doorway, warm under his touch, compared to the cool stone of the wall. When Adam thought of his father this was where he pictured him, peering at a seed tray with one pair of glasses on his nose and another resting on the top of his head, or kneeling next to a bed pulling out interlopers and chatting absent-mindedly to his seedlings as he did so.

If Adam never opened this door then he could keep that picture alive. His dad could be always here, pottering in his garden, just about to take a break and pop inside for a cup of tea. Adam removed his fingers from the handle and turned back towards the house.

–

Bella left Darcy to gather herself, and made her way back into the kitchen. Flinty was sitting at the island, cup of tea in front of her, eyes closed and head resting on hands. She looked up, rearranging her glasses, and smiling briskly when she heard Bella come in.

'Are you OK?'

'Absolutely fine, dear.'

Bella raised an eyebrow.

'Maybe a little bit tired.'

Bella had already worked out that 'a little bit tired' was the closest she was going to get from Flinty to any acknowledgement of illness or fatigue.

'Why don't you go home? You've been here all hours.' Bella smiled. 'And people do keep telling me that you're retired.'

'Oh fiddle faddle. What would I do at home?' Flinty took a deep breath in. 'Right. Veronica thinks lunch is an unnecessary indulgence but I should get on with something for you and Darcy. And Adam, if he's coming back.'

Finally something Bella could help with. 'I can do that. I told Darcy I'd make her something anyway. You finish your tea. If you won't go home and rest you can at least take a proper break here.'

'You don't have to.'

'I don't mind.'

'You don't know where things are.'

'Well you can sit there and tell me.'

'It's really less bother for me to do it.'

They were both being super polite but there was a definite hint of territorial defence in Flinty's attitude. Bella tried a different tack. 'I'm sorry. I shouldn't have told Darcy I'd get her something before I asked you. But, now I have, I feel like I should follow through, you know.'

Flinty hesitated. The appeal to her sense of duty seemed to be working.

'I don't want to put you to any bother.'

'It's just lunch for Adam and Darcy.'

'Aye well, I suppose it's not for the lady,' Flinty muttered.

Bella grabbed the hint of acquiescence. 'What were you planning on making?'

Flinty's expression suggested that she knew she was beaten. 'Well there's eggs in the back pantry, and bacon in the fridge I think.'

'Right. Start me off with where the back pantry is.'

'On the left down there.'

She followed Flinty's directions, and found the walk-in larder. A larder that truly had the potential for greatness, and in reality seemed to mostly house tinned soup, baked beans and some jars covered in a layer of dust and cobwebs that made her feel slightly terrified of checking the use by dates.

She could almost carry out an archaeological analysis of the shelving. At the back of the pantry was the stuff that looked like it hadn't been touched in years. She made a definite decision to steer well clear of that. Then there were the tins. Again there were a lot that definitely weren't super recent, but that was fine for cans, wasn't it? It took her back to childhood and her nan's famous 'mystery teas' which were the contents of whatever the supermarket down the road was selling off because the label had, at some point, become disassociated from the tin. Peaches in sugar syrup and mushroom soup, for example.

Darcy probably needed something a little more obviously edible.

Flinty appeared behind her. 'I should clear this out really. They had a girl came in for a bit after I retired. She wasn't use nor ornament.' She started systematically sorting through tins on the farthest shelf.

'You're supposed to be having a break,' Bella reminded her.

Flinty didn't budge. 'Veg are in the baskets.' She picked up a carton from the shelf beside her. 'And I've got your eggs.'

Bella followed Flinty's instruction to find big ripe red tomatoes and a punnet of smaller tomatoes too, flecked with streaks of orange and yellow.

'From Hugh's garden, those little ones.'

'Hugh at the shop?'

Flinty nodded.

'Have you known them a long time?'

'A wee while.' Flinty laughed. 'Hugh's my brother.'

Bella was still working out the interrelationships of the village. 'And he's married to Anna?'

'Aye.'

Bella tried to make those details stick in her head. 'Well his tomatoes look wonderful.'

'Used to grow our own here. The laird, the old laird, had green fingers.'

'Well so does Adam.' Her brain served up a flash of the orange grove in Malaga, how at peace he'd been among the trees and flowers, and how certain that their place was together.

'I was forever scrubbing soil from under that one's nails.'

Bella surveyed the rest of the pantry. At the very edge of the middle shelf was the carrier Flinty had brought back from the village shop a day earlier. Bread, potatoes, onions, and more fresh veg. Bella could picture Flinty staring into the pantry with the same trepidation she was feeling and just giving up and buying her own stuff and keeping it separate.

It wasn't going to be a fancy lunch, but it would be good honest cooking. She grabbed the tomatoes and a small onion from Flinty's bag. Some fresh herbs would be good, but she could make do. Bella carried her haul through to the kitchen and added mushrooms, bacon and cheese from the fridge to her pile.

She sliced two rashers of bacon into thin strips quickly and professionally. Knife skills were a point of pride for any professional cook and hers had been honed by years and years of vegetable prep in her first kitchen on the lowest rung of the ladder. Her boss had been insistent that anyone who even aspired to call themselves a chef ought to be able to prepare a perfect omelette, and equally insistent that the definition of 'perfect' was individual and specific.

Some people swore by egg whites alone. Bella had quickly concluded that those people were idiots without the palate or discernment to appreciate the warm inviting colour the yolk brought to the finished dish, or, more importantly, the rich, more luxurious flavour. Bella tried, at her grandma's instigation, to approach everyone she met with an open mind and no judgement. People who preferred egg white omelettes tested that ethos close to its limit.

Bella cracked her eggs into a small bowl and added salt and a twist of black pepper before she beat them together.

Aaaa-choo!

The noise behind her made Bella start. 'Bless you!' she laughed.

'What?'

She turned towards Flinty. 'Bless you. Because you sneezed.'

Her companion looked utterly blank for a moment and then nodded. 'Right. Yes. Of course I did. You're using black pepper aren't you?'

'Oh sorry. Are you allergic or something?'

Flinty shook her head. 'No. No. You carry on.'

Bella tossed her bacon into the pan where it sizzled satisfyingly, and left it to crisp up while she chopped her onion and mushrooms. There were a thousand and one techniques for chopping onions without weeping. None of them worked. The only thing for it was to power through. Bella zoned out from everything else around her, absorbed by the rhythm of her knife against the board.

'You're good with that knife.'

'Thank you.'

Bella checked on her bacon, and turned back to her board. The long chef's knife she'd been using to chop the mushrooms wasn't lying on the board. She looked back behind her. Had she taken it with her when she'd checked on the pan? Of course not. She knew better than to wander around a kitchen with a blade in her hand.

'What are you looking for?' Flinty asked.

'My knife.' Bella tapped her board. 'It was right here.'

Flinty looked around and pointed to the worktop at the far side of the kitchen. 'That knife?'

And there it was, several feet away. When had she been over there? 'Did you...?'

Flinty laughed. 'Not me. Poppy.'

'Who?'

'Poppy.' Flinty shrugged. 'I mean we don't know she's called that, but Darcy said she ought to have a name.'

Even in a castle there couldn't be a whole other person clattering around that Bella hadn't noticed. 'Who's Poppy?'

'The ghost.' Flinty seemed entirely matter of fact about this. 'Well one of them. The only one that really bothers us anyway.'

'A ghost moved my knife?'

'Aye. She likes moving things. I don't know why. Must be boring being dead though.'

Bella shook her head. She hadn't been born yesterday. 'Nice try. Messing with the new girl.'

'I'm serious. It was her that sneezed too. She does nay like black pepper.' Flinty looked unconcerned. 'That's probably why she moved your knife. She's not happy with you making her all sneezy.'

Flinty didn't sound like she was joking, which was impressive. Bella would not have suspected her as an accomplished prankster. She decided to play along. 'So, you're saying the castle is haunted? Seriously?'

'Well it's very old. More surprising if it wasn't, I'd say. When Darcy first came here she got this woman in to wave sage about the place and commune with the spirits and that. She reckoned Poppy was a restless Victorian girl. But I don't know. Ghosts are always Victorian aren't they? Especially little girls.' Flinty shrugged. 'She don't mean any harm so we let her be and accept that sometimes your shoes won't be where you left them.'

'Okaaaay.' Bella tipped the now perfectly crisp bacon into a bowl and tossed the onion, and then the mushrooms, into her pan while she added a dash of milk to her eggs and grated a small block of cheese. Once the mushrooms had browned ever so slightly she added the bacon back in, and it was time for the eggs.

This was the pure joy of making an omelette. Through honing and repetition she'd come to understand why so many thought it was the bedrock of good cooking. It came together quickly but every single ingredient needed to be cared for and added at precisely the right moment. Nobody wanted weird flavoured scrambled egg. They wanted something smooth and slightly unctuous. You could add a twist more pepper at this point if you chose. Bella often did, but that was when she was cooking in kitchens not already occupied by a curiously anti-seasoning spirit.

Bella tipped her beaten egg into the pan. The temptation now was to mix and prod and poke but you had to resist, just for the first minute or two. She tilted and swirled the pan to spread the mixture evenly over the bacon and mushrooms, but she didn't stir. To Bella's mind, if you'd beaten and seasoned your egg well enough to start with you had to keep the faith and simply let the heat of the pan work its magic.

And finally the cheese. Another bone of contention. Some people flipped the whole omelette, like a pancake, added the cheese right at the end after cooking both sides, and then folded the omelette to create a cheesy pocket within the half circle of fluffy eggy loveliness. Bella preferred to sprinkle her grated cheese onto the top side of the omelette just at the last moment while the egg on top was still slightly runny, and then fold, without flipping at all, and trust the heat of the pan to cook the final few millimetres of egg and melt the cheese into the whole.

It was when she'd worked that out that she'd finally understood what her old boss meant about every chef having their own individual idea of the perfect omelette. Finding her own hadn't been a test so much as a rite of passage. Less than ten minutes, the most basic ingredients and a lot of care and love. That was the perfect omelette.

'That smells good.' She'd been so lost in the reverie of heat plus ingredients plus care that she hadn't heard Adam come back in. 'I've never really seen you cook before.'

'I was cooking when you met me.'

'You were fending off half a stag do when I met you.'

'While making Crêpes Suzette at table.'

'I was too mortified to pay attention to the cooking.'

She kissed the top of his head as he took a seat next to Flinty at the island. 'And I thought you were hypnotised by my beauty.'

He smiled slightly. 'Sure. Let's say it was that.'

Bella slid the omelette onto a plate and placed it in front of him.

'For me?' he asked.

'No, actually for Darcy, but she's not down yet so I can make her another.'

He looked at the omelette. 'I'm not sure how hungry I am.'

She knew she was staring at him. Since they'd arrived at the airport and Flinty had delivered her dagger to their plans, Bella had become fixated on Adam's face, checking it for signs of distress, or perhaps for signs of hope. Right now he simply looked exhausted. 'You still have to eat.'

'Fine.' He took his first mouthful and closed his eyes for a second. 'That's really good. Thank you Bel.'

'That's OK. I enjoyed making it.'

'I saw. You were in your own world.'

Flinty cleared her throat. Bella realised, with a slight start, that she was still in the room, sitting right there, but somehow fading into the background. 'I was telling your lass how we used to grow a lot of our own vegetables here. Well your father did.'

Adam nodded, but Bella saw his jaw tense a little.

'You used to love that garden. You should get out there.'

He shook his head. 'Too much else to deal with at the moment.'

–

By the time Bella had made omelettes for Darcy, and Flinty – in the face of much insistence that Flinty was fine and didn't need Bella to do for her – and for herself, the atmosphere in the kitchen was almost convivial. Darcy looked brighter for having eaten. Adam felt slightly more himself. For a few minutes, at least, everyone was getting along, everyone was fed, and nobody was asking him to do anything.

'So this is where you're hiding?' Veronica's voice cut through the companionable quiet in the kitchen.

'Not hiding.' He tried to smile. 'Just having lunch.'

'Well thank Flinty, but it's time to get back to work.'

'Nothing to do with me,' Flinty explained. 'All Bella's handiwork. Very nice to be waited on for a change.'

Adam saw his grandmother's jaw twitch slightly. 'Miss Smith made lunch?'

Bella nodded. 'Do you want some? I can whip up another omelette, no problem.'

'No thank you.' She hadn't moved her gaze from Adam for a second. 'And the laird needs to get back to work.'

That was exactly what he needed to do. 'Actually we were about to go out.' He grabbed his fiancée's hand, silently willing her not to give away that this intention was news to her. 'I want to show Bella a bit more of the estate.'

Fortunately she nodded enthusiastically. 'Great. Maybe I'll get a bit further with a proper guide.'

She followed him down the corridor. 'You know I can't actually walk very far, don't you?' she whispered.

Oh damn. Of course. 'That's OK. We don't have to go far.'

'Just looking for a break?'

'Something like that.' He pulled her towards him. 'And some time with you.'

Five minutes later, she was waiting for him by the kitchen door, turning one way and then the other to show off her new footwear.

'You got wellies?'

'After my little misadventure I figured I needed to start dressing for the Highlands.'

'Very nice.'

He took her hand and led the way outside.

'You were so lucky to grow up here.'

He was. He couldn't deny it.

'Darcy said the castle used to be open to visitors.'

He nodded. 'They closed for Covid.' He hadn't got a straight answer out of his grandmother about why they'd never reopened.

'Will we open it up again?'

The 'we' made Adam pause. 'I don't know. I haven't really thought about it.'

'It's so stunning. It would be an amazing wedding venue. Have you ever thought about…?'

Adam shook his head.

'Sorry.' She stroked his arm. 'Getting ahead of myself. We probably won't even be here that long.'

Would they be? 'One thing at a time,' he suggested.

They made their way towards the gate. Bella stopped by the three small steps a few feet away from the back door. 'So is that the dungeon?' She peered down.

'It's not really a dungeon, more a sort of cellar,' he explained. 'With iron bars on the exit.'

'The nearest my childhood got to that was the time out corner at nursery school.'

'We don't send people to the dungeon. Not for like centuries.' He hesitated. 'I think Hugh ended up sleeping in there the night before my dad's wedding to Darcy, but that was just cos he didn't want go home and have Anna see how drunk he'd got.'

They walked slowly away from the castle, ignoring the path up to his father's garden, and following the road towards the burn. 'So, are you going to show me the famous Low Bridge then?'

Why not? That was as good a reason to say he'd chosen this route as any. The riverbank dropped in a shallow slope at first, before getting steeper down to the stream. Adam stopped. The Low Bridge was the heart of Lowbridge. It was the very reason the village, and by extension the castle, were here at all. It was the only crossing point on the Crosan for centuries, until the modern road bridge was built roughly sixty years ago.

'Oh.' Bella came to a halt alongside him. 'It doesn't look like much.'

She was right. The bridge had always been the main route from the estate to the village. As an infant he'd been pushed over here in his buggy by his mother, or by Flinty, almost daily. He'd run across here as a child to play with his village schoolfriends. And visitors to the house had parked across the river and walked over, getting their first glimpse of Lowbridge Castle from the riverside.

He'd been told that the bridge was in need of some TLC, but this needed more than a lick of paint. It needed knocking down and rebuilding from scratch. It was a simple wooden bridge, probably not that different from the first crossing ever built here, but it was wide enough to get a buggy or a wheelchair across, or a quad bike if you really wanted to. Nobody in their right mind would try that now. Adam didn't fancy trying the rotting structure himself and he could see perfectly well that the drop was no more than two feet and the river only a few inches deep.

Bella took his hand. 'A bit of paint, a few new boards?'

'It needs replacing.'

'OK, well how hard can that be?'

The rational part of Adam's brain said not hard at all. He was a professional landscaper after all. He could get the materials at cost and probably even lure a few mates over to do the work for beers and a slap-up dinner. The rational part of Adam's brain was holding on to the controls with its fingertips though. The other part, the part that wanted to run back to Edinburgh and deny that any of this was anything to do with him, was telling him that a broken down bridge wasn't just a bridge at all. It was a symbol of everything that was wrong here. Adam wasn't the laird. His father had been Laird of Lowbridge, and his grandfather, and his great-grandfather before that. They were proper lairds. They had tweeds and elbow patches and grown-up beards. Adam wasn't them. The bridge was falling down. The estate needed someone at the helm who wasn't falling apart themselves. It needed someone with ideas, someone who could make plans, someone who wanted to be here.

Chapter Six

The day of the cremation dawned inappropriately bright and sunny. Birds sang in the eaves around the coach house and the sunlight bounced off the water of the loch. It was the sort of day where the grey stone of the castle took on a warmer hue in the sunshine and the world seemed to be trying to tell Bella that all was well.

The world was wrong.

After much negotiation, mostly conducted by Flinty, it had been agreed that, as the 'real' funeral would be at Lowbridge a few days hence, Adam alone would accompany the funeral director on the long drive to the crematorium. Bella had overruled that in an instant and insisted that Adam would not be going on any such journey alone. Veronica had been entirely unhappy with the notion of some girl who'd just blown in going if she wasn't, and Darcy, quite reasonably, had thought that as his wife she probably ought to have been first on the list anyway. So now all four of them were getting ready for the long slow drive to Inverness.

Bella checked her outfit – a mid-calf length black wrap dress, borrowed from Darcy, on the grounds that the wrap was the only possible option to accommodate Bella's carb-enhanced hips – in the mirror. Adam was sitting on the edge of his bed in boxer shorts and white shirt staring at the black suit trousers draped over the back of the chair in front of him. 'Is it silly?'

'Is what?'

'Getting dressed up to sit in the back of a car for four hours?'

'Not at all.'

'I mean he's not there, is he. I know that. I…' Adam shrugged. 'It's his last journey.'

Bella shook her head. 'Not quite. They're going to bring him back here afterwards.'

Adam nodded. 'Where he will probably sit for all eternity in the back of a cupboard because no one can agree on what to do with the ashes.'

Bella rested her head on his shoulder. 'We'll worry about that tomorrow. For now let's take one thing at a time.'

'You're right.'

'I am. And the next thing is probably trousers.'

–

The hearse was outside the coach house. The coffin was in place with a wreath of blue and lilac flowers resting on top.

Darcy was standing, one hand on the glass, tears streaming down her face. Veronica was a few feet behind, staring straight ahead, expression unreadable. Adam and Bella took their places in the first of the two following cars and waited as Flinty put an arm around Darcy to encourage her into the space alongside Veronica in the second.

They pulled away, up the narrow hillside lane, across the top bridge and back down the far side of the river and into the village.

'Should I have gone with Darcy?'

'And left me with your grandmother?'

Adam sighed. 'Or the other way round. Should we have separated them?'

Bella twisted to try to peer into the car behind. 'They look OK, I think.'

'So they're not actually pulling each other's hair?'

'No. They look quiet.'

Adam nodded.

They drove largely unnoticed along the coastline until they passed the store at the far end of the village. Anna and Nina were standing at the edge of the road, flanked by Netty and Hugh, with Pavel a few steps behind his mother. They bent their heads as the tiny funeral procession drove by.

'Have they always been at each other?'

'Darcy and Granny?' He paused. 'Not as bad as this, but yeah. I don't think my grandmother has ever been that welcoming to a new lady coming in.'

'You don't say,' Bella muttered.

'She's not that bad.'

'Sorry.' Bella was supposed to be supporting him, not sniping at his family.

'Dad was her only son. Maybe nobody would ever have been good enough.'

'Tell me about him.'

Adam turned to look at her. 'What do you want to know?'

'The dad stuff. Not the laird stuff.'

She saw his face relax slightly. 'Well he loved books and science and natural history. Happiest in his...' Adam paused. 'His garden.'

'Was it him that got you into gardening?'

Adam's face tensed. 'He loved walking and other things as well. There was a hint of absent-minded professor about him. Darcy's more outgoing. I think she sort of balanced him out. My mother did too, for a while at least.'

They fell silent. Bella found she wanted to keep the conversation going. The back of this car was a bubble, a tiny echo of that hotel suite in Spain. 'Why aren't you wearing a kilt?'

'Sorry?'

'I thought a Scottish laird would kilt up for this type of thing.'

He rubbed a hand over his plain black trousers. 'I might for the actual service, but…' He shook his head. 'It's stupid.'

'Tell me.'

'I haven't worn the full traditional business for years and I'd kind of thought that the next time would be when I got married.' He paused. 'When we get married.'

Wow. 'I haven't really thought about the actual wedding.'

He picked at some imagined fluff on his sleeve. 'Me neither.'

'Except you've already picked your outfit.' It was nice that he'd pictured it. 'What else did you have in mind?'

'I don't know. When you said we'd do it quickly that sounded great, but then we came back to Lowbridge, and you said it could be a wedding venue, I thought, why not get married here?'

'Would keep costs down. We could definitely give ourselves mates' rates.'

'I would have thought so.'

'I don't want a big wedding.'

'OK.'

'Like all those blokes you were on the stag with. I don't want that thing where we have to invite every kid we were at school with and every friend of every family member whether we like them or not.'

He nodded. 'So who do you want to invite?'

'What do you mean?'

'Well, your grandmother?'

'Of course.'

'Who else?'

Bella shrugged. Who would she want there to see her promise her life to Adam? She'd been close to lots of people over the years but there always came a point where she moved on, and they moved on. She kept in touch, sporadically, with some of them, when she was in the right part of the world and there was the chance of a lazy afternoon drinking beers on a beach somewhere, but mostly she didn't just travel light in terms of how she packed her bags. She travelled light through life. 'I don't know. A small wedding sounds good though.'

'What about...' She could see his hesitation and she knew what the question was going to be. 'Your parents? You change the subject when they come up.'

'Don't have a dad. Well, I do, but don't know where he is. If he's still alive even.' She shrugged. 'Can't miss what you never properly had, so no paternal grandparents or aunties and uncles or any of that either.' She tried to keep her tone light. 'I miss that bit more I think. Maybe I have a big extended family out there somewhere, but I'm never going to know.'

'What about your mum?'

'What about *your* mum?' she shot back. It was a cheap reply.

Adam pulled a face. 'Well, I'll invite her. I have no idea if she'll come.'

'Do you know where she is?'

Adam nodded. 'The address I've got for her is on Shetland. She left because she said she wanted a bigger life, and now she's even more remote than Lowbridge.'

'I'm sorry.'

'It is what it is.'

Bella felt herself physically shudder. She hated that phrase. The passive acceptance that things were unchangeable made her feel sick. 'Has anyone told her about your dad?'

Adam nodded. 'Well, we've tried. No idea if she's read the messages.' He rubbed his forehead. 'I ought to try to call her.'

'I can do it if you want?'

He shook his head. 'No. I should.' He let out a deep sigh. 'Tomorrow though. What about your mum?'

'I don't know. I haven't seen her since I was about thirteen. She flitted in and out before that and every time she came back I was so excited and she'd have all these stories about what she'd been doing and where she'd been, but...' This was the part she'd never said out loud before, the part she'd never even fully acknowledged to herself. 'But I don't think any of it was true.' That was still only a half-truth. 'I know it wasn't. She'd been in hospital, or in some kind of rehab. Or maybe prison a couple of times. Or just off on a bender.'

'I'm sorry.'

'She used to bring me presents from her travels. Stupid gift shop plastic tat that she probably got in Wilkos. But when you're a kid you don't know that do you? So I could let myself believe that this stupid key ring was from

Marrakesh and this crappy little ornament was from Los Angeles or whatever she said.'

'What did you do with the presents?'

'What?'

'The things she brought you – do you still have them?'

' 'Course not.' Ridiculous idea. 'I chucked 'em all out when I realised she wasn't coming back for me.'

'Do you know what happened to her?'

Bella shook her head. 'I'm sure she's still out there somewhere, getting high and fucking people's lives up.' Bella wasn't sure of anything of the sort. Bella's mother had always left her. She'd never stayed. She'd never been reliable. But for the first thirteen years of Bella's life the flipside of that was also true. She'd never stayed, but she always came back. Logically Bella was fairly sure that, if the worst had happened, the news would have made it back to her and her nan eventually. She was less sure, though, which possibility was worse – that her mother hadn't come back because she couldn't, or hadn't come back because she'd chosen to stay away. 'Anyway, I had my nan and that was enough. More than enough.' That part was as true as it ever could be. Bella's nan was a woman worth ten of any other, and she'd taken Bella to places that her classmates in school could only imagine and had instilled in her an energy and a zest for life that she would always be thankful for. 'I was lucky.'

'When do I get to meet her?'

'Soon.'

'What did she say when you told her you were engaged?'

'Er...'

'Bel?'

'I didn't want to tell her in an email. We'll go and see her once she's back home.'

'Where is she now?'

'Somerset I think. She'll be home soon enough though.' Would she? Summer, for Bella's nan, kicked off with Glastonbury and then continued in a haze of festivals, extended visits to friends, and impulse visits to goodness knows where. It was perfectly possible that her flat in Leeds would be empty until the autumn. Bella turned her attention out of the window. 'Do these roads ever get less twisty?'

'A bit.'

'A bit?' That was insane. They were going to be driving for well over two hours, possibly longer if the drivers stuck to a respectful funeral pace.

Adam nodded. 'We're driving right across the Highlands. It's not exactly the M1.'

Bella stared at the continually stunning scenery outside her window. 'Clearly. That's OK. I mean I know it's awful circumstances, but it's nice to have some time together?'

He wrapped her hand in his. 'It is.'

–

The days between the cremation and the funeral service fell into a pattern. Bella got used to not seeing very much of her fiancé during the day. He was up every morning before she awoke and Bella still strongly suspected he wasn't really going to bed at all, but lying waiting for sleep until she drifted off and then getting up again and going back to work.

The first part of the night was different. That precious hour, between returning to the cocoon of the coach house and sleep overtaking Bella, was their time. That was when Adam belonged to her, and they could sail on waves of pleasure back to Spain or up into the clouds, to any place where it was just the two of them together and the world beyond them had no force. But morning always came and, when it did, Bella had to reckon with more complex feelings. She was worried about Adam, but, if she was honest, she was also jealous. At least Adam had something to do. Bella was at a loss. She wasn't built for sitting around and waiting for her man to finish work. She wasn't built for sitting around at all. She knew that people sometimes saw her as flakey. She moved around a lot. She loved to travel, but she always worked. She worked hard and she played hard, so she grabbed any chance to do something.

Which meant she'd done facials with Darcy, who'd been horrified by Bella's beauty routine of 'sunscreen, when I remember, and a glass of water in the morning'. Darcy's reaction was especially mortifying because she'd been lying about the water.

She'd emailed her nan, three times, which was out of character from their once-a-week norm, but all the emails had been vague and non-committal. Having started off not mentioning the engagement or the barony or the castle, it was tricky to casually drop them in now.

She'd walked Dipper until the poor dog looked as though her legs were going to drop off. Together they'd stomped up the road, along the cliff, and around the castle in near endless circuits. Walking with Dipper – simply being in this spectacular, stark, beautiful place – was one of the two thing that were keeping her sane. She'd tracked every shift in the weather, the way the rain made the greens of the hillside deeper and fuller, the way the sky turned dark and heavy before a storm, the way that when the sun broke through it sent glints of light dancing across the sea. A person could spend a lifetime here and never quite see the same view twice.

The other thing keeping her sane was food. She'd cooked every time Flinty had let her, which wasn't very often, but she'd made endless cups of tea for Adam and Veronica and for anyone else that passed her way. She was about twenty-four hours of boredom away from taking up her flask and walking to the village to press hot beverages on a wider range of innocents.

Which meant that her first Ladies' Group meeting was unexpectedly genuinely exciting. The idea that she was someone who was excited about drinking tea with a group of practical strangers in a village lounge was concerning, but was it really that different to beers on the beach in Ayia Napa? Just a different demographic and a different drug of choice, she told herself.

Anna's living room had the sort of homely feel Bella remembered from the very few times she'd been invited to parties with the girls from the new estate at school. Everything was neat and tidy and a little bit floral. It was the polar opposite to her nan's haphazard decorating style of clashing colours and random 'treasures' picked up on adventures.

The bulk of the conversation centred around the fundraising efforts for the community hall. 'What about a talent auction?' Anna suggested.

'We did one last year.' Nina shook her head. 'Only made £500, and we had all that business about Terry Halliwell bidding double for Sandra Deakin to come do his cleaning if she'd do it in the altogether.'

Bella's jaw dropped.

Flinty nudged her. 'Don't look like that, love. Sandra didn't mind.'

'Terry's wife did though.'

'All right then,' Anna brought the conversation back to the point. 'Talent auction but we specify no nudity.'

'Without the nudity we'd only have made £350. What about topless only?' Nina grinned.

Netty whispered something inaudible to Bella. The rest of the group roared with laughter. 'Of course it wouldn't be compulsory,' Flinty laughed.

'Fine,' Nina said. 'Fully clothed fundraising only, but preferably something that'll bring in more than a couple of hundred quid or we'll be at this for decades.'

'How much do you need?'

Nina sighed. 'Forty grand for the roof. That's the most urgent thing, but then really the whole place needs decorating, and it needs a new boiler, and the oven was condemned so we can't do food in there. So I don't know – fifty or sixty ideally.'

Right. 'And how much have you raised so far?'

All eyes turned to Netty. She mumbled a response. Faces fell slightly.

'I'm sorry. I didn't catch that.'

'About three thousand,' Flinty supplied. 'And we've been fundraising for two years.'

'Well we had to spend some getting the big hole in the roof patched until we can do it properly. And then that window got broken so we had to board that up. People want to be generous, but money's tight all over,' Anna explained. 'Nina's right, though. We need something bigger.'

Bella was aware that looks were being exchanged between Nina and Anna, and glances were being thrown towards Flinty and herself squashed together on the little sofa in front of the window. Flinty folded her arms. 'No.'

'What's going on?'

'These two want to go cap in hand to the bloody enemy.'

'The what?'

'The McKenzie estate.'

Bella was entirely lost. 'I don't know what that is.'

'The estate on the other side of the village. They're big and all...' Flinty shuddered. 'Flashy.'

Bella stifled a giggle. Nothing in or around Lowbridge could ever be described as flashy, even the castle itself had a certain tired lived-in air.

'They're very successful, Maggie,' Anna countered. 'They do whisky tasting, and shooting parties, and all that tartan shortbread bollocks for tourists.'

'For Americans with more money than sense.'

'We had thought of asking them for sponsorship. They have a whole thing on their website about community engagement. Forty grand's pocket change to Johnny McKenzie.'

'Maggie's dead against it though,' Nina added.

'I certainly am. What's McKenzie ever done for us? Pushed the MacCellans out of their own home and fenced off a whole lot of land that's supposed to be open to everyone. He's a snake. I'll have nothing to do with him.'

'He's a businessman.'

Netty mumbled what sounded like agreement.

'Quite right,' Nina agreed. 'Maybe Lowbridge *could* do with a bit more of a business head at the helm after...'

The group fell silent. The fury streaming off Flinty was palpable. Nina glanced over at Bella. 'No offence love. I'm sure your man has everyone's best interests at heart.'

Anna nodded. 'Of course. And have you been to the McKenzie place lately? Four quid for a cup of tea. And tartan everywhere. It's like Disney Highlands.'

Netty mumbled a comment.

'Well yes. It is jobs,' Anna agreed. 'But it's not real is it? It's not a community. We do need to get the hall sorted out though. So many groups have had to stop. The village is just...' She shook her head. 'It's not the same without it.'

That seemed silly. Bella knew she hadn't even looked around half of the castle yet but one thing she was sure about was that there was lots of space. 'Why don't groups meet at the castle?'

'I'm not sure the dowager would approve of that,' Anna replied.

Bella bristled. People kept saying that Adam was the laird and things were up to him. 'Well I'm sure the laird wouldn't mind at all.'

Nina shook her head. 'Even so, without the footbridge being useable it's a bit far for people.'

'Most can drive round,' Flinty pointed out. 'And we could put some of the fundraising towards repairing the bridge?'

Bella glanced at her unexpected supporter.

'It'd be nice for everyone at the moment to have a bit more life around the place.'

Back at the castle, Flinty didn't take her customary route direct to the kitchen, but continued towards the dower house. 'I'm going to give the lady's room, the dowager's...' she sighed, 'Veronica's room a going over with the duster.'

124

That meant the kitchen would be free. Bella wondered if she could rustle up enough supplies from the pantry to make a cake, something to cheer Adam a little.

As she approached the kitchen she realised that it was in fact already in use. Veronica was standing at the counter next to the sink staring at a tin can with her lips pursed.

'Are you OK there?'

The tin can – cream of mushroom soup – was standing on the worktop. In Veronica's right hand was a large, plastic handled tin opener. 'What on earth am I supposed to do with this?'

Bella took the tin opener, latched it onto the can, and then twisted the handle.

'Hmm. Well I'm sure these things used to be a lot more straightforward.'

Bella suspected that the basics of can opener design hadn't shifted for decades. 'Maybe.'

Veronica laboured the tin open and peered at the contents. 'It's very thick.'

Bella checked back again. 'It's condensed. You need to add water.'

'It doesn't look like this when Flinty makes it.'

'That'll be because she adds water.' Finally she took pity on her companion. 'Do you want me to do it for you?'

She watched the rare moment of indecision on the dowager lady's face. 'Well if you don't mind.'

The instructions told her to heat the soup with an equal part of water in the microwave. That seemed like it would fall within her cheffing capabilities. She could feel Veronica's gaze boring into her.

'I'm not completely useless in the kitchen, you know.'

The soup bowl in front of them told a different story.

'At least I didn't used to be.'

'It's fine. I like…' Bella looked at the grey sludge in the bowl and hesitated over the word cooking.

Veronica stood back and allowed Bella to take over, for a moment at least, before a third voice interrupted. 'I can do that!'

Flinty marched over.

'I can manage.'

Flinty's hands wrapped around the bowl. 'I usually do it in the pan. I add a bit of black pepper.'

Bella didn't let go. 'I don't mind. I was going to show her how.'

'No need for that. I know how she prefers it.'

Not being the type to back down from a scrap was one of the many things that had got Bella in trouble throughout her slightly chequered school days. *Take a breath*, her nan had always told her. Bella took a breath. It was just soup.

'Flinty does know how I like things,' Veronica added.

'OK.' Bella smiled brightly. 'I'll let you get on then.' She stepped away from the contested soup.

'Did this one tell you about her bright idea?' Flinty asked.

Bella winced. She'd been hoping that the village might move its social and community life into the castle without Veronica noticing. 'I just suggested that some of the groups from the village could meet here, while their hall is closed.'

Veronica's lips pursed.

'And I said I thought that was a great idea. Good to have some life here. Good for Adam. Good for Darcy,' Flinty pointed out.

'Well if it's only for the short term, and they don't get in the way.'

'Of course they won't.' Bella leapt on the grudging agreement, and quickly changed the subject before Veronica could come up with objections. 'I thought you weren't a lunch person.'

'The laird has disappeared off somewhere so I thought I'd get some sustenance so we can get back to it whenever he deigns to reappear.'

'I'm sure he'll turn up.'

Where would Adam be hiding out? It turned out he wasn't so much hiding as skulking. As soon as Bella made it out into the courtyard, he broke cover. 'Bel! Sorry. I thought it might be my grandmother.'

'So you were hiding?'

'Just taking a break. She's been trying to talk me through the figures for last year's lamb sales all morning.'

'Not your thing?'

He shook his head. 'I'm sure I'll get the hang of it. What are you doing? Wasn't it the village ladies' mafia meet-up this morning?'

'It was tea and biscuits.'

He raised an eyebrow.

'No horses' heads were deposited in beds. I'm at a bit of a loose end now though.'

His expression tightened. 'Sorry. I've been a bit preoccupied, haven't I?'

'I understand. Is there anything I can help with?'

He shook his head. 'I just need to get my head around it all.'

Bella raised her arms around his neck. 'Well I shouldn't distract you then.'

He pulled her to him. 'I would love you to distract me.' He stopped. 'But I do really need to…' He glanced back towards the estate office doorway in the far corner of the courtyard.

'It's fine. Veronica's in the kitchen having soup. You've got time.'

He leaned back against the wall of the courtyard. 'I am so very glad you're here.'

'Good.' She moved in front of him, standing in the space between his feet, pressing her legs against his thighs. 'I'm glad too.'

'Really?'

She hesitated.

'It's OK. You can say.'

'I'm not used to having this much free time.' That was unfair. He was working all the hours and she was complaining about being a lady of leisure. 'I'm sorry. It's fine.'

'No. It's not what you expected, it is? Any of this.' His hand was stroking the small of her back, sending a flush of warmth radiating from his touch. 'If you want to go I get it.'

The heat turned to ice. 'What do you mean "go"?'

He stared down at the floor. 'Whatever you need it to mean. You can take my keys and go to Edinburgh, and I'll come over after... all of this. But I know this isn't what you thought you were getting into, so if you need to go, I... I would understand.'

–

She could go. She could choose to be far away from here. She could be back in a busy kitchen. She could be dancing in a field with strangers who had the potential to become best friends. She could be frying prawns over coals on a beach a million miles away from here. But, a million miles away from here was a million miles away from him. Bella shook her head. 'Unless that's what you want.'

'Of course not.' The relief on his face was obvious.

Bella exhaled.

'I want you to be happy.'

'I am.'

He looked unconvinced.

'Well I will be. Wherever I lay my hat and all that.' She took his hand. 'I'm here for you. OK?'

'OK.' He pressed a warm soft kiss to her lips. 'Thank you.'

'You're very welcome. Now get back to work before I really start distracting you.'

Adam disappeared back towards the office and Bella trudged back inside and across the hallway, catching her foot on something in her way and tripping onto her knees. She pulled herself back to standing and retrieved the single wellington that had found its way into her path. 'I still do not believe in you, Poppy,' she muttered.

Chapter Seven

Bella hadn't been to very many funerals in her life. She'd been to one vigil on a beach for a guy she'd met in Mexico who'd died in a diving accident. She'd been to two services at the big crematorium behind the B&Q in Leeds. This one had significantly more tweed than any of those, and none of those memorials had been for people she was desperately close to. Neither was this – she'd never met Alexander Lowbridge – but somehow his death had changed her life.

In the past she'd always left remembrance ceremonies feeling like she had learned something more about the person being celebrated. She'd taken away a feeling of regret for a life ended but also joy for a person who had lived to the full. Alexander's service felt impersonal by comparison. He'd been a good man, Jill had declared, and a conscientious laird who had taken his responsibilities seriously.

The turn-out, and the mutterings of agreement at her comments, seemed to bear that out, but for much of the service Alexander seemed strangely distant. Only when Adam took to his feet did Bella get a sense of the father he was grieving rather than the distant laird. Adam spoke about his father's love of the land, of wildlife, of his garden. He spoke of a man who was happiest with his hands in the soil. He spoke of the way his father had taught him to find his own passion of planting and harvesting and laying out gardens that could bring joy to other families.

As he closed his eulogy, Adam swallowed deeply and inhaled hard, apparently fighting off tears. 'I think it's fair to say,' he continued, 'that I was never the most academically gifted child.' There were a few affectionate laughs in the congregation, but Bella could see Veronica's lips pursing in her peripheral vision.

'And parts of school were really hard. Not the rugby and the tree-climbing, but the maths and the English. I honestly struggled to get through those.' He looked up. 'There are people here who had the misfortune to be amongst my teachers. I can only apologise.' Another smattering of affectionate chuckles. 'But my father believed that if you weren't gifted in one area, that simply meant you needed to find your place and your passion somewhere else. He truly thought that everyone was the right fit for something. Ultimately, he was the right fit for Lowbridge. He loved this place and its people. He loved the landscape and the land itself. I only hope I can live up to the standards he set.'

Adam moved back to his place between Darcy and Bella in the front pew. Bella reached instinctively for his hand, but it was wrapped closed in a tight fist. She lay her hand over this and sent a silent prayer up into the cool chapel air that he would let her soothe him. After a second or two, he pulled his hand away.

They led the way out of the chapel and through to the courtyard, where Flinty had enlisted Nina's help in laying out teas and coffees, along with huge platters of sandwiches, her own lemon drizzle cake and Bella's millionaire's shortbread. The day was bright and sunny, with a hint of sea breeze keeping things pleasant. Slowly, the conversation escalated from a restrained funereal whisper into a more relaxed babble of chatter. Bella moved from group to group, refreshing cups and clearing away empty plates.

At the centre of the largest group she heard Darcy laughing. She seemed to be on better form today, and company clearly suited her.

Bella picked up a cup and saucer that had been left on the cobbles next to a bench.

'Flinty can do that, dear.' Veronica was holding a single finger sandwich and looking slightly disdainfully at the gathered throng.

'Just helping out,' Bella replied.

'Lady Lowbridge! Bella!' Anna and Hugh came over, clutching teacups and slices of cake. 'It was a lovely service. And you've done him proud with this spread.'

'Well that was down to Flinty.'

Bella was sure she saw Hugh's jaw twitch. He turned towards her. 'Maggie said you'd done a lot.'

'Well I mostly did what I was told.'

He laughed. 'Always the best approach with our Maggie.'

A silence settled over the group. Anna cleared her throat. 'We miss seeing you in the village, Ver… Lady Lowbridge.'

Bella couldn't help but feel that the apparently calm, still waters they were swimming through might be hiding dark dangers all of a sudden.

'Everyone does,' Anna continued. Did Veronica's expression soften ever so slightly? 'Don't we Hugh?'

His jaw definitely twitched that time. 'Well I'm sure you're very busy.'

The silence hit again. This time Veronica broke it. 'I heard that you'd extended your little shop into the garden.'

'Not such a little shop any more. You should come and see. You can get all your essentials.'

Bella nodded in agreement.

'I suppose I should. Flinty still stocks the larder though, and she knows what I like...'

'I'm sure she does,' Anna smiled.

Hugh took his wife's arm. 'Well we'd best be...' His gaze flicked around the courtyard. 'We need to talk to...' He floundered again, before he gave up and simply led his wife away.

'Don't even give it heed,' Veronica muttered.

Couldn't if I wanted to, Bella thought. She was still trying to make sense of the conversation as the senior Lady Lowbridge stalked away.

'Bella!' She found herself enveloped in a vigorous, citrus-scented hug from the Reverend Jill, who had Dipper following along in her wake. The dog's instincts for who might 'accidentally' drop half their canapés in her direction was utterly on point. 'How are you doing?'

She looked around. On days like this her brain automatically went into hospitality mode. 'I think we might need to refill the urn.'

'I'm sure Nina and Maggie are on top of it.'

No doubt they were, but it went against the grain for Bella not to be helping out in some way.

'How's your chap doing?'

'OK.' Was he? 'I think.'

'It's a lot of change for him. And losing your father, that can hit people hard. Men especially. They get all these ideas about having to step up and be the man of the house.' Jill looked thoughtful for a second. 'And your lad's expected to be the man of the whole village, isn't he?'

'It's all an adaptation I guess.' But even as she said it something cool gripped her stomach. Adam was the laird. Obviously she knew that. But what did that actually mean? She'd been focused on getting to the funeral, getting through the funeral, and then what? 'I might go and check in with him though.'

–

Across the courtyard, Adam was suffering from what could only be described as sympathy fatigue. He'd had his hand shaken, shoulder patted, and, from one elderly villager, cheek pinched like a podgy four-year-old. Everyone agreed that his father had been a thoroughly decent chap. Everyone agreed that it was a sad loss. Everyone agreed that it had been a lovely service. And everyone agreed that Adam was going to step into his dad's shoes wonderfully. Everyone believed in him. Everyone had faith.

'Lowbridge.'

He winced slightly at the rather formal greeting. That was the way some people still held things should be done. Saying Baron Lowbridge was simply not done. Laird was dangerously colloquial and imprecise. Heaven only knew what fate would befall one who ventured into first names. He nodded at the man approaching him. 'McKenzie.'

'Sorry about the old man. He was a decent chap.' McKenzie shrugged a wax jacketed shoulder. 'Bit behind the times maybe, but he meant well.'

Adam bristled. His father definitely hadn't been a moderniser, but nobody in Lowbridge seemed to mind that.

'I don't know if this is the time to mention this really, but…'

Adam felt a hand slip into his. He turned towards his fiancée. 'Bella, let me introduce John McKenzie.'

She nodded. 'McKenzie? Oh, do you own the next estate along?'

'The one and same.' Adam saw the delight at being recognised in Mr McKenzie's eyes. 'Which was just what we were discussing.'

'Was it?'

'Well in a sense. I don't want to talk business now, but I assume your father had talked to you about our plans.'

Adam knew his face was blank. He also knew that if Ravi were here he'd be whispering urgently in his ear about the importance of keeping a poker face in negotiations. Never let the other person know you are swimming out of your depth. Which was exactly why Adam and Ravi were such a good team. Ravi understood this stuff. Adam understood which plants would thrive in shade. 'Not in any detail,' he ventured.

'Well in short I made him an offer to buy.'

'To buy what?'

'Lowbridge, of course.'

What? Had his father been considering it?

'Given his health, it seemed like a good option all around. And, I'm sure I don't need to tell you about the inheritance tax you've got coming up.'

Actually, he sort of did. Adam's grandmother had definitely mentioned taxes, but it was another of the million things she'd talked at him about and tried to make him concentrate on. It was another column of confusion. 'Anyway, the offer's still on the table.'

Adam was still scrabbling to keep up. 'For the whole estate.'

'Well I can take or leave the house itself.' McKenzie shook his head. 'The repairs and maintenance on my own place are killing me, and that's a new build compared to this old thing.' He laughed loudly at his own humour. 'Not that I'd turn it down. Guests'll pay a premium to stay in a proper baronial castle. It's the land I really want though.'

'All of it?'

'Aye. That's what I offered your father for.'

'And my son made quite clear that Lowbridge was not for sale.' Veronica's voice was imperious as she bore down on the group.

'Lady Lowbridge!' McKenzie smiled broadly. 'Always a pleasure.'

Adam's grandmother didn't reply.

'I'm not sure your son was quite that definitive.'

'Then allow me to be. Lowbridge is not for sale.'

McKenzie stepped away and then leaned back to shake Adam's hand. 'Well, the offer's there if the new laird takes a different view.'

Adam watched Mr McKenzie walk away. Selling Lowbridge. It was, as his grandmother had made absolutely clear, unthinkable, and yet now it had been said out loud it was going to be all he could think about.

'That chancer after your family silver, Lowbridge?'

Adam turned towards the voice. 'Macwillis.' Bella squeezed his hand a notch tighter. 'Sir Iain, let me introduce my fiancée, Bella Smith.'

'Bella!' Macwillis bellowed her name, as Adam knew from experience, he bellowed everything. 'Knew a Bella once. Not biblically. Married a steam engine enthusiast from Hastings.'

Bella nodded. 'I don't know her.'

'No.' Macwillis nodded. 'Don't suppose you would.' He turned back to Adam. 'McKenzie after your place as well?'

'So it seems.'

'Pah. The MacCellans ended up not having much choice. Terrified of the inheritance taxes landing on his daughter I think. Some of us cling on though.'

Adam suspected Sir Iain Macwillis, hereditary chieftain of the Clan Macwillis and current owner of most of Skye and a good sliver of the smaller isles as well, was doing rather more than clinging on. 'It was good of you to come today.'

'Well I liked your old man. And I thought someone should. There's not so many of us around now. Did you hear that the McCullens' new chief lives in Seattle of all places. Runs some company designing, what do you call it? Things for phones.'

'Apps,' Adam suggested.

'That's the badger!' Macwillis nodded cheerfully. 'Good to have you here though. Good to see the next generation keeping the place alive. You're a good man, Lowbridge.'

Chapter Eight

As the last guests drifted away, Bella found her fiancée sitting on a bench at the edge of the courtyard. She slid into the space alongside him, leaning in towards his body. 'How are you doing?'

He shrugged. 'I keep thinking about what McKenzie said.'

'The guy who wants to buy this place.'

'Well not so much this place. More the land.' Adam shook his head. 'That wouldn't be right. Splitting the land from the house. But…' He closed his eyes.

'But what?'

'I know Grandmother isn't having any of it, but McKenzie definitely reckoned Father was thinking about it.'

Bella wasn't sure what all that meant for Adam. 'He didn't mention it to you.'

He shook his head. 'But… honestly I hadn't talked to him that much lately. Nothing happened… you know. I was busy and he was never big into phoning. And he wouldn't go near social media so…'

'So maybe he was thinking about it?'

'Maybe. It doesn't seem…' He turned to Bella. 'Are you OK to walk?'

'Yep.' She stuck out her foot. 'Fully recovered.'

'Then I want to show you something.'

She followed him out of the castle, but instead of turning to the road or down to the riverside, or jumping in the aged Land Rover, Adam turned the other way, across a field on the castle side of the river, and up a steep path. He paused here and there to take Bella's hand and help her scramble up where the path all but vanished and they had to clamber over rocks. Eventually they came to a stop at the top of a high cliff. Bella spun around to get her bearings. She'd walked this way with Dipper before. It was already one of her favourite views around Lowbridge. The ever-changing blues and greys of the sky and the way the colours bounced off the water and deepened and intensified drew her here. Even so she didn't quite know what she was looking out at. The lines between lake and sea and headland and island seemed to blur here, leaving Lowbridge sitting on its outcrop like a single solid thing in the middle of this space between the sea and the land.

Adam took her hand and pointed with his free arm towards the island opposite them. 'That's Raasay. Beyond that is Skye, and then Uist and then… well, America, no Canada I guess.' He turned her around to look back towards the castle. 'This inlet is Loch Abercross.'

'I thought loch meant lake.'

'It does. Kind of.' Adam was suddenly energised, pointing out features as he described the landscape. 'This is a sea loch. Abercross means at the mouth of the cross. It's a bit anglicised but the river is the Crosan, so it's at the mouth of the Crosan. And so originally this would have been Aber Crosan Castle. Like centuries ago, and there would have been a tiny settlement over here. Maybe a few fishermen, not much else, but then the story goes that the first baron fell in love with a girl from the village but her father was dead against it.'

Bella laughed. 'Dead against a baron? Tough crowd.'

'He had her engaged to a nice fisherman's son from the next cottage along. But she loved the baron and he loved her, and he built the very first Low Bridge across the river so he could visit her even after she was forced to marry the fisherman's son...'

'Bastards.'

'Quite. Even after she was forced to marry the fisherman, the baron would still creep into the village to see her, until one day her fisherman husband went out to sea and never came back.'

'That's convenient.'

'Not for him.'

'Fair point.'

'Anyway that meant the girl was free to marry her baron. Not very long after the wedding she had a baby.'

'How long is not very long?'

'Well close enough that nobody was ever quite sure whether the son she had was really the baron's or whether he was the fisherman's boy. Either way, the baron loved him and raised him as his own.'

'Good baron.'

'Yeah. He did the right thing. I mean, assuming he didn't have the fisherman bumped off. There's a lot of that with your early Scottish lairds.'

'Bumping off fishermen?'

'Bumping off love rivals. Any sort of rival really. They were usually rival lairds though.' He shook his head. 'Anyway, my father told me that story when I was about seven or eight years old. The point, he said, was that it meant that we weren't lords over the village. We're not above it. We're part of it. They're part of us. Whether we're descended from that fisherman or not doesn't matter, because we're all part of one thing. We're not in charge of Lowbridge. We…' He stopped.

'What?'

'It sounds ridiculous.'

'We *are* Lowbridge. The village is the house. The house is the land. It's all one thing.'

Finally Bella thought she might be beginning to understand. 'And so selling part of it is hard to get your head around?'

'Something like that.'

She nodded. 'Like when you saw the bridge all broken down.'

'What?'

'Well, the bridge represented how everything's linked together didn't it? The community, and the castle and the landscape.'

'Yes, and not just represented it. It was the connection. Literally. Without it, how does anyone come from one to the other? It's like pulling up the drawbridge and saying, "We're separate from you."'

The understanding that was trickling into Bella's head started to crystallise. 'And selling off part of the land rips the whole thing apart?'

He nodded.

They sat next to one another staring out across the loch. Bella thought she was starting to understand. It wasn't just that the village and the castle and the land were all one. It was that Adam was too. He wasn't the lord of Lowbridge. He *was* Lowbridge.

And that meant they weren't going back to Edinburgh, were they? There was, Bella saw now, no way she could ask him to leave. If Adam was her future, her future was here. She stared out across the bay, and tried to imagine what a life here might look like. Was she ready for her life to be Ladies' Group and community fundraisers and village gossip? Was she ready to spend her days with one man, working to make this castle a place fit for the twenty-first century, working to make Lowbridge come to life and retain its place at the heart of a community, working to make it a place where, one day a very very long time in the future, her own child might become the next Baron Lowbridge?

'What are you grinning at?'

Adam's question pulled Bella out of her reverie. She was grinning, wasn't she? She rested her head against his shoulder. 'I didn't realise that I was.'

Was Bella ready for all that? Maybe that smile meant she was.

'I think I need to see McKenzie's place.'

Bella could understand that. From what she'd heard at Ladies' Group the McKenzie estate was a well-oiled money-making machine, exactly what Lowbridge wasn't. Checking out the enemy was a good idea. Even if they didn't want to go in the same direction, there were bound to be ideas they could repurpose and adapt. Looking out at the view from the clifftop above the castle the possibilities seemed endless. Weddings, weekend breaks, a teashop – a thousand and one ideas were sparking through Bella's mind…

'Let's go then.'

'Right now?'

No. It had been a long and tiring day already, and Bella could see that her fiancé needed to rest. 'Tomorrow?'

He nodded. 'Tomorrow.'

Chapter Nine

'Whyever are you going there?' Veronica was incredulous at news of Adam and Bella's plan.

'Just to see,' Adam explained.

'I heard that they charge four pounds for a cup of tea,' Darcy added in a tone of wonder. 'Tea. Not even coffee. Hot brown water and milk.' She shook her head. 'British people,' she muttered.

'I do need you here. There are things that have to be…' Veronica started.

Adam shook his head. 'When we get back,' he insisted.

They headed out to the Land Rover. 'Can I drive? Like, would I be insured?' asked Bella.

He nodded. 'I think so. And what is there for you to crash into except sheep? And they're our sheep.'

'I won't hit a sheep.'

'You might.' He shrugged. 'They can be really stupid sometimes.'

'Hey. Those sheep love me.'

He grinned. 'No comment. You can drive if you want to.'

She considered the narrow, practically vertical road up to the bridge and the weird clunking noise the Land Rover made every time Flinty changed gear. 'You're all right. So long as you know that I could.'

'Never doubted it.' He started the engine at the third attempt. 'I hate this car.'

Bella was finally getting used enough to the jolting, rocking drive from the castle to the village to be able to look out of the window 'It's beautiful here.'

Adam nodded. 'I know.' He shrugged as he drove. 'It's my normal, though.'

'Growing up in a castle is not normal.'

'It's hardly a castle.'

'It's got turrets.'

He grinned. 'Only quite small ones.'

'And there's a… in the arch to the courtyard.'

'What?'

'The drop-down iron gatey thing.'

'Portcullis.'

'Yeah. My nan's flat did not have a portcullis.'

'It's broken. If you close it down, you can't open it up again.'

'Oh well, hardly weird and posh at all.'

He laughed. 'OK, so it's not a completely ordinary childhood.'

'Did you go to boarding school?' Suddenly the range of differences between them was opening up in front of Bella's eyes.

'Not until secondary school.'

'So eleven? You got sent away at eleven?'

'Only during the week. And that wasn't posh. All the kids from round here did that. There isn't a high school near enough to go in every day.'

'The nearest secondary school is too far away to drive to in a morning?'

He nodded. 'Well, it's about an hour and a half, so you could get back if you had to, but three hours' driving every day is a lot, so yeah, we stayed in the residence during the week.'

'Wow. My school was just round the corner and past the shops. If you were running really late you could climb over the fence at the back of the flats into the playing field.'

'I can't wait to see where you grew up.'

Something about that thought jarred. Adam was a creature of beautiful places. His hair had the assured flop of someone who'd never needed to get it styled because he was raised with the understanding that whatever he did *was* the style. He owned chinos. Bella wasn't sure she'd ever been friends with someone who owned chinos before. She wasn't quite sure what her nan would make of him.

'So have you been to this place before?' Bella changed the subject, she hoped not too abruptly.

'Not since McKenzie bought it. My dad used to be friends with Mr MacCellan though. I think his parents were my father's godparents.'

'What happened to them? The MacCellans?'

'Not sure. Probably moved to a nice draught-free unhaunted semi-detached in Locharron.'

They drove south from Lowbridge village and along the coast for close to an hour, before turning sharply inland until they reached the entrance to what proudly proclaimed itself to be the McKenzie Estate Visitor Experience Hub.

The car park was lined with densely packed pine forest. Bella caught Adam shaking his head. 'What's up?'

'None of these are native. Fast growing, so they use them in commercial forestry, but the wood's as soft as shit.' He pulled her to a stop in front of him, and placed his hands on her shoulders. 'Listen.'

Bella could hear a babble of chat from other visitors and the rumble of cars arriving and departing. 'Listen to what?'

'Exactly. No biodiversity in the planting means fewer insects, means fewer small mammals and fewer birds, means no bird song.'

She listened again. He was right. The forest wasn't exactly silent, but it didn't sound alive.

He moved around to face her and waved his hand towards the offending trees. 'It looks like an ancient forest, if you have no clue what an ancient forest actually looks like, but it's just a stage set.'

They made their way into the Visitor Experience Hub.

'Bloody hell,' muttered Bella. The whole place was festooned in blue and green checks, with lines of bright yellow running through the design. It was a visitor centre that was crying out for a dial to turn the contrast down.

Adam was silent alongside her.

'That's a lot of tartan.'

'Yep.' He was looking around. 'MacCellan tartan as well. Bit of a cheek. Take someone's home, stick your name all over the shop, and then use their clan tartan as window dressing.'

'Doesn't McKenzie have a tartan?'

'Think they have about four.' He shrugged. 'Maybe they didn't match the colour scheme?'

'Good morning. Welcome to the McKenzie Experience Hub!' The woman in front of them was about the same age as Bella but was groomed and put together in a way Bella didn't even aspire to be. She was wearing air hostess levels of make-up.

'Oh, we're just having a look around.'

'That's great.' The woman smiled in a way that somehow still managed to look bored. 'We have walking trails around the woodland, or you can hire bikes, or relax in our top-class eatery.'

Cafe, Bella mentally translated.

'I believe we do also have a very limited number of spaces available on our Silver Whisky Experience at two p.m.' The welcome-bot looked down at her iPad. 'Booking is essential though.'

'We're fine. We'll just get a drink and maybe go for a walk.'

'As you wish. Don't forget to check out our retail experience area before you leave.'

'We won't.' Bella leaned towards her fiancé. 'She means gift shop, right?'

'Wait!' the woman called after them. Bella turned in time to see her speed walking towards them on her high heels, her smile reaching her eyes for the first time. 'Adam? Adam Lowbridge?'

Adam nodded, failing utterly to hide the confusion on his face.

'Fiona! Fiona from school!'

Adam's mouth had fallen open. 'Fi? Fi MacCellan?'

The woman nodded.

'You're working here?'

Her smiled faltered. 'Not a lot else available around here. And it would break Dad's heart if I moved away. I'm the last MacCellan still clinging on.'

'I know the feeling.'

She dropped her gaze to the floor for a second. 'I'm sorry. I heard about your dad. I wanted to come yesterday but John was going so I couldn't get the day off. I'm his right-hand woman. Visitor experience manager.'

'Right. Well, congratulations.'

'It is so good to see you.' She checked her watch. 'Why don't I join you for that drink? We've got so much to catch up on.'

Bella wasn't oblivious to the fact that she hadn't yet been acknowledged by the perfectly mascara'd Fiona, and she definitely wasn't oblivious to the way that this stranger was making eyes at Adam Lowbridge. Fortunately, she hoped, even Fiona couldn't be oblivious to the way Adam's arm snaked around Bella's waist as he nodded. 'This is Bella, by the way.'

'Hi!' Fiona smiled vaguely. 'So a drink?'

The top-class eatery, *one* of the estate's top-class eateries, actually, Fiona explained, turned out to be one of those frustrating types of cafe you often found at tourist attractions that had notions above their station. Everything, the overly tartaned signage proclaimed, was locally sourced and organic and grown within a gnat's whisker of where you were standing right now, and despite that there was very little that a person might actually want to eat.

'Our organic grain bowls are very popular.' Fiona beamed.

Bella scoured the menu board above the counter. What she really wanted was a massive hot chocolate and a slab of cake she could bury her face in. 'What cakes do you have?'

Fiona directed her to a display of 'sweet treats'. Bella appraised them speedily. Everything looked good at first glance, but at second glance the slices were suspiciously neat and regular. 'Do you bake these on site?'

Fiona's beaming smile faltered. 'I think the cakes are bought in. From a local supplier,' she added briskly.

Bollocks, thought Bella. The only way these were local was if there was a secret supermarket cake factory nestled unsuspected somewhere in the surrounding hills. There was no way anything on this table had been baked by an actual human in anything the average chap on the street would recognise as a kitchen. She selected a brownie, more out of professional curiosity than actual enthusiasm, and ordered a cup of tea.

Fiona waved what looked like a staff ID badge. 'I'll get these. Seriously, it's four quid for a cup of tea without the discount.' She paused, like a computer programme momentarily glitching. 'Which reflects the quality of the product produced by our local partners, of course.'

Bella caught the smile pulling at her fiancé's lips. 'Local tea growers?'

'Yeah.' Fiona paused again. 'Well no. I'll get these anyway.'

They found a table next to the full height windows overlooking a pond and a bird feeding station. The bird feeders were a nice idea, at least.

As soon as they were seated, Fiona launched into an enthusiastic reminiscence of the apparently hilarious high jinks Adam had got into at school. Adam nodded politely. Eventually Fiona let out a deep sigh. 'I can't believe you and Olivia didn't go the distance though.'

Olivia? Bella's ears pricked up.

Adam shook his head. 'Oh come on. We were teen-agers. I haven't seen her for years.'

'I know.' Fiona leaned across the table and rested a hand on Adam's arm. 'We were all so jealous of her.' She laughed, slightly too loud and too high. 'We all had crushes on you, you know.'

Bella mentally upgraded Fiona from irritant to would-be rival.

Adam moved his arm away. 'Sorry, I didn't properly introduce you, did I? Fi, this is Bella Smith, my fiancée.'

Fiona's hand darted back across the table like it had been stung.

'You're engaged?'

Adam nodded.

'I had no idea.'

'Clearly,' Bella muttered.

'Adam Lowbridge off the market. You wait until I tell everyone.'

Adam took a sip of his coffee. 'So you're still in touch with people from school.'

'Some of them.' She wrinkled her nose. 'Lots of people moved away. You know for work or whatever, but Liv's in Locharron now. She'll be gutted to hear you're getting married.'

Adam frowned. 'I thought she was living with a woman?'

'They broke up. She's seeing someone else though.'

'Right. So do you think she might be over me?'

Fiona shrugged. 'Maybe.'

Bella grabbed the opportunity to change the subject back to the point of their visit. 'So do you like working here, Fiona?'

'Oh it's great. John's vision has really revitalised the estate. We turned over more than eight million last year.'

Bella heard Adam inhale sharply.

'We employ local people and attract high net worth visitors.'

Something about the way she emphasised 'high net worth' gave Bella the ick.

Adam was looking thoughtful. 'You said you do whisky experiences?'

'Of course.'

'So you have a distillery here?'

'We're more showcasing the range of whiskies available.'

'Right.' He nodded. 'And you still take shooting and fishing parties?'

'Absolutely. A shooting weekend in the Highlands is a really superior option for team building or even a stag do.'

'Bag a stag on your stag?' suggested Bella.

'Something like that. I mean, within the rules obviously. There's a lot of licensing for deer. And you're not supposed to shoot males when they're still in velvet.'

Bella nodded like she knew what that meant, although there hadn't been much need for a close knowledge of game shooting growing up in the housing association flat in Leeds. It was the sort of thing a lady of Lowbridge would be expected to understand, wasn't it? Like the perfectly manicured Fiona MacCellan, daughter of the neighbouring estate, understood.

'And we get a lot of day visitors for the walking trails and the mountain biking. Or just enjoying the visitor experience. John wants to add four-wheel driving and quad biking, but you know what the locals can be like.'

Bella nodded politely. In her experience so far the locals were as mad as a box of frogs. The Ladies' Group would probably be well up for a spot of quad biking.

'Daddy turned the whole of the top hills over to common grazing before John bought the place.' She pulled a face. 'John was a bit cross about that to be honest, but Daddy was within his rights and the solicitors did tell John it would be a bugger, excuse my French, to undo.'

She took a sip of her tea. 'So no quad biking up there. The crofters wrote a long objection saying it freaks the sheep out.'

Bella stifled her giggle. 'Can't be scaring the sheep,' she muttered. Maybe that was why they were so keen to follow her down to the castle courtyard. They knew they'd be safe from Hooray Henrys bombing across the Highlands in over-powered four by fours.

'That's part of why he's so keen to expand the estate over your way. We'd be nearer the coast so we could do sea fishing trips and wildlife watching. And space for the quad bikes. I mean that's all ideas. I'm not here to try to change your mind.' She smiled. 'Will you change your mind though?'

–

Would he change his mind? Adam couldn't answer that question because it assumed he'd made his mind up to start with, when honestly his grandmother had made it up for him. The McKenzie approach was clearly profitable, and it seemed that John McKenzie had the instincts and the drive to make things happen. Presumably he wasn't a man reduced to a nervous wreck every time he was asked to read a balance sheet.

'We don't have any plans to sell at the moment.' Bella had jumped into the silence that Adam had left. That was a suitable neutral answer. Not a no, but not closing the door either.

Fiona shrugged. 'Oh well, can't blame a girl for asking. Imagine the brownie points I'd get if I was the one that talked you round. I guess I should get back to work though. It was lovely to meet you,' she told Bella.

There was something Adam had to ask before he let her go. 'What's it like?'

'Sorry?'

'Working here.' He gestured around the purpose built, entirely characterless visitor centre. 'With it all like this. I mean, this was your home.'

'Well it still is.' Her tone was slightly brittle.

'But everything's so different.'

'We have to move with the times, Adam. That whole thing our dads blathered on about – duty and community and all that nonsense. I mean it's not very twenty-first century is it?' She patted his shoulder. 'So nice to catch up. Can't wait to tell the old school WhatsApp group you're engaged.' She grinned.

Oh no. Oh absolutely no way in hell.

'I should add you to the group. All the old crowd are there. Liv, obviously, but Tommy and Callum and Briony. Everyone.'

'Erm…'

'Go on. What's your number?'

There was no way out, was there? He typed his number into her phone, wondering too late if he should have 'accidentally' mistyped a digit or two.

He waited until she was out of earshot. 'I hate WhatsApp groups.'

'You don't have to stay in it.'

'But I do, cos it gives everyone that "so and so left the group" message so there's no way to quietly sidle out.' He shuddered.

Bella leaned towards him. 'You can mute it. It'll be fine.' She looked around. 'So what do you think? Is this what we should do with Lowbridge?'

'Well we do need to generate more income.' He hadn't grasped much from his endless sessions with his grandmother trying to talk him through the estate finances, but he had grasped that money was important and Lowbridge did not have enough of it.

'Well this place certainly seems to do that. Their cake's bad though.' Bella looked genuinely affronted by this fact. 'There's nothing worse than bad cake. Like bad leeks or something, fair enough. It's a bit of a palaver to make leeks nice. But cake, you have to really not care to serve bad cake.'

'What's wrong with it?'

She broke a piece off her unfinished brownie and handed it to him. She was right. Rather than delivering a rich fudgey hit of chocolate, the mouthful seemed to simply disappear in a second. 'That's sort of plasticky.'

'It's gross. And brownies are so easy. They were pretty much the first thing I ever made on my own.' She broke another piece off and rolled it around her mouth. 'They're super forgiving. If you undercook them they come out fudgier. If you overcook them they're more cakey and you get more crunch on top. So it's still all good. And it's just butter, sugar, chocolate, a little bit of flour and eggs. There's nothing to go wrong.' She pushed her plate away. 'That has never seen a block of butter though, and the chocolate must have been the cheapest they could get their hands on.'

'All the jobs they've created though.'

'I know.' Bella didn't sound impressed.

'Lowbridge needs jobs. There's hardly anyone our age around, is there? Because there's no work.' Aside from Pavel and the Reverend Jill, everyone even close to Adam's age seemed to have moved away a long time ago.

'And maybe this is the way forward. They're attracting lots of people.'

Bella shook her head. 'Yeah but...'

'What?'

'It doesn't feel real does it?'

Adam tapped the table in front of them. 'Isn't it?'

'No. I mean. It's all window dressing isn't it? Like all the top-class eatery bollocks she was spouting.'

'She's just doing her job. It's hard.' He stopped and corrected himself. 'It must be hard to be born into all this and then have it all shift around you.'

Bella wrinkled her nose. 'Fine, well, like the trees, then. You said that was a stage set, not a forest. And this...' She picked up her offending brownie. 'It looks great but there's nothing to it. It's all pretending to be something that they think tourists want, but it's not real. You know what I mean?'

'Yeah. I do.'

Chapter Ten

The day after their trip to spy on what Bella was increasingly thinking of as 'the opposition' it was Ladies' Group time again. The system for deciding where and when the group was meeting remained a mystery, but Flinty always seemed to somehow know. Bella assumed it was something you came to feel 'in your waters' after sufficient years – or perhaps decades – of life in Lowbridge.

Before they went, Bella was set on getting the aberration of a brownie she'd been served the previous day out of her mind. And the only way to get over a bad brownie was to get yourself a really good one. She creamed together her butter and sugar – caster sugar because that was what Flinty had in, but ideally she'd have used half muscovado – while half her chocolate melted over a pan of hot water. Then it was a simple job to combine the chocolate with the butter and sugar, add the flour, eggs and a dash of cocoa and mix together. Finally she chopped the remaining chocolate into generous chunks – no feeble little shop-bought chocolate chips for Bella – and stirred them through the mixture. She popped the whole thing to bake in a low oven for at least half an hour while she sat at the kitchen island with a big mug of tea.

'Oh wow! Something smells amazing.' Darcy sniffed the air in the kitchen appreciatively as she came in.

'Brownies. For Ladies' Group.'

'Oh, I used to love Ladies' Group. I mean, they all thought I was a mad American because I put honey in my tea, but once we'd got past that it was great fun.'

'Why don't you come?'

'Come where?' Veronica appeared in the doorway. The longer she was at Lowbridge the more sure Bella was becoming that Veronica's footsteps made no noise. She never approached. She simply materialised in place.

'To the village Ladies' Group,' Darcy replied. 'Bella's going.' Darcy's tone had hints of a petulant teenager about it.

'Yes. Well.' That 'well' was doing a lot of conversational heavy lifting. *Well* there's no accounting for Bella. *Well* what do you expect from her? *Well* Bella doesn't really count as the lady of the house does she, so does it matter? Any and all of the above could have been the intended implication.

'Well what?'

'Well, you've not been here long enough to really understand these things yet, dear.' Veronica folded her arms. 'If you stick around and marry my grandson…'

As ever Bella bristled at the 'if'.

'…then you'll learn that Lady Lowbridge can't have a foot in both camps. When one joins this family there are certain sacrifices.'

'It's tea and a chat. It's not exactly supporting the forces of revolution.' Although Bella would definitely volunteer as chief cake-maker for the Lowbridge People's Front if the opportunity ever arose. 'And if more groups from the village are going to be coming here it makes sense for me to get to know people, doesn't it?'

Darcy nodded in agreement. 'Quite right. And I shall come with you, Bella. Thank you very much for inviting me.'

With Darcy in tow and a late arrival in the form of Reverend Jill – bustling in with apologies for not making it more often and explanations of the ridiculous demands made of her by needy parishioners, hastily glossed over with a 'Not any of you of course' – Anna's lounge was full to bursting by the time Bella popped open her borrowed Tupperware.

Jill leaned in towards the chocolatey wondrousness. 'I shouldn't. Really I shouldn't.'

The other women nodded. 'A moment on the lips,' Darcy added.

Bella could practically hear the salivating. 'Well I'll pop them here if anyone wants any.'

The conversation kicked off with a fundraising update from Nina. 'So Netty's sponsored silence is underway.'

How could they tell, wondered Bella.

Next to her Netty nodded.

'It's going marvellously isn't it?'

Another wordless nod.

'And we all know what a chatty Cathy she can be, so it's not easy. Anyway, started at noon yesterday so we're twenty-two hours in. The target is seventy-two, and we've got over sixty-two pounds already pledged.'

'Well done, Netty,' Flinty added. 'Sixty-two pounds is great.'

Everyone nodded politely, but it was only polite. Sixty-two pounds wasn't going to get the community hall a new roof. It would barely get their new bridge a functioning hand rail.

Anna leaned across towards Darcy. 'How are you doing, pet? It's hard after the funeral, isn't it?'

'I'm OK, honey. Well, as OK as can be expected. You always think there's more time.'

The other women nodded sagely.

'How's your fella doing?' Anna asked Bella.

'He's all right. We went up to the McKenzie estate yesterday. Trying to get some ideas for Lowbridge.'

'So long as the idea isn't to charge four quid for a cup of tea,' Anna muttered.

'No chance. But I could use your help.'

Flinty and Darcy exchanged a look but the rest of the group looked keen. 'What can we help with, love?' Nina asked.

Bella took a deep breath. This was why she was here. Adam was Lowbridge. She understood that now. That meant that he would stay. It was who he was. And that meant she would stay.

And Lowbridge needed to make money. That would be Bella's project. That would be how she made herself useful. Supporting Adam didn't have to mean being a lady of leisure who turned up to cut ribbons. It meant making Lowbridge work.

'Well ideas really. The McKenzie estate is great for what it is, but it doesn't feel real, you know? There's no community there. It's all...'

'Razzmatazz,' Nina supplied.

'Exactly. But Adam reckons we do need to find ways of bringing more money into the estate, and if we can find a way of doing that that works for the whole community then that would be amazing. So any ideas?'

'Well, we could reopen to visitors,' Darcy said straight away. 'I used to show people round. It was so much fun, and the Americans love that one of their own is the lady of the manor.' She paused. 'Obviously you'll be the lady. I don't want to tread on toes.'

'You wouldn't be.' Bella pulled out her phone and started making a list.

Number 1: Open the castle to tourists

'We'll have to do a good tidy round,' Flinty muttered.

Bella thought the castle was pretty damn tidy already, but she guessed Flinty had higher standards. If people were paying to visit she probably did need to at least put her knickers in a drawer. 'What else?'

'Well we used to do teas at the community hall when the castle was open,' Anna said. 'People would come to you and then come into the village. Can't do that now, though.'

'We could do teas and coffees on the courtyard when it's nice weather?' Darcy suggested.

'Get some big umbrellas and do it all year round,' Flinty added.

Bella updated her list. *Number 2: Cafe in the Courtyard*

'Have you ever looked at getting licensed for weddings?' she asked.

Darcy shook her head. 'I don't think so.'

Flinty laughed. 'You got married at the castle, love.'

'Oh yeah!'

'You don't need a licence in Scotland,' Nina explained. 'The registrar just has to agree that it's an appropriate place.'

'And I can do Christian weddings in the chapel,' Jill added. 'I usually say only people who live in the parish, but I'm happy to discuss it with couples who want a church service.'

Bella added *Number 3: Wedding Venue* to her list.

'Alexander used to lead the bird watching club too,' Darcy said.

'Right. Does that make us any money?' Bella asked.

'Not really.'

Across the room, Netty scribbled furiously on the pad in front of her and passed the paper around the circle to Bella. *Wildlife tours or walks? Tourists love that.*

'OK. Wildlife walks.' Bella added it as number 4 on her list. 'We'd need someone to lead that.'

'Well Veronica's the expert really,' Flinty said. 'She knows every bird you'll ever see out here.'

Everyone paused for a second.

'Maybe we'll have a think about that,' said Bella. 'That's lots to get started.'

'What we really need is better guest accommodation,' Nina chipped in. 'There's two rooms at the pub that people sometimes take for fishing trips and the like, but they're pretty basic. People want something a bit fancy these days, don't they? En suite bathrooms and tiny bottles of shampoo.'

Bella had wondered about offering guest accommodation at the castle, but if they were going to open to the public and accommodate herself, Adam, Darcy and Veronica, could they really afford to make any more rooms out of bounds to day visitors?

'Xander once mentioned the idea of opening up the coach house,' Flinty said. 'Never did anything about it though. It was years ago.' She nodded at Darcy. 'Before your time. I think it was...' She tailed off.

Darcy laughed. 'It's fine. You can mention her.'

'I think it was Adam's ma's idea. She was one for grand notions that never really came to anything.'

'Like being a mother,' snipped Anna.

'I'm sure that's not fair,' Darcy murmured.

The older women maintained a distinctly unconvinced silence. Bella added *Coach house B&B* to her list.

The pent-up ball of energy that was Jill finally snapped. 'Maybe I'll have a tiny piece of brownie.'

She squeezed forward and grabbed the biggest piece from the tub.

'Oh well, if you are…'

'Shouldn't let it go to waste…'

'Maybe just a wee bit…'

Opposite Bella, Netty held up her pad: *Brownie please!*

Bella smiled to herself. Nobody could resist chocolate for long. She smiled again as the group mellowed into a chocolatey silence as the women took their first bites and felt the rich fudgey decadence on their tongues. Darcy had even closed her eyes and leaned back slightly, letting a small gasp of pleasure escape her lips. 'Oh I wish I could bake like this…' she murmured.

Nina laughed. 'I wish my Pavel could bake like this. I've spoiled him. He's so good with his hands but he couldn't find his way round a kitchen to save his life.'

'That's what you should do!' Jill all but punched the air.

'What?'

'You should teach people to cook!'

Bella shook her head. 'I'm not that good.'

'Bollocks.' Jill's cheeks reddened. She flicked her eyes skywards. 'Sorry. You're great. You're a professional chef, right?'

'Well yeah, but I just learnt from my nan and then on the job. I'm not a chef chef.'

'I think you're plenty good enough to teach people who don't know the handle end of a whisk from...' Jill frowned. 'From the other bit.'

Darcy nodded. 'Oh you should. You could do baking classes, and different cuisines, and...'

Could she? The idea of doing something that put her back in the kitchen appealed and sharing her love of food might be fun. 'I don't know. Where would we even do it?'

'Well there's the main kitchen at the castle,' Flinty said. 'And then the bakery and the scullery. There's a second oven in the scullery. Bit old but still works perfectly well.' She frowned. 'You could probably fit six or eight in the main kitchen for a demo.'

'I don't know.'

All of the ladies of the Ladies' Group joined in the chorus of approval for the cooking lesson plan.

'We'll need a name,' Flinty said.

'The Lowbridge Cookery School?' offered Darcy.

'Lowbridge Loch Cookery School?' suggested Nina.

'The loch isn't even called that,' Anna pointed out. 'Not officially.'

'No, but it's what everyone actually calls it,' Nina replied.

Netty held up her pad. *The Highland Cookery School!*

The Highland Cookery School. It had a ring to it. Bella added the suggestion to her list.

–

Adam had to knuckle down. That was so often the case. Adam needed to learn to focus. Adam needed to concentrate. Adam needed to stop his attention wandering and get his head into the estate accounts and administration.

He fought to tune in to what his grandmother was saying. He was sure it was the same stuff she'd been saying every day since he got here, but it hadn't stuck yet and seemed determined not to go in now.

'Since Covid, you see, we haven't had the income from visitors, and the number of shooting and fishing licences was dwindling before that anyway. A few of the locals still fish but your father was loath to put the price up too much for them.'

Adam's father had always preached that the family were the custodians of the land, but the whole community had a right to it. Locals paid peanuts for their fishing rights – barely enough to contribute to the cost of keeping the riverside clean and in good order, which should, Adam reflected, have included maintenance of the bridge.

'Since John McKenzie took over up the way we don't get very many shooting parties. Again, there's only a few of the locals who still shoot. And the younger people don't so much, do they?'

'I guess not.'

His grandmother shook her head. 'So that's something to think about.'

It certainly was. The thing he was supposed to be thinking about was too huge, though. The whole future of Lowbridge – the house, the estate, the village, the title itself – was suddenly resting in his hands. 'Right. Is there anything…' He couldn't say 'smaller' could he? 'Anything more immediate?'

'Well there's the inheritance tax. We can't deal with that properly until we've got the Confirmation, but we ought to start planning for it. Your father had insurance that should cover the lion's share of the inheritance tax.'

'Good?' That was good, right?

'Well yes, but the lion's share isn't the whole amount. We will have a shortfall. I've talked to Mr Samson and we don't have probate yet and that could take an age but we're probably going to be a hundred thousand or so short.'

'How much is the lion's share?'

Veronica stared at him. 'Well, you're inheriting the land, the house, and the cottage in the village, plus all the fixtures and fittings and bits and bobs. I don't know precisely yet, but I would imagine the total bill will be around two million.'

'What?'

His grandmother remained impassive. 'It's a big estate.'

'But…' Figures were not Adam's thing, but they had been his father's, hadn't they? '…aren't there ways around it?'

'There are, which is why he had insurance.'

Dipper padded into the office as she did most days. She snuffled around him, and quickly ambled away, her search for her true master still fruitless. The dog could see what everyone else was missing, but Adam already knew. He wasn't the right man for any of this. 'So how do we raise the rest of the money?'

'Well, when your father inherited I think he sold all the artworks that were worth putting on the market, and he let Macwillis take on the land we held on Skye.' She paused. 'We can use the cash equity but that's only about fifteen thousand, and that will mean we have no reserves at all for anything unexpected.' She tapped her pen on the table. 'So we can ask for payment in instalments, or we could sell an asset.'

'I thought you were dead against selling.'

'I don't mean breaking up the estate, for goodness' sake.' Veronica shook her head like she was talking to a child. 'We do still have one cottage in the village though.'

'Would that cover the shortfall?'

'Close to certainly.'

'And it's an empty cottage?' Years ago they'd had multiple tenants in the village but Adam had honestly thought all the cottages had been sold.

Veronica was quiet for a moment. 'No. It's Margaret's cottage.'

'Margaret?' Oh. 'Flinty?' Adam shook his head. 'We are not throwing Flinty out of her home.'

'No. Well, good. That really only leaves one other option then.'

Adam looked up. Something in his grandmother's tone told him he wasn't going to love the end of this conversation.

'The flat in Edinburgh.'

What flat in Edinburgh? Finally the penny dropped. 'My flat?'

'Well ultimately it's you who owes this bill.' Even Veronica had the heart to look slightly apologetic at that point.

Of course it was. Like everything else it all came back to Adam. He was the hub at the centre of the wheel. 'Right.' He nodded. 'Let's take a break there.'

'There's still lots of…'

Adam was already out of the door. He had no doubt that there were lots of other things he ought to be thinking about but this one was enough for today. To hold Lowbridge together, which was his duty, he had to draw a line under the life he'd built in Edinburgh. Letting go of the flat was like letting go of who he truly was, in the midst of the storm of who he had been born to be.

In the kitchen, he flicked the kettle on and started making tea. Fiona had seemed happy enough and maybe she was right. Maybe estates like Lowbridge did need to modernise. Even if he raised the money for the inheritance tax bill, a house – OK castle, he conceded, silently in his head – like this was a money pit.

He pulled his phone from his pocket. The old school WhatsApp group had thirty-one new messages. He scrolled quickly down. Fiona was definitely the person who'd wanted this group. Her contributions were a steady stream of photos of the McKenzie estate with chirpy comments about the modern Highland life. Everyone else was scattered to the seven winds, living their own lives in pastures news.

Bella and Darcy clattered in from the back corridor. Darcy was chatting and in higher spirits than Adam remembered seeing her. She stopped when she saw Adam. 'Well I'm going to leave you two to catch up!'

Adam frowned as she jogged through to the front hall. 'What's up with her?'

Bella shook her head. 'Nothing. Just some ideas we were talking about at Ladies' Group. She might have got a bit carried away.'

That sounded more like the Darcy Adam remembered bowling into his life when he was fifteen years old in a whirlwind of chatter and modernity, than the pale withdrawn woman he'd been sharing a home with recently. Bella glanced at his phone. 'Is that Fiona?'

'Just WhatsApp. She's like the poster girl for Highland living.'

'What's she saying?' He could hear the edge in Bella's voice.

'Nothing.' He took her hand. 'Why?'

'No reason.'

'Bel?'

'Just, you know, someone like that, she'd be what your grandmother would pick for you, wouldn't she?'

'You're jealous?'

'No! Not exactly. More just…' She shook her head. 'She's perfect lady of the manor material.'

He dropped his phone onto the counter. 'Not for my manor. I don't know if you heard, but I'm in love with someone else.' She let him pull her close. 'Desperately, ridiculously, overwhelmingly in love,' he reassured her.

She buried her face into his shoulder. 'Sorry,' she whispered.

'Don't be.'

'She'd fit in, wouldn't she?'

'I don't know about that.' Did anyone fit anywhere?

He picked his phone up and handed it to her. 'You can read the messages.'

She shook her head. 'No. No. I'm being stupid.'

'OK. Up to you.' He tapped back and couldn't help but notice the two blue ticks next to the message he'd sent his mum. Read but no reply. He stuffed the phone back in his pocket. 'Everyone else is a million miles away.'

'Anywhere exciting?'

That depended on your definition of exciting. 'One woman's a heavy metal singer in Los Angeles, but mostly Glasgow, Edinburgh, Manchester, London, you know.'

All perfectly good places a person could make a life without the pressure to be the perfect laird. 'Not giving you itchy feet?' he asked.

'Nope. This is us. This is where I belong.' She nestled against him and pressed a kiss to his lips. 'Here. With you.'

Here was where he was supposed to be. Everyone agreed. He turned slightly to look out of the back window above the sink, away from the courtyard and out towards the hillside beyond, hoping that focusing on the open space outside would lessen the feeling that the castle walls were closing in on him.

From somewhere through the fog in his head he realised Bella was asking him a question. 'I'm sorry?'

'What have you been up to?'

Back to reality. 'The place is in real trouble I think.'

'How do you mean?'

'We probably can't cover the full inheritance tax from insurance.' He parroted what his grandmother had told him. 'So the suggestion is that we sell my place in Edinburgh.'

'How do you feel about that?'

'It's my home.' He took a seat at the island. 'But this is my home too. So yeah... And even after that I don't know if we'd be making enough money to keep the place going.' That thought almost scared him more than anything else – the thought of Lowbridge slipping further into slow decline, sections of the house being formally closed up and allowed to decay, to hold together an estate and a community that would be dying alongside them. He didn't want to say the next part out loud. She'd been to McKenzie's place with him. She knew what the options were. 'It doesn't feel like I've got a lot of choice left.'

Bella slid her arm around his neck. 'It's OK.'

'I'm letting everyone down.'

'No.' He let her slide into the gap between his knees, and wrap herself around him. 'You're not letting anyone down. It's a lot to get your head around. I've got some ideas though. Everyone does. We were talking at Ladies' Group and we came up with the idea of doing cookery lessons and…'

Adam opened his mouth to stop her, to explain that she'd got the wrong end of the stick, but something about the light in her eyes stopped him. She was excited, like Darcy had been when they'd arrived a few minutes ago. They were fired up about Lowbridge. The problem wasn't the estate. The problem was him.

His phone ringing on the worktop interrupted Bella's explanation of the incredible ideas the Ladies' Group had come up with. Bella moved out of the way to let him answer. He checked the screen and frowned. Another thing he wasn't on top of. 'Ravi, hi!'

'Hi mate, how's it going?'

'Erm… you know. Tough.'

'Look, I'm really sorry to call but Carsons are getting nervy about the plans for their…' Ravi paused and Adam could picture him scouring a set of notes or plans. 'Their innovatively planted garden atrium.'

Adam knew the project. A new set of high-end offices designed to have planting inside running up the centre of the building.

'Danny came to the meeting with me but…' Adam knew what was coming. 'He's not you.'

Danny had worked for Adam and Ravi since their first big project. He was a brilliant landscaper, but he wasn't much of a talker.

'They're asking for an emergency meeting with both of us. Like, if you really can't, I do understand.' There was a strain in Ravi's voice.

'Do you think they'll pull out if I'm not there?'

'Honestly, yeah. They liked your vision for it. Not seeing you in person is making them anxious.' Ravi paused again. 'And we're not booking new work with you away so it'd be a big gap in the calendar. Without this to tide us over we're pretty screwed.'

'When's the meeting?'

'Day after tomorrow.'

Not a lot of time, but the thought of getting back to Edinburgh was a relief, not a stress. 'Fine. I'll come over tomorrow. I'll ring you when I'm home and we can have a planning session in the evening?'

'Brilliant. Thank you mate. I hate to ask, you know, in the circumstances.'

'It's fine. I'll be there.'

He hung up the phone.

'Where are you going?'

'Ravi needs me in Edinburgh.'

'Do you want me to come with you?'

Of course he did. Him and Bella in Edinburgh was what he'd been dreaming of when they were busy falling in love in Spain. Now the idea of her there felt like the world was taunting him with hints of a life he would never have. 'It'll be mostly work,' he said.

'I'd like to see your place in Edinburgh, but I'm probably more use here.'

More use than he was, certainly.

'I'll miss you though,' she pointed out. 'And you need a break.'

He shook his head. 'No time.' Probably there would be time if he could get his head around half of the things his grandmother was trying to show him at anything above a snail's pace.

'One evening before you go. There's a pub in the village, right?'

'Yeah, but—'

'Then I'm taking you for a drink.'

'You don't have to.'

'I want to. You and me painting the town red.'

Adam's horror at the thought of a debauched night at the Mucky Duck must have shown on his face.

Bella grinned. 'All right then. We'll paint the village a very pale pink.'

'That sounds more realistic.'

'It's a date.'

The pub was in the old part of the village, nearest the stream that ran down into the loch. Flinty dropped them off in the Land Rover, ostensibly on her way home, but Bella remained slightly sceptical that Flinty ever actually went home. Whatever time you got up, she was already there, stove hot and kettle boiling.

'It's a long walk back if you don't want to take your life in your hands,' she pointed out.

'We'll be fine,' Bella reassured her, but turned to Adam as she drove away. 'How are we getting back?'

'I'm not sure.' He glanced back towards the water. 'In my head it's still a ten-minute walk over the Low Bridge.'

She took his hand. 'Well if we have to walk the long way it'll add to the adventure.'

'I'm not sure an evening at the Mucky Duck has ever been described as that before.'

Inside, the pub was on the shabby end of traditional. The wood was darkened by years of tobacco smoke, and the velvet on the stools was a little threadbare. The hulk behind the bar was familiar. 'Pavel!'

'Bella.' He grinned. 'And Adam.' He paused, a slight glint in his eye. 'I'm sorry. M'lord.'

'Bugger off, Pav.'

Pavel laughed. 'How are you? I'm sorry I haven't been up since the funeral. I figured you'd be busy with everything.'

'I'm OK.' He turned back to Bella. 'So you two have met?'

'At the village store. I thought you were a builder.'

Pavel nodded.

'And personal trainer?'

'That too.'

'And lifeboatman,' Adam added. 'Water taxi operator.' He frowned. 'Fishing charter operator?'

Pavel nodded again. 'It's good to be busy.'

'And barman?' Bella asked.

'Well since Mr Taggart died, Mrs Taggart was struggling a bit, running this place on her own, so I help out.'

'He helps out every bloody night.' Bella and Adam turned towards the voice. Hugh was sitting at the nearest table to the bar with a pair of men Bella didn't recognise. 'Will you two join us?'

Adam nodded, and Bella was delighted to see Queen Latifah snoozing at Hugh's feet. She raised her head and accepted a little tickle as they installed themselves at Hugh's table with pints of something bearing the McKenzie estate branding all over the tap. 'Do they actually brew this themselves?' Bella asked.

Hugh shrugged. 'I doubt it. Tastes...' He took a sip and paused. 'Well it doesn't taste like beer, but they tied the Taggarts into a contract and it's the only pub we've got

173

so... Anyway, this is Gareth, Netty's husband, and Callum, their lad. And this is Bella and you know Adam, our new laird.'

Bella caught the slight tension on Adam's face at the introduction. She jumped into the conversation. 'You're Netty's husband?'

The man nodded. 'Aye.'

The younger man piped up. 'And you're the famous Bella? I've only been home two days and I'm glad she's on this sponsored silence because she won't stop telling us about you on that bloody notepad. If she could talk my ear would be worn off by now.'

'Oh.' Bella smiled. 'Well I'm glad I made an impression, I think.'

'Don't worry. It's all positive. You're a powerhouse, apparently.'

Bella didn't know what to say to that. She'd always thought of herself as more of a drifter than a mover or a shaker.

'How long are you back for, Cal?'

'Just for the next week. Uni finished and I've got a month or so before my new job starts. Marketing.'

'In London,' his father added.

Hugh sucked the air through his teeth.

'I know,' Callum laughed. 'It's practically France.'

'Worse than France. England.' Hugh glanced at Bella. 'No offence.'

The three men drained their pints. 'We've got to get back,' Callum explained. 'Mum's making spag bol.'

'And I'm only supposed to be out walking this little lady.'

The trio headed out and Bella and Adam settled back onto the bench Hugh had vacated. 'So this is where you did all your teenage high jinx?' she asked.

'Oh no. Mr Taggart was a stickler and he knew everyone's birthdays. He kept a little list behind the bar, so there was no way you were getting served underage. We used to have to nick whisky from our parents' cupboards and drink it on the lochside. Or out in Pav's granddad's boat.'

'You were drinking whisky when you were a teenager?' Bella was impressed. 'Hardcore.'

'Well it's basically your patriotic duty around here.'

'So for this cookery school idea...' she started.

Adam closed his eyes. 'Can we not?'

'Not what?'

'Not talk about the estate tonight.' His expression was one of weariness. 'Just for this evening.'

'Sorry. It's supposed to be a night off, isn't it?'

'That was the idea, yeah.'

'All right then.' She took a long drag from her pint. Hugh was right. It tasted like dishwater. 'What shall we talk about?'

'Tell me something about you that I don't know yet.'

'OK.' What was there? Compared with being a laird and growing up in a castle, Bella's life hadn't been that noteworthy so far. 'There's not much to tell.'

'How did you get into food?'

'What do you mean?'

'What got you started with it?'

She shook her head. 'Everyone's into food. You have to eat, don't you? So, I guess that's what got me started.'

'No. Well yes, everyone has to eat, but you light up when you taste something amazing and when you're actually cooking you're just lost in it. Most people aren't like that.'

Maybe that was true, but it was incomprehensible to her. How could you not get lost in a perfect piece of dark chocolate, just sweet and creamy enough, or in the scent of a chicken, coated with just a dash of garlic, lemon and black pepper, roasting in the oven?

'Did you cook with your mum?'

'Oh God no. She could barely make toast. It was my nan.' She could still see herself back in the kitchen in her nan's flat, rolling out biscuit dough or standing up on tiptoes to take a taste of whatever Nan was cooking from the edge of her wooden spoon. She could remember her nan asking her, 'What else does it need?' She smiled. 'I love that it's never quite the same twice when you cook something. You can take the same ingredients and do the same thing but then sometimes when you taste it, it needs a dash more salt, or a squeeze of lemon, but then other times it's just right already. But you don't know until you taste. I can never get bored of it.' She shook her head. 'I'm sorry. That sounds mad, doesn't it?'

'No. That's how I feel about plants. You do everything you know you should and then you have to wait for the weather and the season to change, and sometimes the soil just isn't right even though you were sure it would be, so you have to change your plan and plant something different. A garden is never really finished, you know. You can always go back in and plant something new or prune something back or move something that's not thriving like it should be. You have to keep sort of listening to it and tending to it, you know?'

'Like a perfect slow-cooked casserole,' she confirmed.

'If you say so.'

They downed two more pints of McKenzie beer, which Bella had to admit improved the more you drank, and talked about nothing and everything. Their bodies leaned towards one another automatically and her fingers wrapped around his as the evening meandered by. Eventually Pavel wandered over. 'You're the last pair standing.'

Adam looked around the pub. At some point the people around them had drifted away. He checked his watch. Ten thirty. 'Sorry mate. Do you want to close up?'

'No rush.'

'It's fine,' Adam reassured him. 'We're walking back so we should get going.'

'You should have said. I just had a dram with Young Man Strachan, otherwise I'd have driven you.'

'It's not a problem. We can stagger through the sheep.' Adam took Bella's hand and pulled her to her feet. 'They'll be delighted to see you, I'm sure.'

'Those bloody sheep.'

Pavel raised a questioning eyebrow.

'They seem to have adopted Bel as their leader,' Adam explained.

Pavel laughed as he walked them to the door. 'So what are you actually up to at the moment?'

'Mostly failing my grandmother's crash course in estate management.'

'Well if you fancy a day's labouring any time let me know. If you're still up to it.'

'I'm still up to it.' Adam was indignant. 'So long as you're not as tough a taskmaster as your granddad.'

Pavel grinned. 'I make no promises.'

Adam wrapped his arm around his fiancée as they made their way out into the night.

'It's such a long walk,' she moaned.

'I know.' It was really too far. 'Why don't we go the short way?'

'The Low Bridge?'

'Yeah.'

'Didn't you close it?'

'Well I put a sign up and some tape across.'

Bella pulled a face. 'I thought that was horribly dangerous.'

'I mean, I wouldn't take a pushchair across it.'

'Right.' Bella rested her head against him. 'Would you go across it at all if you were fully sober?'

That was a very excellent question. 'Probably not.' Adam, however, had the perfect rebuttal. 'But I am not fully sober.'

Bella giggled. 'Neither am I!'

'Come on then.' He led the way down to the side of the burn. The path to the bridge was overgrown from disuse but it was still there and they picked their way through the brambles, giggling and clinging to one another until they reached the bridge itself. If anything, it was in a worse state than Adam remembered. 'So the key here I think is to go slowly, and keep your weight towards the edges where the planks rest on the side supports.'

Bella nodded seriously.

'Cos it's stronger there because...' He knew this. He built arches and bridges. He shook his head. 'Because of science.'

'Yeah. Science,' Bella agreed. 'Who's going first?'

'You're lighter.'

'Right.' She stopped. 'Sorry. Does that mean I should go first to test it out or you should go first cos it's only going to get weaker?'

'I don't know.'

She giggled again. 'I'll go first.'

He watched as she edged her way across the bridge, feet wide to the sides, holding on to what was left of the hand rail. She jumped off the end at the other side and span round, hands aloft in victory. 'Your turn.'

Adam stepped onto the bridge. First step – so far, so good. Nothing was moving underneath him. There were no ominous creaks. He went further. Second step, and then third. It couldn't be more than fifteen, at most, to the other side. Fourth step, fifth. Was that a hint of a wobble under his foot? He stopped still and took a deep breath in. Sixth step, seventh, eighth. More than a wobble now. The wood under his left foot groaned. He knew the crack was coming before he felt it. He hopped his foot up and lurched forward. The movement shifted everything and he landed at first onto the wooden deck, allowing him a blissful moment of thinking it was OK, before the floor beneath him disappeared and he was falling.

'Adam!' He heard Bella squeal on the bank and then she was scrambling down towards him. Their bodies met in the water. She grabbed his arm and tried for a second to hold him up before they both fell, her on top of him, pushing him backwards until he was lying on his back on the bottom of the stream, half covered in water, with a damp, red-faced Bella spreadeagled on top of him. 'Are you OK?'

'I'm fine. Wet,' he laughed. 'Very wet.'

She pushed his damp hair out of his face. 'I don't think the bridge is safe, you know.'

'No.'

They hauled themselves up to standing and clambered up the riverbank, added a layer of mud to their wet legs and hands.

'You're sure you're all right?'

'I'm fine,' he reassured her.

'I was trying to save you.' She waved a hand back towards the water. 'I thought I was being heroic.'

They both fell into another fit of laughter. 'I appreciate the effort,' he managed.

'Come on.' She grinned. 'I want to get you back and get you out of those wet things.'

He took her hand as they walked up towards the coach house, Bella excitedly retelling the drama of the fall from her vantage point on the bank, sharing fits of laughter at the ridiculousness of the whole thing.

Adam glanced back. The Low Bridge was gone, literally collapsed beneath him. It didn't seem that funny any more.

Chapter Eleven

The next morning Bella installed herself at the kitchen island, with Darcy's iPad in front of her (donated in the earnestly stated belief that Bella was going to save Lowbridge), her phone at her side and a notepad open as well. The list of things to do was starting to overwhelm her. Setting up a cookery school would require insurance, and health and safety certificates, and advertising, which meant she would have to pin down specific dates and offers and prices. They didn't have enough useable accommodation rooms yet to offer residential schools, so she was planning one day and half day sessions to start with. But then would anybody come along to those when Lowbridge was about a million years' travel time from everywhere?

And, in addition to all of that, would Bella even be any good at teaching someone else to cook? She cooked as much through instinct as understanding, and that sense of what flavours went well together, whether to cook a piece of meat fast and hot or low and slow, how to treat a simple ingredient to elevate it from simply edible to a delicious indulgence – was that something that could be taught?

'What are you up to?' Adam dumped his suitcase in the doorway to the kitchen.

'Oh, many plans and plots. Are you ready to go?' Bella stood and wrapped her arms around him. 'This is going to be the first night we've spent apart since—'

'Since we met.'

'Yeah.'

He planted a kiss on her lips. 'It's only a few days.'

'I know.'

The sound of raised voices reached them from one of the many coloured rooms on the other side of the front hallway. Adam winced.

'What are they fighting about now?' Bella asked. Since the funeral diplomatic relations between Veronica and Darcy did seem to have calmed a little. Evidently whatever entente cordiale had been reached was no longer quite so cordiale.

Adam shook his head. 'I don't know. Look.' He wrapped his fingers through hers. 'I know you're busy, but do you think you could have a go at brokering some sort of peace there?'

Bella's mouth dropped open. 'Me? Your grandma already hates me.'

'She doesn't hate you.'

She shot him a look.

'Well I think she hates Darcy more. I'm too close to them. Grandmother still sees me as a little boy she can overrule and Darcy is refusing to be the first to give ground.'

She squeezed his hand. 'For you, I'll try.'

Another volley of screaming made its way down the hall.

'I must love you an awful lot.'

'Well it's definitely mutual,' he replied, leaning towards her for another long, soft kiss.

'Ahem.' Flinty was studiously staring at the door frame. 'If you want to get to the train we need to get going, lad. The road to Strathcarron can be awful at this time of year.'

'Yeah. Right.' Adam pulled away. 'I'll be back at the weekend.'

'I know.' She wandered out to wave them off and then made her way back to the kitchen. The iPad beckoned to her, in competition with the yelling from the battling Ladies Lowbridge. She couldn't face them right now. She needed a proper plan before she threw herself into that particular breach.

And a proper plan was not a one-woman endeavour. Bella could well remember coming home from school and finding the living room full of her nan's friends – Tilly from next door, Ginny and Pete from downstairs, Bernie from the sheltered housing across the way, and whoever else had been pulled into Nan's orbit that day – plotting and painting placards and generally readying themselves for the making of mischief. Nan had called the group her Council of War. And, after a flurry of texts and phone calls, Bella was assembling her very own.

Jill was the first to arrive, full of apologies for being late.

'You're not late.'

She checked the time on her phone. 'Oh. I'm not. That's strange. I wonder what I forgot to do.'

Bella eyed the back seat of Jill's four-wheel drive. 'Are those supposed to be somewhere?'

The back of the car was filled with an absolute mountain of pink, blue and purple balloons.

'Oh goodness! The balloon arch for the donkey sanctuary in Locharron.' Jill slapped her forehead with her hand.

'Are they having a fete or something?'

Jill shook her head. 'No. That's the weird bit. The manager just thought the donkeys might like balloons.'

There were so many questions in Bella's head. Why did Jill have a balloon arch to start with? How did the idea even come up in conversation? How did Jill come to be the go-to balloon arch person for the region? She picked just one. 'Do donkeys like balloons?'

'I don't think so.'

'Right.'

'Too late now anyway. I'll tell them I forgot. Would you like a balloon arch?'

Bella shook her head.

'No.' Jill sighed. 'It's not really a thing you get for no reason is it?'

'Unless you run a donkey sanctuary apparently.'

She saw the growing crowd of white woolly bodies as she turned back towards the courtyard. 'No,' she warned them.

Undeterred, the little group of sheep followed her back towards the castle.

'Are they not supposed to be here?' asked Jill.

'No. They should be out on the hill, munching plant life, and I'm sure they weren't here a minute ago.' She eyed the mini-flock suspiciously as they wandered after her into the courtyard.

Jill appraised the herd. 'Do you think sheep like balloon arches?'

'I think these sheep like most things.' Dipper bounded out into the courtyard. Bella rubbed her neck. 'OK Dips. This is your moment. Herd the sheep back up the hill.'

Dipper ambled over to the nearest sheep who didn't bat an eyelid.

'I thought sheep were supposed to be scared of dogs?' Bella asked.

'Well not these ones.' Jill shrugged. 'Or not this dog.'

'She's too soft.'

'She's just good-natured.'

'Dipper!' Veronica's voice carried out into the court-yard, calling Dipper to heel. The dog trotted obediently back.

'She knows who's boss,' Jill muttered. Bella caught her eye. 'I mean that charitably and with love.'

'Of course.'

Veronica appeared through the door nearest the estate office, closely followed by Darcy. 'Oh my goodness,' exclaimed the younger Lady Lowbridge. 'Aren't they adorable?'

'What,' Veronica turned to Bella, 'are they doing down here?'

'They followed me.'

'And you just let them?'

That seemed unfair. 'How do you stop them?'

Veronica shook her head.

Darcy's enthusiasm cut off whatever reply she might have been about to offer. 'They're adorable!' She clapped her hands together. 'Can we keep them?'

Veronica stared at her. 'They're our sheep.'

They were? She did remember Adam telling her that, but Bella had still been imagining some secret hill farmer somewhere. It turned out she was marrying the hill farmer.

Darcy frowned. 'No. Our sheep are out on the hill. They just come down to the barn for lambing.'

There was a barn?

Veronica shot a look to the heavens. 'These ones seem to have taken a liking to Miss Smith.'

'It's not my fault.'

'I don't see why they can't just stay here.'

'For goodness' sake. They can't stay here because there is nothing for them to eat and they…' Veronica waved a dismissive hand. 'Do their business all over the place. And you get rid of them like this.' She took a firm step forward towards the nearest sheep, who edged away. Veronica stepped forward again. This time the whole flock reacted, shuffling towards the gates. Veronica stepped slightly to the side and then strode more forcefully towards the flock, sending them trotting out of the courtyard, past Jill's parked car and back up towards the hillside. She returned a minute or two later. 'Perfectly straightforward.'

'I still don't see why we couldn't have kept a little one,' Darcy complained.

–

Flinty was laying out tea and coffee things in what Bella was rebelliously referring to as the Yellow Room when they went inside. 'Do you need anything else love?'

'I don't think so.'

Flinty made to head back to her kitchen.

'Where do you think you're going?'

'Well you won't want me in the way.'

'I'm not having a Council of War without you on it. And anyway you're the only person Veronica listens to.'

Flinty shook her head. 'I'm sure that's not true.'

'It absolutely is. Please. I need you.'

Flinty sat herself down on the big armchair next to the fire, looking quite like she had always belonged there. 'Well, if you need me, dear.'

Ten minutes later her full council was assembled. Anna had volunteered to take notes. Nina, as ever, had Netty in tow. 'She's still doing her silence love, so she won't be any bother.' Jill settled into the final seat, a small, slightly sagging armchair across from Flinty at the opposite side of the fireplace. A second later she squealed.

'What?' asked Nina.

Jill rubbed her neck. 'Nothing. I just…' She twisted and looked behind her. 'Nothing.'

'OK.' Bella clapped her hands together. 'Thank you…'

'Aaargh!' Jill yelped again and jumped out of her seat. 'Sorry. It felt like someone was behind me.'

The other women stared at Jill's chair suspiciously.

Flinty sighed. 'That's where Poppy likes to sit. She tends to prod you a bit if you're in her place.'

Bella shook her head. 'It was probably just a draught. Poppy isn't real.'

'Have you tried telling her that?'

Actually Bella had. 'She doesn't seem to believe me,' she conceded. 'Poppy's the castle ghost.'

'One of the castle ghosts,' Flinty corrected.

'What?' That was news to Bella.

'She's the only one that really bothers us, but the lassie still doesn't quite believe in her.' Flinty shook her head at Bella's utterly obtuse rationalism.

'Well I do,' Jill said. 'Imaginary people don't tickle.'

Netty held up her pad. *You should do an exorcism.*

'No!' Bella was not having that.

'Why not?' Flinty asked. 'You don't believe in her anyway.'

'But in case I'm wrong, I don't want to be the one throwing a child out of her home.'

Flinty nodded approvingly.

'I'm not really the exorcism type of vicar anyway,' Jill pointed out. 'I could do you a lovely blessing if you wanted though.' She glanced back at the seat and then over at the settee. 'Room for a little one over there do you think?'

Jill squeezed onto the sofa with Anna and Bella. 'Right,' Bella continued. 'Thank you for coming. I hope you don't mind me asking.'

'Not at all,' Anna reassured her. 'It's a long time since we've been up here.'

'You were here last week,' Flinty pointed out.

'True, but you didn't let us in the house, did you?'

'You could have come in to pee.'

'I didn't need to pee.'

'I peed,' Nina piped up. 'I always need to pee. I'm at that age.'

Anna shook her head. 'I'm older than you. I do my pelvic floor though. Bladder like a steel trap.'

'Well bully for you,' Nina muttered.

Anna turned to Bella. 'I'm not writing any of this bit down.'

'OK. Anyway, thank you for coming. I'm really hoping you can help me with two things. The first is how on earth to get this cookery school thing started.'

Nina beamed. 'I'm so glad you're going to do that, dear.'

Netty nodded and waved a big thumbs up in Bella's direction.

'Is she allowed to do that?' asked Anna.

'Do what?'

'Stick her thumb up. I mean that's basically sign language isn't it? Doesn't that count as talking?'

Nina folded her arms decisively. 'It's a sponsored silence, not a sponsored no communication.'

'So if she did sign language the whole time that would be OK?'

'Yeah.'

Flinty shook her head. 'No. Not in the spirit of the thing is it?'

'She can nod and shake her head,' Nina pointed out. 'She's been doing that the whole time.'

Netty nodded in agreement.

'I think Bella was explaining why she'd asked us all here,' Jill interrupted.

'Sorry Bella!' said Nina.

'Right you are.' Anna held up her pen and pad. 'We're all ready.'

'Thank you.' Bella took a deep breath. 'And the second thing is Darcy and Veronica. Lady Lowbridge and, well, Lady Lowbridge,' she corrected herself. 'I promised Adam I'd try to broker a peace between them while he was away.'

Anna sucked the air in through her teeth. 'And when's he get back love?'

'Saturday.'

Nina nodded sympathetically. 'Have you thought of just doing the cooking lessons love?'

Bella had indeed thought of that. It did seem like a much more achievable goal. 'They're at each other's throats, and that will affect the cookery school won't it? I can't have people paying money to come here and having those two screaming the whole time.'

Netty grabbed Anna's pad and scribbled something down. *Some people would pay good money for that.*

The group giggled. Netty probably wasn't wrong.

'Well maybe, but they won't be paying for that. They'll be paying to learn how not to split a hollandaise.'

'Put the fat in slowly and don't let it get too cold,' Flinty muttered.

'My mother used to put a spot of mustard in at the start. That works,' Nina offered.

'Should I be writing this down?' Anna asked.

'No. We don't have to sort out how to make a hollandaise now,' Bella explained. 'That was just an example.'

'Sorry love.'

'It's fine. So Veronica and Darcy, have they always been like this?'

All eyes turned to Flinty.

'Pretty much. I mean Alexander tried to keep the peace between them but even he didn't manage it that often.'

'So what started it?'

'How do you mean?'

'Like, was there something that happened to kick it all off, or have they always hated each other?'

'I don't think Darcy hates Veronica,' Anna chipped in. 'At least I don't think she did to start with, but Veronica can be...' She shot an unmistakeable glance in Flinty's direction. 'Well, a little unbending.'

'She wasn't always like that,' Nina pointed out.

'Really?' Jill, the other 'newcomer' to the village, sounded intrigued. 'What was she like?'

Flinty shook her head. 'It was a long time ago.'

'She was like us,' Anna announced. 'Wasn't she, Maggie?'

'Well...'

'She was. The three of us were thick as thieves.'

'Especially Maggie and her,' Nina noted.

'Yes. Well.' Anna tapped her pen against the pad. 'We were good friends.'

Bella processed that image for a second before the penny dropped. 'Veronica's from the village?'

'Born and bred,' Flinty confirmed.

'Wow.' Jill grinned. 'I think I assumed she was from some other big posh place, you know. Daughter of another laird or something.'

Bella realised she had absolutely assumed the same. Veronica had strong lady of the manor energy. Obviously Bella herself was a blow-in, and clearly Darcy was too, but Veronica exuded the confidence of a woman to the manor born.

'Veronica's dad was a real chancer actually,' Anna continued.

'That's not fair.' Flinty shook her head. 'She's exaggerating.'

'I am not. He'd have tried to sell ice to Eskimos.'

'My mother said he once tried to sell her fish from our dad's catch. They were our fish!' Nina laughed at the memory.

'Sold the old Laird on the idea of marrying his daughter though, didn't he?' Anna pointed out. 'Not that he took much persuading. I never thought I'd see love at first sight, but that night when Alexander and his cousin came to the village dance, he was blown away, wasn't he, Maggie?'

Flinty was quiet for a second. 'I wasn't there. That was the night my mother went into hospital with her appendix.'

'Of course you weren't.' Anna nodded. 'Silly of me to forget.'

Bella had that feeling once again that she was swimming through apparently calm, but actually shark infested, waters. 'Why doesn't she like Darcy though?'

The women looked at each other. Netty scribbled on her pad, *American?*

Jill pulled a face. 'It can't only be that?'

Netty scribbled some more. *No heir?*

Nina frowned. 'You mean Darcy never had kids? Well he's already got an heir, hasn't he?' She nodded at Bella. 'This one's lad. And that would only explain why she took against her later, not right from the start.'

Flinty broke the following quiet with a loud, and pointed, tut. 'For goodness' sake, you're coming at this from the wrong end.'

'What do you mean, Maggie?'

'I mean whatever set them against each other is ancient history now. We need to work out what they've got in common today.'

The group fell silent. Bella shook her head. Darcy was sociable and had the attention span of a toddler on a sugar rush. Veronica was calm, almost unnaturally calm – even when she argued with Darcy it was the younger woman who did all the screaming – and she was reserved, never one to step an inch out of line. 'They have nothing in common.'

The other women nodded. 'Yep.'

'Seems right.'

I agree.

Flinty sighed. 'You're all blind as bats. They've got lots in common. They wouldn't be fighting so much if they didn't.'

'What do you mean?' Bella had definitely learned, during her time in Lowbridge so far, that Flinty knew more than pretty much anyone about the inner machinations of the Lowbridge family.

'Well they're both trying to cling on to being Lady Lowbridge.'

'Both like the airs and graces it gives them,' Anna muttered.

'Nonsense,' replied Flinty. 'They want to be the lady of Lowbridge because they love it here. It means something to them. That's their common ground.' She paused and looked at Bella. 'That and your lad, and his dad. I mean of course Veronica dotes on her grandson.'

Bella couldn't picture Veronica as a twinkly over-indulgent nana.

'But Darcy's always adored him, right since she got here. Even though he was right in the depths of his moody teenager phase.'

OK. So Veronica and Darcy both loved Lowbridge. They had both loved Alexander and they both loved Adam. Maybe Flinty was right. Maybe she needed to appeal to their better instincts and find some common ground rather than try to unpick whatever was at the root of their fighting to begin with.

'It is a very difficult time for both of them right now too,' Jill pointed out.

Everyone nodded. That seemed to be the main thing anyone said to Bella at the moment. It was, everybody agreed, a Very Difficult Time.

'What about the cookery lessons?' Nina asked.

'Yes. Right. Basically we need to do something to raise some money so we can maintain...' Bella looked around. 'Well, all of this, and...' She fell quiet for a moment. 'I really want to try to start a cookery school.' She really did. She could picture it up and running. Residential courses, with students staying in the coach house and learning in the castle. Courses on different types of cuisine. Maybe a write-up in one of the less terrifying broadsheets, with a photo of Bella in chef's whites, standing, arms folded but expression happy and relaxed in front of the castle. That all fell down on two simple problems though. 'But I have no idea if I'd be any good at teaching people, and I don't know how to get started.'

'Well that's easy,' Nina answered straight away. 'If you don't know how to get started, you just start.'

Anna nodded. 'I had no idea how to run a shop until the old grocers closed and we decided to start one.'

'But…' Bella shook her head. 'How?'

'Right.' Nina pursed her lips. 'We can find out if you're a good teacher easy enough. Teach us something.'

'What? Now?'

Anna glanced at the clock. 'I've got to get back so Hugh can drive over to meet the dairy man.'

'Not now then. Tomorrow. At Ladies' Group.' Nina nodded. 'Right. Tomorrow Bella is going to teach us all some cooking. Something simple that we can do at Anna's. It'll be a practice and we can tell you if you're any good or not.'

'All right.' Might as well give it a go.

'And then as for the rest, you just need to get on with it.'

Jill patted Bella's knee. 'If you're nervous why don't you start small? You could do a sort of test day with people from the village. I'll come.'

Nina nodded. 'And I'll make my Pavel come. He could do with learning his way round a kitchen.'

'And there's definitely at least a couple of girls who used to come to parents and tots who'd love to get a bit more confident with their cooking,' Jill suggested. 'And I can rustle up some tame people from my congregations if we need. How many would you want?'

'Maybe eight?' Bella thought about the layout of the castle kitchens. 'That might be too crowded, but if it's a trial run it would be good to see if we can fit that many in.'

Flinty nodded. 'The more we fit in the more profit we'll make.'

'Or the less you need to charge per person,' Jill added. 'Would you charge for the trial day?'

She couldn't charge much, given the very high chance that the whole thing would go horribly tits up on the ground that Bella barely had a clue what she was doing.

'Maybe just cover the cost of the ingredients?' Flinty suggested.

And so they were set. Bella would do a practice of her untried teaching skills at the next Ladies' Group, and on Saturday – actual Saturday, this Saturday, five days away – she would host a trial cookery school day at Lowbridge attended by tame villagers recruited by her slightly worryingly invested Council of War.

–

Adam stepped out of Waverley Station into the noise of Princes Street and felt his shoulders ease and the weight of responsibility lift from his back. Half an hour on the number 26 and he'd be in his flat, his clean unhaunted newly built flat in Portobello. He'd be home.

Ahead of him were four days of his real life. He'd meet with the anxious people from Carsons, and talk them back around to his vision for their building. He'd pick up his car – his functioning, non-antique car – and drive round some of his favourite nurseries in and around the city to source plants for other upcoming projects. He'd check in with Ravi and Danny about what else was in progress. Hopefully he'd even manage to drag Ravi out to the pub for an evening of normality.

This was where Adam fit. And Bella would fit here too. That was one of the most incredible things, on the ever-growing list of incredible things, that Adam loved about his fiancée. She could fit in anywhere. She was a vigorous, hardy sort of plant that didn't need a lot of sun, or a particular soil type, or precisely the right amount of rain. You could pop Bella down anywhere and she was built to thrive.

Adam was a more particular sort of flora. He'd grown up at Lowbridge but, looking back, he wondered if he'd ever truly thrived there, at least outside of the safety of his father's beloved walled garden.

The meeting with Carsons was, as Adam had anticipated, a walk in the park. Ten minutes in they'd entirely forgotten that they had ever had cold feet about the project, and twenty minutes in they were happily commissioning Adam and Ravi to landscape the space to the front of the offices with additional planting. The pair walked out, grinning.

'You don't manage without me, do you?' Adam joked.

'We were getting by.' Ravi shrugged. 'But you know, I'm the numbers guy. You're the plant guy.'

'You know plants.' It was true. Ravi was entirely competent on site when he needed to be, but he was much happier planning and calculating and writing proposals and budgets.

'I know how to stick the plant you give me into the hole you point at.'

'We should go for a drink while I'm here.'

Ravi nodded. 'Yeah. We should.'

Adam raised an eyebrow. 'Really? I thought you'd be rushing home.'

Aside from being Adam's business partner and best friend, Ravi was also a relatively new father to twin girls.

'Sam'll understand. When are you here 'til?'

'Saturday.' Adam saw the tension on Ravi's face. 'Sorry. Everything back there's...' He couldn't even begin to explain.

'I get it. Friday evening then? Foresters?'

'Great. That'll give me time to do some nursery visits and catch up with Danny.'

Ravi nodded. 'He's been taking up a lot of slack the last few weeks.'

From the bags under Ravi's eyes Adam guessed he wasn't the only one. 'I'm sorry.'

'Not your fault. Shit happens.' Ravi stopped. 'Sorry. I didn't mean your dad dying was shit. Well like obviously it is...' He shook his head. 'Sorry.'

'Don't be.' Adam was more comfortable with Ravi's unfiltered chat than with the hundreds of sympathetic head tilts and muttered 'sorry for your losses' he'd been receiving endlessly over the previous weeks. 'Everything'll be back to normal soon.'

Ravi nodded. 'We can talk on Friday.'

—

The next morning Bella slipped out of bed early, and headed straight for the kitchen. Entirely unsurprisingly Flinty was there before her. 'You're up early,' she noted.

'I'm starting Operation Peace in Our Time.'

'What?'

'Peace in our time. Sorting out Darcy and Veronica.'

Flinty sucked the air in over her teeth. 'You know that didn't work, don't you?'

'What?'

'Peace in our time. It's what Neville Chamberlain said right before World War Two broke out.'

She had not known that. 'Well this will go better than that. Hopefully.'

Bella rolled up her sleeves. All the best endeavours in Bella's life started in the kitchen. Today was baking. A lot of pro chefs hated baking. Pastry was notoriously one of the trickiest roles in the kitchen, rewarding precision and attention to detail, and being utterly temperamental to any change in temperature or humidity.

Proper baking – not fancy patisserie restaurant faff – was Bella's first love. One of the few times her nan was ever still was in the kitchen, when she was concentrating on weighing out ingredients or folding batter into gentle fluffy clouds. The process of making a cake or a batch of biscuits still felt, to Bella, like home itself.

This recipe was one of the very first she'd learned and one that she still knew by heart. It was perfect in its simplicity. Flour, butter, sugar, rubbed together by hand and then pressed into a dough. A dash more flour on the worktop before she rolled her dough out into a thick, butter-hued disc. You could cut out shapes now, or fingers, but Bella preferred to shape the disc into a rough circle and chill the whole thing for a few minutes before scoring out wedge-shaped portions, dappling the surface with a fork and baking it as one huge biscuit to be broken up when it cooled.

As her shortbread round baked she opened her phone and scrolled through her email. Her nan was still staying with some Wiccan friends in Somerset, taking a lazy break after Glastonbury. They were planning to head to Cerne Abbas with one of the friends who wanted to sleep out a night on the giant as part of a fertility ritual. Nan joked that she thought she was old enough now to be able to risk it without consequence.

Bella smiled and tapped out a quick reply. 'Still in Scotland…' She hesitated. These two-line messages were a lifeline for both of them, but, not having mentioned it straight away, the size of the 'I'm engaged to a Scottish baron' elephant in the room was rapidly increasing.

She would visit. Once things were calmer here, and the next time her grandmother stayed in one place long enough to make a plan, she would take Adam to meet her in person. 'Still staying on the West Coast.' What else could she say? *In a massive castle*, or, *With the hereditary baron of Lowbridge* seemed like additions that would need a lot of explanation. 'My friend's father died a few weeks ago,' she added, 'so things are a bit tricky but I'm trying to help. Tomorrow the world!'

'That smells good.' Bella looked up as Flinty broke the silence. She was right. The baking aroma that was filling the kitchen was warm and sweet and wonderful. 'What are you making?'

'Shortbread.'

Flinty smiled. 'Risking a Scottish classic?'

Bella hadn't thought about it like that, but she supposed Flinty was right. Shortbread always came in bright red tartan tins with bagpipers or Scottie dogs on them, didn't it? 'It was one of the first things I learned to make.'

'Same here.' Flinty started piling Bella's baking things into the sink.

'I can do those.'

'It's no bother.' Flinty busied herself filling the bowl with water, planting herself firmly in front of the washing up. 'You were cheffing when you met the lad?'

'Yeah. I was working in his hotel in Malaga.'

'Good trade. People will always need feeding.' She had her hands plunged into the soapy water. 'You'll probably not want me under your feet in here then, will you?' There was the hint of a catch in her voice. 'Once you're married and settled. I understand that. I'll not get in your way.'

'Oh. I mean...' Bella wasn't sure what to say. Everyone was very adamant that Flinty was retired, so wasn't she around at the moment because they were having a crisis? That was what people did in a crisis wasn't it? Chipped in. Brought around casseroles. Made sandwiches. Acted as unpaid housekeeper for weeks on end.

'I'll not overstay my welcome.'

'You're always welcome.'

'You're going to be newlyweds. You'll want some time to yourselves.'

Bella heard herself laugh. 'Well you're not welcome to join in with those times.'

Flinty shot her a look. It was a look Veronica herself would have been proud of.

'But you're very welcome here. I mean if we're going to open the castle up more we'll need all the help we can get.' That was true. 'And I was hoping you'd help on Saturday.' The thought of Flinty's reassuringly solid presence for the cookery school trial day was instantly calming.

'Well of course I'll be here for that.'

Of course she would. 'And, from what I can see, you're basically family anyway.'

'Oh.' The noise Flinty made wasn't a word and it wasn't a sob. It was barely a syllable from deep in her throat. Then she shook her head. 'You're very sweet, but no. I'm definitely not part of the family. Mind your biscuits don't get burnt.'

Bella flung open the oven. Her shortbread was a touch on the dark side of golden but should still be delicious. Onto stage two of the plan.

—

Twenty minutes later the three ladies of Lowbridge were sitting in the Yellow Room – still definitely green – and Bella was pouring tea. 'I thought that if we could sit down and talk through a few things then I'm sure we can all get on, can't we?'

Darcy didn't reply. Veronica nodded. 'Of course. I get along with everyone.'

So insolence and denial were her current challenges. Bella slid the plate of shortbread across the coffee table to the other women. 'Biscuit?'

'No thank you.' Veronica shook her head.

'I don't eat carbs before noon,' Darcy told her.

Bella's natural sympathy had been with Darcy as her fellow incomer and the grieving widow, but she was absolutely prepared to switch sides based on attitude to carbs. The shortbread had been her main tool for getting the two women on side. Without food as an offering Bella's social weapons were significantly more limited.

She thought back over Flinty's suggestions from the day before. What was the common ground here? 'Adam asked me to have a chat with you about the whole bedroom thing.'

Darcy bristled instantly. 'So you are throwing me out?'

'Not at all, but he hates two of you fighting all the time.'

'We are not fighting,' Veronica insisted.

'Well we have been a bit,' Darcy conceded. 'Because you won't let it go.'

'Well those rooms are for the current laird and lady.'

'The current laird said he didn't mind.'

The conversation was already getting away from Bella. 'But he does mind that you two aren't getting along.' What would Adam say? No. That was the wrong question. Adam had already tried. He'd tried to keep the peace and be conciliatory and it hadn't helped at all. Bella needed to find whatever it was that Adam wouldn't say. 'And,' she took a deep breath and hoped that her fiancé wouldn't be too furious if – when – he heard about this. 'Only this is Adam's home now and he wouldn't want to have to ask you both to leave.'

Both women stared at her.

'He would never…' Veronica started.

'But Adam said…' added Darcy.

The horror on both their faces made Bella pause. She'd threatened the one thing she knew her fiancé would never condone. 'I'm sorry.'

Darcy was blinking back tears. Veronica looked devastated. So much for her clever strategy. 'Of course he would never… It's just that he really hates you fighting and I promised I'd try to get you to stop.'

'Is it really upsetting him?' Darcy asked.

'It is.'

'Well I don't want that.'

202

'Neither do I,' insisted Veronica, either through genuine feeling or a reluctance to give up the moral high ground to her rival. The older dowager sighed slightly, before picking up a triangle of shortbread and taking a small bite. She closed her eyes. Bella recognised that look. It was the look she remembered seeing on her grandmother's face at the first taste of something new and delicious. It was the simple bliss of putting some-thing delicious into your mouth and feeling it dissolve on your tongue. Whoever would have thought Veronica was capable of such a feeling?

Bella grabbed the moment of pause to move the conversation to calmer waters. She'd made it clear that they needed to sort out their dispute about bedrooms, but she'd let them take a moment to reflect before she pushed again. And it gave her a chance to ask about something else that was niggling at her.

'You both know about Poppy, right?'

Both women nodded as though discussion of the household ghost was utterly mundane.

'Flinty said she wasn't the only ghost.' Bella was still very clear that she did not believe, but at the same time, she definitely wanted to be forewarned if she was likely to meet a Roman legion marching across the courtyard in the middle of the night.

'Oh well of course not,' Veronica confirmed. 'There's the old cook, although I don't think anyone's seen her for years.'

Darcy pulled a face. 'It's just the smell of onions that you can't get out of anything.'

'Quite.'

'And the Grey Lady,' Darcy continued.

'Everyone has one of them,' replied Veronica. 'Grey Ladies are the sparrow of the spirit world. Nice enough but ten a penny.'

'And the headless man!' Darcy's eyes widened.

'There's no headless man.'

'I saw him.'

'You had too much champagne when Adam turned twenty-one and knocked the head off the upstairs suit of armour,' Veronica countered.

'It was a headless man,' Darcy muttered.

Bella bit back laughter. The two women were still bickering, but they weren't shouting. It was progress of sorts.

Veronica took another bite of her shortbread. A moment later Darcy finally succumbed to temptation. 'Oh that really is delicious,' she murmured after her first bite. 'I'm a terrible cook.'

'I used to cook,' murmured Veronica. 'As you saw, I'm out of the habit.'

'We should come to one of your cookery lessons!' Darcy exclaimed.

Oh no. No way. Bella was nervous enough about the idea of teaching a tame group. She wasn't having Veronica there peering over her spectacles at everything.

'What cookery lessons?'

'Bella's going to start a cookery school in the castle kitchen, aren't you?'

'Well...' Bella stopped when she caught sight of Veronica's expression. Where she'd been expecting anger or disapproval or simply pure horror, there was something else. Pleasure possibly. Pride? Maybe even respect.

'What a good idea. I'm sure there's lots of need. People don't learn those basic skills any more, do they?'

'I guess not.'

'So when?'

There was no way she could lie. Veronica would defin-itely notice cars full of students turning up. 'Well I'm starting with a practice day with some locals, just to see how it goes. On Saturday.'

'Awesome.' Darcy grinned. 'I will be there.'

Veronica glanced at her rival. Obviously there was no way she was going to miss out if Darcy was involved. 'As will I.'

Bella forced a smile onto her face as best she could. 'Great.'

Whether it was the shortbread, the guilt of adding to Adam's woes, or the excitement of the cookery school starting, Bella would never know, but something softened Darcy's mood. 'It's not that I'm wedded to that bedroom. I don't want to move to the coach house.' She paused. 'Or the dower house. It feels like being put out of my home.'

Veronica took a sharp breath in. 'I was rather relieved to move over if truth be known. It drew a line under…' She shook her head. 'I suppose it's not essential though. Perhaps another room in the main house.'

Was this progress?

'I have always quite liked the Gardenia Room,' Darcy volunteered.

Bella daren't interrupt the apparent drift towards compromise.

'If Lord Lowbridge is happy with that, I don't see why not.'

Bella had no idea where the Gardenia Room was but she grabbed her victory nonetheless. 'He would be happy with that.'

'Very good.' Veronica nodded. 'We shall organise that straight away.'

—

Bella rushed from the summit with the Ladies Lowbridge and ran into the kitchen to find Flinty pacing and glancing at the clock. 'All your stuff's in the cool box love. Are you ready?'

As she ever would be.

They arrived at Anna's for the Ladies' Group dummy cooking demo with three minutes to spare and were greeted by a large balloon arch in front of Anna and Hugh's patio doors. 'What's that doing here?'

Anna shook her head. 'Jill offloaded it onto Hugh. He's a soft touch. What do we want with a balloon arch?'

'We're going to use it for Netty's pictures,' Nina yelled through from inside the house. 'Netty's sponsored silence finishes at eleven. We're doing pictures of her first words for the Facebook page.'

'Wouldn't video be better?'

'How do you mean?' Nina came out into the garden.

'Well you can't really see that someone's not silent any more in a picture can you?' Bella pointed out.

'I don't know how to put a video in the facebooks,' said Anna. 'You'll have to film that.' She thrust Nina's phone into Bella's free hand. Bella passed the cool bag along the line to Flinty.

'OK. So you want to be under the balloon arch then?'

Nina pulled Netty out through the door, positioned her under the balloon arch. 'Two minutes!' she shouted.

'What?' Bella waved the phone. 'Do you want to go live then?'

'Go what dear?' Nina frowned at her.

'Live. On Facebook? Like stream the end of the silence live?'

Netty shook her head vigorously.

'Oh well, if we can,' Nina said. 'How exciting!' She checked the time again. 'One minute! Everyone in position!'

Everyone in position seemed to mean Netty standing shaking like a leaf under the balloon arch with Nina alongside her bouncing like a hyped-up cheerleader. Bella clutched Nina's phone in front of them, while Flinty and Anna stood to one side chuntering about not having any truck with the modern instaface malarkey, like the women knitting in front of the guillotine.

Bella tapped to start a live video on the Lowbridge community appeal page and pointed the camera at Nina and Netty.

'Are we starting?' asked Nina.

'Yes!'

'When?'

Bella bit back her giggles. 'Now! We're live. You're on!'

'Oh! How exciting. Hello Facebook!' shouted Nina with the intonation and volume of a rock superstar playing Wembley stadium. 'I'm Nina Stone. And I'm here with the one and only Netty Wetherall, who is just seconds away from completing her sponsored silence in aid of the Lowbridge community appeal to raise funds for our new footbridge to link the village and the Lowbridge estate once again! Let's all join in the countdown. Ten! Nine!' Nina waved her arms to encourage the crowd she was clearly imagining to join in.

Flinty pursed her lips.

'Eight, seven, six…' muttered Anna.

Bella did her best to show willing. 'Five. Four. Three.'

Nina, fortunately was generating enough enthusiasm for everyone. 'Two! One!' she bellowed. 'So Netty, what do you want to say now you can finally talk again?'

Netty murmured something that Bella missed entirely, but, out of the corner of her eye, she could see Anna and Flinty nodding. Nina clapped her hands together. 'Well I think we can all agree with that! Thank you everyone who has sponsored Netty, and don't forget that you can still donate on our fundraising page.' She waved happily at the camera as Bella ended the live stream.

'OK. That went out live.' Bella handed Nina's phone back to its owner. 'And then it'll be there for everyone to watch in a few minutes.'

Everyone agreed that that was marvellous, and that Netty had done a great job. Any hope that this might distract the group from the main reason for their get-together swiftly evaporated though.

'Do we need to be in the kitchen for your demo thing love?' Anna asked.

'No. Anywhere with a table should be fine.'

'Well why don't we do it out here then?'

The weather was warm and there was a large metal garden table on the centre of the lawn.

'We might get a few shoppers wandering through,' Anna added. 'But we don't mind that, do we?'

Bella shrugged. What was a few more passers-by to see how bad she was at this?

Anna and Flinty made tea while Bella laid out her demo on the table. There were only five of them including herself, so everyone got their own board with a sheet of pre-rolled pasta on it, carefully passed through the pasta machine at the castle and then floured so it wouldn't stick.

She also set out a Tupperware tub of mushroom filling with five spoons.

'All right then. We're going to do one simple thing so I can practise and make sure I've worked out how to plan everything through,' she explained. 'The task is shaping tortellini.'

Making and shaping pasta was one of those slightly repetitive kitchen tasks that Bella had a strange but deep affection for. Each member of the Ladies' Group had enough pasta to make four tortellini – a task which, in Bella's mind, took about fifteen seconds. She guesstimated the whole demo and practice would only be five minutes.

And that was the first thing Bella learned about teaching cookery. The five minutes she'd worried she'd be struggling to fill stretched to ten and then to fifteen, and that was with women who cooked regularly and who were more than competent following a recipe. In a group, though, they chatted and distracted one another. They looked over one another's shoulders and questioned whether they were doing it right.

Bella had attempted to do one long demo from cutting the pasta into rounds, spooning in the right amount of filling, folding the proto-tortellini into half-moons, and then wrapping them around the tip of her little finger to create the final shape.

Halfway through adding the filling Anna had held her hand up. 'I can't remember all this. Let's do one bit at a time.'

Breaking up the demo into stages meant it took longer but also meant that people didn't have to remember step one while Bella was talking about step four. She might not be able to do that for longer recipes though. 'I'm going to need to do instruction cards,' Bella said.

Flinty nodded. 'You could do little booklets for each session – something for people to take away.'

Nina agreed. 'People feel like they've got more for their money if they've got something to take away.'

Netty added her thoughts to the conversation.

Anna laughed. 'Well I don't think that'll be a problem for Bella.'

Bella could only hope she was right.

After twenty minutes – four times longer than Bella had planned – all her 'students' had a row of four passably shaped tortellini in front of them.

Anna frowned. 'Four's not really enough for a dinner is it?'

'Sorry. I wasn't thinking about that. I wanted something we could do in the time.' Bella pulled an apologetic face. 'But we couldn't do it in the time.'

Maybe the whole cookery lesson thing was a terrible idea. Teachers were organised, orderly people. Bella wasn't a teacher. Miss Smith might be a teacher, but in Bella's mind that name called up one of those very young nervous teachers who only lasted one term before getting eaten alive by the sorts of bottom sets Bella had spent her school days in. Mrs Lowbridge could be a teacher. Mrs Lowbridge sounded positively tweedy and respons-ible. Lady Lowbridge was something else – both entirely unteacherly and entirely un-Bella.

Flinty leaned over and patted her arm. 'That's the point of a practice though isn't it? And look – we've all got little pasta wotnots. I think you did well.'

The rest of the Ladies' Group nodded in agreement.

'So you've got lots to think about for your proper trial day,' Nina said. 'Have you worked out what you're teaching them yet?'

Bella had barely slept for thinking about it. Ideas had been whirring around her head, and she'd spent half the night with her phone in hand, notes app open, jotting down anything and everything that came into her mind. By six a.m., when she'd abandoned the pretence of trying to sleep altogether, she had at least the outline of a plan for the day.

'OK. The basic idea is *The Perfect Stress-Free Dinner.*' She pulled out her phone and opened her menu notes. She had so many ideas, but really everything was going to come down to oven space. There was the big range in the main kitchen, and there were also two smaller electric ovens in the two prep kitchens, which Flinty informed her were originally the castle bakery and scullery. She'd made a note of *bakery* on her ever-expanding list of things that might one day bring income into the estate.

That meant that she could cook eight big dishes at a time, but only eight, so if, for example, everyone made a lasagne then nothing else they made could go in the oven at the same time. Although if the idea was that they were making food to take home for dinner then maybe the lasagne didn't have to be cooked. They could bake her demonstration one for people to taste and they could take their own home with instructions to bake in their own oven. She didn't know why she was fixated on the idea of eight lasagnes. Lasagne wasn't even on her shortlist of things to make.

She tapped into her ideas list and noted: *Cuisine theme meals – Italian, Indian, etc.*

'I was going to do all the teaching before lunch and then have them cook after, but I don't think that'll work, will it?' If the Ladies' Group couldn't retain four simple steps, there was no way her much less kitchen-confident group on Saturday would retain the steps for three different recipes. 'I think I need to break it down into shorter steps and demos and give them written instructions as well.'

'Sounds sensible,' Nina said. 'I love the idea that they get a full meal to take home though. That's great for a full-day session.'

'If you're doing handouts you should have a logo,' Anna chipped in.

Netty nodded silently.

Bella shook her head. 'The trial is in three days. I'll think about stuff like that if it goes well and we decide to definitely go for it.'

'You should have feedback forms though,' Flinty said. 'That's the point isn't it? You might think it's all gone marvellously, but you need to know what the punters make of it.'

'Do I have to give Veronica one?'

'Veronica's coming?' Anna's tone was half-aghast, half-fascinated.

'And Darcy as well.' Bella was still trying to put Veronica's attendance to the back of her mind. 'I think Darcy's quite keen and Veronica didn't want to be seen as less supportive.'

'Or she didn't want to miss out,' Anna suggested.

'Or she's genuinely trying to help with something that might be good for all of Lowbridge,' Flinty added.

Bella could see the scepticism on Anna's face, but she nodded anyway. 'Yeah. Maybe.'

Chapter Twelve

The Foresters was quieter than normal for a Friday night and Ravi was already at the bar when Adam walked in, two pints standing in front of him. They grabbed a table in the corner, out of line of sight from the big TV – because Adam was famously incapable of concentrating on anything anybody said to him while there was a football match between two teams he had no interest in being played anywhere in his peripheral vision.

'I'm really sorry about your dad.'

Adam nodded. 'Thanks.' He shrugged. He still wasn't sure what he was supposed to say when people expressed their sympathy. Claiming to be fine felt like he was disregarding his father's life and death, but nobody wanted to actually hear about how awful everything had turned, did they? All he really wanted to do was change the subject. 'Tell me about your lot.'

Ravi grinned and, as Adam knew he would, pulled out his phone for a rundown of the most recent photos of the twins. Ila and Asha toddling along the beach not more than a hundred yards from where Adam and Ravi were sitting now. Ila and Asha clinging to Sam's hands. Ila and Asha balanced one on each of Ravi's knees. Ila and Asha beaming for the camera with Ravi, Sam and their bio-mum Linzi.

'They've started nursery,' Ravi added. 'Sam doesn't know what to do with himself.'

'What's he working on?'

'Oh, ghostwriting for whatserface. Big tell-all autobiography thing.'

'Which whatserface?'

'Politician woman. The one with the suits.'

'Scottish politician?'

'Nah. English.' Ravi shrugged. 'Anyway he's bitching about the deadline but still not actually writing anything. Same old, same old.'

'What about you?' Ravi put down his pint. 'I'd assumed you'd have a butler to bring us beers by now.'

Adam shook his head. 'You wouldn't travel with a butler.'

'Oh, I'm sorry.'

'A valet maybe.' He grinned. 'Sorry. No man servants. No servants at all. Well there's Flinty but I don't think we're actually paying her.' Given that she clearly hadn't, despite her ongoing protestations, retired, he ought to do something about that.

'Well what's the point in being a baron?'

Adam wasn't sure there was much point at all. 'It feels like a lot of responsibility.'

'It is on your own.'

Oh. Yeah. Adam winced.

'What?'

'It's been a really busy few weeks.'

'I get it.'

'Really really busy,' Adam emphasised, determinedly getting his excuses in first.

'Right?'

'Like so busy it would be completely understandable if a man forgot to tell his best mate he'd got engaged?'

Ravi's pint froze inches from his lips. 'You got what?'

'Engaged.'

'Who to? Sorry mate. I didn't even know you were going out with anyone.'

'Yeah. That's cos I wasn't.' Adam took a deep drag of beer. 'So you remember I went off on that stag thing for Posh Harry?'

'You're an actual laird. You can't call him that any more.'

Probably fair. 'Fine. Well anyway when I was out there I met somebody and we got on and we got engaged.'

'Well I kinda guessed there was someone from the eternally extended holiday.'

Adam nodded.

'I didn't realise you'd brought her home with you though.' He frowned. 'So you met what? Six, seven weeks ago?'

'About that.'

'Wow. I've seen you spend longer choosing border plants.'

That was true. Adam didn't really know how to explain it. 'When you know you know.'

Ravi nodded. 'I guess you do. Come on then. Who is she? When do I meet her?'

Adam found a photo of Bella on his phone, a selfie taken the very first night they'd met, faces squashed together in the frame, lit by the moon and the fairy lights that lined the roof of the beach bar. Ravi grinned. 'Well she's out of your league.'

'Thanks. She's Bella,' he explained. 'She's a chef.'

'And where is she now?'

'At Lowbridge.'

'So she's *living* there? Or *staying* there?' Ravi frowned.

'Staying I guess.' He paused. 'She's got lots of ideas for things we could do there though.' Adam shook his head. 'I don't know. I've had an offer to buy the whole place.'

Ravi leaned back in his seat. Adam knew his friend well enough to recognise that he was thinking carefully, trying to formulate a response that was clear but tactful. It was the expression he had when working out how to tell good people that they didn't have work for them on the next project, or when readying himself to explain to Adam that he had to scale back a design to something objectively less exciting but more in line with the client's budget. 'So are you thinking of selling?'

Adam's instinct was to shake his head, to pretend that it wasn't even an option, but Ravi was part of another world. It was easier to tell the truth here. 'It might be the easiest way out.'

'Do you want a way out?'

'I don't think I'm going to be a very good laird.'

'Bollocks.'

'Everyone's expecting something and it's all on me.'

'Doesn't sound like it is. Sounds like this Bella is already pitching in.'

That was true.

'And it would break my grandmother's heart.'

Ravi paused again. 'You don't only have responsibilities there though mate.'

Adam's chest tightened. Ravi was right. He was needed here as well.

'Like I'm not saying you have to rush back.' Ravi stared at his pint. 'I know it's hard, and you've got to do what you've got to do, but I do sort of need to know what you are going to do.'

'I'm sorry.'

Ravi hadn't finished. 'We need you. The business needs you, which means my mortgage needs you.'

'I know.'

'Sorry. I don't want to stress you out. Ila and Asha miss their Uncle Adam too.'

Adam smiled, even though he knew that wasn't what Ravi was really worried about at all. He was worried about the business, and about the fact that his income was reliant on Adam, which meant that Ila and Asha and Sam were reliant on Adam too. But so was Lowbridge, and that was the rub. Adam had responsibilities everywhere.

Ravi downed his drink, and stood to go for another round. 'Shame you can't be in two places at once.'

Chapter Thirteen

'Stop pacing.' Flinty peered at her over the top of her magazine. 'You're as ready as you can be.'

'We've only got four whisks.'

'Which is why you're having them work in pairs.'

'Is that OK though? Will people expect to be doing all their own thing?'

Flinty put the magazine down. 'It's a trial run. They all know that. They know you're ironing out the kinks.'

'So it is a kink? The working in pairs thing?'

'When you're properly up and running people will mostly come with a friend won't they? So they'll probably prefer it anyway.'

Bella wasn't sure about that at all.

'Seriously, stop pacing pet. You're ready.'

'Am I?'

'You've put the sign up for where to park?'

Bella nodded. 'Where's Dipper?' The vision of a very excitable Labrador bounding into the kitchen and deciding to 'help' popped into her head.

'Spending the day with Hugh and Queen Latifah. She'll be spoiled rotten.'

'Maybe I should check the ingredients?'

'You've checked a million times,' Flinty pointed out. 'Unless someone's crept past us in the last ten minutes and eaten a whole bag of raw potatoes, you're fine.'

'Sorry.' Bella sat herself down. 'I really want this to go well. Like, this would be a proper business. I'd be making a proper contribution, you know.'

Flinty nodded. 'That matters to you, doesn't it?'

'' Course.'

'Why?'

'What do you mean?'

'Why does it matter? I mean I'm not being rude pet, but this isn't your loss is it? If this place was sold. You've only been here ten minutes. You'd move on. Might even help Adam move on too.'

Bella felt herself tense. This was just another version of Veronica's talk about how she didn't belong here. She was doing everything she could. There was a problem here – the estate needed to generate more income – and Bella could help to solve it. That was what mattered. 'I want to help.'

'Fair enough.' Flinty's tone suggested she didn't entirely think that was the whole explanation.

'I want to be helpful.' That was closer to it. 'And Adam belongs here, doesn't he?'

Flinty shrugged. 'Right now I suspect he'd turn the clock back and slip into his life in Edinburgh in a heartbeat if he could.'

No. Adam belonged here. She'd seen it when he'd explained to her about the link between the castle and the village. 'He's just struggling a bit at the moment.'

'Aye. Well I'm sure you know best.' Bella already felt she knew Flinty well enough to doubt that. She didn't think Flinty had ever thought anyone else had known best about anything.

Bella's phone vibrated with a message from her nan. Still in Somerset, debating a jaunt down to Cornwall, or possibly over to France, depending on whether she could beg a lift down to Dover in time to meet the friend of a friend who was catching the ferry.

Bella tapped back the quickest of quick replies.

> Still in Scotland. Tomorrow the world x

She stuffed her phone into her pocket and looked at Flinty. How to head off another round of questions about her intentions towards Lowbridge? 'Anyway, what about you?'

'What do you mean?'

'I mean...' Was she pushing her luck here? 'Adam said you'd retired but you're here every day. Veronica and Darcy would barely manage to boil the kettle without you.'

'Ah well...'

'Ah well?'

'Well I've given it this long.' Flinty looked moment-arily reflective but the moment passed and her usual business-like expression returned. 'Anyway by the time you've finished with them today they'll both be domestic goddesses, won't they?'

Bella laughed. 'They'd better behave.'

'They're much better in company. Usually.'

–

By the time her first eight students had gathered, Bella had read her plan for the day three more times and checked her ingredients twice. She was ready. Or if she wasn't, it was too late to worry about it now. She looked around the gathered faces. Darcy full of excitement and anticipation. Veronica reserved but not actually looking as though she was chewing a wasp. Pavel, the only bloke, quiet but attentive in contrast to Jill's buzzy butterfly chit-chat. The two women Nina had roped in from parents and toddlers were both young, and introduced themselves as sisters, Molly and Katy. 'We bunked off home ec at school,' Katy told her.

'And our mum's an awful cook.'

'The health visitor says learning to cook's good for the little ones though.'

Molly nodded at her sister's comment. 'Otherwise they grow up on chips and dino nuggets. And that's no good.'

'You grew up on dino nuggets,' Katy pointed out.

'Yeah. And I got pregnant when I was still at school.'

'That wasn't cos of the nuggets. That was cos you can't keep your knickers on.'

'She's smug cos she were engaged before she got up the duff.'

Her sister laughed. 'Only about twenty minutes before though.'

'So anyway we want to learn to make stuff that doesn't come out of the freezer.'

'Do your partners cook?' Bella asked.

Both girls squealed with laughter. And then Molly gasped. 'You should do a course for them though. Cooking for useless dads.'

'And useless lads.'

Bella made a mental note. That actually wasn't a terrible idea.

The other two women, who'd been roped in by Jill from her congregation in Locharron, both said they cooked a little bit, but were stuck in a rut of the same five or six meals they did again and again. Figuring those were the two who probably had the least risk of setting fire to their own hair or baking the mixing spoon in with their dessert batter, Bella decided that when it came to time to move some of the group into the smaller prep kitchen those were the pair who could most safely be left unsupervised.

She took a deep breath. 'Hello everyone! Thank you for coming. I'm Bella and this is the very first session at the Highland Cookery School. Thank you for being my guinea pigs. At the end of the day I'd really appreciate it if you could fill in the feedback forms we give you and that'll help us plan how to get this business properly started.'

She invited the group to introduce themselves and tried to remind herself of all the names as they did so. Molly and Katy were shaping up to be quite the comedy double act. Claire and Cath, the women from Jill's church, were friendly and down to earth. Jill introduced herself breezily. She seemed to know everyone already, and had greeted everybody with a hearty hug when she arrived. Even Veronica, who had been wholly horrified by the experience.

Pavel was next. 'Hi everyone. I'm Pav. I think I know most people.'

Claire nodded enthusiastically. 'Pavel did my fitted wardrobes.'

'I did. I'm here because I rely on my mother far too much for home-cooked meals and it would be nice to be able to make something for her for a change.'

The massed ranks of the women in the room let out a small collective 'Aw.' Bella had absolutely no idea how Pavel was still single. It seemed like pretty much everyone in the western Highlands would happily ditch whatever partner they had in his favour in a heartbeat.

That left the two Lady Lowbridges. Darcy jumped in first. 'Hi. I'm Lady Lowbridge, but you all call me Darcy. Now my daddy was a great cook back home. He worked in a diner and he used to say he made the best damn steak sandwich in Manhattan, so he was the cook at home and then…' Her voice tailed off. 'I don't know. Alexander wasn't really big into food and I like to watch my weight so…' She shrugged.

The group fell silent. Bella nodded at Veronica. 'And you?'

'I'm Veronica, Lady Lowbridge. Good morning everyone.'

That seemed to be all they were going to get out of Veronica. 'All right then. Well, welcome everybody. We're going to be making three courses today, and they're all recipes you can take away and make on their own or as part of the whole meal.' She handed around the menu sheets she'd printed out, with Highland Cookery School at the top in neat italics. 'First off then we have pinwheels, which sounds fancy but is basically a little pastry savoury biscuit thing. If it's a dinner party you could serve those as canapés with drinks when your guests arrive or with some salad leaves as a starter. And by making those we'll learn to make rough puff pastry, which you can then use again and again for pies and tarts.'

She glanced around the room. People were listening and nobody looked quite ready to run for the hills yet.

'Then main course will be fish pie with wilted spinach. So that includes a bit of fish cookery, and we'll make a white sauce and a really lovely creamy mashed potato. And you can add more veg into this recipe if you choose to, so great for getting kids to eat their vegetables.'

The two young mums nodded approvingly.

The next stage of Bella's introduction was a little more Lowbridge specific. 'And the fish pie has black pepper in it, so when we get to that point you will see that...' She opened a cupboard and pulled out a pepper grinder. 'All the pepper grinders have these neon stickers on them so they're easy to spot.'

Her students exchanged bemused glances.

In for a penny, Bella thought. 'One of the joys of cooking at somewhere like Lowbridge Castle is that you're in a kitchen that's been in use for hundreds of years. That means that we are...' She couldn't quite believe she was saying this. 'Apparently, haunted. And one of our ghosts, Poppy, does enjoy hiding the pepper. She's harmless apart from that but do please keep an eye on your seasonings.'

Fortunately this warning was met with laughter rather than horror. Bella pressed on.

'And then for dessert, a classic chocolate fudge cake. So this is a spin on a basic cake recipe, which is something every cook should have, but we're going to posh it up a bit with ganache icing so you can heat it up for thirty seconds in the microwave when you get home and serve it as a warm fudge cake.'

'Oooh!' Jill sounded delighted. 'I love chocolate.'

Everyone loved chocolate. That was very much why Bella had chosen it. And across the meal she'd got in a good range of skills for her students to have a go at, but nothing, she hoped, that wouldn't be achievable in the time available. She wanted everyone to go home, not only with an edible meal, but also with a sense of achievement and enthusiasm for cooking more. She clapped her hands together to curtail the chocolate chit-chat. 'Right. First up, puff pastry. We're going to be making rough puff, which is a little bit more straightforward than doing it the fancy way, and honestly it comes out just as good.'

She started her demo round, reminding herself to work in order and talk through what she was doing as she did it. 'The most important ingredient in any puff pastry is cold. As soon as things get too warm your pastry will start sticking and you won't be able to roll it out. That's why we're starting the pastry first, even though the pinwheels won't go in the oven until much later. We're going to roll and turn and roll and turn and then pop it in the fridge and do something else, and then come back for another round of rolling and turning. Basically every time you finish a task during the day, I want you to go and check on your pastry, and if it's cold enough, give it another roll and another turn.'

She set everyone to make their pastry dough and do their first roll and turn. Veronica and Darcy were sent to the second prep kitchen, or scullery as Flinty called it. Bella had a moment of pleasure at the thought of banishing Veronica to the scullery. Claire and Cath went to work in the bakery. Flinty went with them and, straight away, having another person who knew their way around a rolling pin proved invaluable as they both moved from station to station unsticking too warm pastry from worktops and stopping over enthusiastic hands from dropping in tablespoons of salt where only half-teaspoons were required.

By the time everyone's pastry was in the fridge and the group had reassembled for their second lesson, Bella was still pretty much on schedule and starting to relax into her role. Potato preparation was dull. There was no way around that, but Bella did her best to frame it as a basic kitchen skill that everyone should have, and as a chance to develop and hone your knife skills. Good knife skills were an absolute foundation of confident – but also safe – cooking. And her kitchen knives – carefully wrapped and stowed in Adam's hold luggage – had made the journey from Spain to Scotland with her. She talked the group quickly through the basic set.

'What knives should we have at home?' Pavel asked.

'He's happy now he can buy himself something shiny,' Jill joked.

'You don't need all of these. A good chef's knife, as big as you can comfortably work with, is the main thing. That's the most versatile, and if you get a decent one and look after it, it'll last you for years. Decades even.' Bella smiled at the impressed 'ooh' sound that came from the group and she swiped her blade across her sharpening steel. She held up the steel. 'With that in mind, worth buying one of these as well. You can start slowly with it.' She demonstrated the movement at a quarter of her normal pace. 'But a sharp knife is much, much safer in your hand than a blunt one.'

The group started peeling and chopping their potatoes and putting them to boil in salted water. Bella took a stroll around their different stations to see who remembered what to do next. Claire and Cath were definitely her star pupils. As soon as the potatoes were in the pan Claire was wiping the bench down and Cath was collecting their pastry squares from the fridge for another round of rolling out.

Katy and Molly were just as enthusiastic but noticeably less skilled. 'Is this right miss?'

'You can call me Bella,' she laughed, peering at the pair's pastry square. 'It looks OK.'

'It's all lumpy though.'

Bella took the rolling pin and gently pressed the dough. 'Oh, so it is.' She prodded with her fingertip and scanned the ingredients left on the worktop. 'You've still got your butter left.'

Molly gaped. 'Then what did we put in the pastry? We cut it into little cubes like you said.'

The little cubes were, on closer inspection, poking through the dough. Bella stifled a giggle. 'That's cheese.'

Both girls' faces fell.

'It's OK.'

'It's not,' said Katy. 'I said it felt too hard.'

'We did bad!' exclaimed her sister.

'Nothing to worry about. Look. Why don't you roll out my pastry? It's mostly spare. I'll just have to nick it back at the end when I show people how to roll the wheels.'

Molly looked crestfallen. 'Are we the worst you've ever taught?'

Bella considered her answer. 'Well it's my very first lesson. I'm sure I'll have much much worse next time,' she lied. 'Everyone makes mistakes. It's how we learn.'

'I bet most people know the difference between cheese and butter though,' Katy pointed out.

Bella left them to it, and popped the kettle on for their mid-morning refreshments, to be served with the pinwheels she'd made the night before, so everyone could see what they were aiming for. Flinty came up next to her with a tray of cups and a plate for the pinwheels. 'Are you warming the pastries?'

Bella shook her head. They could try their own creations warm at the end of the day and she wanted to show that the recipe was versatile enough to be made ahead.

'It's going very well. Even Veronica and Darcy are getting along.'

Bella had to admit that she'd been slightly avoiding checking on the Lady Lowbridges. 'Sorry. I sort of left them with you, didn't I?'

'That's all right. I know how to handle them. But they were fine. I mean Darcy was doing all the work but they weren't shouting at each other so I think it's going wonderfully.'

'I wondered about splitting them up, but everyone else seemed to pair up naturally.'

'I wondered if you'd put the vicar with one of them.'

Bella had wondered about that too. 'I didn't think she'd thank me for being separated from sexy Pavel.'

Flinty grinned. 'You noticed that as well. She's sweet on him, isn't she?'

'Looks like it.'

'He hasn't got a clue, has he?'

'Not the slightest,' Bella agreed.

'Poor lass.' Flinty found the box of pinwheels in the fridge and set about laying them out on the plate. 'Unrequited love can be terrible,' she added.

Bella had saved what she knew would be everyone's favourite activity of the day for the next session. The idea was that they'd do something really fun before lunch so everyone would be hyped up and enthusiastic about coming back after the break. It was time for chocolate cake.

As she'd anticipated, mixing together the rich chocolate batter seemed to be balm for every soul in the room. She'd toyed with the idea of using a basic sponge mix, but decided in the end to go for something a little more elevated, so this batter included cocoa but also melted chocolate and generous spoons full of soured cream which gave an unctuous moisture to the finished cake and cut through the richness enough to allow you to go back for a second slice. The final little fancy addition to the mix was to separate the eggs, incorporate the yolks first and then whip up the whites before folding in the soft fluffy clouds to create the perfect balance of richness and lightness in the final cake.

Bella loved this recipe. She'd created this final version herself as an amalgam of different recipes she'd found over the years. It was, in her eyes, the ultimate chocolate cake, and sharing it with her little group was actually making her feel quite emotional. It took her back to cooking with her grandma and seeing her nan's pride when Bella completed a task. She realised now that pride had come not only from Bella's achievement, but from the joy of sharing her own knowledge and love of food with someone eager to learn.

By lunchtime, the whole group were, as Bella had planned, having fun and enthusing loudly about their achievements. Well, Veronica wasn't exactly enthusing, but her lips were 10 per cent less pursed than the norm and she hadn't retreated to take her lunch on a tray somewhere far away from the chatter and boisterousness of the dining room. Bella thought she could probably allow herself to relax just a little bit.

Bella was wrong.

–

The afternoon session started well. The group had got along well over the lunch break and even Veronica had been lured into polite small talk with Pavel, who seemed to be able to charm the birds from the trees.

The first task for the afternoon, while chocolate cakes baked in the oven, was to prepare the filling for the fish pies. That was where things started to go a little awry. Bella was in the bakery with Cath and Claire when she heard the yelp of pain from the main kitchen. She dashed back through to find Jill clutching her hand, with blood oozing between her fingers. 'I'm fine!' she announced.

Bella dashed over and inspected Jill's hand. It was just a nick. All her fingers were happily still firmly attached, but the cut was relatively deep. Flinty appeared at her shoulder. 'Oh, that might need looking at,' she declared cheerfully. 'Have you had all your tetanus jabs?'

Jill paled slightly. 'I don't know.'

At the other side of the kitchen Molly and Katy stared wide-eyed. 'The minor injuries clinic at Locharron is open on weekends,' Katy said. 'We had to take Betsy there last month when she fell down a hole.'

Molly nodded. 'It was quite a big hole.'

Bella put all the questions that raced into her head about who on earth Betsy was and how/why/where she'd come to fall down a hole to one side. 'Well let's get a dressing on it for now.'

Flinty was already brandishing a first aid kit. 'I'll just pop something on it and I'll drive you over there, love.'

Jill bit her lip. 'I'm so sorry! I can drive myself. No need to make a fuss.'

She clearly couldn't drive herself, but Bella couldn't leave.

'I'm taking you,' Flinty insisted. She directed Jill over to a stool in the corner and set about unwrapping the wad of kitchen roll Jill was pressing to her hand.

'Oh.' The noise Pavel made was not a happy healthy one.

Bella spun back to check what was going on, and for a moment the kitchen seemed to shift into slow motion. She could see exactly what was about to happen but there was no way she could intervene. Pavel's face had gone extremely white and a shimmer of sweat shone across his top lip. He rocked slightly, and started to open his mouth. No sound came out, and then he was falling, rocking at first front to back and then straight down like a tower block detonated for demolition.

Bella darted forward but she was too slow. The castle kitchen was large for a domestic kitchen, but not large for a man the size of Pavel Stone to collapse without a certain amount of collateral damage. The bowl of melted chocolate in front of him was the first casualty. That sent the whisk spinning up into the air, from where it hit Jill's water glass, which toppled down onto the floor, taking the pepper grinder with it. That distracted Bella from what was happening on Pavel's other side where his fall had dislodged a tea towel, which flicked towards the still-lighted gas ring. A second later flames danced upwards from the stove top.

For a second everyone was quiet apart from a single mournful, ethereal sneeze.

'What the—?' gasped Molly.

'What on earth is—?' Veronica appeared in the doorway. 'Oh my goodness.'

Time slowed and elongated giving Bella a moment to take in every different element of the catastrophe. The blood. The flames. Pavel's bulk prone on the floor. The broken glass. The spatter pattern of melted chocolate giving the whole room the appearance of an unusually tasty crime scene. Bella was seconds away from screaming.

'Right,' Veronica's tone was suddenly brisk, as she surveyed the room. 'You!' She pointed to Bella. 'Turn that gas off.'

Of course. Bella moved on autopilot and did as she was told while Veronica barked out more instructions. 'You girls, grab a tea towel and soak it in water and throw it over here.'

Molly and Katy did exactly as they were told.

'Darcy, help me get this chap flat on the floor and then see if you can hold his feet up.'

By the time Bella had clicked out of her panic, Pavel had his eyes open, Jill's finger was dressed and being held aloft by Flinty, the flames licking the kitchen wall had been extinguished and Cath and Claire were cleaning up the debris from the floor, and joking cheerfully about how they were happy to lick the chocolate off Pavel's torso, purely to be helpful, of course. Veronica surveyed the scene and then clapped her hands. 'All right then. How are you feeling now, young man?'

Pavel pushed himself up on his elbows. 'I am very well.' He smiled slightly sheepishly. 'Apart from feeling a little silly.'

Cath laughed. 'A big lump like you can't cope with a bit of blood.'

'I'll be bruised in the morning, but right now I'm OK.' He nodded at Darcy, who was still holding his feet up in the air. 'I think you can let go now.'

Ten minutes later Jill had been packed off with Flinty in the Land Rover to the clinic in Locharron, shouting reassurances that it was only a scratch and absolutely nobody's fault but her own, and it seemed as though the only non-recoverable loss was a bowl of half-melted chocolate.

'OK. Well, what do you want to do?' Bella found that she was asking Veronica, who seemed to have transformed from reserved lady who was attending under duress to the person in charge. 'Should we carry on?'

'I would say so. I'm sure everyone wants to keep going, don't we?'

Bella was pretty sure that nobody would have dared argue, but the volley of nods seemed to be genuine. 'What about you, Pavel? You've lost your partner.'

'Let's keep going. I can take her some cake tomorrow to make sure she's OK. And I promised my mum I was bringing dinner.'

'Well we'd better not let Nina down then.' Bella took a deep breath to try to damp down the surge of adrenalin.

The rest of the afternoon went well. Everyone was very careful indeed every time they had to chop something, and Bella was very aware that she was running on nervous energy and hope, but her remaining students all completed their tasks and left clutching bowls of food and typed instructions for cooking or reheating at home.

Bella slumped into a stool at the island. They still had a mountain of wiping down and washing up to do. The standards of cleaning up as they went along had definitely declined a notch after the excitement of Jill's injury and Pavel's spectacular faint. But they had got through the day. Darcy came and sat next to her and slid a pile of papers onto the worktop between them. 'I got them all to do the feedback forms.'

'Oh. I completely forgot about that.'

Darcy shrugged. 'Well I didn't.'

A second later Veronica came back in, closely followed by Flinty. 'Jill's all patched up. I dropped her home. She said she'd ask Pavel to bring her over to pick her car up in the morning.'

'Was she OK?' Bella asked. For a second all the thoughts of what might have gone more badly wrong flashed through her head. Jill could have lost the tip of her finger. Pavel could have hit his head.

'She's right as rain. Embarrassed more than anything else.'

'Not as embarrassed as that poor chap,' Veronica noted, but there was an uncharacteristic smile in her tone. 'He was fine in the end too though. What do all these forms Darcy made them do tell us?'

Bella couldn't bear to look.

'For goodness' sake.' Veronica pulled the pile of papers towards her and skimmed the first one. 'People today really do have the most terrible handwriting.'

'What do they say though?' Darcy asked.

'This one's very complimentary.' Veronica flicked to the next form in the stack. 'And this one.' She rifled through the papers. 'All of them really. They enjoyed it. Would love to do it again. Thought it was fantastic value.'

'You did tell them you were only charging them for ingredients didn't you?' Flinty asked.

Bella nodded.

'These two both say they'd be happy to pay full price, and this one says you should do courses for men who don't know anything.' Veronica raised an eyebrow. 'Let's assume they mean about cooking.'

'Was that a joke, Veronica?' The question was out of Bella's mouth before she could check herself.

'I make lots of jokes,' Veronica deadpanned back. 'I'm an absolute barrel of laughs.'

Bella had to turn away from Darcy's gaping expression to compose herself against the fit of disbelieving laughter that was rising in her chest.

'Seems like it went very well, even after…' Flinty waved a vague hand. 'Everything.'

'We should toast our success,' Darcy announced.

'Why not?' Veronica agreed.

Adam pulled his silver four-wheel drive, newly liberated from the parking level at his flat in Edinburgh, to a stop outside the coach house. All he really wanted was to head straight into the coach house and collapse into bed, but the sound of voices from the castle courtyard pulled him through the gateway towards the noise. Flinty, his grandmother and his stepmother were squashed together onto the bench by the kitchen corridor door, and Bella was sitting cross-legged on the cobbles in front of them. All four of them were clutching champagne glasses and talking animatedly, and apparently companionably.

'What are you doing out here?'

Veronica raised her glass in his direction and nodded towards Bella. 'We're toasting this young lady's success.'

'And the Highland Cookery School!' added Darcy.

The first cooking lesson – Adam had completely forgotten. He probably ought to have texted or called his fiancée to wish her luck. He strolled over and planted a kiss on the top of Bella's head. 'That was today, wasn't it?'

'Yeah. Just the trial day. I think it went well though.'

'Give or take a trip to hospital,' Flinty muttered.

235

'What?'

'It was only a cut,' Bella reassured him. 'Jill cut her hand, but she's fine now.'

'Everything else was a triumph though,' Veronica said, which was perhaps the highest praise he'd ever heard his grandmother heap onto anything.

'Only because of you!' Bella replied. 'Seriously, your nan saved the day. When Jill cut herself and then Pavel fainted—'

'And the place caught fire,' Darcy interjected.

'Yep. And the place caught fire, your nan was so calm. She got everyone doing what needed to be done. No fuss. No messing.'

'But then it was Darcy who remembered the feedback forms at the end,' Veronica demurred.

'Which was really the main point of the day,' said Flinty.

'But Flinty was helping all day and it was her that got Jill to the doctor,' Darcy pointed out.

Bella grinned. She looked so happy, so right and so in her element. 'All in all we made a fantastic team.'

That was great. Bella was excited about making something of Lowbridge, and so far she was actually doing it. Of course she was. Bella should be inspiring him. Veronica and Darcy seemed, however implausible it appeared, to have buried the hatchet. Everyone was happy. Everyone was where they wanted to be.

Everyone else, at least.

Chapter Fourteen

Two weeks later the atmosphere at the castle was barely recognisable from the cold empty building Bella had walked into when she first arrived. Buoyed by the first cookery school trial, Bella had pushed ahead with encouraging the village groups that had gone into hiatus, or had to relocate to Locharron while the hall was closed, to meet at the castle itself, and the first sessions were up and running.

As Bella made her way across the courtyard, Nina was putting out play mats and folding chairs for the parents and tots group. 'Maggie said we'd be OK outside today? The forecast looks lovely.'

Bella nodded. 'I'll bring some squash out for the little ones. How many are you expecting?'

'Usually about five or six parents and maybe eight or nine kids. We'd get more if the footbridge was useable.'

Bella thought a version of that thought every time she had to brave Flinty's driving to make it into the village. 'I know.'

'I'm sure my Pavel would help if you need manpower.'

Noted. 'Tea and biscuits for the grown-ups?' Bella asked.

Nina nodded. 'You're a star.'

Inside Flinty was already in the kitchen. 'Nina all right out there?'

'Seems to be. There's someone else in today isn't there?'

'Book club in the Yellow Room straight after mums and tots. Nina runs that too.' Flinty peered at the calendar that was rapidly filling and had become their guide for everything. 'You've put that they're having lunch?'

'Yeah. Just sandwiches and cake. And tea and coffee. They're paying for it.'

'Fair enough. How many people?'

Bella glanced over Flinty's shoulder to decipher her scribbles. 'Eight.'

'That's never an eight. It might be a three.'

'You can't have a book club with three people.'

'Well you can't have an eight without joining your loops up at the top.'

'It's an eight.'

Bella gestured at the tray with a teapot and proper cup and saucer already laid out. 'Is that for...?'

Flinty nodded.

'I'll take it through.'

Veronica was installed in the estate office, three different folders open in front of her, computer screen on, spectacles perched on the bridge of her nose. 'I brought you some tea.'

Veronica nodded towards the only clear square of desk.

'How are things going here?' Bella asked her.

'Ticking over. Our costs are up quite markedly. Printing all your flyers, refreshments for all and sundry.'

The kernel of anxiety Bella had been carrying since the cookery school day prickled at her gut. The detente between herself and Veronica could crack at any moment. 'Sorry.'

Veronica held a hand up. 'But our income is up more thanks to the cookery school pre-bookings, donations from groups, and the charges for refreshments.'

'Right. So that's good?'

'It is.' She pursed her lips. 'At least for now.'

'Where's Adam?'

Veronica frowned. 'I assumed you would know the answer to that.'

That was odd. Bella checked that Flinty was on top of things in the kitchen and headed over to the coach house. Adam was standing by the bed packing a water bottle into a rucksack. He had what looked like work boots on the floor alongside him.

'Where are you off to?'

He grinned. 'Sorry. Was going to come over and let you know. Pavel asked me to help with a landscaping thing he's doing in Portree.'

Bella's local geography was starting to come together. 'That's on Skye?'

Adam grinned. 'You're learning.'

'How are you getting there?'

Adam checked the time. 'On Pav's boat. In about twenty minutes, so I need to get moving.'

'Right.' There was an unease in Bella's gut that she couldn't quite put her finger on.

'What?'

'Nothing.' It wasn't nothing though, was it? 'There's so much to do here.' That was the unease. The castle was suddenly full and busy and they were working all hands to the pumps.

'I thought you had it all in hand.'

Did she?

239

'And Pav's an old mate. You know he asked if I wanted to do some labouring.'

That had been a joke though, hadn't it?

He frowned. 'You're the one who keeps going on about getting involved with the community.'

She was. 'Yeah. Of course. It's fine. Sorry. I just didn't know you were going out.'

He closed the gap between them. 'Sorry. I meant to say but you were up so early, and I forgot.'

'It's fine.' Because of course it was fine. With Flinty and Darcy and Veronica they pretty much did have things in hand, and it was good that Adam was reconnecting with his friends. Apart from his trip to Edinburgh, he'd been holed up in the castle since they arrived. 'I was thinking about the footbridge. What would it take to rebuild it?'

Adam shook his head. 'I'm not sure. I'll have a think about it later.'

Bella accepted the kiss he planted on her lips as he headed out, and made her way back to the kitchen.

–

A day of proper hardcore manual labour was better than therapy. Not that Adam had ever tried therapy, but he couldn't imagine it would do anywhere near as much good as having dirt under his fingernails, sweat running a trail down his spine and muscles that were minutes away from giving up the ghost entirely.

Pavel's crew had accepted him from the outset, with the rapidly bestowed nickname of Posh Lad. That uncomplicated normality, paired with the simple rhythms of working until you were too parched to carry on and then making a cuppa and starting all over again had made for a good day. He pulled his car onto the cobbles outside the coach house, looking forward to a hot bath and then bed as soon as he could manage it.

He stopped in the doorway to the coach house at the sound of voices on the stairs.

'We don't need to move the furniture, for goodness' sake.' That was his grandmother. Adam dreaded to think who she was barking instructions at now.

'But I'm taking the bedside table with me.' Darcy. Of course it was Darcy.

'Well why on earth are you doing that? There's a perfectly good side table in the Gardenia Room already.'

'Which is not big enough. So I need the one from Alexander's...' Her voice broke slightly. 'From Adam's room, and he can have the one from in here.'

'We can discuss that with Adam once we've moved the things he actually needs.'

Adam's bone-tired body did not have the energy to go and find out what on earth this was all about, but he knew that, if he didn't, they would still be bickering at the top of the stairs at midnight. He hauled himself up the steps. 'What are you two doing?'

'Adam!' Darcy looked delighted to see him. 'Tell her you need your own bedside table.'

'I've got a bedside table.' In his flat in Edinburgh.

'No. In your new room.'

'Your proper room,' his grandmother added.

Adam leaned on the wall and closed his eyes for a second. 'Seriously, what are you actually doing?'

He looked past them into the doorway of the coach house bedroom. His clothes were neatly folded on the bed and the suitcase he had brought back from Spain was lying open alongside them. The things he'd brought from Edinburgh more recently were conspicuously absent.

'Didn't Bella tell you?' Darcy asked.

'Tell me what?'

'We sorted out the bedroom thing, so you can move into the laird's room,' Darcy beamed.

'And Miss Smith hasn't had a moment to pack your things up so we thought we'd get on.'

Adam's chest tightened. He was supposed to be pleased. Bella had told him about the peace deal, but he'd managed to stay in denial about what it actually meant for him.

'And you're moving my things without asking me?'

'We were simply being helpful.' There was an edge in his grandmother's voice that would normally make him back off.

'Well it's not helpful.' The rational part of his brain was already telling him that it was just a bedroom, and there was no reason not to move over, and the main rooms in the castle were more comfortable and warmer and, while packing for him was a little intrusive, it was also well-intentioned. The rational part of Adam's brain was losing a lot of arguments at the moment though. 'Leave it. Just leave everything exactly where it is.'

His grandmother opened her mouth, no doubt to tell him that he might be a baron but he had no business speaking to her like that. Adam squeezed past her into the bedroom, slamming the door shut behind him.

Chapter Fifteen

Lowbridge Castle had come to life. They had a full schedule of community groups and small meetings. People were coming and going. Darcy was in her element playing Lady Lowbridge, the hostess with the mostess. Even Adam's grandmother looked at least a degree or two less tense than usual.

Which left the laird himself as the only outlier. Adam knew he needed to take a leaf out of Bella's book. Lowbridge was a foreign country to her, but she'd managed to carve a space for herself as surely as she had in Spain, or as she'd been confident she would in Edinburgh. Bella wasn't second-guessing things. Bella was getting on with it.

If she could find her place anywhere, he, increasingly, couldn't find his anywhere. If he went back to Edinburgh to carry on as normal, it wouldn't be normal any more, would it? Wherever he travelled, the weight of duty on his shoulders would travel with him.

And even without that, would there still be a place for him in Edinburgh? Ravi's updates, since his return to Lowbridge, focused more and more on the things they were doing to manage without him, and less and less on the things he needed Adam to sort out. Which should clear the path for him to stay right here in Lowbridge in the role he was born to. Feeling out of place here was simply not allowed. There was no option but to take a page from his fiancée's book, and just get on with things.

He'd been avoiding the mountains of estate admin, but today that had to change. He grabbed a coffee in the kitchen and headed across the front hallway.

Unusually, Veronica wasn't already ensconced at the desk. That meant that he could look things over without the pressure of someone looking over his shoulder despairing at him going too slowly or failing to understand. But it also meant that he would have to work out what he ought to be doing on his own.

He opened the account book and flicked on the computer. There was a pile of post on the desk. The first was an invoice. He knew how to pay an invoice. It seemed to be all his grandmother ever did. This one was from Pavel, apparently for work on the coach house gutters.

Adam forced himself to focus on the numbers. £55.78 plus VAT, which came, according to Pav's total, to £66.94. He would simply have to take that on trust. No matter how many times Ravi told him working out VAT was easy, Adam found it anything but. He could picture his business partner's incredulous face as he muttered, 'But it's just ten per cent twice.' Adam fell down on not being able to work out 10 per cent once. Actually he fell down on not being able to make the original number sit still in his brain for long enough to get a proper hold of it to do any sort of sum.

Adam logged into the estate's online business banking. Pavel was already listed as a payee. The next part was the part everyone else in the world found straightforward. You typed the amount you wanted to pay in and hit confirm. Even an idiot could do that. Adam re-read the figure and re-read it again. Easy.

Bella walked across the courtyard. It was a beautiful day. An ideal day in fact to take some pictures of the castle and the views of the loch. Her mind was racing with plans for the cookery school. They were going to need a website, maybe a proper printed brochure, definitely some social media presence. This place would make for incredible Instagram photos.

She only had her phone though. The camera was passable but not great. Flinty and Veronica were sitting together on the bench by the kitchen door, Dipper lying happily on the warm cobbles at their feet. Bella had come out from the front hallway, along the side corridor, so they hadn't seen her yet. Would Veronica have a decent camera? She probably would, but it would probably be about a hundred years old and require her to hold up a separate flashbulb while everyone sat perfectly still for three full minutes. It couldn't hurt to ask.

She made her way along the wall towards the two older women, the jutting out stonework of the kitchen corridor still obscuring her from their view.

'You've got to admit she's worked wonders though.' That was Flinty.

Bella stopped. Her brain instantly latched on to the idea that she was the person under discussion.

Flinty chuckled. 'And you weren't expecting that were you?'

'I had no expectations either way.'

'Bollocks.'

'I just hope,' Veronica paused.

'Spit it out.'

'Well a girl like that in a place like this. Sooner or later she's going to wonder what she missed out on, isn't she?'

'You don't know that. She's not…' Flinty's voice trailed away.

'Well we'll see.' Veronica clearly retained doubts about Bella's staying power.

Flinty cleared her throat. 'How do you think the lad's doing?'

'What on earth do you mean?' asked Veronica.

'I don't know. It's a lot to be thrown into.'

Bella almost replied herself. Of course it was a lot to be thrown into, but this was Adam's home. It was where he was supposed to be.

'Of course Adam is fine. He's just adapting.' Bella caught herself nodding in agreement with Veronica.

'You looked at him like a cat who'd brought you a half dead mouse when he turned up with the lass.'

Back to talking about Bella then, and in dead rodent terms. Marvellous.

'I was, perhaps, a little taken aback by the engagement.' Veronica's tone was unruffled.

'Well that's fair.' Both women fell quiet for a second before Flinty spoke again. 'But when you know you know, don't you?'

Another silence. This would be the moment for Bella to make a noise and pretend she'd just come outside this very second, but something about the silence begged not to be broken. And also Bella was really, really nosey.

Finally Veronica replied. 'Margaret, I…' Her tone dropped out of Bella's hearing.

'There you are!' The voice behind Bella was loud and cheery, and was rapidly followed by the distinctive clatter of Darcy's heels across the stones.

Veronica and Flinty jumped up and, Bella vaguely registered, apart.

Darcy continued, oblivious to whatever she was interrupting. 'I couldn't find anyone. Well I found Adam, but he's in a grump staring at numbers and he didn't look very happy to be bothered. You're all out here.'

'Just having a quick cuppa,' Flinty explained, raising her, now apparently empty, mug in explanation.

'And I was looking for a camera,' Bella added. 'I don't know if any of you have a decent one. I thought it was a gorgeous day and there's no groups in until this afternoon. It seemed like a good time to take some pictures for...' She shrugged. She wasn't sure how Veronica would feel about the idea of advertising.

'For promoting the cookery school?' Veronica asked.

'Yeah.'

'Good idea. Didn't Alexander give you a new camera at Christmas?' she asked her daughter-in-law.

Darcy nodded. 'I told him there was no need. I use my phone but he knew I liked taking pictures.'

Bella brightened further. 'You do?'

'Oh yes. I did some modelling back in New York, but I was always trying to chat to the photographers and their assistants. Far more interesting than standing about wearing fancy mascara all day.'

Brilliant. 'Right. You can be our official publicity photographer then.'

Darcy smiled. 'Really? I mean I'm not that good and I don't want to get in the way, and...'

Bella shook her head. Since they'd started getting busy at the castle Darcy had changed from the shadow of a woman Bella had met a few weeks earlier. Clearly she was still grieving, but having distractions and some sort of purpose was helping. 'It would be so useful,' Bella insisted. 'Let's get on with it.'

Adam checked the clock. Paying one invoice and opening the rest of the mail had taken him over an hour. Like everyone Adam had had the dream where he was in an exam and suddenly realised that he hadn't revised, and not only that, but the paper was in an unknown language. All he could hope for at that point was that he woke up before the whole exam hall noticed that he was also naked. Right now Adam was living that nightmare every time he had to look at a row of figures.

He went back to the computer and opened his personal email. The top message in his inbox was from Ravi, with a link to a new housing development to the south of Edinburgh, and a note that the developer was planning low rise blocks of flats and wanted to put roof gardens on top to raise the value of the units.

Straight away Adam grabbed a notepad and pencil and started sketching, roughly at first, and then filling in more detail, noting names of plants and possible materials. After less than half an hour he was ready to snap a picture of the sketch on his phone and message it to his business partner as a starting point for a fuller design. Drawing, thinking about being outside, imagining how the plants he selected would grow and mature, mapping out one idea and then swapping it for something more appropriate for a roof top location – all of those things physically made Adam's shoulder's drop a little and the tension in his chest start to ease.

'It's a lovely day.' He looked up to see his fiancée in the doorway. 'Seems a shame that you're stuck in here.'

'Lots to do.'

She came and looked over his shoulder and the hand-drawn plan in front of him. 'Is this for Ravi?'

'Potential new client.' He glanced over the design. It was rough, but he knew it was good. And thinking about planting made him think Bella was right. 'It would be nice to get outside for a bit.'

'OK. What do you want to do?'

He grinned. 'What about that riding lesson we talked about?'

'Oh.' Her face tensed.

'What?'

'I mean, what do *you* want to do? I'm snowed. Darcy's taking photos for the new website and I need to plan for the first proper sessions, and...'

'Of course. It's fine. I should probably get on here.'

'No.' She shook her head. 'I can make time.'

The landline phone on Adam's desk rang. He glanced at it. It hadn't done that once since he'd been back at Lowbridge. 'Hello?'

The voice on the other end of the phone sounded young, female and slightly stressed. 'Is that the cooking place?'

The what? 'Erm...'

'The cooking school?'

'Oh. Yes. Hold on.' He held the phone out to Bella. 'It's about the cookery school.'

She frowned and took the receiver. Adam could only hear Bella's half of the conversation. 'Yes it is... Yes, we do... We could... Tomorrow?' He tracked the rising panic in her voice. 'Tomorrow tomorrow? Like tomorrow?... Right.' He watched her take a deep breath in. 'Tomorrow. That's fine. Let me grab a pen.'

He handed her a pencil and a used envelope and she scrawled down some details.

'OK then. We'll see you then.' She hung up the phone. 'We've got a booking. For tomorrow.'

'I gathered.'

'Hen party. They were supposed to be going to the McKenzie place but it fell through.'

'How come?'

'I don't know. But I'm making cookies and cupcakes with them from seven until half nine tomorrow. They're glamping near...' She peered at her scribbled notes. 'Ardarrock?'

'Ardarroch,' he corrected.

'I can't do that cee-haitch sound.'

'Well that's being English for you.'

'Shut up. Right. So I'll need to get ingredients in and,' she frowned. 'Baking trays. Cupcake trays. I wonder how many we have? I might have to borrow stuff.' She was pulling her mobile out of her pocket. 'If I ring Anna now she might be able to get everything ready to just pick up in the morning.' She stopped. 'Oh. The riding lesson.'

'It doesn't matter. You're busy.' And it was for the estate. It was good, Adam reminded himself. 'Can I help with anything?'

She shook her head. 'It's fine. I'm on it.'

She kissed him on the top of the head before she rushed away. Adam leaned back in his chair. He could still go for a ride. He hadn't ridden regularly for years but he could ask Darcy and maybe take a trot around the paddock to get back in the groove. Or just for a walk out along the cliff. He wasn't helping here, so why shouldn't he get out of the office?

'What on earth have you done?' His grandmother's voice cut through the remaining embers of his earlier relaxation and sent him right back to feeling wedged into an entirely wrong-shaped hole.

'What?'

'I just had Pavel Stone on the phone. Apparently we sent him over six thousand pounds.'

Adam frowned. 'Did we?'

'Well I didn't, and Darcy said you were in here doing goodness knows what.'

'I paid his invoice.'

'For how much?'

Adam rifled through the pile of papers in front of him and held it up.

Veronica took the sheet from his hand. 'Sixty-six pounds and ninety-four pence.'

'Yeah.'

'Apparently Mr Stone received six thousand six hundred and ninety-four pounds.'

Adam closed his eyes. 'Sorry.'

'Sorry doesn't really help. That will have sent us right to the limit of our overdraft.'

'Sorry.'

'It's only thanks to Bella that it didn't put it past that.'

'Sorry.'

'And thank goodness it was Mr Stone who will, he assures me, pay it straight back. Otherwise that money could simply be gone forever.'

'Sorry.' Adam could hear the petulance in his own tone.

Veronica nodded. 'As you keep saying.'

Darcy bounced in from the hallway, with Bella a second behind her. 'Oh, what about some shots of the laird at his desk?' She paused for a second, her face uncertain, before she nodded brightly. 'Sorry. Still a bit odd coming in here and not seeing Alexander.'

'I know.' Adam really did know. This was his father's place, not his. His father had understood all of this, all of the tiny cogs that kept a place like Lowbridge going. He should be sitting in this chair, not Adam. He looked up into his fiancée's face. 'What are you doing?'

'Taking photos. For publicity, for the cookery school.' She shrugged. 'And anything else.'

'Right. Maybe later.' He couldn't sit here and pretend to be the perfect laird. He looked around the office, grasping for a reason. 'We should probably tidy up a bit first.'

Bella nodded. 'And we should concentrate on outside while it's sunny.'

Adam waited for the two younger women to make their way back outside before he turned to his grandmother. He had to do better, didn't he? Everyone else was chipping in to the best of their abilities and making Lowbridge work. He was the weak link here. 'I am sorry. Show me again how to do it properly.'

Chapter Sixteen

Bella waved a spare baking tray over the set of twenty-four cupcakes cooling on the counter. Only having twenty-four hours to prepare had meant it had taken her until that afternoon to realise that baking cupcakes and cookies and decorating them was far too much to fit in the time. So the new task was making gingerbread, for which Flinty was frantically weighing out individual bowls of ingredients, and then decorating pre-made cupcakes, and then – time permitting – gingerbread decorating.

'Hello! Anyone here?' Jill struggled through the door with a plastic crate in front of her. 'Punch bowl, fruit juices, and a bottle of voddy.'

'Thank you.' Again the short planning horizon had meant that offering cocktails had only come to Bella at the last minute, but it was a hen do, wasn't it? They'd expect something.

'What are we offering the drivers?' Flinty asked.

'Hadn't thought about that.'

'Don't worry.' Jill pulled out her phone. 'Googling mocktails already.'

'Thank you!'

By the time the hens arrived they had alcoholic and non-alcoholic cocktails lined up, gingerbread ingredients ready, and cupcakes (almost) fully cooled. There were six in the group, all in their twenties, all wearing sashes, very helpfully proclaiming their role in the wedding.

Jill was just about to slip out when the bride herself grabbed her arms. 'Reverend Jill!'

'Cecily? I didn't realise this was your do.'

The bride nodded excitedly sipping her mocktail. 'We were supposed to be doing whisky tasting, but I can't cos...' She pressed one hand to her belly and snapped the other to her mouth. 'Oh, for no reason. Just didn't fancy it.'

Jill glanced down at the bride's slightly rounded stomach. 'Well congratulations... on picking a new activity,' she smiled.

'Everybody, this is Reverend Jill. She's marrying us.'

There was a volley of greetings.

'I was just dropping off some stuff. I won't hang around.'

The bride pursed her lips. 'But you've got to. You should stay.' She turned to Bella. 'She can stay, can't she?'

There weren't enough ingredients for another participant, but another friendly face would be welcome. 'So long as she doesn't cut her hand off.'

'What?' The hens stared at Jill, who regaled them with the story of the great trial day blood fest.

'Nothing like that will happen today. No sharp knives involved, I promise.' She gathered the group, drinks topped up, around the island. There wasn't really space for this many people to work but this was as much a party as a cookery class, so letting them all squash together felt more sociable than sending people off to their own little corners.

Bella talked them through mixing the wet and dry ingredients together for their gingerbread, letting the group follow along with her rather than doing a separate demonstration, and then she rolled her dough. 'Ideally we'd leave it in the fridge for an hour before we roll, but we're tight for time, so just make sure you put plenty of flour on the top to stop it sticking.' Once her dough was a perfect pound coin thickness she picked a cookie cutter and cut out a perfect love heart. 'OK. Your go. You can pick whatever shape cutter you like, or...' Bella picked up a standard dinner knife and scored out the shape of another heart with the blade. 'You can fashion your own shapes.'

As soon as the rolling out was finished Bella laid a mental bet with herself on who would go for the obvious shape first. And there it was. Maid of honour, giggling furiously at her gingerbread cock and balls.

The bride glanced at Jill. 'Sorry Reverend. You can't take her anywhere.'

Jill peered at the shape. 'He's got one ball bigger than the other.'

The critique from the vicar delighted the hens. Was that a business idea? Should she invite a member of the clergy to all her cookery nights? Pizza with a parson? Cake baking with a curate?

Ten minutes later the baking trays were covered with a range of cocks, balls, love hearts and one slightly worry-ingly misshapen pair of boobs. 'For equality,' the bride's sister explained.

Flinty popped all of those into the oven, while Bella got things ready for the cupcake decorating. The hens seemed to be having fun, and Bella was starting to relax. Cake decorating was one of her real pleasures in life. People fell in love with food with their eyes long before their tastebuds got a look in, and dessert and afternoon tea treats in particular ought to be beautiful.

Each hen had three cupcakes to decorate and Bella had made up buttercream and fondant to demonstrate two different techniques. First, she showed them how to pipe a perfect buttercream rose on top of their cake. Next she demonstrated using a dash of food colouring in a ball of fondant to make different colours to create a simple graphic on the cake. Bella made a bright yellow sunshine that she laid across the top of her cupcake. For the third cake, she told them, they could do whatever decoration they wanted.

'Cock and balls!' squealed the maid of honour.

'I'd be disappointed if nobody tried it,' Bella assured them.

She walked around the group, helping out and suggesting tips, mostly culinary – how to hold the icing bag up vertically, for example – but some more unexpected. 'Should I try to give it pubes do you think?'

'Maybe not. I mean you have to eat them later.'

The women nodded sagely. 'Yeah. Nobody likes it when they get in your mouth do they?'

Bella ignored the sound of Flinty's sniggers behind her.

By the end of the night the hens were full of sugar and cocktails, carrying boxes full of cupcakes and gingerbread. The maid of honour stopped and hugged Bella before they set off. 'Thank you so much. I was bricking it when Mandy said she couldn't drink alcohol cos of the baby.' She stopped and glanced at Jill.

'I heard nothing.'

'Thank you. Cos we were supposed to go to that big McKenzie place and do whisky tasting. This was way better anyway. I did the whisky thing for our work

Christmas do. It's right overpriced if you ask me. This was so much more fun.'

Bella beamed. Her first official paying cookery school event appeared to have been a roaring success.

—

'That was great.' Jill wiped down the island unit as Bella piled pots and pans in the sink. 'Why don't you leave those a minute?' Jill asked. 'Get yourself a glass of something and take the weight off.'

All of Bella's professional kitchen instincts told her that she'd regret it if she didn't finish clearing up now. By the morning the flecks of dough would be dried onto the bowls and there was nothing worse that coming downstairs to a filthy kitchen. On the other hand, Jill had brought a bottle of red along with her as a 'congratulations' present for Bella's first proper cooking lesson, and the evening was dry and still pleasantly warm.

'OK, but you have to have a glass with me.'

Jill grinned. 'Half a glass. I've got to drive back.'

'Will you have one, Flinty?' Bella asked.

'I'll just take Veronica her cup of coffee, and then I might just have a wee one.'

'A wee what?' Darcy appeared in the doorway.

Jill held up the bottle.

Darcy grinned. 'Well, I came to help clear up, but a glass of wine sounds much nicer.'

They took the wine out to the courtyard and poured two generous, and one tiny, glasses of wine. Jill raised her glass. 'To Bella! A good first night?'

It had been a good first night. She'd done her costings in a hurry, but she thought even with the addition of drinks the night had made them a little profit.

For regular weekly classes she needed seven or eight, but five or six would do while she was still getting the hang of the teaching side of things. 'The first proper course starts next week.'

'I know,' Jill nodded. 'I'm going to be there.'

The first set of six planned classes was aimed at people who already cooked a bit but were stuck in a rut. Cath and Claire from the trial day had both signed up. Reverend Jill was stretching the definition of 'already cooks a bit' but she was very keen and after she was so lovely about the accident at the trial day, Bella didn't really feel she could turn her away. She would be supervising all of her chopping and slicing very closely indeed. Most importantly they had all paid upfront for all six lessons and Cath thought she had two other friends who might want to come along as well.

Bella's phoned buzzed on the bench beside her. *New email from Annette Wetherall Designs.* Bella frowned. She didn't know an Annette Wetherall, did she? The subject line read: *Cookery School ideas* though, so not random spam. Bella opened the email and was met with a screed of text, verbose and chatty, littered with exclamation marks. Bella skimmed through the first paragraph.

> Hi, Sorry to bother you but I was thinking about what Anna said at Ladies' Group about you needing a logo and I really want to help out because we clicked immediately didn't we? You're so easy to talk to, and anyway, this is on the house of course, but there's a couple of ideas attached.

Bella scrolled the very long way down to the end of the message, past extensively detailed descriptions of the design process and where the artist had found her inspiration and how very keen she was to help.

Talk soon! Netty xx

'Netty's a graphic designer?'

Jill laughed. 'As if she ever shuts up about it.'

'She's sent me some logo ideas for the cookery school.' Bella opened the attachment. The first image showed a whisk and rolling pin, crossed like swords on a coat of arms. Scrolling down there were three more similar options with different images to connote the idea of cooking and food, each with the banner *The Highland Cookery School* in elegant letters beneath. Bella held her phone up so the others could see.

'These are fabulous,' Darcy cooed.

They really were. Vintage but not fussy. Welcoming but still classic. Exactly what Bella hadn't known she wanted. She fired back a quick reply thanking Netty profusely for her work and insisting that she would find a way to repay her. A warm, unfamiliar glow came over Bella. Maybe things were starting to fall into place.

'How are you settling in generally?' Jill asked.

Bella paused. She hadn't really thought about it in those terms. She didn't think of herself as a person who settled in places. It wasn't in her genes. Her nan was an old school rolling stone, and her mum… well, her mum didn't have it in her to stick with anything. Deep inside, Bella feared, she was exactly the same. 'I don't know.'

'How did you find it, Darcy?' Jill asked again. 'Coming here from somewhere so different?'

Darcy laughed. 'Different? Lowbridge is so like New York city. You can barely tell them apart.' She thought for a second. 'I always loved it. But it wasn't about the place itself. It was more about finding a place where I fit.' She swallowed. 'I fit wherever Alexander was, and he was here.'

Jill nodded. 'And what about now?' She asked the question gently.

'Well now I don't know. I can't imagine going anywhere else.' Darcy brushed a tear from her cheek with an immaculately manicured fingertip. 'Leaving now would still feel like leaving Alexander. And where would I go?'

'You don't have to go anywhere,' Bella reassured her. 'This is your home.'

'Yours too now though,' Darcy replied.

Was it? 'I've never really had a home.' That wasn't quite true. 'I mean with my nan was home, but we always moved around. Like we were off at festivals or travelling or whatever every school holiday.' She sipped her wine, letting the rich red liquid warm her throat. 'And some times that weren't school holidays too. She would phone and say I was sick when we were actually halfway up some mountain or something. She valued experience over settling down I think.' Bella thought about Lowbridge. The castle. The village. The loch. The hills. The view over towards Raasay and Skye. 'I guess if I'd grown up here I might never have needed to move around though. It's like everything is here.' The views were so big, and the possibilities for what could grow in this place with these people and with Bella felt so endless that she could imagine deciding not to move on. Perhaps she could decide to put down roots. It was the same feeling of certainty she'd had when Adam had got down on one knee – the knowledge that this was her safe harbour. Perhaps Bella could decide not to be her mother's daughter. 'Maybe this is home now,' she whispered.

–

While Bella was finishing her class Adam was accepting the inevitable. Just after nine o'clock, he made his way into the laird's bedroom at the front of the castle. He stopped in the doorway. He hadn't really been in this room since he was very young. As a child he remembered opening his Christmas stocking sitting on the bed, before going downstairs to show his presents to his grandmother and Flinty.

He forced himself over the threshold. Dipper was curled up on the foot of the bed. His father would never have allowed that when he was younger. Dogs were beloved but they were also working animals. Letting the dog onto the bed would be Darcy's doing. She'd softened him – she'd softened both of their lives after Adam's mother left.

Adam scruffed at the back of Dipper's neck. 'You miss him, don't you?' Adam whispered.

Dipper looked up at him, sniffed warily, hopped off the bed and sloped away.

By half past nine he was sitting on the edge of what he still thought of as his father's bed, surrounding by his own packed suitcases. His grandmother had emptied his father's things out of the wardrobe with an efficiency that hadn't allowed Adam to look through any of Alexander's personal possessions. He didn't know if there was anything he wanted to keep. He hoped Darcy had had a chance to take anything that meant something to her.

At half past ten he was still sitting there when his fiancée, apparently slightly tipsy, pushed the door open. She looked at the bags. 'We don't have to sleep in here.'

Adam let himself smile. 'Well I don't think you're expected to sleep in here at all. That would be terribly inappropriate.'

'We were sleeping together in the coach house.'

He shrugged. He wasn't entirely sure about the precise morality his grandmother applied to the whole laird's room, lady's room situation. 'What happens in the coach house stays in the coach house?' he suggested.

'Well your grandmother isn't going to wander in in the night, so I think we're fine.' She stumbled – possibly she was more actually drunk than simply tipsy – towards him. 'We can both go in the lady room if you prefer.'

'Me sleeping here seems to be a whole thing.'

'But if it feels like your dad's room.' She pulled a face.

He slumped forward, resting his head in his hands. 'All the hassle to get Darcy to move and now I can't even sleep in here anyway.'

Bella slid her fingers through his. 'It's not a big deal. It's just a room. We can sleep in any of the twenty-eight other rooms.'

But it wasn't just a room. It was where Adam was supposed to be.

'You look tired.'

He was, but that was unfair. She was the one who had been rushing around. He hadn't done half of what Bel had. She leaned towards him and lifted his chin with her finger. 'Come on. A castle full of bedrooms.' She grinned. 'Why can't we christen them all?'

Adam's breath caught in his throat. She'd done this to him the very first moment they'd met. It had been like standing too close to the sun. 'That sounds like a plan.'

'OK.' She grinned. 'So we're not starting in here.'

He shook his head. 'Definitely not. And we've already done one in the coach house.'

'Two,' she corrected.

He thought back. The light dawned. 'The day Flinty was cleaning and would not stop.'

Bella nodded.

Any plans to sneak in a little afternoon delight at Lowbridge had to fit around Flinty's strict and immovable cleaning schedule.

'I don't think she understands what retirement means.'

Adam laughed, and wrapped an arm around Bella's waist. 'Where do you want to start then?'

'Well you still haven't shown me your actual room, from when you were a kid.'

Adam shook his head. 'No. There's no way I hold on to any sort of sex appeal after you've seen through that looking glass.'

'Well now I have to.' She grabbed his hand. 'Lead on.'

'Fine.' He led her across the hallway and down the west wing corridor. 'Here you go.'

Most of the trappings of teenage Adam were long gone – his carefully pressed school uniform and Iron Man duvet set were things of the past. Bella, of course, alighted on the things that were left. 'You have a wall poster about different types of moss.'

'What can I say? I'm just naturally cool.'

'I didn't even know there were different types of moss.'

Adam sat on the end of the single bed. 'I haven't been in here since we got back.'

'Why not?'

He shrugged. He could say that there just hadn't been any reason to, but that wouldn't be the whole truth. 'I think I knew that in here it would feel like my dad was just downstairs or out in the garden or something. Like I'm still fifteen and he's still around making sure everything's OK.'

'Isn't it nice to feel like that?'

He shook his head. 'It's not real though, is it? I can't just pretend.' He closed his eyes and forced down the wave of emotion that was threatening to overwhelm him. Bella was trying to cheer him up. The least he could do in return was attempt to be cheered. 'Anyway,' he reached for her. 'I don't think we should sleep in here. So which of the many other rooms do you want to check out next?'

She moved to him and kissed the top of his head. 'Well I am going to be a proper lady, you know.'

'I heard.'

'So I do think I ought to find out what it feels like to be properly courted in the official lady's bedroom.'

He shook his head. 'That is not what courted means.'

'Really? I thought it was like a euphemism.'

'No. It means all the stuff before you get married.'

'Well this is before we've got married.' He opened his mouth to argue, but she shut him up with a kiss, entangling her fingers around his and leading him to the other bedroom. Making love to Bella didn't make anything better, but at the same time, and for a short time, it made everything that was wrong disappear.

Afterwards, he closed his eyes and hoped to drift away to sleep. He felt the bed shift beside him as Bella sat up and pulled out her phone. 'What are you doing?'

'Just had an idea for the cookery school. Like could we get a mixologist in and do cocktail nights?' She paused. 'We'd need accommodation, or maybe we could get a minibus and minibus people back to the pub. Or give a designated driver place free?'

Adam listened to her stream of ideas. 'Yeah. Sure.'

'Well which?'

'Whichever you think.'

'But you think cocktails is a good idea?'

'I don't know.' That was the best he could offer. He didn't know what was a good idea. He didn't know what to do for the best.

'I was just asking.' There was an edge to her voice that he wasn't used to hearing.

'I'm sorry. I'm just tired.' He rolled towards her and reached a hand to her arm. 'Can we talk about it in the morning?'

–

Adam woke early, or at least he would have described himself as having woken early if anyone had asked. In reality, he'd barely slept at all, as he had barely slept each and every night since his father's death. He'd managed some rest on those precious few days in Edinburgh but as soon as he arrived back at Lowbridge sleep had eluded him once again.

Eventually, tiring of waiting for Bella to wake up and break the silence with her chatter and warmth, he climbed quietly out of bed and dressed before heading down the front stairs and out of the main door as silently as he could manage. Without thinking he walked around the side of the castle and up the path to the top of the cliff.

That was the place he felt closest to his father – not in the estate office staring uselessly at rows of figures, not with his grandmother or his stepmother who could have shared stories and reminiscences of their own, not with the fiancée who he never got the chance to introduce to his dad – but outside, where he could touch the land that Alexander had loved so much.

There was nothing in the world that Adam Lowbridge wouldn't have given for one more conversation with his father. One more talk might be the key to everything. Adam knew he was failing. He was failing the estate. He was failing his family. He was letting down his father's memory, and now that Bella was throwing so much energy into the life of Lowbridge, he was letting her down as well.

He sat on the ground for what could have been minutes or could have been hours and stared out towards Raasay across the loch, and cried for the uselessness of not being able to ask his dad what to do, and whether he would forgive him for the choice he was considering.

Eventually Adam stood and turned back towards the house. There was a figure standing in front of the locked gate into the walled garden. Adam watched for a second. He hadn't been near the garden for weeks. His grandmother had suggested that he did numerous times but he'd always found an excuse.

He walked down the hillside towards the stranger. It was a woman, and she was bending down, apparently placing something on the ground next to the wall. As he got closer he saw that it was a loosely tied bunch of wildflowers. As he got closer still the woman turned and he caught a glimpse of the shape of her face.

Adam stopped. The woman turned fully towards him and gasped. 'Adam,' she murmured, not quite a statement but not really a question either.

Adam didn't have the words to say, so instead he ran and closed the space between them, letting her wrap her arms around him for a moment, before his bodied tensed and he stepped back. 'Mum,' he said. 'What are you doing here?'

Chapter Seventeen

Adam's mother took a deep breath in. 'I got your message.'

'I sent that a month ago.'

'I wasn't sure if you'd want me here.'

The exhilaration of seeing her was hardening into something more familiar. 'Well if only there'd been some way of finding out.'

'I'm sorry.' He scanned her face, as he always did when she popped back into his life, for some sign of regret or sorrow or guilt for having missed all of the moments when Adam had needed somebody. 'I wanted to pay my respects though.'

They both glanced down at the tiny bouquet, insignificant looking against the solidity of the castle wall.

'This seemed like the best place. I think he loved this garden more than any of us.'

Adam wouldn't let that pass. 'Not more than he loved us. No.'

'Maybe not you.'

'How would you know?'

'What do you mean?'

What did she think he meant? 'You weren't here.'

She wrapped her coat around herself against the early morning nip in the air. 'I got here yesterday, stayed at the pub at Locharron. Didn't really want to see anyone who might remember.'

Adam folded his arms. He wasn't going to offer sympathy for the social awkwardness of wandering back into a community that might well have views about a mother who abandoned her child.

The thought of that last conversation that he would never be able to have with his father lingered in Adam's head. There was another conversation he'd never been able to have. 'Why did you go?'

'Oh sweetie, you don't want to...'

'Yes. I do.'

'Shall we walk?' She set out up the path Adam had come down, leaving him no choice but to follow her. 'I'll tell you whatever you want to know. That's fair, but the first thing is that it was never about you. You were a gorgeous little boy. You were clever and creative and funny.' She was smiling. 'And I thought about you, still think about you, every single day.'

'And?' Because that was obviously only part of the story.

'And it was everything else. I did love your dad. I adored him. He was kind and thoughtful and we were really happy for a few years.'

Still not the whole story.

'But this place felt like a prison. There was a role I had to play, someone I had to be, and I was awful at it.' She gestured towards her unkempt purple-streaked hair and pulled up her sleeve to show him an arm covered in tattoos. 'I mean I'm not really the garden party opening sort.' She half-laughed and then stopped, apparently catching the distinct lack of humour in Adam's expression. 'You won't understand what it's like when you're stuck in a place with all these expectations and you know you don't fit. All I could think about was being somewhere else. It was like I wanted to peel off my skin and climb out of this body and out of the life I was trapped in and float away.' She shook her head. 'I'm sorry. I'm not explaining it very well.'

Adam barely realised he was crying until he tried to speak and felt his throat gulp around the sobs. 'You explained it perfectly. I understand.'

'You do?' He could hear the glimmer of hope in her voice, but he was too wracked with tears to respond.

–

Bella woke that morning with the fuzzy head of just slightly too much wine, and the fuzzy glow of Adam's touch the night before. She lay back, eyes still closed, and remembered the tracks of his fingers over her body, and the brush of his lips against her skin. She let out a small, involuntary gasp as her mind wandered to the urgency and the need between them.

She rolled towards her fiancé and reached out her hand. Adam's side of the bed was cold.

She tried not to feel empty at his absence. He must have woken early and decided not to disturb her. Instead she showered, dressed and headed downstairs. Today was a red letter day in terms of the castle's relationship with the village, at least in Bella's eyes. Other community groups had met here and had a lovely time already, but today was the first Lowbridge Castle meeting for the only group that really mattered. Today the Ladies' Group came to the Blue – still yellow – Room.

Flinty was already in the kitchen, baking bowl in front of her. She held out a teaspoon as soon as Bella came in. 'Taste my buttercream.'

Bella did as she was told. 'Perfect.'

'Really? Because I'll not have Anna say a word about my butterfly buns.'

'I'm sure she wouldn't dare.'

'You weren't there for the demolition job she did on Netty's fruit loaf in 2014. The poor woman barely said a word for months.' Flinty shook her head. 'If you can even imagine Netty not chattering on the whole time.'

Veronica came quietly into the kitchen and cleared her throat. 'I wondered if I might join you all this morning.'

Bella's jaw dropped. Veronica was very clear on her views about the boundaries between the castle and the village.

Flinty nodded firmly. 'I think that's a marvellous idea. The Blue Room at ten.' A glimmer of something naughty twinkled in her eye. 'Of course all those who live here will be sharing the hosting.'

Bella didn't point out that Flinty was baking away quite happily but didn't technically live at the castle.

'So you'll have to help pouring teas and clearing away and all that.'

Veronica paled visibly before nodding. 'I'm sure that can't be too hard.'

Nina, Netty and Anna were all firmly ensconced in the Blue Room by ten to ten. The curiosity and novelty of meeting at the castle hadn't quite worn off enough yet for them to be fashionably late. Jill's lateness, however, was not a question of fashion but of pure chaotic disorganisa-tion, so she rolled in, with a volley of apologies and half-explanations, somewhere closer to a quarter past. 'Sorry. Had to visit Old Man Strachan up past Hartfield.'

Netty whispered something.

Nina nodded. 'She's right. He died two years back. There's just Young Strachan.'

Jill shrugged. 'He must be eighty if he's a day.'

'Right,' replied Nina. 'And Old Man Strachan was a hundred and change.'

'But he died,' Flinty pointed out. 'So they all move up a notch. Otherwise you end up with Baby Strachan and, I don't know, Tadpole Strachan.'

Nina shook her head. 'I don't think that's how it works at all.'

'Was Mr Strachan well?' Veronica's voice cut through the babbling.

'He broke his ankle, so he's making…' Jill paused. 'I don't know, Adolescent Strachan, run around after him.'

Veronica nodded. 'Poor chap. We should send…' She looked at Flinty. 'Something?'

'Flowers?'

'To the Strachans?' Anna laughed. 'Wouldn't know what to do with them.'

'I could make shortbread?' Bella offered.

Veronica nodded. 'Excellent idea.'

Jill approved, too. 'I honestly think they just eat toast and bacon butties up there. I'm surprised they don't all have heart attacks at fifty.' She stopped and glanced at Darcy. 'I'm sorry.'

Darcy nodded mutely. The silence that fell felt heavy and laden with awkwardness.

Flinty cleared her throat. 'Well it'd save all this Old Man debate if they did.'

There was a moment where people seemed to be debating with themselves whether it was all right to break the tension by laughing or whether that would be even more inappropriate. Netty broke first, letting out a booming guffaw that rose from her belly and shook her whole body.

And that, in itself, set Bella off, and then Jill and Anna and Nina and Flinty, and eventually even Darcy. Bella caught sight of Veronica out of the corner of her eye and saw that she permitted herself a small tight smile and a tiny nod of the head, before going back to sipping her too milky tea.

'So we haven't seen you for a good long time, Lady Lowbridge?' Anna turned pointedly towards the elder Lady Lowbridge. 'Making sure we don't damage the good china?' There was an edge to Anna's tone that Bella recognised from her first visit to the village shop.

'Not at all. You're in our home. I simply wanted to extend a welcome.'

'Which is very kind of you.' Jill cut off whatever Anna might have been going to say next.

The other women murmured vague agreement.

'So are we going to see you at more village events?' Anna's tone was softer now, but Bella couldn't escape the sense that there was something underlying it. 'I'm sure Maggie would love to see more of you.' She paused. Flinty was glaring. 'In the village,' Anna added.

'I haven't really thought about it.' Veronica's voice was as cool as ever.

Jill and Darcy exchanged a look. Bella suspected they were every bit as in the dark as she was about what was actually going on here. Netty was staring at her teacup with sudden intense interest. Nina cleared her throat. 'Well I'm hosting a little garden party next week, for the bridge appeal. I'm sure we'd all love to see you there.' She turned towards Darcy. 'You as well Lady, other Lady,

Lowbridge. Gosh, this is going to get even more confusing when you marry the laird, isn't it?'

Bella shook her head. 'I'm sure you can still call me Bella.'

The further pursing of Veronica's lips suggested there would be a conversation about that idea later.

'You know Nina's place, don't you Lady Lowbridge?' Anna was smiling now. 'It used to be Maggie's parents' house. Pavel's got his gym in the back shed now.'

Where on earth was she going with that?

'He does personal training,' Nina added.

'Oh yes, women from all over Lowbridge work up a sweat in there these days.' Anna's face was innocent, but there was definitely something going on that Bella didn't understand.

Veronica looked as though the bee she was permanently chewing had finally decided to sting.

'These fairy cakes are delicious,' Jill announced loudly and non-sequiturially. 'Did you make these, Bella?'

'No. They're Flinty's.'

'Well they're excellent.' Jill smiled broadly in Veronica's direction. 'You're so lucky to have Flinty taking care of you.'

Anna opened her mouth, but Veronica got in first. 'She's a wonderful cook. I don't know what I, well we, would do without her.'

Flinty's face coloured deeper red. Veronica and Anna were still glaring daggers at one another.

The penny in Bella's head refused to drop.

–

Adam knelt on the slightly damp ground, leaning on the outer wall to his father's garden. His mother was sitting, legs crossed neatly in front of her, opposite him. He wasn't sure how long they'd been here like this, but he knew it was the longest he'd spent with his mother in twenty years.

'I know I have no right to say anything.' She leaned forward and took his hand in hers. 'I know I gave up the right to barge in and tell you what to do.'

He shrugged. 'I wish someone would.'

'Well it sounds like you're feeling trapped.'

He couldn't argue with that.

'And I do know what that's like.' She turned her head towards the view up the cliff. 'It's mad. A place like this where everything's so open and so beautiful feeling like a prison, but for me it did. So all I can say is that you can walk away. I did. It was the hardest thing I've ever done.' She extended a hand as if to touch his cheek and then pulled it away. 'Leaving you was...' She shook her head. 'But leaving here, it was the right thing. I would have withered away. I don't know if there'd have been anything of me by now left if I'd stayed.'

Adam shook his head. 'You weren't the laird though. I have a responsibility.'

'You have a responsibility to yourself as well though. You're young. You're single...'

'Actually I'm engaged.'

His mother stopped. He could see shock on her face but then she smiled and nodded. 'Right. Well congratulations. I don't know why I assumed.' She pulled her hand back from his. 'I suppose I still imagine you as a kid, even though...' She pointed at the man in front of her. 'Silly of me. So what does this fiancée want you to do?'

'I think Bella is fine anywhere.' That was the truth. She had an adaptability and an ability to fit in that Adam didn't share.

'So what do you want?'

'I want to be home.'

'Isn't this home?'

Of course it was. When he was in Edinburgh he referred to visiting Lowbridge as 'going home', so why didn't it feel like that now he was here? Because this was home for Adam the child and now he was expected to be the grown-up in every single room. 'It was Dad's home.'

His mother stared down at her knees. 'It certainly was. He would never even think about leaving,' she added with a hint of bitterness in her tone. 'But why shouldn't you? What would you do if you weren't here?'

That was easy. He'd go back to Edinburgh and carry on with the life he'd promised Bella when he'd asked her to marry him. Realistically Lowbridge would be better off without him as well. The McKenzie estate had money and a vision and probably offices full of accountants who would be horrified of the mess Adam was making of everything. He knew his grandmother would be furious, and he was pretty sure Darcy would see it as betraying his father, but without a laird who was worthy of the title the whole thing was hanging by a thread already. Letting Lowbridge go might be the best thing for everyone.

–

The Ladies' Group dispersed. Bella followed Flinty into the kitchen. Veronica and Darcy had tried to help by stacking cups on a tray but Flinty had taken over when Veronica had been defeated by the challenge of making space for the cake plates.

Standing alongside Flinty with a tea towel in her hand and the white noise of the hot water tap filling the sink gave Bella a moment of relative calm. She told herself it was none of her business and she should keep her nose out. She told herself that Flinty's reaction to whatever Anna had been insinuating was a clear signal that she did not want to talk about whatever it was. But there clearly was something. 'Flinty?'

'Yes.'

'What was Anna driving at in there?'

'I don't know what you mean.' Flinty had been wiping the same cup with her washing up sponge for way too long, but she clearly wasn't a woman about to give up her secrets.

Bella thought back over the conversation. *Maggie's always taken care of the Lowbridge women… working up a sweat in Nina's back shed… Maggie would love to see more of you…*

Surely not. But at the same time, why not? It definitely wasn't her place to ask. Bella dried a saucer in silence and tried to think of something else, anything else, to talk about. She told herself not to ask. Who was she kidding? 'So you and Veronica?' she let the question hang.

'What about us?' Flinty's gaze was fixed straight ahead.

'You've known each other a long time?'

'Since we were girls,' Flinty confirmed.

'And… Anna seemed to be implying that you were…' Bella was wishing she hadn't started the sentence.

Flinty put down her washing up brush, flicked the soap suds from her fingers and turned to face Bella. 'Well, spit it out love.'

'…that you were close.'

Flinty didn't budge. 'Well we've known each other our whole lives, like I said. Say what you mean, lass.'

Right. In for a penny. 'Are you banging Lady Lowbridge?'

'No, I am not currently, as you put it, "banging" Veronica Lowbridge.' Flinty turned back towards her washing up.

'I'm sorry.' Bella couldn't imagine now what had come over her. 'I shouldn't have said anything. Anna got me wondering, and it was silly and…' Flinty's reply ran through Bella's mind again. Wait a second. She stared at her friend. 'What do you mean "currently"?'

Was there the tug of a smile at the corner of Flinty's lips?

Bella felt of surge of anger on Flinty's behalf. 'Oh my God! So she was outing you? That's not OK.'

'I don't think she was trying to "out" us, as you put it.' Flinty paused. 'She's protective of me; her and Hugh both are. They think I gave my life up to drag along after her. And maybe I did, but that was my decision. It was never asked for or expected.'

Bella was still processing. 'So, can I ask?'

'You can ask whatever you like. Not to say I'll answer.'

'So when? What happened? Is it still a thing? Are you still into her?' Flinty was here every day, despite claims of retirement. 'You are still into her, aren't you? Does she know?'

Flinty let out a deep sigh. 'Well…'

Whatever she had been intending to say next was cut off by a shout from the front hallway. Bella thought of Darcy straight away. She was the one most given to histrionics. Veronica was more of a cold-hearted assassin type, but it wasn't Darcy yelling this time. Bella dropped her tea towel and ran towards the voices.

'Get that woman out of my house this second!'

Adam was standing by the front doors with a woman Bella had never seen before. Veronica was opposite them with a demeanour that Bella only recognised from nature documentaries. It was somewhere in the region of rabid lioness defending her cub. Darcy came down the stairs and stopped when she saw the newcomer.

'Penny!'

The stranger nodded. 'I was sorry when I heard about Alexander. He was a good man.'

Darcy didn't reply. She was frozen in place on the bottom step.

'Well,' Flinty broke the standoff. 'Why don't we all take this into the Blue Room?'

'No.' Veronica hadn't budged.

'Grandmother.' Adam's voice was tense.

The newcomer shook her head. 'It's fine. I'm not going to stay. I just wanted to meet…' She scanned around the group until her gaze landed on Bella. 'You must be the fiancée.'

'Yeah. I'm sorry. Who are…?'

Bella's question seemed to jerk Adam back into life. 'Sorry. Bel, this is my mother. Mother, this is Bella Smith.'

Adam's mother. She was such an ephemeral figure in the way he spoke about his life that Bella had never anticipated meeting her. She stepped forward and held out her hand, only to find herself enveloped in a hug scented with seaweed and lavender. It reminded her in an instant of the fragrance and soap packs her nan used to make to sell at festivals in the summertime.

Penny pulled back from the hug and looked Bella up and down. 'So how are you finding Lowbridge?'

'I'm settling in.'

'A bit different from where you've been before though?'

279

That was true. Even if Adam had only told her the bare essentials about his bride-to-be there was no arguing with simple fact. Bella wasn't from here. She shouldn't belong, but there was something about the tone Penny adopted – about the way it seemed to imply that they were both the same – that got Bella's back up. She'd run away from her child with no explanation. Only in her darkest terrors could Bella imagine doing that. 'Like I said, I'm settling in.'

'Ow!' Penny shuddered.

'What's wrong?' Adam was looking at his mother with concern.

'Oh. I just felt like something prodded me.' She rubbed the side of her leg. 'Hard. Here.'

'Poppy,' said Bella.

Penny frowned. 'Oh for goodness' sake. They're not still pedalling that nonsense.'

It was one thing for Bella to think that but quite another for this person to come in here and cast aspersions. 'Poppy isn't nonsense.'

'Whatever. She never liked me.'

'No.' Veronica's tone was cool.

Penny turned back to Bella. 'I'm sure moving on won't be a problem for you anyway,' Penny replied.

'I don't have any plans to...' Bella looked past Penny and caught the look on Adam's face. 'What's going on?'

'Maybe we should go and sit down,' Adam suggested.

'We're fine here,' Veronica insisted.

Adam was staring at Bella. 'Can't we go through to the Yellow Room?'

She shook her head. It felt as though a line was being drawn, and somehow Bella was scared that she and the man she loved were going to be on different sides.

Adam took a sharp breath in. Bella could see that he was steeling himself for something. 'I'm going to accept the McKenzie offer.'

He couldn't. 'What?'

'No.' Darcy and Veronica both spoke at once.

'It's his decision,' his mother pointed out. If she was trying to help, it had the opposite effect.

Veronica shook her head. 'It's a family decision.'

'And I'm as much part of his family as you are.'

When Veronica did lose her temper, even with Darcy when the two of them were at one another's throats, she rarely shouted and she rarely screamed. Bella had only been here a few weeks but she already knew that the more furious Adam's grandmother was, the quieter and more definite she became. She almost whispered her reply to Penny, pure rage dancing across every word. 'No. You are not.'

'I'm his—'

'Do not say mother.'

'I am—'

'Where were you when he broke his wrist walking on Hartfield Hill? Where were you when him and Pavel Stone stole Hugh's boat and went for a jolly in Portree? Were you here ringing the coastguard and scouring the loch for sight of them?'

'I—'

'Where were you when he was worrying himself into a frenzy about retaking maths again so he could get into college? Where were you when he graduated?' Finally Veronica raised her voice. 'I asked you a question, Penelope. Where were you?'

'I was going crazy here.' She looked from Veronica to Flinty and back again. 'You were there. You saw.'

'I was.' Veronica's tone softened ever so slightly. 'I understood that you needed some time. But nearly twenty years? You missed everything.'

Penny didn't reply.

Bella kept her gaze fixed on Adam. He hadn't spoken since he'd announced that Lowbridge wasn't going to be all the things Bella had hoped for. The place that she'd begun to think of as home seemed to be shifting under her feet. 'Why?' she asked.

'I can't...' he started.

Bella didn't want to hear, couldn't face hearing. It wasn't just that she was cross with him. She was cross with herself for thinking she could be somebody who put down roots. She was cross with herself for forgetting who she was. Bella Smith travelled light. Bella Smith didn't join groups. She didn't settle down. It didn't matter one bit if she wanted those things or not. They simply weren't for her.

'It's not about you,' Adam started again.

That was evident. Whatever was going on in her supposed partner's head, she hadn't been part of it.

'I have to go.'

'What?'

Bella pushed past Darcy and ran up the stairs.

–

Adam watched her go. His mother and grandmother were still glaring at one another. His stepmother had tears rolling down her face. 'You can't sell Lowbridge,' she whispered. 'Your father loved this place.' She gulped. 'It's home.'

This was why he'd pushed the feeling that he should accept John McKenzie's offer and walk away deep down inside him. He'd known that doing what felt right for him would feel wrong for his family. 'You can stay in the area. We'd be able to afford somewhere for everybody.'

'Live across the river from the crumbling leftovers of the estate while McKenzie's rich idiots barge around the rest of the place like it's their personal playground?' his grandmother asked. 'Well thank goodness for that.'

Adam looked desperately to Flinty for some support. She met his gaze. 'I think you ought to go and talk to your lassie.'

Of course he should. He couldn't fix things here, but he could explain to Bella and he could get her to see that this decision would put them back onto the track that his father's death had knocked them off.

He found her in the lady's bedroom, stuffing her belongings into the rucksack she'd brought back from Spain. His blood froze. 'What are you doing?'

'I've been stupid.'

'What do you mean?'

She picked up the waterproof she'd bought from Anna and Hugh a few weeks earlier and rolled it into a tight bundle. 'All of this. The cookery school. Making plans.'

Adam didn't know what to say. 'I didn't know it meant this much to you.'

'How could it not? I was trying to make things work here.' He'd never seen Bella this angry before. 'It would have been nice to know you didn't care before I let myself…'

'Let yourself what?'

'Feel at home,' she muttered. It was more than that. 'Fall in love.'

'I'm sorry.'

She stared at him. 'It's too late.'

'Wait.'

She watched him take a deep breath in.

'What did you fall in love with?'

'What do you mean?'

'Well you came here because of me, right?'

She nodded.

'And you love it here.'

'Yes.'

'But what about me?'

'What about you?'

He forced himself to ask. 'Do you still love me?'

'Of course I do. And I understand it.'

'What?'

It was what he'd explained to her weeks ago when he'd told her the story of the first baron and the girl from the village. 'You are Lowbridge. I get it. Which is what makes selling even more insane, because...' She stopped as she caught sight of his expression.

'The baron is part of the place. The title. The laird. But I'm just Adam.' His voice cracked. 'I want to just be Adam. I thought you loved Adam.'

'That's not fair. You don't get to make this my fault.' She was yelling now. 'You made a huge decision about all our futures and you didn't even mention it to me.' Bella stuffed the last handful of clothing into her pack, and marched past him. 'Goodbye Lowbridge.'

Chapter Eighteen

Bella's anger carried her out of the castle, across the court-yard, past the coach house and out as far as the road. Then the practicalities of the situation hit her. The nearest station was in Strathcarron. Someone would have to drive her there. She could hardly pop back inside and ask Adam for a lift. She dug out her phone and tapped on a contact. It was answered straight away.

She hung up the call when she heard movement behind her. 'No point going over it all again. I'll be gone soon.'

'That's a shame.'

Bella turned towards the voice. Not Adam. Veronica.

'You think so?' she asked.

'I do.'

'I thought you'd be glad to see the back of me.'

'Perhaps a few weeks ago.' The older woman came and stood alongside her. 'You're quite decided on leaving?'

Bella nodded. She'd been stupid to think that Lowbridge could have been her home. 'I rushed in, didn't I?'

'You did.'

'And now I'm getting my comeuppance.'

'I didn't say that.'

'You didn't have to.' Bella was nothing if not a realist.

'I'm sorry if I wasn't as welcoming as I should have been when you arrived.' Veronica clasped her hands together across her body. 'I know what a role like Lady Lowbridge can do to a person. You have to be the right sort.'

Not a mad hippy from a council estate in Leeds.

'It's broken the hearts of stronger women than you,' Veronica murmured, almost to herself.

'Well it's for the best that I'm off then isn't it?'

Veronica finally turned to face her. 'Is that really what you think?'

Was it? She'd had such big plans. She was going to make Lowbridge the heart of the community. She was going to use produce from the estate in the cookery school, maybe even open an estate shop one day. She was going to… she shook her head. 'What does it matter now? Adam's made up his mind.'

Veronica sighed. 'Well someone has.'

'And you were right anyway.' That was the part that was making Bella really angry. 'I wasn't up to it. I don't know why I thought I would be.'

'Again, I didn't say that. It just strikes me that decisions made in haste can very quickly be regretted.'

'Try telling him that.'

'He's not the only one making hasty choices.'

The sound of a car closing in on them down the hill and pulling to a stop drew Bella's attention away, and headed off the bubbling row. Jill wound her window down. 'You're lucky I was still in the village. What's up pet? You sounded awful on the phone.'

Bella opened the passenger door, and turned back to Veronica. 'I'm sorry. I hope everything goes well, you know.'

And then she jumped in. 'Can I get a ride to Strath-carron? I need to get to the station.'

Jill frowned. 'What's wrong?'

Bella bit back the urge to say nothing. Everything was wrong. 'I need to get away.'

Her new friend nodded. 'Whatever you need.'

A quick web search during the drive over had told Bella that if she made the next train to Inverness and changed there and at Aberdeen she could be in Leeds tonight. Well, not technically tonight, technically very early tomorrow morning, but early enough that she wouldn't have to sleep on a station platform and in thirteen hours' time she could be getting into bed at her nan's flat, far away from Lowbridge, and Adam, and Veronica, and all the silly ideas she'd got into her head about settling down and making a home.

Jill chattered for the most part of the journey. She relayed in far more detail the saga of old Old Man Strachan and young Old Man Strachan and the various women who the different men had loved and lost along the way. 'Apparently there's a young Young Man Strachan who ran off to what they keep referring to as the Big City. I think they mean Inverness.' She shrugged. 'Anyway he's not really to be talked about.'

Bella stared out of the window and nodded, grateful that Jill wasn't asking any questions about why on earth she was driving Bella to the station.

'I have noticed that you haven't actually told me what's wrong.'

Damn. 'I'm fine.'

'No. You're not.'

'I will be.' And she would. Bella always was. She wasn't the type to wallow or grieve or let things get on top of

287

her. There was always something else to do, somewhere else to be. The mistake she'd made with Lowbridge was forgetting that there would always be greener grass elsewhere.

She caught the train at Strathcarron at a run, with only seconds to spare to hug Jill and promise – as Bella always promised when it came time to up sticks and move on – that she would keep in touch. Once on the train she flung her bag onto the overhead rack – never travel with a bag you can't lift overhead on your own was one of Bella's hard and fast rules for life – and threw her body into a seat by the window.

The route closely followed the path of the road they'd taken a few weeks earlier accompanying Alexander on his final journey to the crematorium, but the two Bellas taking those journeys felt worlds apart. The first Bella had been committed to supporting Adam, but even among the grief and the pain it had still been a new adventure. She'd determined to make Lowbridge work, for him, because it was what he'd made her believe he wanted.

Bella today was a ball of rage. She'd put everything into that dream – *his* dream – of a life at Lowbridge and it had turned out that Adam didn't care at all. He was perfectly happy to throw the whole thing away in a second. All that guff about how the laird was the place and the place was part of him had been nonsense. Worse than nonsense. Lies.

By the time she changed at Inverness, the anger had hardened.

By Aberdeen it had settled into a solid certainty.

By the time she was hopping off the university night bus, having persuaded the driver that although she wasn't a student the ethical thing to do was take pity on her, and climbing the stairs to her nan's flat, there was no doubt at all that she'd done the right thing. Settling in Lowbridge had been a crazy idea. Crazier than the time she'd signed up to train to be a paragliding instructor in Peru. Crazier than the time she'd lost her clothes going skinny dipping in California and had to steal a lifeguard's jacket to protect her modesty. Bella wasn't built to settle down. Being with Adam had made her believe that she could be a person who belonged somewhere. But he'd been the anchor. With that cut away she could allow herself to drift or she could take control and make haste away. Bella had no fight left. Flight was all that was left to her.

—

So Bella should be happy, which made the heaviness of her limbs the next morning, and her utter terror at the thought of getting out of bed and facing the day, a little hard to explain. She'd gleaned from the quiet around her that her nan must still be away. The last time they'd messaged, her nan had been in Somerset and Bella hadn't told her she was coming to visit. She lay back down on her pillow and closed her eyes.

The second morning Bella felt much the same. Perhaps, she decided, she was sickening for something. That would be typical, that Lowbridge had left her with a parting gift of influenza, or some strange Scottish castle virus to which wee Sassenach lassies were uniquely susceptible. She couldn't stay in bed the whole time. She could imagine what her nan would say about that. She would say that there were adventures out there that she was missing out on, hunkering down here with her fuzzy head and tired body.

Bella forced herself up and into the shower. Being clean and fresh was bound to make her feel better. There was really nothing finer, in Bella's view, than that first shower when you'd been hiking or wild camping and you could feel the build-up of grime on your skin. This shower was exhausting. Bella filled a water glass, collected a packet of Hobnobs and some tortilla chips from the kitchen, and crawled back into bed.

By the third morning her stomach was telling her that, whatever her brain thought about the situation, she really did have to get up and eat something more substantial, and in her current state there really was only one option. Cheese on toast. It was the simplest, but also one of the most perfect meals Bella knew. Making it was an act of self-care but also a reversion to childhood tastes and needs. She could make a fancy cheffy version with sourdough and three different cheeses and a dash of something a little bit spicy or a little bit hot to elevate the whole thing. Some of her former colleagues swore by Tabasco but for Bella's money you couldn't beat good old Worcestershire sauce.

That wasn't what she was making today. Today she was putting plastic wrapped cheddar onto white sliced bread from the convenience store at the edge of her nan's estate and she was losing the here and now for a moment in the taste of being six years old and off school with a cold, on those simple days where cheese on toast made everything seem a little bit better.

'What are you doing here?' Her nan's voice carried through to the tiny kitchen from the hallway as she bustled in dropping bags and coats in her wake.

'Aren't I welcome?'

'You're always welcome. I just didn't know you were coming. How long have you been here? I'd have come back sooner if I'd known.'

'No need to.' Not that it was true anyway. Bella's nan kept her own schedule. She had ever since Bella had been old enough to pack up and bring along. She'd never let niceties like school term dates or paid jobs hold her back. She definitely wouldn't have rushed back on Bella's account.

'So is this mystery man with you?'

Bella stopped. She hadn't told her nan about Adam. 'What man?' she asked.

'Well you scurried your way back over here from Spain without a hint you were planning it, so I assumed there was a man. Or a woman?' she asked.

Bella couldn't lie to her nan. She always saw through it. It was her superpower. 'It didn't work out.'

Her grandma nodded. 'So that's why you're back here.'

Bella tried to smile. 'Just until the next thing pops up.'

'All right then. Any idea what the next thing might be?'

Bella shrugged. She'd run from Lowbridge. What came next was... was what?

Her grandma was still looking at her. Bella knew that look. She braced herself for what was coming next. Even though she hadn't lied, she also hadn't entirely told the truth. Eventually her grandmother nodded, and stepped back. 'Well I'm going to go and have a bath. Been on the road all day.'

'You got new wheels?'

She shook her head. 'Nah. Got a lift with a Cornish escapologist heading up to Edinburgh. Nice lad.' She grinned. 'Bendy.'

'I do not want to know how you know that.'

'I had him stretched out right across that back seat.'

'Nan!'

Her grandma laughed. 'I dropped my glasses under the passenger seat. He bent round to get them for me.' She sighed. 'Not that I'd have said no to a bit of the other, but he said that having sex drained his focus for getting out of handcuffs before he drowns so what can you do?' She rubbed her eyes. She looked tired.

'Are you OK?'

'I'm fine.' Her nan looked Bella up and down. 'Can we say the same for you though?'

Chapter Nineteen

The knock on the bedroom door would have woken Adam up, if he'd actually managed to sleep at all in the last seventy-two hours. Mostly he'd pretended to sleep and when he'd reached the point where it seemed as though he couldn't get away with that any longer, he'd slipped out of the coach house – where he was resolutely staying – and walked as far as he could away from Lowbridge, away from the village, away from the family, hoping that if he walked and walked he would tire his body enough that he would have no option but to fall asleep. Perhaps he even hoped that if he walked far enough he would walk right back to her.

Flinty pushed the bedroom door open and wrinkled her nose. 'Oh. When did you last open a window in here?'

Adam had no idea, and an overwhelming desire to tell her to go away, but he knew better than that. He had a strong suspicion that Flinty didn't consider him too old or too grand to be put on the naughty step if he talked back to her. She put the tray she was carrying on the dressing table. 'I brought you some tea. I was going to bring you breakfast, but then I thought if I did that you'd have even more excuse to hide in here.'

'I'm not—'

Flinty's look silenced him, because he was hiding. Of course he was. 'You need to talk to them.'

'To who?'

'Your grandmother. And Darcy. You walked in, announced that you were selling the estate, had a shouting match with your lassie and you haven't spoken to anybody since. Have you spoken to her?'

'Bella?' Adam shook his head. He wanted to, like he'd wanted to run after his mum and tell her not to go all those years before. But, just like that time, he was terrified that nothing he could say would be enough. And this time, it was all his fault.

Flinty shrugged. 'Well you can't avoid everybody. Your mother hasn't been back in touch?'

Adam wasn't sure whether that was a statement or a question, but he shook his head. 'She said she was going back to Lerwick.'

'Typical.'

'What?'

'Well barrelling in, causing all sorts of trouble and then buggering off again.'

'That's not fair.'

Flinty raised an eyebrow.

'She didn't make me decide to sell.'

'No, but I'm sure she didn't discourage it.'

Adam had never fallen out with Flinty in his life. He'd had typical teenage rows with his dad, his grandmother could be impossible to please, and Darcy's exuberance had clashed with Adam's adolescent moods more than once, but Flinty had been constant. Always there willing to patch up scraped knees without too many questions asked. 'It was my decision,' he insisted.

'All the more reason you need to be over there explaining and working out what happens next then.'

'I will.' He watched Flinty automatically start tidying the space around her, folding his clothes into a neat pile on the chair. 'Are you cross with me too?'

'Not my place to be cross with anyone.'

'But you think I'm doing the wrong thing?'

She smoothed his jeans onto the pile. 'About selling? I have no idea. But lying about here in bed with your family over there not knowing whether they're coming or going and...' She hesitated. 'Well yes, I think you're messing things up a bit now.'

That hadn't been what she'd started to say. 'What else?'

She shook her head.

'Say it.'

'Well, and with your lassie goodness knows where.'

'She decided to leave.'

'Oh fiddle-faddle. She did this. I didn't do that. It's all nonsense. If you love somebody you find a way to be near them. Life's too long to live it any other way.'

Adam didn't reply, which he imagined Flinty would interpret as agreement.

'Oh by the way, I'm going to take your car out to go to the village. It's ever so comfortable to drive.'

'I know.'

'And all the doors work,' she added. Flinty passed him the mug of tea. 'Now get up, get dressed and bloody well start getting on with things.'

—

Adam hadn't done what he was told, at least not straight away. In fact for the next few hours he'd done the exact opposite, not out of stubbornness, not even out of a pretence that Flinty was wrong, but out of pure paralysing

295

fear. He'd failed spectacularly at being the laird and he'd failed at being Bella's partner. He'd promised her a life he couldn't deliver.

Having made the decision to sell up and walk away, he'd been able to tell himself that things would get easier. He'd been able to tell himself that the decision was an end point.

But of course it wasn't. It was a beginning of something else for everybody and he was still responsible for working out what that should be.

And now he was responsible for all of that alone.

His phone rang on the side table. He pounced on it, desperate to see Bel's name on the screen. He swiped to answer anyway. 'Ravi?'

'Hi. You OK?'

'Oh you know.'

'I just wanted to say I was sorry.'

What did Ravi have to be sorry for? 'How come?'

'When you came over here. I feel like I put a bit of pressure on you and that wasn't fair. You've got enough going on.'

'You didn't put pressure on.'

He heard his best friend clear his throat. 'Yeah. I did. And, you know, we do need to work stuff out with the business, but we will. And we can muddle through until then. I can send you stuff remotely, or you can come over when you can. It's all...' He sighed. 'We'll make it work.'

'Ravi, mate, you don't have to say that.'

'Yeah. I do. I talked to Sam and he said I might have been a dick to you.'

'You weren't.'

Ravi laughed. 'I might have to put you on speaker so you can tell him that.'

'I'll text him.'

'Please do. Seriously though, you're the girls' godfather and, well, we don't have that many people.'

Adam understood. He'd never met Sam's family but they'd reacted badly to their son coming out. Ravi's family were more supportive but his parents had moved to Mumbai around the time Ravi left college.

'Like, whatever happens with the business, you're family. All right?'

'Thanks mate.'

'Right. Well sorry if I was a dick and sorry if that was too mushy.'

'It wasn't. Thank you.'

'No bother.' Ravi paused. 'I mean we're partners aren't we? You don't give up on people just cos things get difficult. Anyway, if there's anything we can do for you over there, you let us know. Right?'

'All right.'

He hung up the phone, and checked the rest of his notifications. The old school WhatsApp group was on fire with chat, started not by Fiona, for a change, but by a classmate who was now a weather presenter on BBC North West. She'd posted a picture of the view from her city centre apartment.

> Can't lie. Woke up craving some open
> space and some highland air this morning.

The replies had come thick and fast. Person after person yearning to be out on a boat on the loch, or walking in the hills, or just hanging out in the village pub with nowhere to be and nothing to do.

> I'm back in Lowbridge and I sometimes wish I wasn't.

He hit send before he had time to think or censor himself. He wasn't likely to run into these people any time soon.

The first reply came almost immediately.

> Oh mate. I guess the grass is always greener, isn't it? I don't think it matters that much where you are. It's the people who make it home, isn't it?

The sender, Callum, who Adam remembered as a slightly shy but personable enough lad, added a picture of a woman pushing a tiny red-haired toddler on a swing set in what looked like a suburban back garden.

Callum was right. It wasn't the place that mattered. It wasn't the role. It was the people. It was one person.

Adam took a deep breath in. Ravi wasn't giving up on him. And Flinty hadn't either. The least he could do was get out of bed. He got up. He got dressed. He headed towards the castle fully intending to make his way to the estate office, sit down with his grandmother and have a proper talk about what happened next.

Instead his feet carried him around the outside of the castle to the gate in the wall that he'd been avoiding since he first came back. The wall that enclosed his father's pride and joy, the place he'd been happiest in life, the place Adam had always felt close to him, and the place he hadn't been able to face entering since he'd returned to Lowbridge, not to see his father, but to bury him.

Adam pushed the gate open and stepped into the walled garden.

He was greeted by a riot of life. Adam knew – of course he knew – that gardens had to be tended and maintained to remain in their neat borders and boxes. And he knew that it was summer and that plants needed nothing more than light and rain to grow up with vigour. But, nonetheless, he'd been imagining nothing but cold barren ground, and plants shrivelled and dying without his father's care. In his head the lifeless abandoned garden was a picture of Lowbridge itself without Alexander there as laird – neglected, not cared for, withering away.

He walked to the centre of the plot, trailing tendrils of green brushing against his legs. Sure. A lot of what was here was not what his father had intended but it was here, regardless of intent or design, and it was thriving – joyously, vibrantly alive. There were tomatoes, bright and red and almost ready to harvest. Runner beans, rapidly going to seed but here and defiantly surviving. He'd missed the asparagus entirely, but that in itself made Adam smile. He warned his dad years ago when he'd first planted it that the asparagus picking season lasted about twenty-five minutes and not a moment longer. The marigolds his father liked to dot between the rows of vegetables were in full flower, loud and bright and full of sunshine.

A pair of sheep ambled through the gateway and started chomping happily on the produce in the nearest bed. Adam didn't even try to chase them away. This garden had been intended to grow food for the residents of Lowbridge. It felt right that at least some of them were enjoying it now.

Adam turned around, trying to take in the explosion of greens and reds and yellows around him. The garden was alive. With a little bit of care and love it could be wonderful again. It could provide produce for the cookery school. It could work as a proper market garden. It could supply the village store. It could…

Adam stopped. Of course he wasn't going to do any of those things.

'What are you doing out here?' Darcy came from the open gateway, picking her way past the sheep and across the gravel pathways in her wedges. 'I haven't been out here since…' She folded her arms. 'Well you know.'

'Me neither.' Adam held out his arms. 'But look. Everything he planted.'

Darcy nodded. 'He was good with things that needed tending.'

'He was good with all of it.'

Darcy snorted.

'What?'

'Well, I mean I loved your dad. I love your dad, but he wasn't good at everything.'

Compared with Adam, Alexander had been a paragon.

'I mean he was good at the estate stuff, managing all that side of it, but he hated having to make nice with the parish council and host big dinners and all of that. He only did any of that because he was too scared of Veronica to tell her no.'

That wasn't true. Adam's father had been the perfect laird. Organised. A natural manager, but also a genial host, at ease in any company.

'We had a little code at all those parties. If he mentioned New York or the Mets or, I don't know, the Statue of Liberty or something it meant he needed me to come and be American at people.'

Adam shook his head. 'What does that mean?'

'You know, all teeth and tits and bubbliness so he could sink into the background.' She smiled. 'Which was fine. All of this is too much for one person on their own, so we helped each other out.' She folded her arms across her body. 'I wish he'd let me help more. I used to be a dab hand with a spreadsheet.' She smiled. 'Oh, come on. I know I say I was a model but most models are admin temps most of the time.'

A quiet descended over them, punctuated only by the buzzing of bees between the marigolds and the dull background hush of the waves in the loch.

'I'm sorry,' said Adam eventually.

'What for?'

'For selling this place.'

'It's a done deal then?'

'I mean I haven't actually contacted McKenzie yet, but I'm decided.' He looked over his father's garden again. 'I was decided. I'm sorry for not talking to you all about it first though.'

'Like father, like son,' Darcy murmured.

'What?'

'Making big decisions without talking to anybody. Asking for advice wasn't exactly your dad's strong suit either. Like he was fine with my being the social butterfly of the team, but he never talked about anything else that was worrying him.' Darcy shook her head. 'I miss him.'

'Me too.' Everything at Lowbridge was something Adam wanted to tell his father about. He was telling himself that back in Edinburgh the gap where his father was supposed to be would feel less pointed somehow.

'He wasn't good at asking for help though. Those last few months, he was—' Darcy's voice broke a little. 'He was tired. I told him to go to the doctor.'

'Grandmother said it was a heart attack.'

'Yeah, but I don't know. Maybe if he'd asked for help they would have picked something up. Maybe if he'd slowed down and rested more. Maybe if I'd made him.'

'It wasn't your fault. He never even told me he was feeling ill.'

'He wasn't ill exactly. Just not himself.' He could see her welling up. 'I love him so much. Still.'

'I know.'

'Where does all that love go? What am I supposed to do with it?'

Adam tried to blink back his own tears.

'And I'm angry too, but I can't be angry with him now, can I?' She wiped her eyes. 'Why didn't he go to a doctor or at least say something to me if he wasn't feeling right?'

'I don't know. He always told me everything was fine too, no matter what.' Adam ought to have known something was wrong.

'He never wanted to worry anyone. He absolutely hated the idea of letting people down. Especially you.'

'Why me?'

Darcy took deep breath in and turned to face him properly. 'Well because of your mom.' She said it like it was the most self-evident thing in the world. 'He couldn't bear the thought of anyone hurting you like that again, especially not him. Whatever happened, so long as it was all right for you, that was enough for him.'

Adam stopped fighting the tears.

'I wish I could ask him what to do now.' That was the bottom line. Adam needed someone to tell him if he'd made the right choice, but how could he ask Darcy or Veronica when it was their home? He'd let Bella believe it was her home too, and he'd betrayed them all. 'But I can't ask him and I don't know what to do on my own and whatever I do, I'll be disappointing all of you. Especially him.'

'Don't be stupid.'

'What do you mean?'

Darcy wrapped her arm around his shoulder. 'You all get so wrapped up in the duty of the thing. This place is glorious. You and your whole family are so lucky to have it and be a part of it and you spend your whole fucking time worrying that you're not good enough.'

'I really don't think my father worried about that.'

'Balls. I don't think any Lowbridge son ever feels up to his daddy's standard. If you all stopped trying to uphold something from the generation before and got on with how you want to do things now I think everybody would be a lot happier.'

'Isn't that what I'm doing? By walking away?'

Darcy sighed deeply. 'I don't know. If it's what you really want, but…' She looked around the neglected, unkempt, yet still blooming garden. 'I think you could do amazing things right here, if you just let yourself accept that you're good enough, and that's all you need to be.'

Chapter Twenty

Another two days passed with Bella going through the motions. She'd put on proper clothes and let her nan drag her along to an anti-war sewing circle, and a 'save the swans' riverside litter pick. She moved around the kitchen with no sense of joy, aware that her nan was watching her intently. 'Bella darling?'

Her nan was sitting at the tiny kitchen table, sipping a mug of oversweetened tea. 'What?'

'I think it's time we talked about what you're really doing here.'

'Nothing. I'm making a snack.'

'You're making sad cheese on toast,' her nan pointed out. 'Which you also made yesterday and the day before. You're depressed.'

'Eating cheese on toast does not mean I'm depressed.'

'Comfort cheese on toast does. You went and got plastic cheese specially didn't you?'

'I'm fine.' Bella laughed merrily to prove her point, which even she could hear did sound a little bit strange.

'No. Come and sit down.' Her nan pulled out the mismatched chair alongside her. 'What are you running away from?'

'I'm not running away.'

'Then why aren't you still in Scotland with mystery boy?'

'I told you. That didn't work out.'

Her grandma narrowed her eyes slightly. 'And why haven't I seen your phone in your hand since you got here?'

'What do you mean?' She knew exactly what her grandmother meant. Normally when she was back home she was glued to her phone, messaging people to find her next opportunity, scrolling job sites for interesting gigs in interesting places.

'You know.'

'Just taking some time out. Like a digital detox.'

'Bella, you're avoiding something. Or someone.'

'I'm not.' Bella stormed out of the room, marched into her bedroom and found her phone in the bottom of her rucksack. She turned it on in front of her grandma with a flourish. 'Look. Not ignoring anything.'

'Good.'

Bella's skin physically prickled as she waited to see what notifications popped up. Had Adam tried to call her? Had he messaged? Not that it mattered. She wasn't desperate for him to call. She wasn't in limbo because she'd run away without a word; every inch of her wasn't desperate for him to call her back. That wasn't who she was at all. She'd done her best. Things hadn't worked out. And now she'd moved on. She wasn't about to get hung up on what might have been.

She slammed the phone down on the kitchen table. She wasn't looking at the notifications. She didn't need to. She wasn't waiting for, or avoiding, anything. It was just a phone. Her phone trilled. Once, and then twice, and then again and again.

Her grandma raised an eyebrow. 'Are you going to get that?'

Bella shrugged. 'I'm sure it's not urgent.'

'You can look.'

'I don't need to look.'

Her nan raised her hands in a signal of surrender. 'All right then. Well I'm out to Maya's for the meditation circle this evening. I'll be back about nine. Unless you want to come.'

Maya was one of nan's longest standing friends and a lynchpin of their local social circle. Normally Bella would go along and let everyone coo over where she'd been most recently and where she was heading next. She shook her head. 'I'm fine here.'

She waited with a level of self-control worthy of a much better woman until she heard the click of the Yale lock as her grandma closed the front door behind her, before she picked up her phone. The waiting proved, didn't it, that she was genuinely chilled about who might have called or messaged.

She swiped away a couple of unused app notifications and a demand that she updated a whole load of other stuff and concentrated on the list of messages and missed calls. Six missed calls. Three from Darcy Lowbridge. Two from Flinty. And one from Veronica. Nothing from Adam. Not that she cared. That was over. Better for everyone that he didn't get in touch.

She opened her messages. Jill was at the top of the list. Six new messages. Bella read them quickly backwards from the most recent.

Today: Call me?

One day ago: Don't want to keep bothering you, but are you OK? Don't want to intrude but hope you're all right. Let me know if you need to chat.

One day ago: Missing you here. Hope you'll be back soon. The prayer group missed your cakes!

Two days ago: Just been up to Lowbridge to deliver the study books for prayer group. It's not the same without you. I'm sure everyone misses you.

Two days ago: Just checking in. Hope you're all right xxx

Three days ago: You're barely on the train and I'm already texting. Hope you're OK. Keep in touch and let me know if you need ANYTHING!!!!

Jill was a sweetheart, obviously, and it was kind of her to say that everyone missed her, but she was a bloody vicar. She had to be kind didn't she? It was basically part of her job description. And not everyone had tried to get in touch with her.

She flicked down to the next message from an unknown number.

> **One day ago:** Hi. This is Cath from the cookery school. Hope you don't mind but Jill gave me your number. Me and Claire had great fun doing trial day. Darcy said the evening course was paused for a bit. I'm really sorry to hear that. I wanted to talk to you about something you said you might do for lads who know nothing about cooking. I really want to send my two boys – well they're 19 and 22 but still boys to me! They can barely light the hob. You would work wonders. See you soon x

Flinty next.

> **Today:** Where are you? Seriously, people need you here. You can't just bugger off.

> **One day ago:** Where are you?

> **Two days ago:** Where are you?

> **Three days ago:** Where are you?

Well that was direct. The last unread message was from Pavel. That one took a second to open. It was a picture message of Nina grinning at a massive chocolate cake. Bella scrolled down to the caption.

Tried your recipe again without the blood
and fire and it turned out great. Mum loved
her cake. Thank you!

Bella half-smiled at Nina's beaming expression. Next she
had to bite the bullet and listen to her voicemails. Only
two new messages. The first was from Darcy. 'Hi Bella. It's
Darcy.' She giggled tinnily on the recording. 'I mean you
know that, don't you? I saw you put my number in your
phone, so it'll have said who called you. Or will it? When
you get a voicemail does it just say the number? I'm not
sure. Anyway it's Darcy. Which you definitely know by
now. Oh my goodness. Listen to me! Anyway I know you
were a bit shocked when Adam said he was selling, and
well we all were, and I know how much work you put
in, and what it's like when you're not from a place like
this at all, and you're trying so hard to fit in and make it
work, so we all understand if you felt a bit overwhelmed
and needed to get away. But we're worried about you.
And... well Adam is...' She stopped. 'We're all worried
about you. Just let us know you're OK sweetie. OK?'

Adam was what? Clearly not sufficiently devastated at
her disappearance that he could be bothered to call her
himself. Adam was obviously fine. Better, if anything,
without her.

Second new message. 'Bella, it's Veronica. I don't know
what you're playing at but it's frankly ridiculous. Phone
me back.'

Bella deleted the message. Veronica was not the boss of
her. She turned her phone face down on the bed, because
she wanted to, not at all out of some strange feeling that
Veronica was in the phone and might somehow rise up
out of it and tell her off for not following instructions.

Adam spent the rest of the day in the garden. He cut back weeds, started harvesting produce that was at risk of turning overripe. He tied up the tomatoes and the peas and beans. It was after ten when the light finally began to turn hazy and he stepped back to assess what he'd achieved. There was still work to do, lots and lots of work, but that was always true in a garden. One of his father's great pieces of wisdom was to tell him that a garden was never finished. It was a living breathing thing that you merely took care of and tended. There'd always be more to do tomorrow.

He was wheeling a final barrow over to the compost pile when his grandmother came into the garden. Adam braced for the lecture on why he was wasting his time out here when there were things to be done. Instead she sat silently on the old bench next to the gate and simply waited for him to join her.

'I'm surprised you haven't been out here more since you came back.'

'I couldn't face it.'

'And now you can.' Veronica nodded. 'Time changes things, doesn't it?'

He knew where this was going. 'You think time will change how I feel about selling Lowbridge.'

'Perhaps.' She brushed an imaginary piece of lint off her trouser leg. 'I didn't say time changes everything though, did I? I suppose it all depends how you really feel about this place. And how Miss Smith really feels.'

He wished that question was still relevant. 'I don't think Bella's coming back.'

'Have you asked her?'

She'd been very clear how much he'd let her down already. 'No.'

'Then shall we not rush to conclusions? Time, as I say, can change a lot of things.'

Veronica in reflective mood was unnerving. 'I thought you'd be furious with me.'

'I was.'

'And now?'

'I'm mostly cross with myself.'

'Why?'

'I could see how hard all this could be for Miss Smith. I didn't think about how it might be for you. One assumes that those who were born to this somehow know how to manage it all.'

Adam almost laughed. 'I should though, shouldn't I?'

'I think coming here is different for everybody, but then we can't really avoid putting our own experience onto everyone else. For Darcy, you see, Lowbridge was an escape. For your mother, it was a trap. And for your father it was a duty, which he took very seriously, but who am I to say that he wouldn't have been happy, happier even, somewhere else entirely?'

Adam couldn't picture that. His father, in Adam's memory, had been the epitome of the idea that the laird and the place were all part of the same whole. 'What is it for you?'

'What do you mean?'

'What is Lowbridge for you?' he asked again. 'Escape or trap?'

'Oh. I...' She shook her head, and Adam thought for a moment she was going to demur, briskly change the subject and move on. 'Perhaps both,' she said. 'You know that I grew up in the village.'

Adam nodded. He could remember being taken to see Great-Granny Hetherington, Veronica's mother, when he was a tiny child.

'So in that sense I didn't move very far at all, but it was still a different world. I was very young and I wanted...' She shook her head. 'I wanted certain things that I think would have broken my mother's heart, so accepting your grandfather's proposal felt like a way out.'

Adam stared straight ahead, not meeting his grandmother's eye. 'Did you regret it?'

'Regret is a waste of time. And I had your father and then he had you and I loved being involved in running the estate and planning events, but one wouldn't be human if one didn't wonder about the road not travelled.'

'What should I do?'

She shook her head. 'I can't tell you what to do.'

This time Adam did laugh. 'When did that start?'

His grandmother shot him a look.

Adam watched Dipper's progress around the garden for a moment. She darted up and down the rows, stopping to sniff and scuffle out interesting scents here and there, before settling in front of the door to his father's potting shed. 'She's still looking for him everywhere.'

Veronica followed his gaze. 'Perhaps she is. Perhaps she'll find him, or enough of the memory of him to carry on.'

'Do you miss him?'

His grandmother shook her head. 'Missing him isn't the right word. It's not enough. I know I can be a little...' She glanced at her grandson. 'Well, anyway. He was still a child to me. I don't quite know who I am here without him.'

'You never seem like you're struggling.'

'One does what one must to keep going.'

Dipper padded away from the shed and trotted over to their bench. Adam ran his hand over her back. 'What if I'm not good enough?'

'How do you mean?'

'I can't stop thinking that this place isn't right for me.' That wasn't it. It was so close, but it wasn't it at all. 'That I'm not right for this place,' he corrected. 'How do you know?'

She reached over and took his hand. Adam froze slightly. His grandmother had never been one for hugs or passing touches. She turned his hand over in hers and traced a fingertip over his dirty soil-laden nails. 'I think you're exactly where you're supposed to be.'

'I can't just be a gardener here.'

'Why ever not?'

'Because I have to be the laird.'

Her face softened. 'Actually I really shan't tell you what to do this time.'

'Really?'

'I am sorry to disappoint. I will say, though, that when I was young I felt as though I had a very stark choice. One path or the other. Black or white. But time does change things. The world is different now. Things that were unthinkable when I was a girl are commonplace. Don't get yourself into a trap because you think things have to be wholly one thing or the other.'

'What will you do if I do sell?'

Veronica let out a long sigh. 'I think I shall do the same thing either way.'

That made no sense. 'What?'

'I have had a good life here. I raised my son, but he's gone now.' She shook her head slightly as if willing away tears. 'I'm hoping it's not too late for me to take a detour along that other road.' His grandmother patted his hand. 'I'll let you get on.'

Dipper raised her head to watch Veronica go and then settled herself back down at the Laird's feet.

–

Bella didn't cry. She never cried. It was a point of pride, and occasionally disbelief when she told new friends in bars in far-flung places.

But she was crying now. Big violent sobs were shaking her whole body and she had no idea why. She'd made the right decision. She'd reached the end of the road in Lowbridge and it was time to go. There was no point dwelling on any of it, and dwelling on things was not at all Bella's way, and yet the tears were falling down her face in a vast and unstoppable flood.

'I knew you weren't all right.' Her grandma was standing in the doorway to Bella's room.

'I thought you were out.'

'I was. Now I'm back.'

'You're early.'

Her nan shook her head. 'Actually I'm late.'

Bella checked the time. Half past nine. That couldn't be right. She couldn't have been sitting here with tears streaming all evening.

'What happened up in Scotland, love?'

'Nothing.'

'Bollocks.' Her nan sat down on the bed next to her. 'Your aura's all squiffy and you're lying to me. You never lie to me.'

Her nan always knew.

'You told me the first time you got high and the first time you got laid, and trust me, that was not a story any grandmother needs to hear. So what aren't you telling me now?'

'There's nothing to tell.'

'Humour me.'

Bella wiped her nose on the back of her sleeve. 'Everything got messed up, and things had run their course. So I came home.'

'What's messed up?'

She might as well tell her. There was no point keeping it herself, but where could she even start? 'It's too hard to explain.'

'Well we're not in any hurry. You can take your time.'

Bella took a deep breath in. Her nan wasn't going to let her get away with breezing over the details. 'So I met this guy in Spain…'

One hour, two glasses of wine, and eleven exclamations of 'An actual castle?' later, Bella had got past the point where she'd set about saving the fortunes of the Lowbridge estate, and up to the point where the cookery school was past its rather eventful trial day and starting regular classes, and where the castle was bustling with community groups and meetings. That's where Bella stopped.

Her nan refilled both their glasses. 'Go on.'

'It's stupid.'

'I said, go on.'

'I… I was starting to feel like I could make a home there.' Bella waited for her nan's inevitable laughter.

'What's stupid about that?'

'Seriously? Settling down. Making a home. It's not exactly our style is it? You raised me to be an adventurer.'

'Adventure doesn't have to mean moving around the whole time. We had plenty of adventures right here.'

'I guess.'

'And I have a home.' Her nan smiled slightly tipsily. 'You, darling, are my home.'

Bella rolled her eyes.

'I'm serious! Anyway, it sounds like everything was going marvellously. What on earth are you doing back here?'

'It turned out,' Bella's tone hardened as she explained, 'that Adam didn't want any of that. He walked in one day and announced that he was selling the whole place.'

Her nan frowned. 'And he hadn't talked to you about it?'

Bella shook her head.

'I am so sorry. I can't imagine how much that would have hurt.'

It had. It had hurt so much.

'And it was a complete shock?'

'Well I knew he'd had an offer, but I never thought he'd take it.' Bella sipped her wine. 'I thought he was happy.'

Her nan took a long sip of wine. 'Well, not perfectly happy I wouldn't think.'

'Why not?' Adam had every reason to be happy. He had a castle. He was an actual baron. He said he loved Bella and she was working so hard to make everything work.

'Well his father just died, for one. And you said his business partner in Edinburgh needed him back there.'

'Well yeah, but…'

'What happened to make him actually decide?'

'I don't know.' It had all been so out of the blue.

'You didn't ask?'

'I…' Had she asked? 'Well his mum turned up. I think Veronica thought the whole thing was her fault.'

'Is he close to his mum?'

'I don't think he'd seen her since he was a kid.'

Bella's nan let out a long sharp breath. 'I love you darling.'

'I know.'

'I'm going to say some things now that you might not want to hear.'

Bella steeled herself. This was why she hadn't talked to her nan. It was because, although she knew she'd get sympathy and she knew she'd get love, she would always also get truth.

'Well, his father died, he gave up his whole life to move back home, he's grieving, trying to adapt to this whole new role, and then the mother he hasn't seen for decades shows up out of nowhere and he freaks out and his fiancée leaves him.'

'That's not what happened.'

Her nan's voice was soft. 'Which bit did I get wrong?'

Bella went over the steps her grandmother had laid out. 'Well, it's not so much wrong as…'

'As not the way you see it, which is fine. It doesn't mean you're wrong either, but you promised this lad you were going to be part of his life.'

'Which means he should have talked to me before he decided.'

Her nan nodded. 'Of course he should. Should you have talked to him before you did a bunk though?'

That was different. 'He made this huge decision without mentioning it to me. It was like none of what I'd been doing mattered to him.'

317

'And that sent you fleeing down here with your tail between your legs.'

'And why's that a surprise? It's what I do, isn't it?'

'What do you mean?'

'I run away when stuff gets tricky don't I? Never stay in one place for too long. Pick up and ship out as soon as stuff gets hard.' Bella took a deep swig of wine. 'Like mother, like daughter.'

Her grandma shook her head. 'Is that what you think?'

'Well if the cap fits…'

'You are nothing like your mother. Your mother is an addict. Simple as. When she's clean she's great. She loves you. Loves us both. When she's using she's lost. I nearly broke my own heart trying to fix that and I only stopped when something more important came along.'

'What?'

'You. I couldn't make things right for your mam, but I could take care of the only thing, apart from the drugs, that she really loved. Looking after you was the only thing I could do for her, and it was easy. I fell in love with you the second I saw you.'

Bella let her nan squeeze her hand. It didn't change anything though. 'I'm still like her in the running away though.'

'You don't run away from things.'

'I do.' Of course Bella did. 'I never stay in one spot.'

'Because you're running *towards* something.'

What? 'What do you mean?'

'Well you went to Spain cos you were offered a job there. You went to Brazil because you met people who invited you to that festival. You went to Scotland because you…' Nan hesitated. 'Because you fell in love?'

Bella could see her knuckles whitening from her grip on the glass. 'But it didn't work out.'

'Are you sure you gave it a chance?'

That wasn't fair. 'I did everything I could. Adam…' This was the thing that had sent her away, wasn't it? 'Adam gave up on us.'

'Did he?'

'He chucked everything we were doing away.'

'And that was awful. Of course he should have talked to you.' Her grandma stroked Bella's hand. 'Grief can take people differently though.'

'He didn't seem like he was grieving that much.'

'Unless he's made of stone I promise you he was, and if he wasn't letting it out then it was sitting, waiting somewhere in here.' Her nan pressed a hand to her own chest.

'But if he really loved me that should have been enough.'

'That's not how grief works, darling. I mean it must have been an insane couple of months for him. He lost his father, and then his mother turning up, and suddenly being responsible for this whole estate and everything.'

'I tried so hard.'

'And then you ran away.'

'I couldn't make it work.'

'Look.' Her nan stood up and got a second bottle of wine from the fridge. 'I can't tell you what to do. If you really think this thing is over and you'd rather walk away that's your decision.'

'Yeah. It is.'

'But I am going to make you hear me out. You told this chap you were going to marry him.'

'It was a holiday romance.'

'Shhh.' Her grandma snapped her fingers together in a 'button it sunshine' gesture. 'I'm not done. You told him you were going to marry him. That's a commitment. And that means that it's not about trying to make it work. It's about dealing with whatever happens regardless of whether it works out like you pictured it or not.'

Bella knew better than to talk back to her nan, but she'd had enough of being lectured from Veronica. 'I'm not taking romance advice from you,' she muttered.

'Very wise.' Her nan nodded. 'But I'm not talking about romance. I'm talking about a commitment. Like I made to you.' She reached out and touched Bella's cheek. 'I was fifty when your mam first left you with me. I wasn't looking to raise another baby, but I loved you with every bit of me and I committed to making it work, to being the person who would never leave you struggling. That was my promise. When you said yes to this posh lad's proposal, that was yours. If you'd actually gone down the aisle with him you'd have signed up to sickness and health and better or worse, wouldn't you?'

'I guess.'

'And he does one, admittedly huge, screwed-up thing a few weeks after he's lost his dad and you decide he's given up on you.'

'He didn't even talk to me about it.'

'I hear that.' Bella's nan narrowed her eyes. 'What else is there?'

'Nothing.'

'Really?'

Well, there was the thing that had been sitting deep in Bella's gut since the very moment she walked away from Lowbridge. Bella closed her eyes.

'Tell me.'

'I think maybe I got caught up in the estate and the village and all the things we could do.'

'And?'

'And, before I went he kind of said I was more in love with Lowbridge than with him.'

Her grandmother nodded. 'And was he right?'

'No.' The certainty of Bella's answer crystallised something inside her. 'No. I love him.'

'What about him?'

'I love how good he is with his hands.'

Her nan shook her head. 'I don't think I need those sorts of details.'

'No. I mean, he's practical. He's a gardener, and he can just sort of look at a plant or a piece of land and know what it needs. He nurtures things.' Bella shook her head. 'That sounds silly.'

'Not at all.'

'And he thinks about things. Too much probably, but he doesn't just rush in. He weighs things and he worries about letting people down.'

Her grandmother placed her hand over Bella's. 'It sounds as though deciding to sell would have been really difficult for someone like that.'

'That's what I don't understand.'

'So maybe if you talked to him?'

'You think I should go back.'

'I think that's up to you.' She paused. 'What was the hardest thing when your mam used to disappear when you were a kid?'

'Not knowing. Like when she was here I never knew how long she'd stay and then when she went I never knew if it was for good this time.'

Her grandmother didn't respond.

'This isn't the same.'

'No, but you have a chance to at least give him some closure. And you too. And then you can see what you want to run towards rather than turning into someone who runs away.' She sat back. 'Which is not who I raised you to be, young lady.'

Chapter Twenty-One

No amount of wine would shift Bella's nan's resolve that she had already stepped far too close to telling her grand-daughter what to do and was going to say no more, but there was no pretending she didn't think that going back to Lowbridge and at least talking things through was the better choice. And part of Bella, the part that had said yes to Adam's proposal, the part that had let herself get excited about the cookery school, the part that had even thought Veronica might have been softening to her, knew her nan was right.

But the other part of Bella was giving as good as she got. She could totally get closure via text message. Lowbridge was a really long way away. She'd only just got here. It would take her a full day to get back.

Bella's credit card had just about enough wiggle room on it to override the practical considerations, and she knew that Nina or Jill would be happy to put her up if whatever went down with Adam meant spending the night at Lowbridge Castle wasn't an option. The practical objections were no more than the opening act.

Next came petulance. Adam was the one who'd kicked off this fight. Why should Bella be the one to go all the way back there to make things right? She was the one in the right. He should be begging her to come back.

It wasn't only him she'd run away from though, was it? It was Flinty and Darcy and Jill and the whole village. It was the cookery school students. It was all the promises she'd made, not just the one when she'd said yes to Adam's proposal. That promise was the big one though. She hadn't said yes to the village or to the estate or the cookery school. She'd said yes to him. Yes to the way he looked at her like nothing else mattered. Yes to how much he cared, about her but also about everything around him. Yes to how he saw beauty in things she would otherwise pass by without notice. Yes to how hard he tried to be a good man. And she'd run away from all of those yeses.

Her brain still had one more card to play. And it was a good one. It was the trump card to beat all trumps. It was the royal flush of objections. Fear. What if the whole community blamed her for running away?

And then the even bigger fear, the deepest terror. What if Bella went back and Adam didn't want to see her at all?

Bella drew herself up to her full height and glared at herself in the mirror. 'Then at least you'll know,' she told herself. She could do this. She could go back and look Adam in the eye and know whether he was her future.

'What time's your train?' Her nan was in the bedroom doorway.

'Half past.'

'So you'll be going for the quarter to bus?'

Bella nodded.

'Right then. Well I'll be on my way over to Manchester tomorrow, for Bob's living funeral thing.'

'He's having another one?'

Her nan nodded. 'Bad bout of flu last month. Convinced himself he weren't much longer for this world.'

'But he's better now?'

'Completely, but why cancel a party?'

Bella shook her head, gathered up her rucksack, and pulled her nan into a hug.

'If it doesn't go how you're hoping you can come down to Bob's thing,' her nan reminded her. 'And call me if you need me.'

Normally Bella would wave away that instruction with a cheery reassurance that all would be well. Today she nodded.

Her nan squeezed her hand. 'Tomorrow the world pet.'

'Tomorrow the world.'

—

Bella hauled her rucksack down the stairwell, across the square of concrete at the centre of the group of flats and out to the bus stop on the main road. The bus from the station ran out to here, did a loop around the big roundabout at the top of the estate and then headed back into the city centre.

She leaned against the weird half-seat thing along the wall of the bus shelter and checked the time on her phone. Three minutes to wait. The digital display board, installed at great expense to inform travellers of the precise location of the next bus, told her brightly that no information was available at this time. She glanced down the road. The expanse of concrete and tarmac almost startled her. She was an animal of the city, but part of her brain was screaming for wide open skies and deep sparkling sea.

She blocked out the view and scrolled through her phone, not really taking in what she was reading, thinking instead about what exactly she was going to say to Adam when she made it back to Lowbridge. If she hadn't been so absorbed she might have noticed the vehicle pulling into the bus stop. She might have heard the door opening and slamming closed. She might have been less shocked when she looked up.

Adam.

He was standing next to the estate's antique Land Rover, parked entirely illegally in the bus stop. His hair was messed up and his face etched with tiredness. She moved to him without thinking, her body responding to his presence.

'You're going somewhere?' His eyes were fixed on the stuffed rucksack that was still in her hand.

'I was going to go and see you.'

He half-smiled, the same half-smile that had melted her the first time she'd seen it. 'I'm not there.'

'Clearly.'

They stood opposite one another in silence for a second. Bella needed to say something. She'd thought she had hours on trains and buses to pin down the details. 'Adam—'

'Bel—'

They both stopped.

'Can I go first?' Adam asked.

'OK.'

'I'm sorry.'

The knot in her stomach unclenched a notch. She let herself press her body against his and wrap her arms around his neck. For a moment he responded, pulling her closer and burying his face in her hair.

And then he pulled away. 'Please. I've been planning this the whole way here. I'm sorry. I...' His voiced tailed off. 'I'm sorry. I'm going to be a coward and do this bit first.'

'What?'

'Look, I wasn't going to show you these. I didn't want to put pressure on you but, I've got some letters from people.'

'What do you mean?'

He pulled a handful of papers from his jacket pocket. There were notes from everyone. Flinty. Darcy. Pavel. Jill. Anna and Hugh. Cath and Claire. Molly and Katy. Nina and the parents and toddlers, complete with handprint artwork from the kids. All asking her to come back, all telling her how much more alive Lowbridge had become since she'd been there and how much they missed having her around.

The final letter was in a sealed envelope addressed to Miss Bella Smith in neat cursive writing. Bella slit it open.

> Dear Miss Smith,
>
> I believe I might owe you both an explanation and an apology. I have come to see that I did not always make your time at Lowbridge easy and I fear that you might have come to the conclusion that this was a result of some antipathy towards you on my part.
>
> On the contrary, I sought — misguidedly perhaps — only to protect you. I know, better than most, what can happen to young women full of life who give their futures to Lowbridge. I was once one myself, and everyone said how very lucky I was that the laird would choose to court a butcher's daughter from the village. And I was lucky. My husband was kind and took care of me and our son very well, but I closed off a part of myself when I married him and took on the role of his wife.

I still wonder what that girl I used to be would make of me now. I fear I would be the most awful disappointment to her.

And then when my son married Adam's mother and she couldn't bear the role that was thrust on her, to the point that she ran away from her own child, and then he brought Darcy back from America, it felt as though the story was constantly repeating itself. Yet another fiery, lively, woman closed up inside the castle.

Perhaps I couldn't bear to see you trapped in the same way. It has been pointed out to me that I might have read these other people's stories through the tinted lenses of my own. Darcy assures me that she never felt for one moment trapped but loved, not only by my son, but also Lowbridge itself. I wonder whether I should allow you and Adam the space to write your own story and not impose my own upon you.

In short, then, I apologise for any coolness you might have felt. I do hope you will come back to Lowbridge. You brought a certain light and vigour that we have, I now see, been missing. If you choose not to return, then I hope you make that decision for the best possible reasons and will find happiness wherever your life might take you.

Yours,

Veronica, Lady Lowbridge

'Did you read this?'

Adam shook his head. 'I wouldn't dare.'

She handed the sheet of paper across and waited while he scanned his grandmother's lines. 'Oh, my poor grand-mother.' He frowned. 'Did you feel like that?'

'No. I felt like you'd abandoned me. And like I'd done everything I could think of to make things better but it wasn't working.'

'All the stuff you did worked brilliantly though.'

She shook her head. 'It didn't make you happy.'

'Oh my God. No. I'm grieving. I was lost in my own sadness. You did nothing wrong. It was never up to you to make me better. It's only up to you to be there with me. If you want to be.'

The flicker of hope that had sparked when Adam appeared in the middle of the sprawl of tarmac and concrete ignited into a flame.

'I let everything get on top of me,' he continued. 'And I was so caught up in how awful I was feeling that I didn't think about you. And… I'm so sorry. That's the most important thing. I got caught up in myself, and I lost sight of you – no, of us – and I'm sorry. If it's unforgivable, I understand, but I want you to know that I know I screwed up. And if you give me a chance we can do it all differently. I'll be there next to you, no matter what.'

He was right, but also not right at all. 'No. You were grieving. I freaked out and ran away.'

'Why were you coming to see me, Bel?'

'To say…' To say what? She glanced up the road. 'We should move. The bus will be here soon, and you're parked in the way.'

He nodded. 'Where to, then?'

Bella hopped in the car and directed him towards the parking bays at the foot of her nan's block. 'Why didn't you bring your car?'

Adam shook his head. 'I let Flinty drive it to the village once and now I can't get her out of the thing. She's seen how the other half live. Or how they drive anyway.'

'You drove all the way down here in this thing to avoid an argument?'

'Not just that.' He patted the steering wheel with one finger and the corner of his lip twitched up. 'Perfectly good car this. You just have to know how to treat her.'

They fell into a silence that seemed to be waiting for big meaningful words. Bella filled the quiet with chit chat, narrating the short journey. 'So that's where I fell off my bike and broke my wrist. And the bus stop where you found me, that's where you get the bus into town. Well really it's the one on the other side, but then you have to cross the dual carriageway so it's easier to just get it there and…'

Adam cleared his throat. 'Bel.'

'Yeah.'

'We're here.'

She stared at the grey building in front of her. 'So this is my estate. Bit different to yours.'

'A bit. Fewer ghosts maybe?'

'Probably. Nan reckons Mr Herbert next door still bangs on the wall when she makes too much noise though, but it's more likely just that she pisses the new people off too and…'

'Bel, why were you coming to see me?'

The things she could say flew through her mind. She'd been angry and sad and confused. But sitting next to him now there was only one thing that felt right. 'I'm sorry, too.'

'What for?'

'I thought being on the same team meant working towards the same thing, but it's more than that.'

He unclipped his seatbelt and twisted to look at her.

'You were right that I got caught up in Lowbridge and forgot a little bit about you.'

'Right.'

'But you were wrong about that meaning it wasn't you that I was in love with.' Bella swallowed hard. Bella was not a weeping person. 'It was all for you, really...' This next part was hard. 'I think my mum wasn't really around and dad not at all, and I know my nan loves me and I adore her but she was all about teaching me to find my own way and be independent and fly free, and I'm not sure I know how to be on the same team as someone.'

'Do you want to learn?'

'I...'

'Simple question. Yes or no?'

'I feel like we've been here before.'

He glanced out of the window across the expanse of grey. 'Well not here exactly.'

'Orange grove in the Spanish sun. Car park on a York-shire housing estate. It's all the same.' Bella half-laughed.

'Is your answer the same?'

She nodded. 'Yes.'

He closed the gap between them in an instant, leaning awkwardly over the gearstick, pulling her into his arms and pressing his lips to hers. She sank uncomfortably into the embrace for a second. It would be so easy to let this play out. Being in Adam's arms felt right. It had always felt right, but they'd rushed back from Spain with so much unsaid. And her nan was right. Bella was someone who ran towards things. She placed her hand on his chest and pulled back. She asked him the question she should have asked weeks ago. 'But what do you want?'

'I want you.'

That was the right answer. She believed it was true, but they both needed more. She leaned away from him, turning to stare out of the windscreen at the bins behind the flats. 'What do you want your life to be? Where do you want to live? What do you want to do with Lowbridge?'

'So long as it's with you, I don't care.'

'Yes. You do.' Rushing towards the 'yes' would be easy, but 'yes' wasn't a life. Yes was a good intention. A marriage started from that, but if she wanted the forever, rather than just the next three-month stopgap, it needed something more. 'You decided you were going to sell the whole place without talking to me about it.'

'I know.' He leaned forward putting his head into his hands. 'I should have talked to you weeks ago. I hate being the laird.'

'What?' How could you hate something like that? Adam was the kingpin.

'I'm awful at it. I keep messing stuff up in the office and I don't know what I'm supposed to be doing. You're great. You have all these ideas and plans and I felt like I was drowning and I couldn't say anything because everyone was expecting me to be in control of everything.'

'You could have talked to me,' she insisted.

'I thought I had to be able to do it all on my own.'

'You don't.'

'I know. Darcy thinks I've been too hung up on duty and trying to be the sort of laird I think my father would be proud of.'

Bella hadn't thought of it that way. 'Is she right?'

Adam nodded. 'It's more than that though. My father was there for me when mum went. It's hard to explain, but when your own mum goes... I don't know. Mums are supposed to be there no matter what, aren't they? That's what everyone assumes, and when she's not it leaves this sort of…' He jabbed his hand against his gut. 'Hole.'

'I know.' Of course she knew. 'I think a bit of me never quite lets me feel safe anywhere, because I don't quite believe it won't get ripped away.'

He buried his head into his hands. 'And then you started to feel safe and I ripped it away. I'm so sorry.'

'No. You should have talked to me.' She wasn't letting that go. 'But I need to find a better way of dealing with problems than just packing a bag.'

'I do the opposite. I try to hold everything together and be the person everyone else needs me to be.'

'Until you can't any longer?'

He nodded.

'I think we've both learned not to rely on other people,' she suggested.

'But the people were there. My dad. Your nan.'

'Even your nan.'

He smiled ever so slightly. 'Each other?'

And that was what she truly wanted. 'Each other,' she confirmed.

'So what now?'

'What do you want?'

What did Bella want? 'Before I came to Lowbridge I'd never really thought I would ever put down roots, you know.'

He shook his head. 'I'm nothing but roots.'

'But it was starting to feel like home,' Bella admitted. 'I let myself get excited about our lives there.'

'It's going to be so much work to make the estate work, and I don't know how much help I can be,' Adam countered. 'I'm useless in the office. It's embarrassing. I

333

can barely even check a bank statement without wanting to scream. The numbers don't sit still for me.'

Another thing slotted into place. 'Like number dyslexia.'

'Is that a thing?'

Bella nodded. 'There's a proper name for it.' She reached for her phone.

He stopped her. 'We can look it up later.'

'Sorry. Yeah.' That mattered, but it wasn't what they were supposed to be dealing with right now. Right now was about him and her and whether the crazy promise they'd made on a hot afternoon in Spain meant something in their real lives. The last thing Bella wanted to do was force Adam into a life that made him miserable. 'If you don't want to stay at Lowbridge, I won't try to make you.'

'I actually think I might not hate it, but we would need to find a way that works for us, and I don't want to give up my business in Edinburgh. They only really need me for the design stuff, so if I went over maybe one week a month and then worked remotely, that would keep things going and maybe bring in a bit of money. If I stayed with Ravi and Sam, we could even rent out my flat.'

'So no big city bolt hole if we wanted to run?' she pointed out.

He shook his head. 'And at Lowbridge I need to be more honest about what I can do. The gardens. The land. Not sitting in an office.'

'What about the inheritance tax though?'

'We don't even have the final bill yet. Maybe the insurance will cover it. Maybe we can make enough to set up a payment plan.' He shrugged. 'Maybe I don't have to have all the answers worked out straight away.'

'But we'd commit to staying and working them out together?'

He paused. 'I can't be the sort of laird my father was, or my grandfather.'

'You don't have to be,' she reassured him.

'I might need you to remind me of that.'

'And if I promised to do that?'

'Then I think Lowbridge could work.' He leaned forward and angled his body towards her. 'So you can see yourself doing this in another five or ten or thirty years' time?'

'Well I do think the cookery school could work, and maybe we could do a tearoom in summer, and…'

Adam was shaking his head. He still wasn't convinced, was he?

'What?'

'I meant doing *this*?' He pointed from her to him and back again. 'This. Not the estate. Not the cookery school. Nor Darcy or Flinty or the Crazy Women's Tea Club.'

'That's not what it's called.'

He raised an eyebrow. 'Not any of those things. Us?'

The two of them. Together. Not a passing romance. Not the next stop on the adventure. A team for good or ill for as long as they had. Bella nodded. 'Us.'

Finally she did close the space between them, wriggling and half crawling across the seats to press her lips to his. Bella's safe harbour was here, where it had always been, with Adam.

They stayed like that for a long time, gearstick digging into her thigh, shoulder pressed up against the steering wheel, before Bella finally pulled away. 'So we're going back to Lowbridge? Together?'

'If you want to.'

Absolutely she wanted to. 'All those things I planned. I want to make them work.'

'OK.'

She grinned. 'But mostly, I want to marry you. If you'll still have me. Do you still want to be my husband?'

'Yes, Bella Smith. I would like that very much, so long as you promise that I never have to look at an account book again.'

'Deal.'

She bent her head for another kiss, and then paused. 'So are we going to need to hire an administrator or something?'

He laughed. 'Apparently Darcy is an admin wizard, and is pretty much chomping at the bit to take over the accounts.'

'Like Veronica would ever let that happen.'

Adam laughed again, a proper rumbling chuckle that went all the way through his body. 'Actually, that's something else I need to tell you about.'

Epilogue

The grassy bank that led down to the Low Bridge was bustling with visitors and locals alike. Bella scanned the scene. People were milling around, chatting and sampling the drinks and canapés that Flinty had strong-armed Molly and Katy into handing out in freshly pressed black skirts and white blouses. Dipper was lolloping between the groups of guests, helpfully hoovering up any crumbs that were dropped. Claire and Cath had appointed themselves unofficial cookery school ambassadors and were singing Bella's praises to anyone who would listen. Anna and Nina were overseeing proceedings with an attitude somewhere between proud mother hens and imperious sergeant majors. Darcy was charming the pants off a rather mousey looking man from the local tourist board, who seemed thoroughly delighted to be talking to the actual lady of the manor. Everyone, it seemed, was in their element.

Bella stopped in front of the new wooden sign they'd erected at the entrance to the castle. Netty was already admiring it. 'The artwork you did looks amazing,' Bella told her.

'Happy to help.' Netty smiled as she went off to refill her glass.

'I heard her!'

'What?' Bella felt a touch in the small of her back, accompanied by a waft of familiar aftershave.

'Netty talked to me, and I understood.'

Adam looked blank. 'OK,' he nodded slowly. 'And that's exciting because…?'

'It's just I can never normally.' She shook her head. Bella didn't need to explain. It was enough that it had happened and she knew. She looked around the gathered friends. 'It's going OK?' she asked.

'It's going brilliantly. Those little pastry things are amazing.' Adam leaned in and kissed the nape of her neck.

'No snogging. Your grandma's on her way over.'

'As is yours.'

The two women hadn't exactly seen eye to eye since Nan's arrival, but Bella was overjoyed to have her here for their big moment. She pulled her into a hug. 'Thank you for coming. Are you having a good time?'

'I'm having a great time. That Iain fellow with the very red face wants to take me out on his boat and show me his salmon farm.' She turned to Adam. 'I'm assuming that's some sort of posh Scottish euphemism.'

Adam shook his head. 'That's Sir Iain Macwillis, and I think he has an actual salmon farm. More than one probably.'

Bella's nan looked momentarily disappointed and then rallied. 'Well I don't think I've ever been to a salmon farm before. Every day's an adventure isn't it?'

'Tomorrow the world?' Bella asked.

'Always.' Her nan squeezed her hand. 'For me anyway. I think it's time for you to let the world come to you.'

Darcy extricated herself from the tourist board man and joined the group, followed a second later by Flinty, who fixed Veronica with a hard look. 'Have you properly told them yet?'

'Not exactly.'

'Well then.'

Veronica rolled her eyes. 'Very well. So I don't want any fuss or nonsense, but, as I said to Adam already, I've decided I'm moving out of the dower house.'

'You know you don't have to,' Adam replied.

'I know I don't have to, but I wish to. I will be moving into a cottage in the village.'

Flinty cleared her throat very pointedly.

'I'm getting to it, Margaret.' Veronica flushed. Bella had never seen her flustered before. 'I will be moving into Margaret's cottage in the village. With Margaret. As, well...'

Bella could not risk a look at Adam's face. She was too scared the shock she was feeling would be mirrored there. Be cool, Bella, she told herself. Be cool.

'As her companion.'

'I'm her bit of rough,' Flinty added.

Bella's nan recovered her composure first. 'Well that's great news, I'm sure. It's never too late for a fresh start, is it?'

'Fuck me...' Darcy hadn't quite got the 'be cool' memo.

'OK. Well, erm, congratulations,' Adam managed. And then he hugged his grandmother. Bella watched the old woman stiffen and then relax just enough to pat his back.

'Thank you dear.'

Bella stepped forward. She remembered the words in Veronica's letter about closing off a part of herself. She hugged her soon-to-be grandmother-in-law gently. 'I'm glad you're happy,' she said.

'Yes, well. This is all well and good, but there are speeches to be made and this day is about the two of you, not about me, so...' She nodded at Adam. 'Off you go.'

Bella followed the love of her life onto the tiny raised platform they'd erected next to the bridge and watched as he turned on the microphone and called for quiet.

'Ladies and gentlemen, thank you all so much for coming on this very special day for me and for Bella and for everyone here at Lowbridge. It's fantastic to have so many of you here to celebrate with us and to sample a few little tasters of Bella's amazing cooking. I'm not going to go on, but I do want to ask you all to raise a glass to the most incredible woman I have ever known. She's positive when I lose hope. She's practical when I get my head stuck in the clouds, and willing to dream big when I'm overwhelmed by the details. She takes things in her stride that would floor any lesser soul. And I'm so unbelievably lucky to have her as my partner, not just here at Lowbridge, but in life. Ladies and gentlemen, please raise your glass to Bella Smith!'

She looked out across the faces. New friends and old. New family and her grandma who'd supported her all her life.

Adam returned to the microphone. 'And, as so much of this is her doing, I think it's only right that she gets to do the final honours.'

He waved her forward. Bella shook her head. He was Laird Lowbridge, and for the first time he looked as though he was finally comfortable living the role. She wasn't anybody. In front of the stage Pavel clapped his hands together and called out, 'Bella! Bella!'

Others started joining in. She shook her head but accepted the inevitable and took the mic from Adam, grabbing his hand with her free one at the same time to keep him close. If he was going to make her do this, then he was going to be at her side while she did. 'Thank you everyone. OK then. Well not much more to say, other than thank you for coming to our launch party, and…' She looked around in a panic, until Darcy dashed forward and thrust a pair of scissors into her hands. Bella leaned down from the platform and dragged the microphone cable towards the ribbon they'd strung across the newly rebuilt Low Bridge. 'I am delighted to declare the New Low Bridge, and also the Highland Cookery School, open for business!'

The guests clapped and cheered. Glasses were raised. And on the stage Adam pressed his lips to hers. 'Next time we stand up in front of people and give speeches it'll be our wedding.'

'I know.'

'No cold feet.'

'Freezing feet. We're outside in Scotland at night!'

'You know what I mean. You're not going to run away again?'

'Never.' She looked around. This place, these people, this man. Bella Smith had, finally, found her home.

Author Letter

Hello lovely reader. I'm assuming you're lovely. Readers generally are, but in the interests of making clear that everyone is welcome here, hello to any nefarious readers too. I'm so grateful that you've chosen to spend your money and your precious reading time on Bella and Adam's story. Their relationship is one of my favourite sorts of love story. I adore taking people who don't look like they would fit together but somehow just do, and then forcing them to work out how on earth they're going to make that work.

I also had a blast writing the whole Lowbridge community – Veronica, Flinty, Darcy, Nina, Netty, Pavel, Jill, Anna, Hugh, and, of course, Poppy, Dipper and Queen Latifah. I had so much fun with pesky spirits, sheep and hen parties, and I really hope you had fun too.

Life can be tough for all of us, in different ways at different times, and I've had days when just turning on the news feels like another wave of horror I simply cannot manage. And in those moments funny, joyful, romantic stories matter. They remind us that people can be, and often are, brilliant – kind, generous and driven by love. They remind us that things can, and do, end well, and they provide a place where we can just be happy for a little while.

I hope this book does that for you, and I hope you'll join me again to go back to Lowbridge to revisit some old friends, and meet some new ones, later this year.

Amelia x

Acknowledgements

Thank you first of all to everyone at Hera Books, especially my editor, Jennie. Her ability to point out things I have utterly messed up in a way that somehow sounds generous and endearing is a thing of genius. (Or witchcraft. Honestly, I'm leaning towards witchcraft.) Thanks as well to everyone who has worked on bringing this book into the world – Keshini, Dan, Kate, everyone involved in sales, marketing, cover design and editorial. You are all genuinely tremendous.

I think I say every time I write acknowledgements that writing a novel can be a very solitary undertaking, and my writing mates are the backbone stopping me turning into a total dribbling mess every time I start a new one. So thank you, as ever, to the magnificent women of the Naughty Kitchen – baubles of fabulousness every single one.

And, finally, thanks babe. The patronage of the arts thing you've got going on is very much appreciated.